Widely acknowledged as a prolific and gift
previous novels include *The Third Child,*
Soldiers, *Body of Glass* (winner of the Arth
Longings Of Women, *Braided Lives* and *City*
Piercy is also a celebrated poet whose most
published in Great Britain are *The Art of Bles*
in Bone (Five Leaves), launched at the International Poetry Festival in London in 1998. She lives in Wellfleet with her husband, the novelist and painter Ira Wood.

Also by Marge Piercy:

Fiction:
Going Down Fast
Dance the Eagle to Sleep
Small Changes
Woman on the Edge of Time
The High Cost of Living
Vida
Braided Lives
Fly Away Home
Gone to Soldiers
Summer People
Body of Glass
The Longings of Women
Storm Tide *(co-written with Ira Wood)*
City of Darkness, City of Light
Three Women
The Third Child

Poetry:
Breaking Camp
Hard Loving
4-Telling
To Be Of Use
Living in the Open
The Twelve-Spoked Wheel
Flashing
The Moon is Always Female
Circles on the Water
Stone, Paper, Knife
My Mother's Body
Available Light
Mars and Her Children
What Are Big Girls Made Of?
The Art of Blessing the Day
Early Grrl
Colors Passing Through Us

Memoir:
Sleeping With Cats

Non-fiction:
So You Want to Write *(co-written with Ira Wood)*

First published in Great Britain in 2005 by
Judy Piatkus (Publishers) Ltd of
5 Windmill Street, London W1P 1HF
email: info@piatkus.co.uk

First published in the United States in 2005
by HarperCollins Publishers Inc., New York.

This edition published 2006

A catalogue record for this book is available from the British Library

ISBN 0 7499 3633 9

Set in Times by
Phoenix Photosetting, Chatham, Kent

Printed and bound in Great Britain by
Mackays of Chatham, Chatham, Kent

SEX WARS

Marge Piercy

1868

ONE

VICTORIA WAS READING the enormous book their landlady on Greene Street kept in her parlor. She was lying in bed with her temporary lover, Charlie, who was sleeping in on his back, snoring lightly. She doubted anybody else had bothered with the book, for some pages were still uncut—the Orations of Demosthenes, a great Greek speaker Victoria had begun to dream about since she and her sister arrived in New York. She could see him clearly at times and once in a while she began to hear his voice addressing her, a deep, resonant voice that thrilled her. She had seen visions and heard voices since she was a child. The same was true of her sister Tennessee, but Tennie was willing to fake it on demand, while Victoria refused. She considered herself chosen for some high magnificent fate. If life so far had been hard and sordid at times, she knew it was all about to change. She could feel it. Her voices strengthened her. They made her special in spite of her troubles.

A telegram from her husband Colonel James Blood lay on the night table. In two days, he was joining the sisters in New York. She knew it was only a matter of time before the rest of her Claflin clan found them. Money, they always needed money. Her father Buck had taken her on the revival circuit since she was old enough to stand, project her voice and fascinate a crowd; then Tennie with her clairvoyant act had taken over. The family cooked up patent medicines and practiced magnetic healing. Both sisters were good at the laying on of hands, which might prove useful if their plans, worked out in the Midwest, came to fruition—as they must. The sisters and James had carefully studied Cornelius Vanderbilt, as much as they could learn from a distance. He was their best hope.

Charlie was stirring. She put the leather-bound book beside the bed, half pushing it under. He was a reporter on the *Sun* whom she had run into at a spiritualist meeting. He was a good informant on the city—the Tweed ring, the flavor of the different newspapers, the scandals, where the wealthy lived, rode in their carriages, ate. He had served as a correspondent the last year of the Civil War, but now he reported on politics. His limp ginger hair falling over his high forehead, he snuggled into the pillows with a wide yawn that showed his plentiful gold teeth. She was not tremendously moved by Charlie—as a lover he lacked talent—but he had much to teach her. She wanted to keep him as a friend. When she was sure she had his attention, she touched the telegram and sighed heavily.

"What's wrong? Bad news in the telegram?"

She handed it to Charlie, saying nothing.

"Oh, rot. That is bad news. But maybe you can get away sometimes? There are some very pleasant houses of assignation I use sometimes."

"Let me see how things work out. Perhaps after a while. Especially if I introduce you as a friend, or as someone interested in Tennessee. That would make things easier for us."

She had not lied. If she told the truth, that she and James believed in free love, her lack of sexual interest might hurt Charlie's feelings. She genuinely liked him, but there was no spark. He was too plodding a lover, with—as was the case with so many men—no understanding of a woman's body. They did not know how to find, let alone stimulate, a woman's spot for pleasure.

Fortunately, he had to run off to work. Tennie was waiting in the hall for him to leave. "Listen, I met the most wonderful woman last night." Tennie looked absolutely radiant. Her beauty was quite different from Victoria's own—not that she was vain, but being beautiful had clear advantages. Victoria's face was chiseled, refined. Her hair was dark and her complexion fair. Tennie was voluptuous and high-colored, with auburn hair and a figure men always wanted to get their hands on. All seven Claflin children had different appearances, although there was no doubt with their hyperreligious mother Roxanne that Buck was the father. He wasn't faithful, but Victoria was certain their mother was. Roxanne might be considered touched, as people said, but she had managed to feed them all under hellish circumstances, and she had loved them in her own way. She had never denied their gifts. Nor had Buck. He simply exploited them.

"So tell me about this woman." Victoria sat on her bed, mending a peacock blue frock of Tennie's. Victoria liked to wear black while her sister went in for vivid colors. Victoria sewed well—in fact she had tried to make a living at it in San Francisco, but it paid so poorly, she had gone on the stage instead. Tennie paced back and forth in her chemise, crinoline and corset that pushed her breasts high—up and out.

"Annie Wood. She runs an elegant whorehouse on Thirty-fourth Street. Only the real toffs go there. She's getting rich fast, because the toffs talk about the stocks and their investments. Annie chats them up and has her girls do the same, then she invests. It's a place the girls are treated swell, Vickie. You have to meet her. She's sharp."

"Maybe today. The Colonel is coming tomorrow." Victoria's second husband had been a real colonel in the Union army during the Civil War, and he had the wounds to show for it. He had returned from the wars scarred both inwardly and outwardly, uncomfortable in his life and no longer able to enjoy sex with his wife. He had come to see Victoria in her professional capacity as a magnetic healer about his headaches and had confessed his problems to her. The moment he had walked into the parlor where she was receiving patients, she had jumped as if something hot had been driven into her spine. It's the man, she thought. She wanted him at once. She felt the spirits within her commanding, Yes! Tennie and she both had a healing touch in more ways than one, and on that very first visit she had taken care of his sexual problem. He could not always perform, but he was satisfied now. He encouraged her to take lovers, but he did not trust himself with any other woman unless there was some clear advantage—perhaps a woman who might back a scheme of his. He had left his conventional marriage and gone off with her.

He was a bright man with radical ideas. It was a time of ferment for many. She had missed him while he was clearing up financial matters in St. Louis, but now they would be together. He had spent considerable time polishing her manners and appearance as they had journeyed around the Midwest giving séances and healing the sick and troubled. She could pass as a lady now.

"Yes, this morning on the latish side," Victoria said musingly. "I'll meet your Annie Wood. Bring some of our medical items. Perhaps the ladies of the house would like to try them. We could deal with some of the better houses. James can handle the business end if the contact works out."

Tennie nodded. "If all else fails, it wouldn't be a bad place to work. It's done up like a mansion in New Orleans, where Annie comes from. The food is real Creole cooking, and the furnishings are plain elegant, Vickie. Even to the paintings on the walls. Not your barroom nudes but tasteful, everything first-class. Her clientele includes bankers, stockbrokers, doctors, lawyers, judges, politicians, you name it. . . ."

"Cornelius Vanderbilt? Does he go there?"

"As far as I can learn, he doesn't go for prostitutes. He used to chase governesses. He doesn't pay, although he can be generous. They say he's worth at least ninety-five million."

Among their aims in coming to New York was meeting Cornelius Vanderbilt—meeting and conquering. They had certain advantages that might pique his interest. His power and money certainly intrigued them. "Charlie says he has the manners of a pig. He spits tobacco on the floor. He eats enough for an elephant, very rich food that's shortening his life. He likes women but he's having some problems now. He's eighty. And he's still trying to contact the spirit of his mother."

"I'll see what I can do," Tennie promised. "I bet I can move the old geezer."

Victoria shook out the dress she had mended. Her sewing was excellent, tiny stitches no one would be able to see. "I'm sure his mother is eager to communicate with him. We'll have to see what we can do. By the way, from what Charlie told me, the gossip is that he likes full-bodied women."

"Okay. Then it's up to me." Tennie shook her loose auburn hair. "Let's try it."

"James won't be here until tomorrow evening. His train gets in around eight. Vanderbilt has his open office hour at five. We'll get there by four to be sure we can see him." She had pumped Charlie on everything he knew about Commodore Vanderbilt. "He'll only give us five minutes. So if we can't hook him in five, we're out the door." Victoria let herself fall back on the chenille bedspread. "I do so hope we can seize his attention. We need him, but we have to persuade him that he needs us."

The brothel was one of those newish brownstones speculators were building on block after block. It looked much like every other house in the row—none of the posters of whores or the ladies hanging their titties out the window Victoria had noticed farther downtown. A hefty butler who probably doubled as bouncer answered the door, then passed them on to a colored maid in pristine starched apron who grilled them on their purpose. Finally they were led to Annie Wood.

"Yes, I'm Louisiana born and bred," Annie said. She was a slender blonde in her thirties with a low sweet voice. She wore white lawn with a cashmere paisley shawl thrown round her shoulders. "I grew up on a plantation up the Mississippi from New Orleans about forty miles. We had a magnificent house, but it was burned in the War Between the States."

They were sipping coffee with chicory in the conservatory, a pleasant room with a glass dome and tropical plants, banana trees, orange trees, oleanders, azaleas. There were small brightly colored birds in cages among the greenery. They sat among the flowering plants sipping café au lait from fine china cups with a design of peacocks.

"Is that what brought you into the business?"

"Have you ever sold your body, Mrs. Blood?"

Sold? she thought. Lent, perhaps. "Call me Victoria. And I kept my first husband's name, Woodhull. I think 'Blood' has certain connotations that aren't appropriate for me."

"You didn't answer my question."

She decided to be truthful, for Annie interested her. "When I was an actress, we were expected to permit liberties from well-to-do gentlemen after the performances."

Tennie said, "My daddy Buck used to have me take men to bed, and then he would bust in and blackmail them. We must have done it a hundred times. He'd be swearing I was a virgin and all. Sometimes we'd get run out of town."

Annie nodded, her blond curls bouncing. "The old badger game. There's houses here where that's the real source of income."

Victoria said, "Now I prefer to select my lovers, but sometimes a woman has no choice. I don't judge prostitutes and I'm not out to save them. If I had my way, they'd make a good living and so would every other working woman."

"Are you for woman's rights, then?"

"Of course I am. Aren't you?"

Annie smiled and offered more coffee. "I know the chicory is an acquired taste. I like coffee with warm milk and lots of dark sugar."

Victoria found the chicory bitter but decided against saying so. She liked this woman, this madam. She wanted her as an ally. "It's delicious. . . . I answered your question but you ignored mine."

"I always say, when I have to tell men anything, that my family lost their money in the war and that my parents were killed. But the truth is I was seduced the year I came out and my lover abandoned me, my father disowned me."

How she had wished at times that her parents had disowned her. The very word itself reeked of privilege. Did the poor ever "disown" anyone or anything? "A madam has much more power than a working girl does."

"And a house is much healthier and safer than working the streets. Try the dark sugar. I'm fond of it. I don't like overrefined white sugar. It has no flavor."

"So your gentlemen like the mulatto girls?"

"I have ten of them and ten white girls. I dress them as Southern belles. They all bring in good money."

Victoria pointed to a statue, the only one in the conservatory. It depicted Daphne struggling to escape from Apollo and turning into a laurel tree to avoid rape. "That's an unusual subject for a brothel."

"Some of the men consider it stimulating."

Victoria tapped the table. "That's not why it's here, is it?"

"You have brains as well as beauty. I rarely meet women with such an edge. . . . That's sex to me. No romance. Just rape or escape."

"You don't take lovers any longer?"

"Lovers?" Annie laughed shortly. "There's no love in men. But there certainly is profit."

"I think we're going to be friends, Annie. I find your company very satisfying."

"We're both businesswomen, I declare. We can be friends and we can share a common interest in making ourselves secure in our finances, Victoria. We've both been poor, and neither of us would care to be so again."

THAT AFTERNOON VICTORIA had a vision as she lay in her bath. Having grown up without indoor plumbing, with a falling-down outhouse and a rusty pump at which to fill a bucket for every watery need, she loved long hot soaking baths, scented oils and thick bath cloths and thicker towels.

She loved steam rising to the mirror and a shelf of fine lotions for afterward. But at the moment they were living in a boardinghouse, and they were only allowed to bathe on alternate days.

She saw herself addressing a great crowd in an auditorium. She could see the oak lectern before her, people cramming every seat and leaning out of the balcony that ran across the back. She could feel herself straightening her notes and her heart beating on her breastbone in fear, but when she began to speak, her voice filled the space. In the vision men threw their top hats and derbies in the air and women applauded and wept—for her, Victoria Woodhull. For her.

Even in the vision, she was only the messenger. Demosthenes taught her to speak, but the spirits spoke through her. Yes, she had to make money, she had to support her family and her children, who were coming with James, poor broken Byron and dear Zulu Maud, her children from her disastrous first marriage. But beyond making money and taking care of those for whom she was responsible, she had a further calling, a duty to the voices who spoke through her. She was more than the sum of her parts. She was the portal for powerful voices from beyond who were calling for a new world, new freedom, an opening for light and hope, for women, for children, yes, for men who cared also. She had certainly experienced man troubles, but unlike Annie, she was not embittered. The sexual act committed in freedom and loving-kindness sustained her, gave her strength and tapped energies most women were not lucky enough to enjoy in these silly times. She wanted to bring that freedom and joy to other women. She had never let herself be debased as their daddy Buck had debased Tennie. No, her sexuality was her power because it was in her control.

Someone was tapping on the door and she rose from her bath, thinking herself like Venus rising from the sea. "Just a moment, please." Botticelli's Venus, a reproduction Annie Wood had hung in the parlor where gentlemen were first received and shared champagne with the ladies of the house while a stately gentleman played softly on the piano. That Venus was fair-haired, unlike her. Soon she would have a magnificent house for herself, her sister, husband, children and whomever else she needed to take in and provide for—there would be others, there were always others. She had been making a living for herself and others since she was eight.

Victoria dressed with care in ladylike black silk with touches of white lace, Tennessee more flamboyantly in magenta silk with a turquoise shawl. Victoria disliked very tight lacing, but today they helped each other pull the corsets in and in. They examined each other with a critical eye. "We'll do," Tennie said. "Too bad we don't have some jewels. Ladies always have jewels."

"Soon we will. They mean nothing to me, but they're a sign, as you say. An emblem of status."

The flunky ushered them into Vanderbilt's inner office. "What can I do for you, ladies?" The portly old man was stuffed into a chair that barely fit him. He was a big man still, with a high forehead where his hair had receded and a penetrating dark gaze. He sat in his chair like a bear brought into the parlor, his shoulders and arms those of a man who had done hard work in his time. He wore old-fashioned clothes, a dark and rumpled suit coat and white cravat. Victoria doubted he had thought twice about his clothing in the last forty years. He still made a powerful presence. In his prime, she might have found him attractive. Tennie still would. The smell of money and power would work for her, as it didn't for Victoria.

"We've come," Victoria said in her clear contralto voice, "to offer our help to you. We are both spiritual adepts who have had great success over the years in putting people into communication with their loved ones who have passed over. We are also magnetic healers, again with years of successful practice. I want to put you in communication with your mother, and my sister is going to ease some of your physical problems. You'll tell us when you want us to start."

They both beamed at him and Tennessee leaned a little forward, flashing him some cleavage.

"That's quite a tall order, my dears. Quite a tall order. I've gone through forty mediums over the decade since my mother passed on, and I've had paltry success. Most mediums are scallywags and frauds. And the same with healers."

"Therefore, if we can't help you, you can say goodbye. We won't charge you."

"Everybody charges. What's your racket?"

"If we help you, you'll help us. If we can't help you, then we're off and you're none the worse for it. But if we do assist you in the spiritual and physical ways I've mentioned, then you can decide what you want to do for us. How's that for a bargain? No risk to you."

"What about you, the redhead? You haven't got much to say for yourself." He inserted a wad of chewing tobacco into his jowly cheek.

"I'm more of a physical worker," Tennie said, imbuing the statement with innuendo. "I can help you, but not sitting across a desk."

He spat on the floor, watching their reaction. Victoria allowed none to show. She had grown up around enough taverns to be used to men spitting tobacco juice wherever they felt like it, in a spittoon, often on the floor or whatever else got in their way. Charlie had warned her about the Commodore's less genteel habits, so they were prepared. Neither of them was put off by rough males; their father Buck was a tough rascal and a hard-drinking man. Nothing that Vanderbilt, who had a reputation for chasing servant girls around his mansion, was likely to pull would shock either of them.

The factotum who ushered the visitors in and out appeared, but the Commodore waved him away. The man backed out of the room like a courtier in the royal presence.

"If you'll appoint a time," Victoria said while Tennie was giving him the eye, "we'll come to you at your home. You'll see exactly what we can do."

"Next Monday at nine in the evening. Do you know where I live?"

Of course they did, but Victoria shook her head. "We've only just arrived in the city. Do you have a card?"

"Write it down, dear. Ten Washington Place. This office backs onto my house."

Victoria had been looking around the office. A large stuffed tabby cat stood on top of a row of cabinets. Vanderbilt was not known as a kind or sentimental man. He had grown up on a Staten Island farm, and farmers saw cats as barn animals. But he had been a sailing and then a steamship captain. Captains often had cats. To have a cat stuffed he must have regarded it highly. "Even your ship's cat has a presence here. A very benign one."

"Pouncer. Sailed with me to Nicaragua and up the river they said I couldn't navigate in a steamship. During the gold rush. Best damned cat for ratting I ever knew."

"A handsome animal." Victoria rose and motioned to Tennie to do the same. "We'll see you then. Thank you for your time. Next time we meet, you'll thank us." They swept out in a rustling of skirts.

She would have liked to take a horse cab but it would cost. They sat on a stoop to put on more sensible shoes from Victoria's commodious bag, then walked downtown toward their boardinghouse. Victoria could walk miles when necessary. It was a dry mild evening with a hint of freshness in the rank smoky air, perhaps coming off the river. Victoria took Tennie's arm as they strolled. The smells of roasting corn and frying oysters and sausage made her mouth fill with saliva, but there would be some kind of food back in the boardinghouse. Watery stew with a few pieces of leathery something. Times were hard, but Victoria was convinced they would soon be less lean. Like so many others, she had come to New York to make her fortune, but she had the wherewithal to succeed. Her voices had told her she was to lead a great crusade, but she would need money to do that. And money to keep them out of the stinking warrens of poverty. They would not only survive in this hard place, they would thrive.

They picked their way through the teeming streets, lifting their skirts carefully to avoid the offal and horse shit. As they walked downtown, the sidewalks grew crowded with men shouldering each other returning from work, whores accosting them, pickpockets working the crowd, carts loading and unloading, vendors selling oranges, hot corn, oysters, coffee and chestnuts, girls crying their wares of matches or flowers, street musicans tootling or sawing away or loudly singing. They ducked out of the way of carriages and once a thundering water cart from a company rushing to claim a fire. Twice sporting men accosted them—young men on the prowl—but Victoria clutched Tennie and they slipped away. Arm in arm, she and her favorite sister marched on. She had stolen Tennie away from Buck to save her—the other sane and bright member of their family. Together with her husband James, they would be formidable.

TWO

FREYDEH GOT UP before dawn as usual. The Silvermans always woke her, even on the rare morning when she might have slept in. She had a straw mattress in the windowless kitchen, three dollars a week. The baby was already crying to be fed. The girls and Mrs. Silverman had to get breakfast for everyone before they started making paper flowers in the front room, the only room with windows and some natural light and ventilation, where the boys and male boarder slept. Freydeh washed quickly in a basin she filled a third full from the bucket hauled up the night before from the pump in the yard behind the tenement—to finish before the men rose. It was always a race because

Karl the twelve-year-old would try to catch her with her blouse open or her skirt rucked up. She ate her bread, smoked herring and tea sitting on her cot, and then she was off to the pharmacy, leaving the tiny flat with its eight other inhabitants.

It was the best job she had found since arriving in New York six years before—years of selling old shoes from a pushcart, then bread, then aprons. Like her, her boss Yonkelman was one of the few Jews from the Pale—the Silvermans were German Jews, who often seemed more German than Jew. They didn't even speak Yiddish, but rather German, and they winced when she spoke. Yonkelman wasn't bad to work for. He didn't try anything funny. He was an elderly man in his fifties, once tall but now stooped, shiny bald on top but bristling from his brows, his chin, his nose, his ears. He had a sick wife he was crazy about, who used to do the job Freydeh did now. He paid Freydeh more than she had ever earned, which wasn't much but every bit helped her survive and save a little—a few pennies a week.

But the best thing about this job, she thought as she worked at her new task of grinding materials for pills, was that she got ideas how she might do something that would let her see ahead further than the end of the week. She wanted, oh, she wanted a place of her own. She wouldn't mind taking in boarders like the Silvermans, like the other two places she had lived in New York, but she would be the woman who got the money and kept the couple of rooms the way she wanted them kept. A place of her own: she dreamed of that day and night.

That loudmouth Izzy White came in. White! He had changed his name to be more American, he said. He was shorter than she was, a little wizened as if something in him had dried out or been pickled in brine, but his voice was that of a barrel-chested ogre. Even when she was in the back room doing inventory or preparing pills and medicines—something Yonkelman trusted her with more and more—she could hear Izzy the moment he barged into the shop.

"So how many gross you want this time, Yonkelman?"

"Four gross this week. But these better be good ones. My customers, they complain if they break. That's no good for them, no good for me. I can go back to getting condoms from Colgate, I can do that anytime."

"Sure, at twice what I charge you. So sometimes the rubber isn't so good, but I do a pretty nice job. I include a gross of the fancy ones—I make fancy *and* cheap."

She looked quickly for one of those little mirrors Yonkelman sold.

Then she brushed her hair hard, pinched her cheeks and rubbed at her lips. She had never been a beauty—that was Shaineh in her family, who took after their mother, and not their father, as she did. But she had a good full figure and Izzy had an eye for her. Not that that would do him any good the way he wanted, not in a thousand years. But she liked to get him talking. Making condoms was a great way to make a living. Now that was something a woman could do in a kitchen, and soon Freydeh would have her own house, maybe in Brooklyn, and live like a queen.

Every time Izzy came to pester her, she got him to talk more about how he did it and afterward she wrote everything down in a little notebook. She wrote in Yiddish. Her English was not so good yet. She had learned to read and write, her mother had insisted, so she could keep accounts for her mother's business—making and selling vodka out of a shed. Her father had been a woodcutter, like her dear dead Moishe.

"Now a woman like you," Izzy said, sitting on the counter so they were eye to eye, "you have to miss the comfort of a husband to warm your bed. A big healthy strapping woman full of juice, still young enough. . . ."

She had loved Moishe since she was sixteen and they were married under the chuppah. She had seen him around for years because he worked the same as her father in the forest cutting timber. But they had never exchanged five words before they were betrothed by their parents. Although her parents had barely one coin to rub on another, they'd had no trouble finding a husband for her because she had a reputation as a hard worker and she could keep books. So while Moishe as a woodcutter had not been considered a great catch, he had a job and her parents could never afford a scholar or a rabbinical student for a husband. Secretly she was glad, because she didn't want to be the sole breadwinner in the family. Women had to work of course, but if she had one of those fancy husbands studying Torah or halachah all day, he would not have brought in enough to buy stale bread.

She had been afraid on her wedding night, but Moishe had been gentle with her. He had been with the whores in the brothel by the river many times and he liked women and their bodies. He loved her body and made her love his. Many weeks, no matter how tired they were, they had joined their bodies far more often than required for a man who did physical labor, according to Talmudic law. She had been rich with joy, but until they had come to this city, she had never conceived.

That was her great grief, the lack of a baby from Moishe, her love, but she wasn't about to have a bastard with Izzy, so he could just forget it—but no, better he went on hoping she would fall plop in his arms like a ripe plum off the trees in the orchard near the shtetl where she had been born. A ripe purple plum just about to split its skin with sweet juice. He could hope all he liked, but what she wanted from him was information. Every time he came back to flirt with her, she learned more. Yonkelman let Izzy pester her because he wanted Izzy to give him a good price on condoms, and he thought she was a lure for that. So they all played their little games on each other and it went on week after week. Izzy wasn't about to lower his price, she wasn't about to let Izzy tumble her, and Yonkelman wasn't about to start buying his condoms from Colgate.

"So how is your business going? You still have your nephew helping you cook the rubber and fill the molds?" she asked.

"He's a *starker,* eats his weight every night, but he works good, so I should complain?"

"You told me sometimes he overcooks the rubber. So how can you tell?"

Lucky for her, Izzy liked to talk and she was happy to listen. When he finished his explanation he launched into a long story about how some other widow was making eyes at him, and that was a woman who knew a good thing when she saw it.

Freydeh sighed, and Izzy moved nearer, thinking he had gotten through her reserve and she was pining. With a little laugh she swung out of his arm and away. "I got to get back to work or Yonkelman will toss me into the street and somebody else take my job, Izzy. So let me get back to it."

"He's not going to fire you, you work too hard. You do two jobs. Even his wife, good and pious as she is, he never let her mix the medicines. So give me a little kiss."

"Give yourself one for me. Now out of here." She gave him a semi-playful shove.

"You're a strong woman, Freydeleh. Sometimes I think you could pick me up and carry *me* over the threshold."

Some men were put off by her strength, the strength of her father who cut trees all day in the forests near Vilna, the strength of her mother who bore eight children and saw three of them die before their second year. But some men like Izzy liked a big strong woman, and tough for him, because her pushing him out of the back room was the closest he was ever getting to her.

When Yonkelman closed the pharmacy at four for Shabbos, she had to go over to Hester Street and buy a chicken for the Silvermans and herself.

One chicken would make soup for all of them tonight, and Mrs. Silverman had asked her to pick it up, pluck and cook it for them because she had to finish a whole box of the flowers and deliver them to the manufacturer before sundown. The baby had been sick and Mrs. Silverman, who looked forward to the Shabbos shopping that included gossiping with friends she never got to see otherwise, had to pass off the job. Freydeh didn't mind. On a mild April afternoon, she'd rather be in the street because inside smelled even worse.

Hester Street was curb to curb with people, a mass of pushcarts and women haggling and pushcart vendors, men and women and sometimes children, shouting their wares. The sound rose between the narrow buildings like the roar of a waterfall of voices. In the forest where she had gone to take her father bread and cheese and an onion, sometimes he was working near a stream tumbling down in a waterfall. How clean the forest had smelled.

She made herself remember the pervasive stench of fear, the tightness in the belly when she had to walk by a group of peasant men, the goyim who surrounded them in the Pale, where they were forced to live crowded together. The fear of their violence. Here she could work freely at what she could find. Here there were neighborhoods where she might be attacked but others where she felt safe, and she could even go up to the shops on Fifth Avenue and walk around staring in the windows like any rich lady. Here she could earn money and put it away little by little and send it off to her family whenever she had enough to mail a money order. Here she could sometimes go to night school and improve her English and learn. Here school was free to children, and surely Shaineh would be married by now and have children she could care for as soon as she could send them all passage money. Those children, her nieces and nephews, would go to school and be educated, girls as well as boys. She had made the right choice and soon others from the Pale would see. They had been pioneers, Moishe and she, for they had read a book about America and they had burned to go and be free. They had been carried out of the Pale of Settlement where Jews were forced by the czar to live, hidden under sacks of grain. Then they sailed from Danzig, changed to a ship in Hamburg, landed at Castle Garden and finally, finally entered. As they stood at the rail of the steamer entering New York Harbor, after only a twelve-day crossing instead of the forty days before steamships had been put into service, she had taken Moishe's hard hand in her own. "Like your namesake, you've led us to the promised land. But unlike him, you're going to set foot in it and live out your life here."

She sighed, making her way in the melee of bodies gesticulating, bargaining, prodding, shouting. She had been right, but she had not guessed how short that life would be. She straightened her shoulders and plowed into the crowd. Enough of this sad musing on what was gone like water to the sea. At five six, she was taller than almost all of the women and a good many of the men—her father's legacy—but it was still hard to see ahead of her in the press. Mrs. Silverman had not given her enough for a good chicken, but she would see what she could do. As a female boarder, she not only paid her rent, she was expected to watch the baby, the younger children when needed, to run errands, to help with the laundry, to cook on occasion. Still, it was much better than the last place she lived.

She had just tried bargaining with two different purveyors of kosher chickens when, as if the thought had conjured him up, she saw Big Head Wolf, her previous landlord—a con man and sometimes a thief, who had tried to press her into service in his scams. She thought of turning away but he had seen her. "Freydeleh, Freydeleh, you look blooming and bright. Got yourself a new man?"

"Good day to you, Big Head. What I do is none of your business."

He seized her by the elbow. "You still owe me two dollars."

"You took my necklace. That covers all debts."

"I want my two dollars." He let go of her elbow, leaning toward her with a little grin. "Of course, if you don't want your letter from your family . . ."

"You got a letter for me? Since when?" For more than a year she had heard nothing from her family back in the Pale. She had sent money for her parents to emigrate, but she never heard from them. She wrote again and again without an answer. So much could go wrong in the Pale. Troubles could descend like the plagues of Exodus, on the good as well as the wicked.

"Since some time ago while I'm waiting for my two dollars you owe."

"You can't keep my letter from me. That's my property."

"But I can forget where I put it."

"You got me over a gulley, Big Head. I want that letter. Those are my only people. Don't you care about anybody but yourself?"

"I care about my two dollars you owe. Pay up and I'll give you the letter."

"I don't trust you."

"Okay, come by Sunday in the evening and give me my two dollars and I'll give you your letter." He gripped her elbow again. "Deal?"

She hated to give him anything, the man who had stolen her only necklace, one her mother had given her when she married, but she needed that letter. Maybe it said they were coming. Maybe they were on their way. "All right, I'll come by after work, around eight, nine. We run late at the pharmacy. Will you be there?"

"If I'm not, give it to Pearl. I'll leave the letter with her. You give her the money, she gives you the letter."

SHE WAS NERVOUS ALL through Shabbos. She went to the shul with the Silvermans because it was easier to go than not to. Moishe and she had been freethinkers, socialists, poor as they were, among the enlightened ones. She did not believe in all that nonsense, but she kept kosher anyhow. At Wolf's, going to shul was one thing she didn't have to do, but the Silvermans were better people. They were honest, they were hardworking, and if they worked her hard too, she understood why. Mrs. Silverman was so skinny she could sit with her younger daughter two to the same chair. The oldest daughter was just as thin and pale as if the sun never touched her, and it scarcely did, for she worked all day and into the night with her mother and sister making those flowers to be pinned to ladies' bosoms or stuck on their floppy hats. They all had light brown hair worn down their back in braids, all the girls and even Mrs. Silverman. When Freydeh had arrived in New York, she had been shocked how many good Jewish wives wore their own hair, but now she was used to it. After the second month, she left off her wig, letting her own hair grow out, thicker than it had been before she married, a dark reddish brown Moishe said was the color of good tea.

She was on edge the next day at the pharmacy. Sunday was always a busy day. Lots of hangover preparations, mostly for their non-Jewish customers who knew how good a pharmacist Yonkelman was. He was better than most doctors at figuring out what ailed a sick person and what they should have—better than the cruel bleeding and poisons and purges regular doctors believed in. He sold pills too for female troubles—which meant somebody got knocked up and needed to get rid of the baby. All the pharmacies sold condoms, pessaries, womb veils, forty different douches, all to prevent conception or end it. Most pharmacists made those kinds of pills, but Yonkelman got his from Madame Restell, who sold pills and performed abortions out of a fine row house on Greenwich Street. Carriages were always pulling up to her door and veiled women in fancy clothes climbing out. Madame had a sliding scale, expensive for the elite and cheap for working women. Every so many weeks, Yonkelman would send her down to Madame or to her husband Charles Lohman, who had his office around the corner with a doctor's plaque. He made up the pills. He was no more a doctor than Madame was, but that hardly mattered. Madame knew what she was doing, a big buxom woman with a head of beautiful dark hair, always dressed in silks as fine as any of her clients. Women preferred to go to women. Every woman in the shtetl knew there were times to have a baby and times not to. It was all part of what women did for each other at home, herbs for this and that, potions, midwifery, the lore women passed on generation to generation. When you had female troubles, you turned to a woman. Women were always running to male doctors here, but she didn't trust them. They hadn't saved Moishe. Besides, a male doctor wasn't decent.

At last they were finally closing. She rushed through the streets so fast her breath stabbed her. Fortunately, she didn't bother with corsets and those stays American women wore. They couldn't bend over or lie down in them or even sit comfortably. She wove her way through groups congregating around every stoop, gathered in the street, men smoking, women gossiping, kids chasing each other or looking for something to swipe. Street arabs like her friend Sammy were running errands or shooting craps or holding some toff's horse while he visited a whore.

Big Head's apartment was in a rear tenement on Cherry Street, up on the top floor. He came and went across the roofs sometimes. She labored up the steep dark steps, hopping over puddles of urine and sticky stuff that looked like blood. Something was dripping at the back of the second-floor hall. The smell of cooked cabbage, rancid grease, unwashed bodies made her put her hand up to her nose, although she ought to be used to it by now. Back in the shtetl, she could always step outside and the wind would carry the evergreen scent of the woods. Here outside smelled as bad as inside. She had to walk to the river to smell something fresh, and even then, half the time it smelled like sewage or slaughterhouses or tanneries.

Big Head wasn't home, but his wife Pearl opened the door. She was pregnant again, wearing a loose wrapper with a stained apron over it. "Another three months to go, eh?" Freydeh eyed Pearl's belly. She had helped deliver enough babies to know.

"What you want, anyhow, coming around here all of a sudden after the way you moved out!" Pearl tossed her red hair and turned to plump her behind into a chair.

"Big Head said he got a letter for me. I came for it." She slid past Pearl into the kitchen and stood, hands on her hips.

"He said, you pay us the three dollars you owe us and then I give you the letter."

"Two dollars. And he took my necklace."

"Three dollars. Big Head says you got to pay interest from owing it so long."

"Two dollars is all I got." She took the greasy dollars from her pocket and flattened them out to show Pearl.

"Big Head says three."

"Okay, well I tried. The letter is probably nothing but a series of complaints anyhow, it rained too much, the winter was too long, our cow died, I got rheumatism. To read somebody's stale grief isn't worth money I don't got."

Freydeh gave the woman a big false smile showing all her strong teeth and then swung on her heel, marched out slowly but steadily and slammed the door. Then she stood outside it, her heart tapping its hammer on her breastbone, her clenched hands wet with sweat. She took another three steps, trying to hear if Pearl was moving behind the paper-thin wall, but there was too much noise.

The door flung open. "Well, all right, all right. Don't keep me standing here," Pearl yelled. "Out of the goodness of my heart, I'm giving you the letter for the original two dollars you owe us. Now give me the money and take your dirty letter. Oh, and this is one of yours that came back. See, I saved it for you."

Freydeh grabbed the two letters and ran down the stairs. She did not dare stop to read the letter—it was dark already and the gas lamps that weren't broken gave a faint illumination to the unpaved streets. Fortunately a lot of people were out. The night was mild for early April. She ran the five blocks to the Silvermans', and not until she was in their front room did she dare take the letter and tear it open. Mrs. Silverman and the two older girls were at the table making flowers, as usual. They wouldn't be able to stop till they fell asleep, they got so little for each piece.

She moved near their candle and read. It wasn't her mother's writing. Her mother always wrote the letters. This hand was more ragged than her mother's neat tiny writing. Her father? No, the letter was signed by Shaineh. Why Shaineh? By the light of the flickering candle, she leaned to read. Her hands were making the paper soft, she was sweating so. She smoothed out the crumpled paper. It was dated eight months ago, August 1867. In Yiddish it said,

Dearest Sister Freydeleh,

I have the worst news for you, forgive the messenger, but you have to know what came down on us. First our brother Eliyahu went off to the new lands where the czar is promising much land and seeds to plant, if Jews will go, so he took his wife and their little boy and he went. We have written and written to him, but we have heard nothing and we fear the worst.

Mama and Papa got cholera in the epidemic this summer. Mama got sick first and Papa caught it from her, trying to save her and little Yakov. I was away because Mama had apprenticed me to a seamstress. But I never learned nothing about sewing because she had me taking care of her twins and cooking and cleaning and treated me like a servant. So I didn't get the cholera but everybody else did except Sara and her family, who are fine.

Mama and Papa were going to emigrate this fall on what you sent them, but we used up some of the money burying them all so there was just enough for one. Sara said I should be the one to go. She has taken over Mama's vodka business and her husband is working for a miller so she says she is set and I should go to America and live with you and make money and then I can send back enough for all of them to come over or else Eli and his family if they came back from that place where the czar sent them. As for Shlomo, nobody has heard of him since the czar took him for the army and maybe we never will, it's in the hands of Hashem.

So I have made arrangements to get out of the Pale the same way you did. I am traveling with a family from Minsk so I should be safer than if I went off alone. Papa had betrothed me to the Sibivitz middle son but he got taken by the czar too, so they called it off. So I got no ties to keep me here and I want to go and be useful and have a good life there.

I am leaving in time to get a ship from Hamburg 20 October before the winter comes and the seas get too rough and dangerous. The ship I am supposed to go on, it's called Die Freiheit. I think its name is a good omen. Things have been so terrible here, people ate their shoes, cooked them in water for soup and got deadly sick. We had to eat our last cow. There was no choice. We were dying of hunger. But we did that and then the cholera came, so what was the use sacrificing Daisy to survive when nobody did?

So I expect to be in New York around the end of October to embrace you and let us blend our tears for all the troubles of our family and the loss of Mama and Papa, who worked so hard and gave us so much love.

Your loving sister,
Shaineh

Freydeh put the letter down in shock. Her mother, her father, her little brother, all dead. All gone from her forever. It had been hard enough to leave them, knowing as every emigrant knew, that she might never see them again. But now they were truly gone and she had not been there to nurse them, to bury them properly, to mourn them. Her father had been such a force in her life, working in any weather, risking his skin to bring them enough for bread and fuel. Her mother worked from before dawn till long after dusk. Her mother was the fire in the hearth, the light of the house. Singing at her work, always singing, and the children learned those songs as early as they could mouth the words.

Then Freydeh groaned aloud. Shaineh had presumably arrived at the end of October and there had been no one to meet her. She had probably made her way to the address she had from before, but Big Head would not have helped her. Freydeh had taken care that Big Head didn't know where she moved, because she didn't trust him, because she wanted nothing to do with him and his gang of thieves.

She had sent more money in the last letter and her new address, but Shaineh must already have left. She opened her own letter carefully. It looked as if it had been rained on, dropped in the dirt and smeared with something. But her letter and the last money order were still inside. It was amazing that no one had pilfered it, torn it open, taken the order and cashed it, some Pale version of Big Head. There were enough of them. When times were hard, there were always crooks to make it still harder.

She put her head in her hands in despair. Shaineh, her beautiful youngest sister, had come to New York alone and no one had met her. So what had happened to Shaineh? All that could go wrong swirled in Freydeh's head. She had to find Shaineh, but how?

All right, the first thing was to find out when the ship had come in and whether Shaineh had truly been on it. She needed to talk Yonkelman into letting her leave work to go down to Castle Garden and make inquiries. Even the prospect of dealing with the immigration people gave her a stomachache, but she must do it, and soon. If she could afford a lawyer, this would be easier, but she couldn't, no use fussing about it. Her English was just not good enough. She had been studying and studying, sometimes even in the pharmacy during slow times. The Silverman girls helped her. They didn't even have accents. Of course, who could hear their own accent? She would still sound like a greenhorn, she didn't doubt it.

She could take one of the street kids from the neighborhood with her. That kid Sammy she sometimes shared a little bread with or gave a penny for an errand, he was bright. Sammy was a good kid—as good as he could manage to be. She'd get Sammy to go down to Castle Garden with her and then she would be sure the immigration people and the people from the Hamburg line would understand her and she would understand them. It was a plan. Not much of one, but the best she could do. She had to find Shaineh, and so she had to start someplace.

She knew that in part she was involving Sammy because she had feelings for him—barefoot in all weather, half starved, getting by on garbage and luck, filthy, ragged, scorned, invisible like thousands of others who lived on the streets of this city. They broke her heart. She wanted a child so passionately, and there were all these children just thrown away. She'd look for Sammy right now—even though it meant going down to the street. She knew where he slept—the passageway between two tenements the locals called Pig Alley. She stood up, made her explanation to the Silvermans. Mister had gone to bed with their son. The youngest girl had fallen asleep with her head on the table. Missus and the two older girls were still making flowers, their fingers bleeding as usual by day's end. When the candle guttered out, they would finally go to bed. In the meantime, she would find Sammy and persuade him to accompany her down to the Battery on her quest for real, hard information about Shaineh. It was a weak plan, but she could not see where else to start. She had to find her sister, and she was months late looking. Anything could have happened to Shaineh, anything.

Over the year and five months she had been living at the Silvermans', she had come to know Sammy. Boys grew up fast on these streets. They slept where they could. Their bodies turned up in the mornings and were hauled away and buried in an unmarked pauper's grave. Nobody said goodbye. Nobody missed them, except perhaps a younger kid whom they protected or an older kid who had protected them. There were thousands in these streets, sleeping in alleys, in filthy second basements, in halls and by fences or in sheds. Everywhere she went in the city, there they were, the unwanted, the sloughed-off kids.

Pig Alley was a narrow unpaved slot between the six-story tenements that lined the street. Sammy had built himself a little hut against a wall, cobbled out of builders' scraps and boxes, with a horse blanket he had probably stolen for his bed. He was huddled there, sucking on a bone he had found someplace—a bare bone but better than nothing. She approached him slowly—he was skittish—and held out a heel of bread she had saved, as she might approach a dog encountered in the street.

"Sammy, it's Freydeh. I brought you a little bit of bread. I need to talk with you."

He gobbled the bread and then listened, squinting up at her. He had brown hair a few shades lighter than hers—she thought, but it was hard to tell because of his filth. He was scrawny and tough, but he looked years younger from being so short. He wasn't sure if he was ten or eleven.

"Can you help me?"

"Gimme a quarter."

"I'll buy you some secondhand clothes to keep you warm, that's what I'll do."

He hesitated. He'd rather have money, of course.

"And I'll buy you something to eat on the way."

Finally he nodded approval, and she arranged to meet him in the morning. She smiled slightly as she climbed back upstairs. He had no idea what she was going to do to him. His father had died of typhus when he was little, his mother had married again and bore at least two more babies to her new husband, who beat him. Finally he ran away. They had not bothered to look for him. Nobody had ever wanted him, except for the gang of boys he hung about with in the street or somebody needing him to do something for them—mind a horse, carry a package, send a message, run to the store. He had always been honest with her. She appreciated that. She knew it was silly of her to take an interest in a street arab, but she liked Sammy. Who did she have, anyhow? Until she could find Shaineh, she had no family. She thought Sammy was a cut above the little thieves of the neighborhood, and when she had a bit of extra food, she shared it with him.

Before they started downtown, she bought him a used pair of trousers and a used jacket. He stank so they would have trouble in the offices where he was going to be her spokesman. She made him stand in the yard by the privies while she scrubbed his face and hands with a bit of cloth. Sammy cursed, enduring the cold water and her harsh scrubbing at the pump in the muddy yard between the tenement she lived in and the rear house. Then she had him put on the second- or thirdhand trousers. "*Le'mir geyn,* Sammy—let's get going." Sullenly he followed her.

She had worked hard on her English, but she knew she still spoke with a thick accent. Most of her life was conducted in Yiddish or in German and, once in a while, Russian. Opportunities to practice English were few, for most business of the pharmacy was conducted in Yiddish or German. Sammy spoke Yiddish of course and German too, but he had been born here and spoke English like a native. He had even gone to school for a couple of years, before he went on the streets. He could read and write English, but not Yiddish, and he had not stayed in school long enough to learn to write a cursive hand. When he had to write something, he printed.

They took the horse-drawn trolley downtown, crowded as always. Sammy kept smoothing his new clothes—new to him—and she saw him trying to catch a glimpse of himself in the reflection off the windows. She waited till they were off the trolley and then rehearsed him. "Now, you're my little brother and you live with me at the Silvermans'. That's the best thing to tell them. *Nu, mach snell.* Hurry!"

"I could be your son."

"You could be." She smiled, putting her hand on his bony shoulder. "You like that better?" She would have had to have borne him when she was sixteen if he was eleven, but such early births were not uncommon, back in the Pale or here.

The offices were near the docks, on a cobblestone street with many signs for makers of sails and other gear for ships. Where the docks came up to the street, the bowsprits of ships stuck out overhead, among the wharf shipping sheds and ferry houses on the water side. The street was thick with wagons loading and unloading from warehouses, draymen shouting to get out of the way, roustabouts heaving boxes and barrels. Sailors went lurching past and an occasional natty officer, one in uniform with a lady in a mauve overdress and bustle as big as a bushel basket sticking out on her behind, sashaying along. Over her head she held a matching parasol. A Negro servant walked behind them carrying a satchel and a cloak, and behind him came a cart loaded with four trunks, pulled by a weary gray horse. On the land side of the street stood offices of maritime brokers and lawyers, sail lofts, occasional restaurants. The nearby taverns were dark and rowdy and dangerous. It was said that a drink called the Mickey Finn could knock a man right out so he could be robbed or shanghaied aboard a ship leaving port. The offices of the steamship company, however, were clean and orderly, with many clerks at high desks writing rapidly on ledgers and foolscap. Freydeh and Sammy stood there for what felt like hours before anyone spoke to them.

Sammy introduced himself. "My mother and me, we're trying to find my aunt Shaineh Leibowitz, my mom's youngest sister. She was supposed to come over on one of your ships, the *Freiheit,* but we didn't get the letter until this week. It went to the wrong house."

The clerk made them wait around, but finally he found Shaineh's name on the manifest of the *Freiheit* that had arrived in port on November 9 of the previous year. Shaineh had really come. Of course they had no idea where she had gone or what had happened to her. When they left the office, Freydeh covered her face and leaned on the stones of the building. "Poor girl. What did she think when I wasn't there for her? What could she do?" She stared out over the gray waters where a huge steamship low in the water was being drawn by a tug toward the Hudson.

"You know how those people from the boardinghouses around here, they try to grab the luggage of the greenhorns and drag them off to board with them."

"I don't think she spoke a word of English. She must have been terrified."

"But, Freydeh, wouldn't she go to the address she had?"

"If she could figure out how to get there, sure. But Big Head never told me she came by, and Pearl didn't mention it. So I wonder if she ever got there."

"How much you trust that crook?"

"Not a pinprick worth, believe me."

She had planned to go to immigration next. The clerk at the Hamburg line told her they would have a record if Shaineh had been denied immigration and gone back. "A girl alone," the clerk had said, "probably they'd keep her for a few hours, but there's no record they sent her back. They don't like young women traveling alone. Still, providing she had your name and address, they'd take that into account."

She decided to sit for a moment and think about what they should do. She bought a couple of hard-boiled eggs and some hot corn cakes and coffee from vendors and they walked into the park to eat. This park by the Battery had been closed to ordinary people for years when this had been a fancy neighborhood, but now anybody could sit in it. In the center stood a bandstand. Middle-class people liked to promenade there and listen to concerts. Sometimes there were rallies or parades, as there had been the day Moishe and she had arrived. The people in fancy clothes had glared at them as they staggered out of immigration.

The wind was strong here but it smelled better as they sat on the bench eating their lunch. Seagulls swooped down on them crying out like street arabs in hopes of grabbing crumbs—but they weren't about to leave any. They watched ships pass each other off the Battery, most of the sailing ships going toward the East River, most of the steamships into the Hudson. The masts of the sailing ships stood up in a forest of poles above the warehouses and shops of sailmakers and outfitters. The horns of the steamships blared as smaller fishing vessels and ferries crossed their path. It looked like chaos but every vessel seemed to go where it intended.

The immigration center was an old fort roofed in with a high round three-level room ending in a cupola with a huge flag flapping in the rough wind. It had been a concert hall between being a fort and being what it was now. To one side stood an employment exchange in a long shed. The hawkers were already out, waiting to hire likely-looking men at cheap wages. The boardinghouse keepers and brothel recruiters were beginning to mass by the huge double doors of the fort, where the immigrants would pour out.

"There's a ship, look, bringing the greenhorns. Pretty soon the folks will start coming out. That's when the boardinghouse keepers swarm them. We can ask if they remember Shaineh."

"We can try. You're a good boy, Sammy."

"Not so good. I got to get by what way I can."

"So do we all."

A decision was forming in her. She was always making plans, it was her nature. She had to try, always. "The only good thing that's come out of all this pain is that I have some money now, money I saved for my parents and my family to come over. I sent them the money order but it came back." Freydeh licked her fingers for the last taste of the corn. "I have enough once I get this money order cashed to get my own place. Then when I save up more, I'm going to start my own business."

"What kind of business?" Sammy squinted at her. She couldn't even say if he was fair or ruddy or dark, although she had tried to clean him up. He needed a real bath, a good scrub-down. Baths were hard to come by except in the summer when the pools in the East River were open.

"I'm going to make rubber condoms."

Sammy laughed. Then he squinted at her again. "You serious?"

"There's money in it. I know a gonif makes a living at it. I can do it as well as him. And you're going to help me, Sammy." She had noticed the squinting before. She wondered if he needed glasses. Of course he wouldn't know if he did.

He turned and glared at her. "Don't make fun of me."

"You want to live in a box in Pig Alley?"

"I get by."

"Barely. You're a smart kid, Sammy. I got nobody to look after till I find Shaineh and I'm going to need help."

"Like what kind of help?" His eyes were fixed on hers now. He sat rigidly, waiting to hear what she would say. "I can do anything."

"I'll need help making the molds. We buy the rubber in sheets. I'll do the selling, to establish customers, and you'll do a lot of the deliveries. I can't be making the stuff and running around delivering it too."

"But after you find your sister, you won't need me."

"For all I know, Shaineh is married by now. She was the pretty one in the family. Looking at me, you can't picture her. She was slighter than me, very light brown hair, with a face like a flower, Sammy."

She stood, paced for a moment, sat back down on the bench. "And how do I know if she'd want to work for me? She might be a seamstress by now." She sighed, putting her hand on his arm. "Sammy, I haven't seen her since she was twelve—just a couple of years older than you are now. So what do I know from nothing about her? She's my kid sister and she's lost somewhere in New York—and that's all I know."

"Bad things can happen when you're all alone."

"You know it." And she was sure he did. She wasn't about to ask. Better he should keep those things to himself, not to be ashamed. "Okay, let's go to where the boardinghouse keepers shout their wares to corral the poor people staggering out."

The boardinghouse hawkers were lined up waiting, although nobody had come through the doors yet. She and Sammy pushed from one to another, describing Shaineh, mentioning the ship she had come on, the date she had landed. They had almost given up when they found one enormous red-faced woman who smelled like soup.

"I remember her. She wasn't interested. Then that evening, she came staggering in, exhausted. She couldn't find you. When she finally got to the address you'd given her, they said you didn't live there. So she came back to me. I remember her because she was so pretty and little and she cried so."

"Is she still living with you?" Freydeh took the woman by the arm and she must have grabbed too hard, for the woman flinched.

"Watch it! That hurts."

Freydeh let go. "I'm worried about my sister. Is she with you?"

"She ran out of money, so she had to go."

"Where?"

"How would I know?" The woman was glaring at Freydeh, rubbing her arm ostentatiously.

"Didn't she leave a forwarding address?"

"How long do you think I keep that? I'm one woman running a boardinghouse full of people who come and go, who sneak out without paying their bills, who eat like pigs at the trough. You're lucky I remember her at all." She turned and dived back into the milling crowd of hawkers and the confused immigrants staggering out with their battered luggage and bags and bundles on their heads, on their backs, clutched to their chests like babies. Women in shawls looking as scared and overwhelmed as she had felt six years before.

She sat back on a bench with Sammy, her head in her hands. "Sammy, what would you do if you were Shaineh and dumped down in the city without no one to care for you? Where would you go?"

"Girls go on the streets all the time, just for that. 'Cause they got no home, no money, no friends."

"Sha! I won't think that. She could go to a shul for help. Go back to the neighborhood where she expected to find me and where at least some people speak Yiddish and start asking. That's what we'll try next."

"Are you really going to cash that money order?"

"You bet I am. When I find Shaineh, I need a place to put her, I need a place to work from, and you need a place to sleep too, if you're going to help me." She tried to make herself sound more cheerful than she felt. Whenever she imagined Shaineh alone and friendless and lost on the streets of the city, she panicked. "So are you in?"

"Of course I'm for it. If you really mean it."

She stood, motioning for Sammy to walk with her toward where they could catch a horsecar uptown. She was a little sorry to leave the trees, their buds just opening into tiny leaflets. The smell off the water was a combination of salt and sewage, freshness and decay. It felt good to have wind in her face, trees over them, but it was time to go to their neighborhood. As they left the park, ladies drew their skirts aside as if their passing could soil the fine silks. Gentlemen strolling along, pipes in their mouths, expected them to get out of the way. Now they were back on cobblestones slippery with horse urine and manure. Sailing ships stuck their sprits overhead, some with carved ladies. Big truculent-looking steamships loomed over, stories high. "I hate living in other people's kitchens, sleeping in chairs, sleeping on the floor. This is blood money. I saved it a penny at a time to bring my parents over. Now they're dead and Shaineh's lost. But if I work for myself, I can look for her without begging Yonkelman, Oh, please, mister, please, let me have Monday off, please, sir."

"I thought you liked working in the pharmacy."

"It's better than being a peddler or making flowers like the Silvermans. But I just get by. I can just scrape up a tiny bit each month to save. The way it is with me now, I'll never get ahead."

"What do you really want?" Sammy swung around to stare at her, his hazel eyes startling in his face reddened and weather-beaten by his days and nights on the street, ingrained with dirt and coal dust in spite of her earlier scrubbing.

They waited for a horse-drawn streetcar, in a crowd of others collected on a corner. "I want a little house. I want to be independent. I want Shaineh to live with me."

"Don't you want to marry again? The guys say that's what every widow wants."

"I loved my husband. I don't know if I can love another man that way. What I want, I can work for." They pushed onto the trolley and it was too crowded to talk for the half hour it took for the streetcar to shove its way through the mobbed streets. After they had gotten off and begun to walk again, she said, "There's this woman I heard speak, Ernestine Rose, and she's all for women. She says we're the equal of men and we should keep our own money and we should be treated equal by the law and in the courts. She's a Jew like us, a rabbi's daughter who fought and won her inheritance in the courts. I liked hearing her talk that way. She made me feel like I could do anything."

"Until you get slammed down again," Sammy muttered.

"You get knocked down, you get back up. Nobody's going to help you up. Except if you have a good partner and good friends and a good family. Then somebody will help you. Otherwise, if you fall and you don't get up, you'll be stepped on, you'll be run over and die in the street. Understand me?"

"I got no family."

"Ah, but you have something better. Me." She clapped him on the back. "I will find Shaineh, I swear it. But now we got to figure out how to get my money back out of this stupid piece of paper." She touched the money order in her bosom. She would not let go of it for anything till it was turned into real money. Gold coins, not paper money. Until then, she would sleep with it, she would eat with it, she would wear it to work. It was her future and Shaineh's and Sammy's too. Their future in a single piece of paper.

THREE

MONDAY MORNING EARLY, Henry Stanton caught the train for the city. In Elizabeth's spacious house in Tenafly, New Jersey, there was a room for her husband, but it was far easier when he stayed at the flat in Manhattan. Once their parting embrace would have been passionate. Now they spoke a lukewarm goodbye, she waved perfunctorily and returned to her breakfast.

"Has Mr. Stanton gone?" Susan stuck her head around the corner, ready to retreat. Susan preferred when Henry wasn't around. He demanded too much of Elizabeth's energy, and since his misconduct in the customs office, Susan had allowed her contempt for him to burgeon. Susan's family, the Anthonys, were Hicksite Quaker, unyielding in their moral views.

"Gone to the city. He won't come out again for a couple of weeks." Elizabeth took another pastry from the platter Amelia had set out. Amelia was more friend than servant, a Quaker woman who had been her housekeeper for a quarter century.

Susan grasped her hand. Elizabeth glared. Susan's bony hand was tight around her more fleshy wrist. "Mrs. Stanton!" Susan employed that starchy formality even when they were alone, in spite of their twenty-five years of intimate friendship, often sharing Elizabeth's house. "You must not gain more weight."

"I enjoy my food. Heaven knows how we fight battles every single day, every week, every month, every year, every decade. . . . You're badgering me about food the way you used to badger me about the conjugal bed."

"Every time Mr. Stanton bothered to come home, you'd end up expecting again. Why couldn't you abstain? For a moment of pleasure, you once again plunged yourself into an exhausting round of child-rearing."

"I enjoyed it, Susan. I was still in love with him. I liked making love with him. I didn't wish anything to interfere. . . ." She could never make Susan understand how crazy she had been for Henry—her knight—full of courage, facing down mobs of pro-slavery zealots, fighting passionately for abolition. He had been tall and handsome with a resonant voice, a fine speaker. If now he was shopworn with bad political compromises, she could still remember when he had seemed the epitome of bravery. "I liked motherhood, or I wouldn't have had so many. Anyhow, there's never been a woman so happy to reach menopause. Not that I ever had trouble in childbirth till the last. The midwife used to say I dropped babies like a mother cat birthing kittens."

Susan made a sour face. "You took more care with your children than that!"

Amelia came in with some darning. She winked at Elizabeth from behind Susan's narrow back, laying a letter on the table. "This came for thee, Susan."

Elizabeth grabbed it, for the address was printed Susan Bitch Anthony. Another hate letter. They both got enough of them. She tore it in two and tossed it with good aim into the wastebasket. "I just meant the birthing." Neighbor women in Seneca Falls—even the Irishwomen down the hill among the factories and tanneries—used to come to her for remedies for whooping cough and colic. She never lost a child. She crossed her arms over her full bosom, smiling. She did not know another mother who had not lost babies or children, including her own mother, half of whose children had died. She had not minded being the one who knew best, the woman who had mastered running a household and rearing healthy bright offspring.

Susan frowned. "Yes, you can always call on your authority as a respectable married woman, mother of a tribe."

"Well, she's been a good mother to them all," Amelia said. She didn't interrupt often, for she had the Quaker sense that she should not speak unless the spirit moved her. She was a quiet but strong presence in the house. "She can love with clear eyes that see what each one needs."

Elizabeth patted Susan's shoulder. "My dear, don't let them get to you when they call you an old maid. You have your freedom, the way I never had for all those years of choking domesticity—years I'd never have survived without you. I simply would have exploded with frustration and rage and you'd have had to scrape pieces of my innards off the ceiling. And the truth is, Susan, you'd have made a perfect wife if you'd wanted. You had proposals."

Susan let that thin but warm smile of hers spread across her face. "We've always helped each other. You're the brains, Mrs. Stanton. I'm but your mouthpiece."

That was how it had been for many years, but Elizabeth had observed now that she could travel after a decade housebound in Seneca Falls, she was the better speaker. She could sway a crowd more easily than Susan could. Time after time, they would make the same points, and people would say they agreed with Elizabeth and disagreed with Susan. She knew she came across as motherly and warm, that she had the ability to think of a little witticism in the moment. Susan, who was kind and generous to a fault, never had been able to joke on her feet or tell the anecdote that made something real to people—unless Elizabeth in writing her speech inserted stories. But Susan had the organizational talents she lacked—the ability to sit endlessly in committee meetings, to steer proposals through the maze of subcommittees, to disagree without causing rancor and continue pushing for her agenda without seeming strident. Susan had her own genius. Susan could function in an organization behind the scenes as Elizabeth never could.

Susan rose and walked to the windows, open to the May morning and the garden. The scent of lilacs drifted in. Bees were humming in the honeysuckle outside and Elizabeth could hear mourning doves roo-coo-cooing in the big maples. "We must do something to move things forward. Our movement's stalled like a carriage in the mud." Susan paced as if consumed by her own energy.

"Let's go out to the porch." As they strolled toward the door, Elizabeth snagged the pastry. Susan was thin as a pole, but Elizabeth enjoyed her girth. She felt her appearance was more grandmotherly and thus less threatening because she was plumpish—with curly hair and a great laugh—a useful façade for a lifelong revolutionary. She had been a flirt in her younger days, and she still carried herself with that ease, the confidence of someone often called charming.

For a few moments they rocked in silence, looking at the side garden where a smattering of jonquils were still in bloom among bloodred and white tulips. This house was twice the size of hers in Seneca Falls—two full stories and a smaller third story, with six pillars in front. It was not one of the fashionable carpenter Gothic houses going up all around her but simple and grand in an older style. Susan was frowning. "We should never have agreed to amalgamate the Woman's Rights Society with the Anti-Slavery Society. We thought we were all for universal suffrage, but they have other priorities. Once again they're pushing women to the end of the line—telling us to be patient, forever and ever, amen."

For two decades Elizabeth and Susan had given their energy, their passion to abolition. "I supported Wendell for president of the society. I intend to remind him at the convention." Elizabeth folded her arms and sniffed the lilacs. Somehow that scent was the same color as the flowers, lilac indeed. Wendell Phillips had been a friend and ally since 1840, at the anti-slavery convention in London, when he had supported the women's desire to be seated as delegates. That defeat had been Elizabeth's first awakening to her situation as a woman. Wendell was a handsome man who liked women and she got on with him. She was convinced she could get him to support woman suffrage.

"You're far more impressed by Wendell Phillips than I am, Mrs. Stanton."

"He's of old Brahmin stock, but he's given his all to anti-slavery. Let's see if he pays his debt to us. I swear on the heads of my children, Susan, I won't let our sex be put off this time."

"This meeting is crucial. . . ." Susan turned to beam at her. Her face could soften remarkably. At such moments, she was almost handsome. "Well, are you going to address my typographers? Have you made up your mind yet?"

Susan was organizing the women typographers into a union. "If you really want me to."

"Why do you let Henry come out here?" Susan returned to the earlier point of disagreement between them, in her dogged way.

Susan would never understand the bond between them that, frayed as it was, made her forgiving. "I've had seven children with him. I'm financially independent finally. We live separately. What good would it do to create a fuss?"

"You should never have married him to begin with."

"I hadn't met you or Lucretia then. I was living with my father, who wouldn't let me do anything political." After she'd addressed the New York legislature on married women's rights, he never forgave her for speaking in public, calling her a harridan. He had only reinstated her in his will shortly before he died. "Henry was the breadwinner then—not that he ever earned a lot of bread." She laughed. Even the house in Seneca Falls on the outskirts of town overlooking the tanneries and mills—a plain house she had come to loathe for its isolation—was only theirs because her father had paid for it. "I can't imagine life without my children. Sometimes I've wanted to run away from them and the constant problems and chores. But I never did and I never will. They give me great pleasure. They tether me to the wheel of life."

"You could do with a little less tethering."

Susan was capable of passionate friendship but had never really been in love. It was not that Susan lacked domestic virtues. She could cook and clean and sew and manage a household, if not as well as Elizabeth—who was not convinced anybody could do it as well—then sufficiently to fill in. How often Susan had come and taken over so she would be free to write a speech or a paper making their position on some issue clear. If it had not been for Susan, how would she have endured her marriage, really? Henry was never around when she needed him. He had not been present during the birth of any of their seven children. He loved to travel, so he arranged his life to spend vast amounts of time doing it. He always seemed to find work that required him to be elsewhere. And elsewhere he had usually been, until the scandal in the Customs House forced his resignation from his last grasp at public life. He missed the limelight now. He had a minor position at the *Sun,* writing about politics, and a small law practice in the city. He was jealous of her fame, but she ignored that.

No, she had been married to Susan as well as Henry all those years. Susan had given her the support she needed when she felt as if her brain would burst her skull with the tedium of cooking meals for a big family every day, managing the scant help, dealing with laundry and sicknesses, creating her own medicines and poultices and salves, bringing in and putting up fruit from their orchard, sewing for an army, cleaning and cleaning and cleaning and cleaning again. Indeed, Henry without ever acknowledging it had been married to Susan too, for Susan had run his household when Elizabeth couldn't—something the children understood, who had grown up calling her Aunt Susan and giving her the love she had always given them. Susan and she had their disagreements, but Elizabeth never doubted they were far stronger together than separate. When they both agreed, they were always right.

Now her youngest Robbie was screaming, so Elizabeth trotted in search of him. He was nine. He had been huge at his birth—twelve and a half pounds—and he was still big for his age. Big and awkward. He had been climbing in a weeping willow tree and had fallen. She examined him quickly with a practiced hand for injuries. "You didn't break anything. You'll have a big purple bruise on your knee. A comfrey poultice and you'll feel like new. Come."

He was badly shaken from the fall. She put him on the sofa in the back parlor wrapped in a quilt she had sewn with women friends back in Seneca Falls, and set him up with a jigsaw puzzle of *Washington Crossing the Delaware*. She never made the boys ashamed to cry, although Henry had tried. Venting emotions was good for both sexes. Her own emotions—anger, love, passion—were the engine that drove her through all the obstacles an unjust society could throw in a woman's path.

Susan left for the city and the washing began. Amelia had already fired up the boiler, so the water for the linens was hot. They took turns stirring the suds into the water and then stirring the load with a huge wooden paddle. Amelia started the bluing cooking on the coal stove while Elizabeth rinsed the first two loads. They had a hand wringer that got most of the water out of the less delicate things—the sheets, towels, tablecloths, underclothes, towels, rags. Then Amelia joined her and they hung the damp clothes on lines from the back of the house to the carriage house—not that they had a carriage, but the family occupying the house before her had. They would get done as much as they could today, then resume tomorrow.

Finally the next evening, she sat at the dining room table to begin the speech for the women typographers. Amelia was still ironing. Elizabeth passionately hated ironing, especially the goffering iron that was needed for all the ruffles and little tucks. Four different irons were used for all the linens and clothes. She would focus on the economic disadvantages of women. Yes, and she would talk about divorce and child custody. Some suffragists—the Boston ladies in particular—seemed afraid of working-class women. Elizabeth liked them. Susan was actually more ladylike than she had ever been. Elizabeth was made of coarser, more earthy stuff and understood women's physical needs and desires while longing for a world in which they could achieve fuller expression without danger, without fear, without condemnation. She had always liked her body and felt at home in it, enjoying the pleasures of the flesh, enjoying riding and dancing. Susan was abstemious by nature. Elizabeth did not want a life of bread and water and stones.

When she'd first been with Henry, they had been disciples of Graham, who advocated loose clothing, cold rooms, lots of exercise, whole grains and avoiding meat and fats. He also advocated sex no more than twelve times a year. They had not stayed on Graham's program long. The porridge and whey routine had gone out the window, but she retained her belief in fresh air, exercise and loose clothing. She had worn the bloomer costume for two years, but she found that no one could hear what she was saying for the commotion a woman wearing pants seemed to cause. Reluctantly she abandoned its comfort.

When this draft was finished, Susan would transcribe it, for no one else could read her handwriting. She'd developed a terrible handwriting early, perhaps to keep her diary a secret from her stern mother. Or perhaps it had always been that her mind leapt ahead and her hand ran raggedly after to try to capture her thoughts. She scrawled and rushed on with that same feeling she used to have on horseback, a sense of being fast as the wind and conquering distance; that was all she could do to change the world so far. So quickly she wrote on.

FOUR

NTHONY LEANED FORWARD, placing his hands on his knees and peering into Edward's face. "My mother was the purest soul I've ever known. She was a saint, Edward. Losing her when I was a boy of ten is something I've never gotten over and never shall. But while she lived, she taught me to be a true Christian."

"I'm sure she was a remarkable woman, my friend. But the roles open to a young man in Manhattan are a far cry from the world of a ten-year-old on a farm in Connecticut. What did your mother know about living in a great metropolis?"

"Here are more temptations, more sinners and more ways to sin. But the way to live righteously is exactly the same." Anthony found the city frightening at times, but he never imagined returning to rural poverty. He must make his way here or not at all. They both stopped talking to watch a four-in-hand pass with matched horses, some rich guy off to an important appointment. The coachman in front and the footman standing on the back of the carriage wore livery of red and blue.

"There's the good life." Edward knocked his pipe out on the edge of the stoop where they were eating bread and cheese for lunch. Anthony thought smoking a filthy habit that could lead into temptation, for some of the so-called tobacco shops in lower Manhattan had a bevy of prostitutes on call or available in the back room, as he'd learned when Edward stopped for pipe tobacco. "Sometimes I feel you just don't see what life offers, Tony—may I call you that?"

"Don't. I like my own name. It's more dignified." No one had called him Tony since his mother died. It was too intimate for anyone else to use. "Life offers chances to sin, but they're only useful to build your strength of character by resisting." Perhaps it was futile to try to save Edward, but Anthony could not give up. Edward reminded him of his own brother Samuel, who had perished tragically of wounds received at Gettysburg on Barlow's Knoll. Samuel had died slowly and in great pain over the course of a week, although Anthony had prayed for him day and night. Anthony had enlisted in the Fifteenth Connecticut Infantry to replace his brother. Because of Samuel, Anthony could not stop trying to reach Edward. Edward was his only friend so far in this strange city.

"Anthony, you're twenty-four, right? Have you ever had a woman?"

"Had? You mean in the carnal sense?"

"Is there another way to have a woman?"

"Of course I haven't. Purity is not only for women."

"You'll make some woman a good husband. If you ever get close enough to one to marry her." Edward winked at him.

"But on what we earn, when can we think about marriage? Twelve dollars a week. Out of that we pay room and board, our clothing, transportation, and I have to give some to my church on Sunday—"

"The boss has you going to his church in Brooklyn. All the way on the ferry there and back every Sunday. Isn't that a little excessive just to lick his boots?"

"It's a decent church. I feel at home there." He liked strict hellfire and brimstone sermons, just as in the Congregational churches of his childhood and the commanding revivalist preachers that had swept through, saving everybody again and again. That was real religion, religion that smote him to his bones. The fear of hell could make a man feel truly alive.

"Ah, Anthony, tonight after work, come with me to the Melodeon. It's a concert saloon. There's a fight on tonight and Katie Sullivan is going to dance with her Girly Girls. Enjoy yourself for once."

"You go there every Friday night." For Anthony, it was as if Edward plunged into darkness and vanished. Was it his duty to accompany him once, to see what so fascinated his friend? Maybe it wasn't as bad as he suspected. Maybe he was unfair to Edward.

"Because it's fun, Anthony, fun."

Anthony was eyeing Edward's pocket. Something yellow with printing on it. Edward succumbed to the dirty books that were sold everywhere in the neighborhood where they worked, on Pearl Street. Anthony had tried to reason with Edward before and gotten nowhere. Edward's reading would have corrupted a far stronger soul.

"It's a good-time place. Let yourself loosen up for once. Relax with the boys."

Anthony passed those concert saloons, drab as empty warehouses by day, lit up at night with every window ablaze, men staggering in and out and women too on the arms of ruffians, sometimes alone as only a lady of easy virtue would appear. He should investigate. "All right, Edward. I'll go with you tonight after supper."

Edward clapped him on the back. "You won't be sorry! New York has a lot to offer a young man, even sports like us with scarcely two dollars jingling in our pockets. There's lots of pleasure to be had by sporting men, Anthony, a whole world of excitement. We work from eight till eight, and we deserve some fun."

It was time to go back to work. They were both shipping clerks in a big dry goods importer, working at adjacent desks and going home at night to a dingy boardinghouse eight blocks away. Edward and he would probably never have become friends if they did not share that walk every day from boardinghouse to work and back again. Every day together they ate meager lunches that left them hungry. Edward was like the men in Anthony's regiment in the Union army, who had teased him unmercifully, mocking his religion and his temperance, one of whom had actually knocked him down when he spilled his daily rum ration on the ground rather than passing it on. He had to fight Reddiger then. The ring of men gathered around them, one on the lookout for the sergeant, egging on that bully, jeering him. They had expected Reddiger to squash Anthony, although they were both big men. The men had mistaken blustering, drinking, whoring and playing cards on the Sabbath for real manhood.

Anthony could admit to himself how much satisfaction he had taken in laying Reddiger on the ground. He had proved that godliness did not make him a marshmallow. Years of hard chores on the farm had given him power in his arms and shoulders. He had sparred with his older brothers many times out behind the barn.

Not that Edward was a bully. No, he was simply weak, like so many of his fellow soldiers had been, without backbone to resist the temptations surrounding them. Prostitutes followed armies, and even the officers accepted that as a fact of life instead of a way to moral death—sometimes with the terrible diseases God would smite them with, actual death. Corruption sent out tentacles a hundred different ways, through obscene books, postcards and picture books the men passed around to each other and kept in their mattresses, through rum they drank and cards they played, the constant gambling, the dirty jokes they told as if nothing was worth laughing at that did not degrade women or insult anyone with faith.

Normally Friday he would go to the YMCA on Varick Street. He had come to know the work of the YMCA when he was in the infantry. The YMCA was one of the groups in the Christian Commission that sent Bibles, ministers and religious tracts to the front, along with blankets. When his fellow soldiers mocked him, he sometimes found solace with representatives of the commission. One minister had aided him in setting up regular prayer meetings in his company, but often he was the only attendee. It had been a frustrating time. When he arrived in the city with exactly five dollars in his pocket, and that borrowed, he quickly found the YMCA, whose officers helped him to his present job—such as it was.

After the usual greasy supper at their boardinghouse—unidentifiable meat in watery gravy topped with lard and eked out with turnips and mushy cabbage—he allowed Edward to take him by the arm and steer him in the direction of the Bowery. Anthony seldom walked there with its garish gaslights and huge crowds jostling each other off the pavement. The street was chockablock with carriages and wagons among the pedestrians. Women arm in arm accosted them as the two men struggled through the crowd. Many of the men and women were poorly dressed, tenement dwellers he judged, but he saw many young men, clerks, apprentices, office workers like the two of them. Anthony turned his face away from the advances of the wanton girls, but Edward bantered with them. On they went to a place where a placard proclaimed grog and dancing. It cost them twenty-five cents to enter, although Anthony noticed a separate smaller door for women, who apparently were passed in free.

Smoke, bad air, the smell of unwashed bodies and cheap perfume choked him, made him dizzy so that he wanted to flee, but he plowed on, following Edward to a seat. Waitresses in harem costumes sidled among the tables with trays, occasionally stopping to flirt with a man who bought them a drink. Sometimes they sat on a man's lap wriggling in a manner he could only suppose was some kind of obscene activity. Up above on a balcony, women hung over the edge and called to men at the tables. They wore low-cut dresses and little else, being uncorseted, with their hair hanging loose and wanton. This was the kind of place those obscene books Edward bought near their office led him to frequent.

Edward ordered a whiskey for himself and soda for Anthony. Anthony would not stoop to alcohol even to blend in with the ruffians who frequented this place. Why would Edward waste his scarce money here?

A brawny man whom everybody seemed to know as Charlie the Chopper announced that a fight was about to start. A space had been cleared in the center of the room for two men stripped down to long underwear and undershirts to square off with bare knuckles. The fighting did not bother Anthony, although he knew prizefighting was illegal. At least the worst the men would get out of it would be a battered head or a bloody nose and bruises. Still, he could not share the half-mad excitement that swept the room. Even women were jumping up and down rooting for their favorite, Dan the Drayman, who was fighting a bigger man called Hooting Tommy. Tommy was bigger, but Dan was faster and more experienced as a fighter, Anthony judged. He had a good jab and an unexpected uppercut that staggered the bigger man. Anthony idly wondered if he could take Dan. He had a mighty jab of his own, honed in his army scraps. He noticed that Dan dropped his hand after he hit Tommy, leaving himself open. Yes, he could take him.

Anthony watched the audience instead. Certainly the bloodlust they were screaming out was unedifying, but less appalling than the open sexual lust he had observed before. At least for the length of the fight, even the ladies with their bosoms mostly bare hanging over the balcony stopped trying to entice male patrons and egged on the fighters. The fighters were ill matched and Dan got his man down not once but three times. The third time Tommy was out cold. He was hauled off to the alley. Dan raised his bloody hands in triumph and was given his purse. Then he passed among the crowd in his underwear with cap in hand to collect what people would give him. Several women embraced him.

Charlie the Chopper got back on his chair and bellowed, "Drink up or clear out, boyos! In half an hour, Katie and her Girly Girls'll dance the cancan. Let's all have a drink and toast the serving girls and have a good time."

A fight broke out near the bar that ran the length of the immense room. Two burly men who appeared to be official bouncers quelled it. Charlie mounted his chair again to shout that he would not tolerate fighting between the patrons unless it was an official fight. The bouncers threw out the three men involved, and what passed for normality in the saloon resumed.

Anthony observed a regular passage of men up to the balconies. The women disappeared into curtained alcoves with their clients. Edward introduced him to four other young men, employed downtown by importers or law offices, clerks come to the city like himself from respectable and God-fearing families—here in this den of shame where women were garishly painted and men handled them at will. Some seemed much too young to be selling their bodies. Others looked too old to be salable, but all seemed sought by men who should know better. One of the women took a seat on his right. He suspected that Edward had motioned her over, for he bought her a drink. Drinks for the women cost more than for the men, Anthony noticed. She put her arm around him, leaning close, her bosoms loose in her gown. He froze.

"Don't be afraid, dearie. I won't hurt you. I know something about young men, and what they need." Her breath reeked of beer and she smelled unclean. She put her warm moist hand on his thigh, then stroked his manhood through his trousers.

He was ashamed by his reaction. He closed his eyes for a moment and thought of the eternal fires of hell. "I'm not interested." He pushed her hand away.

"Sure you are, dearie. I can feel you. You're just scared." She tried to touch his manhood again, but he caught her wrist.

"What I fear is what I should fear. Please let go of me." He disengaged himself and stood.

"Then I won't waste my time on you. Maybe you like the boys better, um?" She flounced off to pester someone else.

"Anthony, you passed up a golden opportunity. Sally's a good whore. You could do a lot worse for your first time."

"You've been with her?"

"When I can afford it." Edward looked after her longingly. "She knows I don't have the wherewithal tonight."

The air was foul and getting thicker. He drank his soda and ordered another. He tried to discuss the place objectively with Edward, but his friend was accosted by another young man who began arguing the merits of various terriers used to fight rats in pits. Such fights offered an opportunity for gambling, as did, he gathered, dogfights and cockfights.

Charlie the Chopper mounted his chair. "Now the main event of the evening for all you sporting gents. Here comes Katie Sullivan and her Girly Girls ready to dance the cancan. And afterward, if you're up to it, you can buy the girls a drink and drink in their charms."

The woman who led the way out for three others was red-haired and sharp-featured, no spring chicken, dressed in a bright red outfit with several petticoats which, as the pianist started banging out some rancid ditty, she began kicking high up, turning and kicking some more, and finally holding her leg high above her head as she turned on one foot, hopping awkwardly. All four women including one who looked barely sixteen and had no more curves than a rake were kicking with great vigor but little grace, screeching out some incomprehensible and repetitive lyrics. Anthony suddenly realized that they were exposing their most private parts. Blushing, he turned away to fix his gaze on the tabletop scarred with initials and phrases from a dozen penknives. Around him men were rising to their feet and cheering, pounding the tabletops with their tankards, whistling and clapping. So this was how Edward spent his Friday evenings. Anthony despaired of saving him. Edward was too far gone, he suspected, for any arguments, any pleas to reach him. Anthony stood and made his way out. Edward didn't notice. He was banging on the tabletop with the worst of them, shouting like a wild beast.

The air in the city was never pure, but compared to the stinking filth he had been breathing, it felt clean as a country brook. He drew deep breaths into his lungs, appreciating the breeze off the East River as he marched from the Bowery. It was too late for Edward. He had already succumbed. But there were thousands of Edwards, impressionable and innocent young boys crowding into the city as Edward and he himself had in order to better themselves—and better was not what happened. It took courage and a deep sense of what was right to stand against the ubiquitous sporting culture the city offered to young men—a tribal thing, appealing to their lowest passions but making it feel as if such activities were the only way for a man to become a man. He had seen the clerks passing around the sporting papers that featured reports on the "best" whorehouses and gambling hells. He longed to be a sword in the hands of the living God to smite the corrupters. For a moment as he walked south, he felt weak and almost silly, swearing battle with everything around him. Then his resolve stiffened and he thrust back his shoulders. Edward was wrong about the way to be a man. He would go his own way, the right way, even if he lost the only friend he'd made in this wild and dangerous city.

FIVE

ICTORIA MET HER HUSBAND James's train. It was the Vanderbilt line, New York Central, which she viewed as a good omen. Both her children arrived with him, Byron, her toothless idiot son, at fourteen unable even to speak, her daughter Zulu Maud, just turned seven. "I swear, you've grown in the three weeks since I saw you!"

Zulu flushed with pride. Her braids hung halfway down her back. Neither of her children had inherited her looks, but she loved them. Byron was sweet, more like a pet than a son. Zulu was fiercely loyal to her mother and would do anything to please. Victoria embraced them; then Tennie went off in a cab with them while James and Victoria collected the luggage. "Did matters go well?" James asked, taking her arm. He carried a satchel while a porter brought along his trunks.

"We've made a slight connection. What happens next depends on our interview with him tomorrow." She held up her free hand with crossed fingers.

"It must go well." James frowned. "Did you remember everything we studied and agreed upon?"

They ambled along slowly, for Colonel Blood had received half a dozen war wounds during the campaigns of the Civil War, one of them in his thigh. Preferring his skill to the dangerous mercies of the camp doctors, he had dug out the bullet with his own knife. He would always have a slight limp, but he carried himself with military bearing. She had met a number of men who styled themselves Colonel; Vanderbilt himself liked to be called Commodore. But James really had been a colonel, and a heroic one. He was an attractive man, with longish dark hair, regular features, a dark beard that left his finely modeled chin bare. He was tall and lean, dashing in spite of his limp.

Before the war, he had been a conventional man in a conventional marriage with a conventionally respectable job. He was auditor of the city of St. Louis and held the presidency of a local railroad. He had married well and lived a prosperous bourgeois life with his passive, placid wife and two daughters. But for the war, he might have continued so.

The war had shattered his sense of human possibilities. A quiet abolitionist, he had enlisted early and fought hard. He had seen men slaughtered around him, their bodies soaking the mud red, their limbs smashed by cannonballs, their skulls broken like eggs. When he returned a hero, he could not fit back into his old life. He was haunted by the dead. He saw ghosts, who sometimes tormented him and sometimes seemed fiercely eager to communicate. He could no longer make love to his wife. He felt estranged from her and everyone he had known. When he fell in love with Victoria, he was ready to discard all he had ever cherished or worked at or owned—and he did. He ran off with her. Later, being a man of probity, he returned, paid off his debts, divorced his wife and gave her his earthly goods. There was a core of cold intellect in him that Victoria both respected and sometimes regretted, for it kept him from the sensual abandon she knew herself capable of. Still, they were well mated. He was not possessive, for the ideas he held of free love and free union were far more important to him than possession of her.

"And how is Tennessee?"

"Well and eager. She has plans for the Commodore."

Colonel Blood had agreed to take Tennessee in when she had fled the Claflin clan. Tennessee had been supporting the family for years and—sick of that life—longed for something better, so James had willingly taken her under his protection. He was not interested in Tennie the way men usually were. He was too much in love with Victoria, and he liked his women slenderer and brighter, but he understood Victoria would not rest until she had freed the sister she loved.

"Did you bring me more books?" She squeezed his arm gently. His arm could pain him where he had been wounded in yet another battle. He had begun systematically educating her. In school, she had been an excellent student, but Roxanne and Buck were always pulling her out to be hired as a domestic servant, to care for the younger children, to front Buck's traveling circus of patent medicines and wonder cures. She was sure her clan would show up on her doorstep as soon as Tennie and she had established themselves. Victoria took as given that she and Tennessee would always have to support the Claflin family. They had grown up in a state of siege with whatever neighbors they had at the time, always the respectable element gossiping about them, trying to get rid of them. So they stuck together, family first. She had grown up with neighbors pointing at her, whispering about her family, insulting her. They were pariahs. "You were able to raise some money?"

"Sold off some stocks I still had. Where are you bivouacked?"

"In a cheap boardinghouse. It won't do. We need a decent address."

He slapped his waistcoat. "We can get set up quickly. I'll work on it tomorrow. Find a flat or a brownstone."

"Tennie and I have made friends with the keeper of a high-toned brothel, Annie Wood. She knows how to furnish a place elegantly but cheaply. I'm going to visit her tomorrow late morning when she rises. We sometimes take coffee together in her conservatory."

"I look forward to meeting her."

"She's a Southerner but don't get your back up. She has a lot of colored girls working for her, and she treats them better than most madams treat their white whores. She takes care of her girls, and she pays off the police and the politicians handsomely—two hundred dollars monthly for the police alone—and gives them a free ride once a week, so there's no danger of any of the girls ending up in the Tombs."

"The tombs? You mean, dead?"

"That's what they call the jailhouse here. A big ugly building that looks vaguely Egyptian. May we never see the inside of it!"

"Why should we?"

"You know my family."

He grunted assent, hailing a horse cab and tipping the porter. "Where should I look for a place?"

"I don't want to be too far from Vanderbilt." She lowered her voice so the cabbie would not hear. "I took a lover—a newspaperman from the *Sun,* Charlie St. James. Newspapermen tend to know the politics of a place and the useful gossip. I don't want to continue the liaison—I want to turn him into a friend. So when you meet him, be uxorious, if it wouldn't offend you."

"Certainly. Maybe I can befriend him." He cleared his throat to announce a change of subject. "What have you been reading?"

"The Orations of Demosthenes."

"Did you read the Suetonius?"

"On the train." She leaned her head on his shoulder. "What a nasty lot they were, the Roman emperors. I shouldn't like to have caught the eye of Nero or Caligula. Anyone with that kind of power is too dangerous."

"Is Vanderbilt dangerous?"

She thought for a moment. "To anyone who crosses him." She remembered his famous letter to the men who forced him out of one of his steamship companies during the gold rush: *Gentlemen, you have undertaken to cheat me. I won't sue you, for the law is too slow. I will ruin you. Yours truly, Cornelius Vanderbilt.* "He needs to win. But he's not a brooder."

"Is he interested in you?"

"Tennie is what he wants. I couldn't do it, frankly. I can't fake it."

"And Tennessee can?"

"Sure. She faked spiritual séances for years, and before that, the gift of tongues. She's a good actress—"

"I bet you were a better one."

"My gift was rapid memorization. Tennie would have been better at acting. She has the gift of talking herself into being interested in a man if he looks like a good idea. She's an easier person than I am. She has fewer spines."

"And less of a spine."

"Don't underestimate her, James. She's stronger than you think. She's been through hell and come out unblemished." Victoria laughed. "After all, she's lost her virginity something like fifty times."

IN THE MORNING, James went out to look for suitable lodging. She told him to try Great Jones Street. She had no particular reason except that the name popped into her head, and she took it for a spirit communication. The name had a magnificent ring. In the meantime, she and Tennie prepared some products Annie might find useful.

Victoria loved to take coffee in the conservatory with Annie. She was even growing accustomed to chicory. Today the bread was made with dates. Strawberry and quince jams, marmalade and honey in silver pots offered themselves on the silver tray. Something sweetly scented was blooming.

Tennie spread out the products they had brought. "Vaginal sponges presoaked in vinegar. They're pretty good at preventing conception."

Annie was wearing one of her many morning robes de chambre, this one in pale lavender gusseted and trimmed with row upon row of lace. Someday soon Victoria would have such fine costumes instead of plain white cotton nightdresses. Annie was asking, "Can they be reused?"

"Of course. You wash them after every time. The reason to presoak is that everything's ready to go." Tennie clapped her hands.

Victoria took up a red bottle. "This is a preparation of cloves. It's a bit numbing—fine for reduction of pain in the female parts. So often there's abrasion and discomfort from so much activity. The cloves numb, but if the man penetrates, then there's a feeling of warmth." She would not put anything over on Annie, since she wanted her as a friend and wanted her trust. She described the items, careful not to claim too much.

"He thinks she's hot for him, but she actually feels less." Annie smiled, motioning for more coffee.

"In short, yes."

"Sounds good to me. What's that?" Annie poked an elegant finger at a bottle of colorless fluid.

"One of three colognes we produce. This is a mixture of rose and verbena." Victoria held the bottle under Annie's nose. "A lot cheaper than French perfume. We have one that's muskier."

"I'll try a few bottles of each. Let you know how they go over with my girls."

One of the colored girls in a French maid's uniform appeared. "Miss Mansfield is here to see you, Madame."

"Show her in, Marguerite." She turned back to the sisters. "I give all my colored girls French names. Josie Mansfield is Jim Fisk's mistress. He set her up in grand style, but she still visits me. She gives me tips on the stock market."

Victoria frowned at the name. Fisk. He and another man, Gould, controlled the Erie Railroad. A manipulator of the market. A big spender. Vanderbilt's enemy.

The maid showed Josie in. Victoria hung back, not wishing to embarrass the woman by recognizing her unless Josie was willing to admit they had met. Josephine Mansfield was a full-figured woman with hair as dark as Victoria's and fine ivory skin. She was dressed in the latest fashion, a striped silk skirt and a vivid green weskit over a lacy underblouse, a mantilla over all. Victoria thought her attire a little much for noon, but obviously Josie liked to flaunt her prosperity as well as her figure. She had large melting eyes and a pouty mouth.

"Annie, that man is driving me crazy—" Josie stopped abruptly as she noticed Tennie and Victoria.

Annie introduced them. "The sisters are medical adepts. They were just showing me some items that could be useful to my girls. Want to try the cologne?"

"He buys me French cologne by the vat. Thanks anyhow."

Then she looked hard at Victoria. "Victoria Woodhull! Remember me?"

"Of course! I could never forget *you*." Victoria turned to Annie and Tennessee. "We met in San Francisco." Josie was a nitwit but bighearted and without malice.

"We was both actresses. You was in *New York by Gaslight* and I was playing in *The Robber's Revenge*. Both of us up there in corseting that pushed our tits up to our chins with dresses cut down to here."

"And those parties with idiots pawing us afterward."

"You could memorize a part in a flash. All us girls envied you, how you could read it once and then go pour it out word perfect."

"I wasn't much of an actress. You were a lot better."

Josie giggled. "It does me in good stead with old Jim, believe me."

"You can put up with a lot if a man is generous," Tennie said.

Josie winked at her. "You get the picture."

"We've all been there." Tennie was ingratiating herself with Josie. Actually neither Tennie nor Victoria had ever been kept. Rather both of them had kept their families. Victoria had supported her first husband, the drunken doctor Canning Woodhull, for most of their disastrous marriage.

"He's good to me. But ladies, when he gets on top, it's like being fucked by a hippopotamus. He may look the dandy with his fancy clothes on and his diamonds flashing, but once he strips down, you want to avert your eyes—and I don't mean from modesty."

"A beauty like you could do better, then," Victoria offered.

"Not likely. He spends money like water. I can't complain of his generosity. He buys me jewels and clothes and furs. I have a fine house, but he lives in it with me, and that's a little more of him than I like."

"He isn't married? You should marry him," Tennie said.

"He has a wife—Lucy—who lives in Boston. He never says a bad word about the lady, but they don't share a bed and don't even share a roof. He keeps her in high style and they both seem to like that arrangement just fine."

"Does he talk to you about the market?" Victoria asked.

"Constantly. Ask Annie if I haven't helped her put away a pot of money for a rainy day. Sometimes he's wrong, but not often. Believe me, not often."

Annie nodded. "But Josie doesn't invest."

"I like to spend too much. I like to live well, ladies, that's my aim in life. I hide a little away, cash here and there where I can lay hands on it if I need it, but I'm not into the care and husbandry of money like Annie." Josie laughed. "It's just not my thing. I don't breed horses or dogs or money. I just like to have it around."

Maybe Josie could prove useful to her, Victoria thought. "What I need is to know where I can furnish a house cheaply but with some refinement." Victoria turned to Annie. "I was hoping you could help me."

By late afternoon, James had leased a brownstone on Great Jones Street, just as she had envisioned. It was vacant and theirs at once. Tennie and Victoria were so eager to get out of the boardinghouse that they moved into the house that evening, sleeping on the floor with their trunks the only furniture and their coats for beds. James sent a telegram to his brother in New Jersey telling him where he was, and they put their names under the doorbell outside.

"Central heating—hot water rises into the radiators. We'll need someone to come in and stoke the furnace every morning," James was explaining politely, knowing they were not accustomed to bourgeois living. "But we don't have to think about that until fall, when we should have money in hand to pay a couple of servants and a cook. This house has two water closets. The stove in the kitchen heats water."

Victoria was well pleased. These were luxuries she had never known, although they were a matter of common comfort to James. Even though they had to go into debt, it was important to furnish the place well—to project an air of money. Unlike Josie, she had no desire to spend for its own sake. Shopping was not her favorite form of entertainment. Yet she liked the woman for her frankness, her direct sensuality, her boldness. While Victoria preferred to maintain a certain dignity and greatly prized intelligence, what she most disliked in women was pride in what they weren't—pride in being passive, silent, put upon, pride in having no desire they would acknowledge. A so-called good woman often appeared a cipher, defined by what she wasn't and what she never had done and perhaps refused to let herself imagine ever doing. Josie had been molested by her stepfather, who later pandered her to other men until she ran away. Josie and she had met in the tawdry world of San Francisco theater and given each other advice and information on openings and auditions.

Victoria saw herself as a multiplicity of possibilities, some of which were surely better, healthier, more satisfying than others, but there was little of which she did not imagine herself capable. She could see herself leading an army. She could see herself addressing Congress. She could see herself leading a congregation—hadn't she done so already in tent revival meetings as a child? She could imagine herself as Cleopatra or Joan of Arc or Queen Elizabeth or Boadicea. She felt she contained within herself a hundred vital magnificent women in potentiality. If she had taken the lot passed out to her at birth, she would still be back in Ohio doing other women's laundry, married to a drunk. At fifteen she had no idea what she was getting into, but she had understood clearly what she was escaping. Marriage to Woodhull had seemed a step up from her family, leaving her free to try to make her way, even if she had to drag him along.

Byron went right to sleep, curled up on the floor like a puppy. They must get beds. Everything had to be done as soon as possible. They had an address, and that was a start.

THE EVENING ARRIVED WHEN the sisters had their appointment with Cornelius Vanderbilt. His foursquare house was furnished in the style of a generation earlier, with maudlin or fleshy undistinguished paintings on the walls and a row of silver and gold steamships sailing across the marble mantelpiece. The Commodore was impatient to begin, probably mistrustful. He was a hard man. No woman had ever succeeded in rounding his rough edges. His wife must be somewhere on the premises, if she had not gone off visiting relatives or to a spa. Apparently visitors seldom beheld Sophia, who was also his cousin.

Victoria requested that the gaslights be turned off and candles lit. They gathered around a table at which the Commodore usually played whist. There were certainly spirits here. Victoria could feel the tingling. "You were haunted by ghosts but they can no longer enter. I feel them just beyond. A boy and a man."

The Commodore jerked to attention. "Don't you bring them back. I paid good money to get rid of them."

"Don't be afraid. They can't enter here. Someone has blocked them."

"The only real medium I ever hired. She got rid of them, bless the old witch."

"But there is someone who wants to speak with you."

"Is it my mother? You said you could reach my mother."

"There's someone else who wants far more vehemently to speak with you. A man in the prime of life. Pale."

"Pale! Is he coughing?"

"He says you are thinking of how he passed over, but now he has no cough, no disease, no pain."

"It's my son! George Washington Vanderbilt. My youngest son. My good boy."

"He served in the Civil War. He is standing in his uniform now. He says he knows my husband, Colonel Blood. But he wants to ask you about . . . about a horse. Does that make sense?"

"He had a favorite horse. Oh, Georgie!" The big man's voice broke. "Silversides. He's fine, Georgie, he's in my stable right in back. I take him out riding and I think of you, always, Georgie, I think of you. I keep him real fine. He's curried every day."

"He says he knows you love your horses and you're good to them. He says you take too many chances, however, when you are driving them on Bloomingdale Road."

Vanderbilt snorted. "Tell him to mind his own business. I like to drive fast. It's one of my pleasures. Nobody can handle horses better than me."

"He says he knows that. But there's something about a train?"

"I like to cross the tracks just in front of the five twenty-two. Nobody else can do that. The horses know me and they know I won't let it hit us. It just gives the crowd a scare. You know, people come out there to watch us race. We have to give them a thrill. And I win my races nine times out of ten."

"He thinks you take too many chances on your afternoon rides. He watches over you, but he can't help you. He says to tell you he's happy where he is. He's advancing along a path that feels good to him and he has found a spiritual mate there. He hopes you find someone to ease your loneliness. He knows that in spite of all your other children and your wife, you're lonely. He feels that strongly and that too worries him. That worry is holding him back on his path."

The Commodore seemed shaken and moved by the séance.

"I'm exhausted," she said. "If you don't mind, I'll just lie on the sofa and rest."

"You don't go in for table-rapping or the whooshing or ectoplasmic spirits other mediums have tried on me."

"That's all fake. I have no need for any of that. I just open myself to the voices, and if someone wants to come through and communicate with you, I listen and tell you what they say. No rapping, no Ouija boards, no materializations, no strange music. I can't command the spirits. I can only tell you what they want me to. I'm sorry to disappoint you, because I couldn't make contact with your mother this time."

"Don't apologize, little lady. To hear from my dear son was fine enough. He was my favorite and he died too young of tuberculosis he caught in the war. He was the best of a sorry lot."

"Now it's my turn, old boy," Tennie said. "Let me start with your neck."

Victoria lay on a sofa in the next room to give Tennessee privacy with Vanderbilt. She would start by massaging him and then move on from there as his responses indicated. Mesmeric healing. Her electrical hands. Victoria dozed off on the velvet sofa as she waited patiently for her sister to finish.

Tennie was flushed when she woke Victoria. "He's going to take me in his carriage tomorrow when he goes to race his horses on Bloomingdale Road."

Vanderbilt ordered his coachman to take the sisters home. They gathered their stuff and left. Tennie showed her a fifty-dollar gold piece. Victoria took it. "We'll buy some furniture. I gather it went very well indeed."

"I eased his muscles. I eased his tension. I got him up and then I got him down. All in a night's work. He wants to take us to dinner the night after next. I don't think the Colonel is invited."

"He won't mind. He wants to see his brother in New Jersey."

"Then it's all for the best." Tennie stretched luxuriously. "I only wish we had a bed at home so I could sleep well instead of huddling on the floor in a coat."

"Tomorrow. Thanks to our skills tonight, tomorrow we'll have beds of our own." Something she had promised herself since childhood, when she had shared a mattress with four of her siblings. "We will each have our bed, our bedroom and our privacy." That was dignity. Victoria knew she had refined taste, for she had studied ladies and worked out a vision of what was appropriate for her new life—nothing showy, nothing overblown, just fine stuff in dress, in furnishings, in decorating. The house would not impress Vanderbilt, for likely he would never see it. No, it was for others whom eventually she would meet, artists, intellectuals, politicians, those who thought deeply, spoke well and made things happen.

SIX

FREYDEH COULD TAKE over her new apartment May 1, a traditional moving day in New York. The evening before, she sat late on the stoop outside the Silvermans' tenement. Families were moving because their leases were up, because they couldn't pay the rent and were leaving on the sly, because they had found a better or cheaper place. Even after dark, people were dragging their goods through the streets, over the cobblestones and wood planks, through mud and puddles from yesterday's rain. Early the next morning, Sammy and she hastened up and down the nearby blocks for odd pieces of furniture discarded here and there. They rescued two ladder-back chairs and a kitchen table only slightly burned.

Now on the great day itself, Sammy and she moved her effects. Sammy had nothing that didn't fit in the pockets of his dirty cutoff pants or couldn't be hung in the patched sack he wore around his neck to keep his few coins in. She had been storing the good secondhand pants and jacket for him. Her stuff fit into a hamper and a basket. They borrowed a cart from a peddler who was laid up with a broken foot. He was glad for a few coins for the lending of the cart. They had to make a detour as two blocks were flooded a foot deep from backed-up sewage—that happened a lot after heavy rain.

They were moving to Allen Street, a fifth-floor front—always the best since it faced the street and not the privies, with a high rent of eighteen dollars a month. In layout it was like the Silvermans'—the airless bedroom just big enough for a bed and a chair, the dark little kitchen with a fireplace that had a coal stove piped into it to warm them in the winter, plus a fireplace in the largest room, the front room lit by the only windows. The flat even had a fire escape—the back apartments never did. The previous tenants had left a rickety little table and a kerosene lamp that had lost its glass lantern, plus a chair that needed fixing—one leg broken. She would have to buy a bed, a couple of mattresses and a table big enough to work on. The bedroom had pegs in place for hanging clothes. The kitchen was well equipped with shelves some previous tenant had banged up. She had her own chamber pot, some dishes and pans from when she had been married, a knife, two forks, four spoons, three glasses and two cups. The first things she sent Sammy out to buy were a bucket to haul water and a basin to wash in.

They took turns toting their effects up the four flights so that the cart or its meager contents would not be stolen. A cart was a useful thing. Somebody who owned a cart could set up as a peddler or make a little money moving other people's belongings. People moved a lot down here. They hoped for a better place, they moved to get away from prostitution or thievery, they moved because they couldn't pay the rent. In hope and in despair, they moved.

Within a week of asking around and putting a little sign in their window, they had a boarder, Mrs. Stone, a widowed German Jew from Bavaria. She seemed to think that counted for a lot, but neither Freydeh nor Sammy had the least idea where or what Bavaria was. She spoke German rather than Yiddish, and her English was better than Freydeh's, although not as good as Sammy's. She thought it was. She said that Sammy spoke like an uneducated lout. Freydeh did not like her, but she needed the money Mrs. Stone would pay her every Friday afternoon. Mrs. Stone was a seamstress, but not a dressmaker. She did alterations. She too would be working in the front room.

She was two years older than Freydeh's twenty-seven years, but looked five years older. She was skinny as a lamppost, a head shorter than Freydeh and freckled like a trout. She used a pince-nez when sewing. She considered herself psychic and was always trying to impress Sammy or Freydeh with her powers. "Mark me well, that Mrs. Shapiro is pregnant again. And her barely recovered from the last one." She shook her head. "That Mr. Fiedler has some bad news coming to him within two, three weeks, you wait and see." That was a reasonable guess, since almost everyone in the tenement would have something bad to worry about in the next week, in the next month, every month in the next year.

Freydeh had not quit her job at the pharmacy. Until Sammy and she had the business started, they needed every penny. Freydeh had talked Yonkelman into hiring Sammy to run errands and deliver medicines to people too sick to come in. It paid pennies, but it was something and it kept Sammy busy. The street still had its lure for him. His old pals would try to seduce him into schemes every few days, although it was better since they had moved.

Their first attempt at vulcanization was a disaster. The rubber got too sticky and when she went to peel it off the mold it ripped. The next batch was too runny. So far her condom business was costing her money, not making it. Mrs. Stone complained of the smell. "Go sit outside if you don't like it," Freydeh told her.

Freydeh was waiting on a woman in the pharmacy who needed pills for dyspepsia. The woman asked, "So are you the one who took in Mrs. Stone?"

"She's my boarder."

"I am wondering, is this the same woman I know? Middle-aged, maybe thirty. Skinny like a stick. With freckles."

"Yah. A widow who does alterations."

"Widow, my elbow. Her husband ran off with another woman. They say he may be in the South."

"If she drove him crazy like she does me, no wonder he took off."

"She's a gossip, so watch out."

So I'm well warned, Freydeh thought to herself. But we all have to get along. That's how it goes when you share a too little space with strangers. They don't stay strangers. You learn how dirty they are, what doesn't work so good in their body, every little habit and quirk and tic, you learn it all.

Their experiments with vulcanizing rubber sheets they bought were costing them, but she was convinced they would master it. If it was easy, every other fool would be making condoms in their front rooms. She would not give up. It was only a matter of practice until they could produce usable items. She was convinced it was the right move, a trade a woman could carry on, one she could do in her kitchen and make a decent profit.

When she figured out what they were doing, Mrs. Stone had plenty to say. "It's no trade for a respectable woman."

"This respectable woman wants some money. I don't want to live my life out in darkness and bad air."

"You're young enough to marry again. Believe me, I would if I could. A woman needs a man."

"I need a trade to support me. A good living so I can live good. A man I don't need. I got a boy, that's good enough."

Sammy didn't like Mrs. Stone and she despised him. He found little ways to be mean to her, hiding her sock, breaking the thread when she left a piece of work, spilling the chamber pot near her bed. In her turn, she made it clear she thought him a thug from the street. Freydeh tried to keep peace between them. Sammy had a mean streak when he felt someone disrespected him. It came from years in the street, where to overlook an insult was to invite a beating.

Sammy and she had tried going from boardinghouse to boardinghouse describing Shaineh, to no avail. Sammy shook his head. "We'll never find her like this. We need a picture. A picture we can show people."

"I don't have a picture of her. I don't even have one of me. It wasn't like here, where there are photographers in the street ready to take your likeness."

"Then we need to have someone draw a picture of her."

"But I haven't seen her since she was twelve."

"So you got to tell what she looks like, to guess the best you can." Sammy knew far more the ways of the city than she did.

"We'll try it." She clapped him on the shoulder. "You're a good boy, Sammy. You got brains." He also, she discovered, had lice. She had to douse him with kerosene and then pick at his scalp to get rid of them. There were enough bugs in the tenement without having lice as well.

The following Saturday, they walked to the Bowery. They had to wait in a cloud of dust and stink because a herd of cattle was being driven through the narrow street toward the slaughterhouse on the East River. "Be careful where you step," she warned when the drive had passed. On the Bowery, in the mass of humanity and carts and trolleys and horses, they found a street artist. They were always about the streets between the hot-corn girls and the orange and match peddlers—artists who cut silhouettes and, in this case, a woman who did pencil sketches—usually someone sitting on the stool she provided. After haggling over a price and once walking away, Freydeh got the artist to agree to try to draw a picture of the woman Freydeh would describe, and to correct it as Freydeh described Shaineh.

"Light brown curly hair. No, not loose curls like that. Tight. Like ringlets."

"Frizzy?"

"If you want to call it that. Thinner. She had a small waist. Not like me, with my hips and my *tuchus*. Make the chin more pointed. Triangular like a cat—make her face that way. The eyes bigger. The mouth smaller."

A portrait was emerging. Freydeh wondered if it would bear any resemblance to her lost sister. She was just trying to guess how the twelve-year-old Shaineh would fare as an eighteen-year-old. She knew from family letters that Shaineh was remarkably pretty. She trusted her mother's judgment, for her mother had never insisted that she or Sara was pretty, only that they were strong healthy girls and would make good wives and mothers. Freydeh didn't have a lot of faith in the drawing, but now they had something they could show people. People just didn't listen when she went into a long description of what she thought Shaineh looked like. A picture could hold their attention while she talked.

They began their search again farther downtown, closer to the Battery. Down here were lots of businesses and warehouses as well as boardinghouses, and to judge by the women leaning out the windows with their bosoms flopping free, lots of whorehouses as well. She wasn't afraid of the whores. She had grown up near the whorehouse on the river. The only Jews allowed to travel freely out of the Pale in czarist Russia were prostitutes—Jewish prostitutes being in high demand. Some women like Mrs. Stone would draw up their skirts when they saw whores as if the sight of the women would sully them, would soil their clothing.

She squeezed Sammy's callused hand. "Here things are hard, but you have some kind of a choice. Where we come from, no hope, no chance, no luck. Just hunger and danger."

"There's plenty of both here, Freydeh."

"True. But there's other things for Jews here. I know, a cart could run us down in the street, a coach could trample us. We could catch the cholera or consumption. But maybe not. Don't we have a place to live now? Our own place?"

He nodded solemnly, eyeing a girl who was eyeing him. A young whore of perhaps thirteen. "First time in five years I get to sleep inside regular. Sometimes a bunch of us would work for Shifty Bean and he would let us all sleep on pallets in his second basement, under the place where he prints the numbers tickets. But there were rats and it was wet, really dark and drippy." He was still gazing at the girl, who was motioning to him, wriggling her ass.

"That girl is just a child," Freydeh said. "How can this happen?"

"Toffs like kids to do it with," Sammy said knowingly. "They think they can't get the clap from them. The girls know they can't get a baby yet." He and the girl were still making eyes.

She grabbed his arm and dragged him along. "None of that for you. You start in now and it will stunt your growth. You're small enough. You got to grow some before you start thinking about women and getting yourself into trouble."

"I know all about men and women. I seen it done, you know. I'm not a baby."

"If you don't want to be the size of a little boy your whole life long, you forget what you know till it's time to use it."

He was silent for a few minutes. Then he said softly, "I wish I would grow. Big guys get all the respect."

"Not necessarily. You look at some of them prizefighters, and they aren't always the biggest gonifs. Sometimes a little guy can take one of them by knowing how to hit where it hurts."

The first boardinghouse, the woman lost interest when they told her what they wanted. "I got to clean up after these pigs. I only rent to men."

The next boardinghouse took women but not Jews, never Jews. They were too dirty.

"We bathe once a week, missus. When was the last time you took a dip?" Freydeh yelled over her shoulder.

They had been at it for three hours and were about ready to give up when a woman came to the door of what had been a Federal mansion before all the carriage trade moved uptown. "I'm not running a boardinghouse, darling, but let me see that picture." She studied it carefully. "I know her."

"Is she here?" Freydeh clutched herself.

"She worked for me for two, three months a year ago winter. She came to me scarcely speaking a word of English and really hard up. . . ." She read Freydeh's face. "Not as one of my girls, darling. She was a housemaid. Sometimes it's better if they can't speak English. They don't comment on what's going on and they work for less. Come on in. I have her name written down in my desk. We can see if it's your sister."

The house was weirdly painted, all purple and black and with odd tinkly curtains of beads. Whips were hung on the wall of the parlor. The madam, a pretty plump lady with auburn hair in curls around her face, sat down at a neat old-fashioned desk and began to look down a ledger. "I keep track of everyone who works for me, as well as my customers and my girls." She was wearing a bustle that collapsed when she sat, a purple-and-black-striped overskirt and a bright green satin petticoat trimmed with black lace, a fitted velvet jacket with black frogging and green kid gloves. She removed them to lick a finger and turn the pages.

She motioned Freydeh to an overstuffed plush chair. Freydeh sank into it, her hands clasped across her belly. She tried to breathe normally, dizzy with anticipation.

"Here it is." The madam showed her the ledger. The name was written Shayna. Shayna Leebowish. "Is that she?"

Freydeh nodded, unable to speak. "But she doesn't work for you now?"

"She wasn't comfortable with what goes on here. She appeared to be a virgin."

"You didn't . . . You didn't want her to work for you, I mean as one of your girls?"

"Too fragile." The madam looked Freydeh over. "You're more the type we can use here. We're not a common house. We specialize. You saw the whips. Some men like to be spanked or whipped or punished. Some want to do the punishing. Either way, we need strong girls."

"Thanks, but I'm going into business for myself. I'm going to make condoms."

"Really. You could do worse. I hope you find your sister."

"So Shaineh quit?"

"She cried a lot while she was here. She'd cry in her bed at night, and the other girls didn't like it. It was depressing. And she was always afraid of the men. . . . Now, she wasn't a great seamstress, but she could sew. I used her to fix my girls' costumes. There's a lot of wear and tear on clothing in this business."

"Do you know where she went?"

"No idea. She took her bundle and went out the door, and that's the last I saw of her." The madam stood. She was shorter than Freydeh by a head. "Good luck."

They walked a few buildings along the street and then sat down on a stoop. "Well, that was odd," Freydeh said. "At least we found her trail, no matter how cold."

"Freydeh, what's with those whips? I thought it was a whorehouse, but I don't see what she does with the whips. I don't get it. . . ."

"Neither do I, Sammy. Maybe it's better we don't understand. I think maybe it's better we just forget what we heard except for the part about Shaineh."

"So there's a thousand places she could be working as a seamstress. Is that what she was in the old country?"

"Mama apprenticed her to a seamstress, but she complained that she was just doing chores for the family. So I don't know if she really has skills."

"Well, there can't be more places that give out piecework for sewing than there are boardinghouses—or whorehouses." He looked back over his skinny shoulder.

"This is New York. There's a lot of everything. We just have to find the right one."

Sammy was silent. He had that look he got when he was upset. She knew it by now. He showed a sullen withdrawal when he was disappointed or afraid of being disappointed. She left him alone as they walked north, having decided not to take the horsecar and walk—saving money, avoiding the chaos and shoving. Once they came out of the district of warehouses, lines of wash were hung over the side streets, thicker than the tangle of telegraph wires in the main and business streets. Broadway when they crossed it, dodging among stalled carts and wagons and carriages, was a crisscross mess. Policemen were shouting at the draymen and coachmen trying to untangle the vehicles going every which way and slamming into each other. It happened every day.

Finally she said, "But things are looking up for us, no? We have a place of our own. The boarder helps pay the rent. We found cheap beds and they don't have bedbugs. We have enough to eat. We managed to pick up Shaineh's trail."

"We're never going to make the rubber right."

"Sure we are. We have to practice some more. Nobody's born knowing how to vulcanize rubber. Izzy, who comes to Yonkelman's—"

"He's sweet on you."

"Yah, that and a cigar will get him a smoke. Izzy has a tiny brain in his noggin, shaking around like a few seeds in a gourd. If he can do it, so can we."

"Otherwise you got no use for me."

"Sammy, I took you in and you're staying. That's just how it is. I got no family now except Shaineh. You're stuck with me."

He squinted at her, half disbelieving, half wanting to believe. She wondered again if he had weak eyes. At some point she could get a doctor to check his vision. But not yet. Doctors cost money.

SEVEN

HORACE GREELEY WILL never forgive what I did at the New York constitutional convention," Susan said as she sat going over the bills from printing the *Revolution*. They were in the offices of the newspaper in the Women's Bureau, a large town house on East Twenty-third owned by a sympathizer who let them use the space rent-free. It was airy with thick carpets and white walls hung with portraits of Lucretia Mott and Mary Wollstonecraft. Susan managed the office, paid bills, hired the women printers. Elizabeth was editor and wrote most of the copy about everything from factory women to woman's rights in France. "That's why Greeley's *Tribune* is attacking me."

Elizabeth put down her pen. "It got his goat, all right." Greeley had been scheduled to give his negative report on woman suffrage, lumping women with lunatics and idiots and felons as not able to handle the vote. George Curtis, one of their supporters, stood and asked to present a petition in favor of woman suffrage, headed by Mrs. Horace Greeley. That had seriously embarrassed Horace.

"He turned on us long before that." Susan gave a dismissive shake of her head. Then she sighed. "We don't have enough in our poor little account to pay half these bills."

Elizabeth was trying to fit all the articles she had written and commissioned and that had come in voluntarily into the narrow confines of the six pages they could afford to print. They had a reasonable number of ads this time, but since Elizabeth refused those for patent medicine—the most lucrative—ads couldn't support the paper. She had written about the condition of women tailors, about divorce reform, suffrage in Wyoming, women homesteaders. "Should we go on printing Train's articles?"

"He gave us the money to start. The Brits still have him in prison. We should give him the benefit of patience until he's a free man again." Susan knew Train better than Elizabeth did and was prone to defend him from their days sharing a platform and the hardscrabble travel around Kansas, often facing hostile audiences together.

"He gave money to Irish independence and went to jail for them. That's where his heart is now. We shouldn't entertain fantasies about more aid from your Mr. Train."

"He's not *my* Mr. Train. I was saddled with him, but he and I made the best of it." Susan's mouth formed a thin line of annoyance.

When Susan had been in Kansas canvassing for a suffrage amendment, she had been set up by people she trusted from the radical Republicans and anti-slavery movement to travel and speak with an Irishman, George Francis Train, eloquent but flamboyant and eccentric, traveling around Kansas in purple gloves and top hat and frock coat. Train had a hard time keeping up with Susan, but his dedication to woman's rights had been genuine. After their journey, he had been so impressed with Susan he had given them funds to start their own newspaper.

It had come out in the New York and Boston papers—Greeley and his *Tribune* were particularly gleeful—that Train was a rabid pro-slavery Democrat. Susan was tarred with Train's views and attacked by former Republican allies. She and Susan were considered political liabilities now that the fight for Negro suffrage—Negro *male* suffrage, as Elizabeth kept pointing out—was close to being secured. The Republicans were running the overwhelmingly popular General Grant for president.

Elizabeth wanted to get the newspaper together and quit for the day. They were scheduled to go to dinner at the Tiltons'. They slept in the city when they were putting out the paper, but tonight they would cross to Brooklyn. "Do you think the Republicans arranged for you to work with Train to discredit you?"

"We'll never know, Mrs. Stanton. But they've deserted us."

"Deserted us, reviled us, trampled us. But at the rights convention we're going to fight back." Elizabeth paced to the window, her skirts swishing. Absently she picked a loose brown hair from Susan's dress as she passed. "We should hurry it up. We don't want to be late."

The ferry cost two cents and ran often. At this time of night it was crowded with working people in shabby clothes. The better-off went home much earlier. Susan and Elizabeth were packed in with carts, wagons, horses, a coffin. Brooklyn was a middle-class city of respectable families, tree-lined streets, large houses, many churches and more than its share of ambitious politicos, of whom Theodore Tilton was certainly one. Even President Lincoln had visited the Tiltons. Elizabeth and Susan often took the ferry over for a social and political evening with Theo and his wife Lib.

It was Theo who greeted them at the door, not the maid. Theodore Tilton was a handsome man, something of a poet who dressed the part with long flowing blond locks and Byronic shirts, towering over them all at six feet three. He wrote mostly for an important church newspaper—church newspapers had as large a readership as the leading secular papers. He was passionately involved in Brooklyn and national politics. Like Susan and Elizabeth, he had been stalwart for abolition for more than a decade and supported woman's rights. He was a protégé and ghostwriter for Henry Ward Beecher, the charismatic preacher of the important Plymouth Church in Brooklyn. Special ferries ran on Sunday, Beecher's Boats, people called them, to bring Manhattan churchgoers over to Brooklyn to hear the great Beecher sermonize about the forgiving God of Love, so different from the hellfire Puritanism most had been exposed to in childhood. Elizabeth hoped to make sure Theo and Beecher would support them in the convention and not allow woman's rights to be sacrificed. Both men were important liberal voices people would listen to. They had been bosom buddies for years, but lately Elizabeth had noticed a strain between them. She was curious but assumed it was political in origin. Theo had been spending a great deal of time in Washington of late because of the attempt to impeach President Johnson, something he had worked for.

The Tiltons occupied a double-frame row house in Brooklyn Heights. It was sumptuously furnished, although the paintings—reproductions of oils—ran to the sentimental and bombastic with Roman motifs. The furniture in the front parlor was decorated with carved cherubs' heads. Lib was flitting about when they arrived. She greeted Susan warmly and Elizabeth more warily. Lib was also named Elizabeth, a petite attractive woman, with shiny black hair and large dark brown eyes framed by lush lashes—a good wife and mother, presumably, but an odd match for the intellectual activist Tilton, as she seemed naïve. Then, Elizabeth did not think Lib had been given much of a chance to develop her own ideas. She seemed to be mostly maidservant to Tilton, who was all for woman's rights but treated his own wife like a wayward child and constantly complained that Lib simply did not know how to run a house in a manner he thought befitted a man of his stature—and pretensions. Sometimes he rebuked her in front of company for her lack of intellectual pursuits, but Elizabeth could not see that he gave her time or encouragement to pursue any. Lib was very involved in Plymouth Church, a respectable outlet for her interests.

Lib felt comfortable with Susan. Now she pulled Susan off to see the children. Elizabeth was aware that Lib did not really like her. They had been invited to spend the night. She should take advantage of this visit to win over Lib, for it struck her as preposterous that she should be close to Theo and distant from his wife. Susan thought Lib had potential; she spoke of her as emotionally rich and not unfriendly to woman's rights, although a bit afraid of women who might overly impress her brilliant husband. Theo had affairs, it was whispered. She had heard of certain liaisons, often with bright and political women, unlike the timid, housebound Lib.

Lib should be brought out, Elizabeth decided. She would work on it, a small side project that would delight Susan. Susan had repeated to her something Lib had said: that her husband might think her silly and stupid, but the great Henry Beecher thought enough of her intelligence to show her whatever he wrote for her critiquing—that is, when Theo did not ghostwrite Beecher's material. The Reverend Beecher liked to write upstairs in the Tilton house in a sitting room with a stained glass dome, the room Elizabeth agreed was the most charming in the rather ostentatious house.

For the moment, it was Theo they needed. He had come up with the original idea of combining the Anti-Slavery Society and the Woman's Rights Society into one organization. Both groups of the disenfranchised would gain their rights together. No group should gain equality at the expense of the other, Elizabeth had said countless times. The women had listened, but she was not sure the male abolitionists had digested her plea. It was shameful that she should be subject to laws she had no part in electing representatives to create, to pay taxes for a government not responsible in any way to her, unable to testify in court or sit on a jury or sign legal papers—in other words, she was a child in the eyes of the law. Taxation without representation, indeed.

After a long evening of discussion in which at times Elizabeth thought they had convinced Theo and at times was sure they had not, Tilton brought out his chess set in which the figures were medieval knights, bishops in regalia, the queen a regal figure, the castles with turrets. Susan went off with Lib while Elizabeth settled in to play. Tilton loved chess. Elizabeth enjoyed the game and usually beat him. Tonight her mind was distracted by the coming convention. The real battle sapped her interest in the mock one. Tilton was pleased with himself for checkmating her twice. He lay back in his chair beaming. "I knew my game had improved. I can take you now."

Elizabeth resisted telling him that his game was the same as ever but her mind had been elsewhere. She simply congratulated him. And to think Henry complained she had no tact.

He wanted to talk about something, she could tell. She waited for him to open up. He did, seemingly flustered. "Do you think it's possible for a good woman, a saintly woman like Lib, to have . . . what I might call sensual feelings?"

"Of course," Elizabeth said simply. "Women can enjoy the conjugal embrace as warmly as men."

He winced. "I can't believe that. Lib has always been cold . . . until recently. I don't know what to make of her now. It upsets me."

"Why? Pleasure is something for both parties, don't you think? Why shouldn't a woman feel desire?" She certainly had.

"Don't you think that's unnatural in a woman, with all her modesty, her inborn purity? Maybe it's a kind of disease."

"It's a natural function, Theo. Accept it and rejoice in it." But she did not think he was prepared to. How strange that a man who had sought the embrace of several women she knew about should cringe at his own wife's ardor. Men talked and wrote so much poppycock about women, it was no wonder if Theo felt confused.

THE AMERICAN EQUAL RIGHTS ASSOCIATION convention turned into a brawl. Elizabeth and Susan were not the only women up in arms at the abandonment of woman suffrage and the insistence, which Elizabeth's old friend and houseguest Frederick Douglass supported, that this was the hour of the Negro and that the hour of women could be put off. A woman delegate stood up to shout, "We want a party that will adopt a platform of universal suffrage for every color and every sex!"

Elizabeth thought she had persuaded Wendell Phillips to support them. By midafternoon she realized he had tricked her.

"By mixing these movements, we will lose more for the Negro than we can gain for the woman," Wendell thundered.

Elizabeth felt electric with anger. "May I reply to your argument with just one question: Do you believe the African race is composed entirely of males?" She was angry, hot and cold at once—passionately furious and coldly resentful. She would never forgive him for lying to her. Delegates were on their feet screaming while the chair pounded his gavel for order. People were throwing the agenda and programs in the air and trampling them underfoot. The aisles were clogged with knots of men and women confronting each other.

Elizabeth had been supposed to be elected on the new slate of officers as vice president, and Susan was to be on the executive council. But mysteriously, when the slate was announced, their names had disappeared. That was meaningless to Elizabeth. She did not want to be an officer of this society, now, tomorrow or ever. She stood and walked out, with Susan at her heels.

"They sold us out." Elizabeth shook her head slowly, leaning on Susan's arm as they paced in the hall outside where they could hear the new slate being voted in.

"You let Wendell Phillips seduce you." She imitated him, with that sly way she had in private, "My family has been around since 1630, so pay heed to what I advise."

"He can turn on the charm. I'll never trust him again." Elizabeth sat down heavily in a chair in the hallway outside the room where they had just been handed an overwhelming defeat. She found that sense of betrayal familiar, an old sore reopened. Yes, a betrayal that had happened when Henry and she eloped and then sailed for England with Henry's Liberty Party comrades to learn about the aftermath of British emancipation in the West Indies, to discuss strategy for ending slavery altogether.

In London, the newly married couple stayed in a boardinghouse with other American delegates, including the female Anti-Slavery Society representatives. Lucretia Mott, a plainly dressed abolitionist speaker and Quaker minister, wife and mother of six, was there, as was Wendell. The question of whether to seat the women delegates caused a huge floor fight. The faction with which Henry, who had been elected secretary, was allied rejected them. Wendell won her approval by protesting. In the meantime, the women were stuck behind a railing off to one side. Debate went on for hours. Clergymen from both sides of the Atlantic said participation by women would be shameful and immoral. The men supporting the women—who weren't allowed to speak—argued that the women had been duly elected in America. Wendell moved to seat the women but was defeated by a huge majority. The women were allowed to remain as spectators only. Elizabeth was furious. The tone of the speeches against women was frankly insulting. Elizabeth assumed that Henry had voted to seat them.

Two days later, she was walking with Lucretia in St. James's Park admiring the swans when Lucretia said, "Have you forgiven Henry?"

Elizabeth turned to her in confusion. "Forgiven him for what?"

"Voting against us. Voting with his faction not to seat us."

"I didn't know. I didn't know, Lucretia." No, she would not lightly forgive him.

Lucretia was more than twenty years older than Elizabeth, but they felt like sisters, joined in their politics, their tastes, their courage. Elizabeth had been appalled that the movement to free the slaves could not endure freeing women to speak and vote. She felt debased. The rest of the time in London, Lucretia and she spent their days together, at the convention, visiting schools and prisons, museums and restaurants, shopping and sightseeing. Henry was not overjoyed by her intense friendship with Lucretia or that she was now an ally of the opposing faction to his. That was the first betrayal this fiasco brought back. In spite of more than twenty years of working together, the men had no intention of releasing their hold upon women who were once again consigned to sitting on the sidelines.

"How could they turn on us so?" Susan wrung her hands. "How could they forget all those years of fighting side by side?"

"Maybe that skirmish with Wendell just before the war meant more than we thought at the time." Elizabeth closed her eyes for a moment, remembering the runaway wife who had come to Susan for help. Juliet Pettibone was married to a Massachusetts state senator who had beaten her badly when she confronted him about his other women. He took custody of their children and had her confined to a mental institution. She escaped, managed to take her daughter and flee. Susan brought them to Elizabeth, who hid them in the backyard gymnasium she had built in Seneca Falls, between the house and the apple orchard. She had put it up because little girls were not encouraged to exercise or included in calisthenics and because she did not want her sons hanging around billiard parlors in town. The older boys were now away at a school run by abolitionist allies in New Jersey. She told her younger sons and daughters that the gym was off limits because of an infestation of hornets, the same story she told Henry on his infrequent stays at home. Juliet and her daughter lived there for two months. Eventually the younger Stanton children met them and she swore them to secrecy. In the meantime, Wendell was pressuring them to produce the woman, whom he and Garrison saw as a fugitive from the law. When Susan argued that it was the same as harboring fugitive slaves, both men were furious. Wendell had sat in her parlor only a hundred yards from where mother and daughter were eating their evening meal and berated her for putting the abolitionist movement in jeopardy by interfering in a man's family. Elizabeth and Susan had hidden Juliet until they found a place for her in the Wyoming Territory. They scraped together the money and sent mother and daughter off to a new life. Wendell had not understood their position then and he didn't understand it now. It was time to stop trying to persuade him.

"We'll have to go it alone," she said to Susan as they proceeded slowly down the hall arm in arm, hearing the boom of voices through the closed doors of the auditorium. In anger, Elizabeth kicked over a brass spittoon, lifting her skirts away.

"What do you mean?" Susan stopped, turning to face her.

"We can't count on men. We can't count on congressmen or senators, we can't count on judges or newspapermen. We must build a movement of women, controlled by women, with women officers and a women's agenda."

"I agree." Susan clasped Elizabeth's hands.

"We'll start our own organization. I won't be controlled!"

Susan stood tall and proud as a flagpole. "We'll put our rights in the forefront and we won't give an inch." She seemed to shine with courage and will. Sometimes Susan looked absolutely handsome, almost radiant. It was a beauty, Elizabeth thought, that came entirely from within.

"Precisely. . . ." Elizabeth beamed at her, squeezing her hands back. "Now let's go to the *Revolution* office. I want to tear up the issue I was laying out and put out a call for rebellion. We're going to war. I feel a need for some downright honest fighting."

EIGHT

VICTORIA WAS NOT immensely pleased but hardly surprised to answer the door of their leased town house—they had no servants yet so she was answering the door herself—and find her father Buck standing there.

"Give your old daddy a big kiss, Vickie. I had a mite of trouble finding you, but I kept on it like a hound dog on a trail and here I be. Glad to see me?"

"Of course. . . . Where's the rest of the clan?"

"They be coming any day now, soon as I tell them I found you. I bet Tennessee's here too."

Victoria sighed. She would do her best to protect her younger sister from their father's schemes. "She is."

"But I bet she misses her days on the open road with her daddy. Those were the times. From Cleveland to Memphis, from Cincinnati to Wheeling, we rode our wagon and we cleaned up good." He stepped forward and eyed her. "You're looking a little peaked but right handsome. Nice dress. Must have cost a pretty penny. You got yourself a sugar daddy?"

"We have someone who may help us. I'm not his mistress."

"Is Tennessee?"

She wasn't about to tell him anything he might decide to cash in on. She wouldn't permit his trying to blackmail the Commodore, who would crush him like a beetle. "She just flirts with him. We're operating as mediums."

"That's always a good in." He surveyed the room, strolling back and forth. "Bare as a baby's ass in here. No money for furnishings, eh?"

"We're working on it." The parlor had only a green plush love seat and a mirror. They were expecting an Oriental via Annie Wood that recently graced one of the Seven Sisters' fancy brothels. That sister had just changed her decor. Victoria waved her hand at the wall. "We have gas laid on. Also water and central heating."

"Central heating? I hear tell that's unhealthy. Chokes you up."

"I think freezing half to death the way we always did is harder on the health." She turned away toward the fireplace, which was only for decoration. "James and the children are here too, of course." Buck hated James for taking Victoria away and then protecting Tennie. Those daughters had been his to use for profit, and now James was in the way. Roxanne didn't like him any the better, for she was jealous of the influence he wielded over Victoria. She and Utica had been Roxanne's favorites, as Tennie was Buck's. Roxanne had tried ineffectually to protect her from Buck, but never to the point of truly angering him, or he would beat his wife just as hard as his kids.

"We can all double up, darlin', don't you worry about us."

"I'm not. We have the entire house."

"You can't tell me your Colonel is paying for all this."

"We expect to be doing right well here." God, she was slipping back into idioms she never used. "We've started selling chemicals to the better houses of pleasure."

Buck lit up. "That's just fine, little darling. I can handle that."

"I'll tell you which ones you can handle. A few of them have to be dealt with by Tennie or myself."

"Where is my sweet child Tennessee?"

"She's out at the moment. Taking the air." Tennie was riding in the park with Vanderbilt. He liked to race his bays every day flat out. He had terrified many a passenger over the years. Most men would only ride with him once. But Tennie understood the rules of the game, claiming vivaciously to enjoy the racing as much as the Commodore. It was not exactly a lie to say Tennie wasn't his mistress. He couldn't perform the sexual act, but Tennie gave him release in her daily massages. Tennie was not looking for lovers. She said she'd had enough of men to last her a few years. She wanted money, she wanted comfort, and she wanted fun. Vanderbilt was good for most of that. Victoria just had to keep Buck out of it.

Three days after Buck telegraphed them, they arrived, her mother Roxanne, her sisters Utica, Polly, Margaret Ann and children. They must have been packed and waiting, either back in Ohio or in some wayside town after their money had been exhausted, run out of another town by the law.

"My sweet baby daughter!" Roxanne, shorter than Victoria, embraced her tightly. "My angel. I been missing you something terrible." She was wizened like an old raisin, her eyes squinting from poor vision.

"Where did you get that black eye, Mama?"

"Some fool give it to me. Like the Good Book says, if he smite ye on one cheek, turn the other."

"It wasn't Daddy?"

Roxanne was examining Victoria closely, touching her hair, fingering the material of her dress. Now she made a circuit of the room. "Was some sinner who said our cancer medicine made his auntie die. Where's your darling babes?"

"Upstairs. I'll show you."

"Is that Colonel man around still?"

"He's my husband, Mama. He's working over in Jersey today with his brother."

"Some husband. Can't even walk straight."

"Come." She took Roxanne's callused hand. "Let's go to Zulu Maud and Byron." As a child, she had been tremendously close to Roxanne, who encouraged her visions, her voices, her trances. She had felt as if Buck wanted to use her powers to make money, but her mother truly believed. Her first husband hadn't been the only drunk in the family. Roxanne liked to hit the bottle. Utica was addicted to opium, but also liked to drink until she collapsed. They were blood, and they had hidden each other from vengeful lovers and furious wives, from bill collectors and sheriffs. When she was close to dying after Byron's birth, Roxanne had nursed her back to health. She was alive today because of her mother, and only because of her.

Slowly she was putting the house together. She did not trust Roxanne's taste or Buck's, but she entrusted them with shopping for simple necessities—straight chairs, a kitchen table, pots and pans and cutlery, baskets and buckets. Her mother knew a bargain when she saw one, and it was always a good idea to keep her and Buck occupied. Both Tennie and Victoria were getting money regularly from Vanderbilt. Victoria had established contact with his favorite son and his mother. But she needed a lot more than what the Commodore was giving them if she wanted to establish herself as a power for good, as the spirit of Demosthenes had bade her do.

She never permitted anyone but Tennie to accompany her to Annie Wood's. They had struck a deep connection. She felt at ease with Annie. They confided their plans for the improvement of their lives far more frankly than Victoria shared with anyone except Tennie. Although Tennie liked Annie, when she accompanied Victoria to the brothel there was a lot of laughter and gossip but little serious discussion.

The same boisterous mood prevailed when Josie Mansfield dropped in. Victoria liked Josie, even if she was a bit simple and greedy. She would pass on what she heard Fisk say about the stock market and his machinations only because she liked the attention it brought and because she thought it made her seem knowing. That precious information meant little to her.

"I don't have to bother with that stuff," she said. "Jim takes care of me. I don't need to be worrying is the market going up, is the market going down, does Daniel Drew have a corner on this or that. They sneak around behind each other's backs. I think the only people Jim is completely open with is that weird little partner of his, Jay Gould, and me. But he's generous to a fault. He gave his coat to a beggar he felt sorry for. Just this week, he gave me pearl earrings the size of dice. The trouble is they hurt my ears, or I would have worn them over for you ladies to see."

"There's a trick to heavy earrings," Victoria said. "Place a little disk on the other side of the ear—it balances the weight and keeps them from falling off."

"I'll try that."

Victoria knew that Vanderbilt was extremely interested in anything Fisk was involved in. Fisk and Gould were the only players who had ever taken Vanderbilt. He had been trying to buy up Erie stock after collecting six or seven railroads. He intended to take it away from Gould and Fisk, who controlled the stock and the board. But Gould just kept printing more stock. Gould flooded Vanderbilt with Erie he kept gobbling up until finally he realized he would never get enough to control the railroad, because Gould would make sure there was always more. They had taken the Commodore for seven million—not that he would miss it, but he didn't like to lose. She wasn't about to let him know how she had obtained her information. She must figure out how to feed him what she learned, just a bit at first till she was sure that what Josie and Annie were telling her was accurate.

Of Annie's sources, she was reasonably confident. Champagne flowed freely in Annie's brothel, and the girls were encouraged to coax the gentlemen to chat about their business affairs and politics. This was no five-minute house. Often the girls were hired for the evening, and some had regular appointments with a certain man every Tuesday or Friday. After the client left, the girls were instructed to write down everything relevant they remembered. Annie wouldn't hire an illiterate white girl—Victoria's own mother was illiterate—and she liked them on the bright side. Of course, many of the men liked to boast and make much of their activities, but over time, often Annie could guess who was exaggerating. Some of the mulatto girls had learned to read and write illegally under slavery or had been born free. Those still illiterate, if Annie thought them smart, she would hire. Then she'd have them study with a young man who had the run of the house on Mondays—the day they were closed—in return for his tutoring the girls in the mornings before the brothel opened for business. It occurred to Victoria, and made her smile for an instant, that Vanderbilt couldn't have gotten a job with Annie since he could scarcely read a paragraph. Anything longer than a sentence or two he would abandon. His secretary read letters to him. Tennie and she took turns reading the newspapers aloud while he lay on his couch cursing the idiocy of politicians and people in general.

"I heard it through the grapevine that you sisters have snagged the Commodore. But he's tight as a five-year-old's twat. You won't get much out of him for your troubles." Josie fanned herself.

"So far, so good," Victoria said. "I'm consulting the spirits for him. The physical work is up to Tennie."

"You used not to be so fine!"

"I'm not his type, Josie. Tennessee is. He likes a bit more flesh than I can offer. I hear he was a skirt chaser in his youth."

"His youth ending yesterday, maybe?" Annie Wood laughed. "He isn't one of our customers or any other sporting house. Usually he chases governesses. That's a sign of great laziness or great miserliness. He never gives away a penny. Can you squeeze blood from that stone?"

Josie chimed in, "Jim told me a story about him. Some years ago he was interested in a governess. His wife wouldn't go away for a while, so he had her committed to a madhouse. Other people say he did that because she wouldn't leave Staten Island and move to Manhattan. But he sure did have her locked up. Finally William, the oldest, got some doctor to swear there was nothing wrong with her and got her freed. But she's stayed out of his way since, Jim says."

"We dine with him regularly. He doesn't give us diamonds or fine gowns, but he does pass over cash. He's had mediums on call for years. When he wants something for himself, he puts out the money."

"Mediums?" Josie laughed. "Jim doesn't believe in that bunk, and neither do I. Table-rapping. Scary noises."

"I do believe in the spirits. I've felt their presence many times. Why be surprised that the next life touches at least tangentially on this one?" Victoria leaned back in her chair, a little defensive.

"So he really believes in all that?"

Victoria was very careful what she said about Vanderbilt, for she felt if it got back to him they'd lose their sponsor. She said only what she felt he would not mind others knowing. She had heard him tell several people about his communication with spirits. "He was haunted by a ghost some years ago, that was how his interest began. He sleeps with dishes of salt under the four legs of his bed to keep them away. A medium he used to consult told him to do that." She did not add that one ghost was that of a boy his coach had run down in the street, and the second ghost was a signalman killed on his line whose family he had refused to compensate. Those were the spirits he wanted kept away.

"And everybody thinks he's so hardheaded. Each man has his weakness," Josie said. "I'm sure glad that Jim's is me."

As Victoria was leaving, Annie gave her the usual list of the chemicals and preparations her girls would need. Their business had grown slowly at first, but seemed to be burgeoning lately. One madam told another. It was a second source of income. Victoria didn't like being entirely dependent on Vanderbilt's largesse. Any patron could change his mind; every one did eventually. She confided in Annie that she was determined never to be forced to go to bed with a man she did not want for himself—because he was attractive to her physically or because he was intelligent, knowledgeable—a man who could teach her something she passionately wanted to learn. Love was a malleable thing; after all, she had loved some real losers, like Dr. Woodhull. Sex was too powerful to use for gain. It was an overwhelming force that linked her to deeper powers, and she intended to go only where its magnetism pulled her. She could never endure sexual contact with Vanderbilt, even if it had been her he had pursued and not her sister.

James was working for his brother, who ran a press in Newark. He commuted via the ferries, staying over several nights a week. Today Buck was out with the rest of the clan. Victoria had suggested they go sightseeing, recommending the Croton Reservoir—Fifth Avenue from Fortieth to Forty-second Street—a huge Egyptian-style edifice that resembled a fort. It had towers on the corners and granite walls over forty feet thick. It was a popular place for a promenade, strolling on top of those walls looking down on the city. The clan's absence gave her and Tennie time to discuss how to begin slowly and gradually feeding the tips she got from Annie and Josie to Vanderbilt.

"His mother," Tennie said. "He has enormous respect for his mother. When he had that huge steam yacht and sailed to Europe, he made the captain give a twenty-one gun salute as they passed her place on Staten Island. He thinks she was one shrewd lady. She lent him the hundred dollars that started him on his career."

Tennie rather liked the Commodore. Old boy, she called him to his face, and he preened in her attention. She felt she could handle him. "He's falling apart, sure, everything from top to bottom is wrong with him. He lived hard and he's paying the price. He eats as if food were going to vanish from the earth in the next hour and leave only stones to gnaw on. You've seen him shovel it in."

Indeed, they dined with the Commodore regularly, when he ate more than both of them together times four. He would consume several dozen oysters, most of a ham and roast beef and pudding besides, with maybe a turkey leg or two thrown in. "You must improve his habits. We want him to last a while."

"I'm working on it. I've got him to cut back on his smoking. He enjoys my scolding him. It makes him jolly."

"As long as you can manage him. I couldn't, frankly. And as long as you're comfortable. I don't want you doing anything you don't want to."

"Don't worry about that. I've been with some real oafs, Vickie, and more than one brute. The old boy's okay. He can be really mean when he wants to be, but with me he wants to be warm and almost cuddly. I like the way he treats me. I'm not interested in being kept like Josie. I want money, not presents. I want my own life to come home to. Unless he marries me, of course. That I'd go along with."

"Be careful. There is one very alive Mrs. Vanderbilt."

"She's not that alive. They haven't shared a bed in thirty years."

"They shared one pretty vigorously before that. Eleven children, is it?"

"She stays up in her part of the house. All the times we've both been there, you ever seen her?"

"Never. Are you saying she doesn't exist?"

"I caught a glimpse of her once, going out as I was coming in. She simply nodded at me and got into a maroon landau and the coachman drove her off—visiting one of her daughters. The Commodore is a stone-cold miser with his daughters. They aren't real Vanderbilts, he says, and he begrudges them every dollar."

"He was crazy about George, the son he has me communing with."

"Well, if he did love George, that was his only kid he has any feeling for. All those children, and he couldn't care less. She's his cousin, you know." Seeing Victoria's blank expression, she added, "His wife. He says that was a mistake and that's why all his kids except the dear departed George are idiots." Tennie shook her head. "He says his wife isn't well."

"They all say that. She doesn't understand me. She's on death's doorstep. We haven't been together in thirty years. She has a lover. Or she has no interest in sex and she doesn't mind. . . ."

Tennie laughed from the belly, that infectious unladylike bellow of amusement that always made Victoria smile. When she caught her breath, Tennie said, "Yeah, I never had a client in the old days who said, I love my wife, she understands me just fine. We get along perfectly. I just want to fuck."

"Did Mrs. Vanderbilt strike you as unbalanced? Remember, Josie said he had her committed to an insane asylum."

"He said he'd figured out how to get her to stay out of his way. She didn't look crazy, but then, how does a crazy person look?"

"Be careful what you say around Buck and Roxanne and the rest of the clan."

Tennie sighed, propping her round chin on her folded arms with their luxurious dimples showing above her chemise. Her dress lay on the bed ready to put on to dine with Vanderbilt. "I do watch my step with the old boy, Vickie, 'cause I don't think he's the forgiving sort."

THE GASLIGHT WAS DIMMED and only candles were burning, the way she liked it. She opened her mind and waited until she felt a spirit approaching. She believed in communicating with those who had passed over, some recently, some long, long ago. She experienced them in visions and when their minds brushed hers. The spirits did not care for loud noises or too many people. Theirs was a more tranquil, harmonious existence. But it was possible to mentally urge the spirits to communicate certain facts or ideas. After all, the dead were not stupid. They kept up with what was happening in their families.

Vanderbilt sat up expectantly across the round table from her. She liked to use a round table and had requested one. He had this table delivered that they'd used ever since, with a black cloth over it and a candle burning in the center. Tennie sat to her left, Vanderbilt to her right but farther away.

Victoria had discovered the power of being a medium when she was still a child. Women were not supposed to speak in public. But if they were spiritualists, they could collect an audience and make a decent living, or they might be really good at it like Laura Cuppy Smith or Cora Hachen, who worked the lecture circuit. Otherwise, only actresses could stand up in front of an audience and get paid instead of punished, but mediums were far more respectable. Mediums were almost holy, vessels for the spirits of those who had passed over. People came to mediums wanting reassurance, comfort, information. They wanted to be told they were not guilty. In most families, half the children died in infancy or early childhood. Their parents wanted to hear that the children were in a good place and happy, perhaps that they were still growing up there, and that their life on the other side was better than their life had been in this world. People wanted to be told the eternal hellfire that preachers had threatened them with did not exist; that the afterlife was much like this, only better. Almost every family had lost a young man in the Civil War, and they wanted to hear that their dead were doing fine on the other side.

Victoria had learned to be skilled at reading people's postures and small, often involuntary movements, unconscious reactions with their eyes, their mouth, their hands. She began with a kind of droning evocation, intended as much to put Vanderbilt in the mood as to do anything for the spirits. When she had him intent but relaxed, expectant, she went into what she thought of as her higher state.

"Someone is here. O spirit who wants to approach Cornelius, O spirit of a loved one perhaps, speak! Hear my voice, heed my plea, and speak to us. . . ."

At this point Tennie would make a kind of sound with a rattle she kept under her skirt. She had attached it to her leg before they sat down, so that she could make the sound when they were holding hands around the circle. Afterward, she would pass it off to Victoria while she had her intimate time with the Commodore. The rattle—filled with dry beans and sand—made an unearthly sound. It was just to create a mood. The spirits didn't mind and it helped create the kind of quiet receptivity she needed.

Victoria altered her voice. She could feel the spirit nearing. She could feel the power moving through her. She spoke in the voice she had learned by trial and error made Vanderbilt think of his mother. "My son . . . my son. . . ."

"Mother? Are you here?" He sat forward, clutching her hand till she winced.

"I am here, son. I'm glad you are beginning to take care of yourself. My son, often you take better care of your money and your horses than of your own body."

"Well, we all get damned old, Mama. I'm no brawling youth any longer."

"You will pass over to me in God's good time, but in the meantime I want you to take better care of your body."

"Do you have any news for me, Mama?"

"Yes, my son. You have been having trouble with the jackals of Erie."

"Fisk and Gould and Daniel Drew. Damned sons of bitches, blast them to hell. I could eat their balls for breakfast, Mama."

"You sound the same as you ever did, son. But don't despair. Something is about to change, I can see."

"What, Mama? Am I going to beat them?"

"I don't see that, son, But they are going to come to you. They are going to come begging an end to the wars of Erie. I can see that."

"When, Mama?"

"Time is not the same here as it is there, my son. I can't tell you when. Now I'm tired. You know this is difficult. I will speak with you again soon, my son, soon."

"Mama, don't leave me yet. Don't go."

Victoria let her head droop. She was silent. There, she had got her message across. Vanderbilt would be prepared for what Josie had let drop, that Fisk and Gould were hoping to settle with the Commodore. They weren't about to turn over their profits, but they were seeking some kind of compromise that would let everybody go home with a piece of the Erie pie. They were tired of the battle of corrupt judge versus corrupt judge, constant payoffs. They were tired of bribing legislators wholesale and piecemeal. They were tired of their toughs from the Irish gang in Chelsea against Vanderbilt's gang of hired Dead Rabbits. It was time to end the Erie War. They must reach a negotiated peace. Now Vanderbilt would have time to prepare, to expect the approach of the two men who had fleeced him with watered stock for months and taken seven million of his hundred million. He could not forgive that. But he could get some of his own back.

The Commodore was extremely pleased. He bussed her on the cheek and handed her fifty dollars in gold. "If they come to me and offer me a deal I can live with, then Erie will go up. I'll keep you posted. Maybe I'll give you some of the wallpaper they fed to me when I was trying to gain control. Yes, if what you say comes true, I'll give you both some Erie stock."

NINE

SINCE HIS PROMOTION, Anthony had lost touch with Edward. Now Anthony was a salesman in women's notions—ribbons, laces, embroideries, sewing supplies. He worked wholesale, not door to door, contracting with the new enormous stores like Stewart's and Lord & Taylor and with many smaller shops throughout Manhattan and Brooklyn. Other salesmen were jealous he had been given such a choice route when usually beginning salesmen were sent off to remote regions where they had to travel from town to town. Getting that stellar route might have had something to do with his joining the same Brooklyn church as his boss. Or perhaps his boss thought he was of good character—as he tried to be.

He felt at home in the Reformed Church in Brooklyn Heights, for its straight and narrow approach resembled the churches of his upbringing in rural Connecticut. None of that loose and anything-goes smarminess of pastors like Beecher over at the Plymouth, that should be named the Wide Mouth, for wide and spacious was the road to hell. He went not only to services on Sundays, a half-day affair, but also to prayers two nights a week. In his childhood, his family had gone to church twice on Sundays and his saintly mother had conducted prayers every morning. In his loneliness and isolation, he needed the church. At least there he was visible. People greeted him by name. The pastor took an interest. "You should marry, young Anthony. A man is only half a man until he has a wife of his own. And children."

He was making twenty-five dollars a week from commissions. He was saving what he could, but he doubted he could afford marriage. A wife was an expensive proposition. Still, he needed one. Living in boardinghouses offered too much temptation, bad food and too little in the way of virtue and seemliness. His boardinghouse keeper was a respectable widow, Mrs. Hanley, who took in only male boarders, but many of them were loose in their morals and spent their evenings in what they called "the sporting life"—as Edward had.

He felt a pang of guilt when he realized he had completely forgotten Edward. Edward had not been ready to pay attention to his warnings, but perhaps by now he would be more open. Anthony had a duty to look up his friend and see if he could yet be saved. On one of his excursions to lower Manhattan, he stopped by their old boardinghouse. "Is Edward Lorrilard still living here?"

The woman shook her head. "Not that one. You won't find him here or anyplace else."

"Did he leave the city?" That would be a good sign. Edward, like himself, came from a small town, in his case in upstate New York.

The woman heaved a great sigh, as if she cared, although Anthony knew her to be a hard case who cared about nothing but her oaf of a daughter and money. "He's left the city, all right, Mr. Comstock. He's left this earth."

Anthony grasped the woman's hand. "He's departed? What happened to him? He was only twenty-five."

"Got into a drunken fight over a tart, he did, and her pimp stabbed him. It was a scandal, but they never caught the tart or her pimp—they got clean away and nobody would point the finger at them. Poor Mr. Lorrilard. Cut down in his youth and for what?"

"For what, indeed. . . . Thanks for the information, although it's not what I was hoping for." He went home, stricken with a mixture of guilt and a kind of queer satisfaction in having been so right in the warnings he had given Edward.

On the way to the dry goods firm the next day, he passed the establishment he had noticed in the old days in the basement of a building on Warren Street. CONROY SPECIALTY BOOKS. BOOKS FOR YOUNG MEN. ADVENTURE, COWBOYS, LIFE ON THE OPEN ROAD, FRENCH BOOKS, SAILORS' STORIES, EXPLORERS, LIFE IN A TURKISH HAREM, CONVENT LIFE REVEALED. Dirty books like those in yellow wrappers that Edward used to carry around and read when he could sneak the time, when work was slow. Anthony stood before the door clenching his fists in anger. This demon sold hell to young men.

Every day he glared at the store as he passed. This man Conroy could openly advertise, corrupting the souls of young clerks. Conroy had seduced Edward away from respectability and the desire for the love of a good Christian woman, all the values he had been raised in, as had Anthony, back in the moral societies of rural and small-town America. Conroy had seduced Edward to his death. Something had to be done. Anthony owed it to Edward's memory, dear Edward who was so like his dead brother Samuel, and now untimely dead himself. Dead and forgotten by almost everyone, but not by him. He would avenge Edward. He would put Conroy out of business.

Finally, after two weeks of brooding and fuming, he went to see George Graves, chairman of the Y on Varick Street, where Anthony spent many happy and fruitful evenings. There he had attended lectures on avoiding obscenity, and the most recent speaker had mentioned some kind of legal remedy. He had to wait for an hour for Graves to see him. He used the time reciting speeches in his head. He had come to respect Mr. Graves for his piety and his good works. He would confess to Graves his desire to find justice for his murdered friend. He would never know who the pimp was who had stabbed him, but he could punish the man responsible for Edward having been in that vile place in the company of a prostitute. No doubt that degraded woman was much like the ones who had swarmed their table the one night he had been persuaded to accompany Edward to that concert saloon.

At last Graves opened his office door and waved him in. "It's good to see you, Anthony. But why the long face? Is your job going badly?"

"Not at all. I have a choice route. But I am in a quandary." He pulled up a chair that Graves pointed to and spilled out the story of Edward Lorrilard.

"So you want to cause trouble for this Conroy. You say he's a purveyor of pornography?"

"Openly so."

"You want to close him down? You're determined?"

"I am, sir."

"If you're serious, you have a good shot at it. We finally got an obscenity bill with teeth through the legislature this year."

That was what the lecturer had meant. "Can we put him in jail?"

"You can try. It's a law for the suppression of the trade in obscene materials—illustrations, ads, articles of indecent or immoral use. We've been working on this for years, Anthony, years. Officers can seize obscene books and indecent objects. If an indictment is forthcoming against Conroy, all his stock will be destroyed."

"That's thrilling, Mr. Graves. The power is there to be used."

"You're determined to proceed?" The man looked skeptical.

"I am."

"Well, this is how you might go about getting him. It may be a bit distasteful, but it should work—providing the police cooperate. They don't like to arrest these fellows. But I know a captain who will act—if you go through with it."

Anthony could tell Graves thought he was made of words and not deeds. He would show him. Still, his work kept him from confronting Conroy for nearly three weeks. It was a busy season for women's notions—moving into warm weather when different styles of attire were worn by ladies. He was kept hopping, and although when he retired for the night he thought of Edward and vowed to bring Conroy to justice, he could not pry the time from his schedule. It was a profitable time for him and his commissions, but he had to admit, when he studied his bankbook with the long columns of very small amounts, that at this rate it would be years before he could acquire a wife. He saved a nickel here, a quarter there. He was a successful salesman, but his commissions did not amount to enough to set him up as he wished to live.

In spite of his good relationship with his boss, he was going to look for something that paid more. It came down to that. Move on or atrophy. He saw clerks in the offices of the dry goods firm who had withered at their desks, never married, never had children—husks of men. He looked too at the older salesmen, always on the road. Sometimes they took to drink or women. Being away from home so much, either they had never taken the time and trouble to court a good woman and marry or they had some poor drudge at home but enjoyed the company of more exciting women in hotels across the country. He did not want their lives. Although he was good at sales and knew a great deal by now about women's notions—more than most women could boast—he could not say he found his work satisfying. If he failed to sell his notions, would it make a bit of difference to anyone except himself and his sad little bank account? It was trivial work that accomplished no higher moral good, did not improve men's souls or the society in which they lived.

One night he woke from a nightmare, or was it a vision? Edward was standing hip deep in flames shaking his finger at him. Edward was burning and cursing him for not seeking revenge, for not keeping other young men from his fate. Anthony was covered in cold sweat and shaken. He had been sent that dream as a prod. He was sure he could smell burning flesh, like scorched bacon.

Finally the day came when he could get back to Warren Street. He checked his wallet and marched down the block. The place next door to Conroy was just as bad—purveyors of rubber goods. Everybody knew what that meant. Filthy business, all of it. But he had a special grudge against Conroy.

He felt queasy as he paused outside Conroy's establishment. LATEST PAUL DE KOCK, 100 NIGHTS IN A GIRLS' SCHOOL. He forced himself down the steps and inside. It looked like any other bookstore, just racks and racks of books. The first ones he saw as he veered to the left were books about fishing and the out-of-doors. He stared at drawings of trout until he regained his nerve. Then he came upon anatomy books. Drawings of the inner organs, the digestive system, the circulation of the blood, and yes, here was a cutaway of the male reproductive system. He did not doubt that the female reproductive system would be likely sliced asunder and laid out on the page to tempt impure thoughts in the heedless young.

"Can I help you?" It was a middle-aged man, completely bald with bright blue eyes and a big smile, perhaps six inches shorter than Anthony and slighter of frame.

He could not very well say, Sell me a piece of pornography, please. The sign came into his mind. "I'd like the new Paul de Kock."

"You'll find it a most satisfying read. He's a very popular author." The man was so depraved he might have been talking about the book on trout. "We can scarcely keep him in stock." The man bustled behind the counter and slapped down a book in a yellow wrapper, much like the ones that Edward had insisted on reading.

Anthony paid him and asked for a receipt. The man seemed surprised—probably buyers of pornography did not usually want a written record of the transaction—but he obliged Anthony with a receipt that said what the book was and how much it cost, with the name of the bookstore printed at the top.

Before he proceeded, Anthony decided he must study what he had bought, to make sure it was evil and to understand his prey. He took the book home, well hidden in the portmanteau in which he carried samples, and that night in his room he read it cover to cover, going without sleep to carry out his mission. A weaker man would have succumbed to the solitary vice, but he resisted. It was as vile as he had imagined. Young girls, supposedly innocent, tampered with each other and then were seduced by teachers, ministers, their own parents. Each scene was dirtier than the last, with couples leading to threesomes and then vast orgies. He finished it by dawn. That he had not touched himself made him feel strong. He had tested himself by fire and not been found wanting. He could enter the flames and not be burned.

Anthony marched to the relevant police station. He asked for a Captain Curtis, for Graves had told him he might receive satisfaction from this man as he might not from a run-of-the-mill policeman. Captain Curtis kept him waiting half an hour, but he was patient, reminding himself of his mission and the satisfaction it would bring him to see Conroy punished.

Finally Captain Curtis met with him. "What can I do for you? Has someone harmed you?" He was a burly man, as befitted a policeman, with muttonchop whiskers beginning to gray, a prominent square jaw and bushy brows.

"Someone has harmed the community in the eyes of God and man." He drew the dirty book from its plain wrapper and slammed it down on Curtis's desk. Beside it he placed the receipt. "I bought this piece of filth at Conroy's Books on Warren. This violates the law passed this year against obscenity."

"Right you are. Are you willing to swear out a complaint? I know about the law, but we haven't had an opportunity to enforce it."

Anthony held his tongue. After all, on any day they could easily have done what he had and coaxed the evil Conroy into selling an illicit book. That they had not bothered to do so made Anthony feel that he had a duty to fulfill because they were shirking theirs. "I'm ready. Will you accompany me?"

Curtis looked annoyed but rose at once. "I'll get a constable and we'll arrest him in his den."

So the three men, Anthony and Captain Curtis side by side and the constable just behind them, marched the several blocks to Conroy's establishment. When Conroy understood what was up, he responded with anger. "I'm not doing any harm. Look at the streets around here. There's dozens selling racier books than mine."

"The more shame to all of you. Aren't you going to cuff him?"

"Not necessary," the constable said. "He's not a rough one. He'll come along lamb-like. Just down to the station house."

Curtis said he would send a couple of men with a wagon. Anthony sat on the stoop to wait. He was not going to take a chance that they'd let Conroy go with a cheap fine and he'd come right back and open up his den. He sat there for two hours until a dray pulled up drawn by a swaybacked piebald horse, with two policemen in uniform sitting on the box. From how often he was kept waiting, he felt how unimportant other men judged him to be. Anthony helped them load books. He made sure they took the anatomy books also, although one of the policemen said they were perfectly legal. "Well, they oughtn't to be."

He was sure that both men had slipped a book or two into their pockets, but he could not prove it and he did not have the right to search them. They were probably past vulnerability. He was here today to save the young clerks who frequented the neighborhood, not case-hardened police who might well be on the take. He was sure from their attitude of amusement that if he had gone to them with his complaint, they would have put him off. Anthony went home exhausted but satisfied. He had done his duty. He felt as if others should see in him as he passed a certain authority, a light of rectitude and strength. No one seemed to notice, but he felt the difference in himself.

When he reported back to Graves, the older man shook his hand warmly and clapped him on the back. "If we had more with your courage,

Anthony, this city would be a far safer place for innocent young men who come here to make their fortune and too often lose their souls."

"I would like to do more, sir."

"There's always more to do of the Lord's work, Anthony. But you should marry. It's the only way to avoid temptation in the long run."

"I would like to, sir. But I'm only a salesman. Matrimony is expensive."

"That it is, young man. You have no idea how expensive." Graves sighed. "If it's not one thing, it's another. It never stops."

"I would like for it to start, sir."

"With your stalwart faith, how can you doubt?"

Nice words, but Anthony was left to return to his dismal boardinghouse as impoverished and lonely as ever. He could imagine a blissful married love, but he wondered if he would ever reach that state. All he saw ahead of him were hardscrabble times in the dry goods trade and boardinghouse after boardinghouse into old age. He felt trapped in a path that led nowhere.

TEN

RS. STONE HAD MOVED out. She said it was improper for Freydeh to manufacture such things. She would not even pronounce the word. She could not have her good name linked with such an enterprise, but Freydeh heard on the street that Mrs. Stone's cousin had a room for her over in Little Germany where they ran a family beer parlor. She could help out and get her room and board free.

They needed the space now far more than they needed a boarder. Freydeh bought the pure rubber in sheets from a dealer, saying that she was manufacturing dress shields. Probably he didn't believe her; certainly he didn't care. They hung the sheets over a rack. Then they would take a sheet and spread out the rubber on a metal table they bought from the widow of a doctor. They cut the pieces to various sizes, then fitted them over forms they had made. Then they dipped the condoms into a vulcanization solution made from sulfur and white lead from the pharmacy so that the condoms would not be affected by temperature or become sticky. That was when they had to cook it on the stove.

She had learned lots of American words for condoms. Sometimes they were called capotes or baudruches or safes, French secrets, English letters, cundoms, cundrums, rubbers, gents protectors, skins, sheaths or envelopes. Some men preferred caps that covered only the head of the penis, but they were more difficult to make and had to fit very tightly. What Sammy and she made were full-length sheaths. Condoms were still made of intestines, but those were mostly inferior to rubber—except for the goldbeaters, thin and fine as silk. That took skill neither of them had, and they had no access to slaughterhouse products. First they had to master the process of vulcanization, sizing, sealing the edges. Finally they succeeded in making some product. Sammy tried what they considered their first successful condom, pouring water in. "No leak. Look, Freydeh. Watertight."

"So, Sammy, we done it. Now we only got to produce a whole lot of them and then we start trying to sell them."

Then he began to snicker. "This would be one weird-looking gent who could wear this."

Freydeh sighed. "We have to cut better. Yah, he'd lean far to the left and bulge in the middle. I think we need cutting guides. Like dress patterns."

"It's hot work."

"So is working in a laundry, but if we can make a bunch of them and sell them, we'll do a lot better than that. . . ." She wiped her forehead with a cloth dampened in the water Sammy had poured back into the enamel basin. "Did you ever go down to the river and bathe? Mrs. Goetz was talking about that—how they have bathing piers set up in the East River."

"Yeah, I done that. They only open them in the summer, and they don't like you to hang around too long. But it feels good on a day like this."

"They say it may rain tomorrow and cool things down a bit. . . . In my old village, we used to bathe in the river, us girls. There was a *mikvah* of course—a ritual bath. But I liked the river better. It wasn't no big river like the ones you have here. It was twenty feet wide and ten feet deep. I never felt so free as when I was splashing around in that river."

"It's great in the river here. Maybe we can go tomorrow?"

"You go, Sammy. You're still a kid. You should have some fun. I'll stay here and cook rubber."

"You should go too. It gets awful hot in these tight streets. Stinks too, worse than the rest of the year. It feels good to cool down for a little while."

"Maybe. I'll see."

"You work all the time. You work for Yonkelman six days a week. You come back here and you work on the rubber. Then when we have any time we can get away, we go running around looking for Shaineh."

"Is the life too hard for you, Sammy?"

"I only run errands. Sometimes he just sends me back here. Sometimes I sit around waiting. It's easier than what I was used to on the street. But you, you're like one of the horses that draw the trolleys—you'll work till you drop in your tracks."

"That's sweet of you to worry about me." She mopped the sweat from her forehead. It was running down her back, gathering under her breasts. "It's just I can almost see what I want, but it's still so far away, I'm running all the time to get closer. But okay, I'll go with you tomorrow. We'll dip ourselves in the river and wash the sweat off. I promise. Now we have to work faster. We can't do one every hour."

"Every hour! Freydeh, it took us a month to do this one."

Mrs. Stone had told her she should not let Sammy call her by her given name, but she did not mind. Mrs. Stone kept saying he should be grateful. No, she wasn't sorry to have that woman gone. She didn't worry about Sammy taking advantage of her. They needed each other. They had settled in like a real family. It made her life less bitter to have him there. She felt from him in return a strong loyalty. Gratitude could turn sour, could turn into envy or resentment; she had seen that before. But loyalty was something that could last, like a well-made pot. Forget about boarders. She needed to put all her effort into trying to get launched in her new business. She didn't want anyone interfering, telling her she was a bad woman. She didn't think it wrong. Most women had more babies than they could raise or handle. Childbirth was dangerous and infants were fragile and weak. Children died in this neighborhood every day of a dozen diseases, they died of hunger, they died of thirst, they died of beatings, they died of the cold—half before they reached the age when they could care for themselves, ten or eleven. A good many of them were thrust out or ran away, like Sammy. No, she didn't think something that might limit childbirth was a bad thing. She wished she had children, but most women had the opposite problem, far more babies than they could feed or care for. People like Mrs. Stone could not succeed in making her feel guilty for the work she had chosen.

The next afternoon, Sammy reminded her of her promise. She was embarrassed. "What do people wear?" In the shtetl, she and the other girls had simply hung their clothes on a bush or spread them out on the rocks. They would post a lookout, who would come in later and be replaced by one of the girls who had splashed around already. Finally she put on her cotton dress. It needed washing anyhow. She would wear the dress into the water. She wanted to be modest. Flaunting her body was not the way her dear mother had raised her.

She was nervous as they trooped to the East River, passing through the German section where both goyish and Jewish German-speaking people lived mixed up. Then they had to pass through the Irish section. Sammy clasped her hand in his and his other hand closed around a blackjack she had seen him slide into his pocket. Often Jews were attacked in these streets. They walked quickly through air like heavy woolen blankets pressing on them. They could smell the fat-rendering vats and the reek of blood from the slaughterhouses. Acid rose in her throat and she swallowed it down. "Maybe this isn't such a good idea, Sammy."

"Just keep walking like you own the place. And don't talk. If they hear you, they'll know you're Jewish. Keep quiet if anything happens and let me do the talking."

Kids on stoops eyed them suspiciously and groups of men turned and watched them. But the only hail they got was from a couple of guys who yelled obscenities at Freydeh, saying what they would like to do to her. She only knew that because Sammy briefly, gruffly explained and they walked faster.

At last they got to the baths. She was nervous about how it would be. Sammy went in one door and motioned her to go to the women's door. It was free but the towel cost a nickel. A German woman was blocking the entrance until each woman paid. Then she was handed a towel—thin as a piece of paper but it would do, it would have to do—and the German waved her through.

The baths were out on a pier in an elaborate floating building, the women's on one side and the men's on the other with high wooden fences enclosing them off from each other or from any observer. A square pond was open to the water below and the sky above. She walked gingerly along a floating dock that moved under her feet, that rolled with each passing boat. There was no collection of bathing beauties in fancy long woolen suits here, such as she had seen in the windows when she had strolled along Fifth Avenue. These were stout neighborhood women and their children, splashing about the way she had with her sisters and friends, in her own little river back in the Pale. They were dressed any which way in whatever they dared get wet. The German woman at the door had told them all in German and English they could not wash themselves, but everyone was doing so anyhow, as best they could. She had a little piece of soap with her, made from suet and wood ash from the fireplace. For once all the women were getting along, the Irishwomen, the Hungarians, the Germans, the tough American-born. She heard two women speaking Russian and dog-paddled over to them. She suspected they were Jews because she had not met a Russian in New York who wasn't. Yes, one of the women was still wearing the shaytl, the wig worn by all married women back in the Pale except for a few freethinkers and prostitutes.

She greeted them in Russian and then in Yiddish, so they would know who she was, and she told them where she came from.

"Is that near Vilna?" the younger of what she guessed were two sisters—the one not wearing the shaytl—asked her. "We're from Odessa."

"About three hours' journey by horse. Have you been here long?"

"A year last month. It's lonely for us. So many many people and so few speak the mother tongue. I'm Giborah. That's Hetty."

They compared notes. Giborah was unmarried. Hetty's husband worked as a peddler and so did she. Giborah had been betrothed, but her fiancé had been murdered. "Which shul do you go to?" Hetty asked her.

Freydeh didn't want to admit she didn't go to shul. "I went to a German one on Allen Street, Beth El, but it was strange. All in German with little Hebrew and no Yiddish. All the melodies were different."

"I know what you mean," Hetty said. "We go to a tiny shul in a storefront on Orchard Street, but it's real."

"She means like we're used to at home," Giborah said. She was maybe two, three years younger than Freydeh and so thin there was just skin over the bones of her hand. Her hair was light brown and almost straight. Her gray eyes were watering from the river—it was none too clean, but it was better than not being washed. Hetty was round. Her face was plump, her chin perfectly rounded, and her eyes were gray-blue. Giborah did most of the talking for both of them.

Freydeh reminded herself to thank Sammy for making her come to the river. Maybe Shaineh had found that shul. She had always been a good girl and attended regularly with their parents and other siblings, long after Freydeh refused to go because it was superstition and she was a bold freethinker. There were not many of their countrymen here in New York, so if

Shaineh was looking for a shul where she could feel at home, that might be a place she would visit. Maybe ask for help. "I would love to go to your shul with you. It would make me feel more at home."

Giborah squeezed Freydeh's shoulder with her bony hand. "You come along, absolutely. You come to our flat Friday just after supper. We live at 71 Grand over the kosher butcher. The fourth floor back. You find us and we'll walk to the shul."

Hetty nodded. "It's good to find a landsman, believe me. You come."

Freydeh promised she would be there Friday next week for sure. She would try not to hope too strongly, but she could not help wishing it were next Friday already. She used her little bit of soap, washing herself through her clothes and washing her hair, long and dark and heavy, loosened on her shoulders and then soaking wet. She wrung it out like a mop and then pinned it back to dry. The day was so hot, it should dry fast and then she could put it up properly. It was not seemly for a woman her age to go about with her hair loose. Men would stare.

The attendant was calling to them. "You been in long enough. Come outta there. Your time is used up."

"There's enough water in the river for all of us and ten times more," Freydeh called back. Hetty and Giborah were scrambling to the planks to get out, but Freydeh was not easily intimidated by another woman. She had the confidence of her physical strength.

"Your time's up. Now come on out or I'll take a hook to you."

Hetty and Giborah were motioning to her to come out. She did not want to shock her new friends by making a scene, so serenely and slowly she paddled to them and hauled herself out of the water. She could dry herself sort of with the towel, although of course almost all of them had to put their wet clothes on again, as she did. All but Hetty. She had brought a voluminous black gown she could step into, making her wet clothing into a bundle she could carry in a basket. Freydeh suspected they had more money than she did—three of them working. Someday she would have more than three dresses, two wool and one cotton, and maybe even a bathing costume.

When she got outside, Sammy was waiting for her, his tattered clothes steaming in the sun. Like her, he had gone in as he was. The women looked at him with disapproving glances. "This is Sammy," she said. They looked from her to him. There was little physical resemblance. "He's my adopted son."

Hetty nodded. "Parents dead?"

"Yeah." Sammy preferred that story. But he was staring at her. When they had walked a block, he said, "That was a big lie you told."

"Not such a lie." She shrugged under her wet dress. Water vapor was rising from her as if she were a stove with a kettle heating on it.

"I don't know what that means." He kicked a stone into a puddle of horse urine. The streets around here weren't paved. In hot weather, the wind blew dust into the faces of pedestrians like them.

"It means we're a family. Unless you don't want to. You don't have to."

"For how long?" His chin was still dug into his chest.

"Families are forever. Till they die." She looked around carefully. "We have to pay attention. We're in the Irish now." She touched his arm.

She stopped to buy eggs. They came in fresh every morning but she had to buy the cheaper ones, packed in brine. The better eggs were packed in bran. Someday.

When they came into their hot and airless rooms, they sat down across the table they ate on. Sammy was sulky. Another would have thought he was angry about what she had said, but she knew him better. He was afraid. Afraid to hope. Afraid she did not mean it. She had come to feel strong affection for him. If she was never to have children of her own body, then she at least could take in a child who needed a family as much as she did. But she wouldn't push things. They sat there in silence for a while and then she said, "I'm going to change into something that isn't sopping wet."

She went back to the airless little bedroom. Her body felt clammy, even chilly under the wet clothes, but a few minutes out of them would restore her to being too hot like everyone else on the bottom of Manhattan. "If you felt like going down to the courtyard, you could bring up a bucket of water and we could sit with our feet in it. That would give us a little relief."

He thought about it, head propped on his hand. "Okay." He did not move for several minutes, but finally he took a bucket and went out to climb down the four flights of steps.

Below in the street, a drayman and his helper were trying to remove a dead horse. It had been worked to death, poor thing, and died of the heat or thirst. It was as skinny as Giborah from the river, but still weighed more than two men could easily shift into the wagon. The horses pulling it were not happy and kept snuffling uneasily. They knew what they were expected to carry off, and they did not like it. Some fellow feeling among horses for their fallen, she thought. Horses she was not comfortable with. Cows, chickens, sheep, those she knew familiarly. She had lived with them. But horses were something else. Dangerous feeling. A man up on a horse felt superior and had an advantage. But horses were not to blame for how men behaved once astride. Horses were probably good creatures left on their own.

Across the street, every fire escape was loaded with people. She had tested theirs carefully, and when Sammy came back they could sit out there. When the sun began to set, they could go back to work on their rubber project. They were not natural chemists, either of them, but she was determined.

Loud voices brought her to the window again. A fight had broken out between two groups of young men, so far only a matter of shouting and strutting, but those scuffles could turn deadly fast. They were all in their shirtsleeves, brandishing their fists and shouting in German. She could understand them, but the reason for their fury was obscure. Something about a debt owed for a bad bet. Bored men could always find something to fight about. Sammy should have been back up by now. The last thing she felt like doing was going down four flights of steps to look for him, but the fight could turn violent any moment. If he was her foster son, the way she had said, then she had to look out for him. Never mind that as a street arab he had seen hundreds of fights and probably been in plenty himself. That wasn't his life now, and she could not let him risk getting hurt by standing too close. Even watching a fight was dangerous. She heaved herself out of the chair and went down the steps, as quickly as she dared in the dark. In the stairwell, it was always midnight. Hot and dark and steep, without a breath of air other than fetid smells.

As she had suspected, there was Sammy on the stoop with the full bucket beside him. The door was open to the street and he was watching as the first blow landed. All at once it was a tangle of shoving and punching bodies, shrieks and curses. She grabbed him by the shoulder and drew him in.

"Hey, I want to watch."

"Upstairs you got a good view and no trouble. Come on." She took the bucket from him and pushed him ahead of her down the hall, up the stairs. She could tell he was annoyed, but she was bigger than him and he could not get past her to climb down. Realizing he was stuck, he began to run up the steps in order to get to the window in the flat.

He reached the room a good two minutes before her, puffing along with the full bucket and careful not to spill any. He was out on the fire escape already. She put down the bucket and climbed out beside him. One man was swinging a club. Another went down cursing and after a moment she could see a comma of blood seeping out from under him. Another was kicking a man who had been pushed down on one of the stoops. From a window above a woman threw down the contents of her chamber pot on the fighters, splattering them. They cursed at her.

"There's more where that came from!" she yelled in German. "Now go back where you belong and let our lads alone."

"Who says this block belongs to you, bitch!" The man shouting up at her was suddenly smashed in the face. His teeth exploded.

"Brass knuckles," Sammy said knowingly.

Suddenly they were all scattering and the man who had fallen now lay in a widening spiral of dark blood, the back of his head caved in.

Freydeh took Sammy by the elbow. "Look. That's how the street life ends. If you ever think it's boring with me, look at that poor stupid lad bleeding out his life. I don't want that for you. Do you want that?"

Sammy was staring down, his mouth fallen open. "I knew him. He ran numbers out of a parlor on Orchard. He used to give me little jobs sometimes."

The draymen had come out of the courtyard where they had taken refuge and went back to trying to lift the dead horse into the cart. When they finally had it loaded, they picked up the corpse of the numbers dealer and carried that off too. If he wasn't dead already, he soon would be. It was all the same to them. Just garbage to haul.

ELEVEN

"Mrs. Stanton, you've alienated folks by what you've said about ignorant Negro men having the vote while women are denied. How can you say that, being such a close friend of Frederick Douglass?" Susan stood over her with arms crossed.

"I feel betrayed. We fought for their rights, but they won't stand with us for ours." She winced as if struck. The pain was still raw in her. Frederick kept saying it was the hour of the Negro, but apparently not of Negro women. "He's far from ignorant. There isn't a better orator in the country."

"Nonetheless, we must watch whom we alienate."

Elizabeth sighed, cheek against hand. "Contributions are drying up." Since they'd started the National Woman Suffrage Association, they had not drawn donors. Women who could afford to give judged them too controversial.

"Money is the least of our problems. My Quaker upbringing has taught me how little I really need." Susan smoothed down her plain gray dress.

"My dear Susan, you may not need money, but the movement does. The press costs money. Paper, printing, postage. Meetings eat up money. Conferences run on money. Travel is expensive—railroads, stages, hotels, meals. Publicity for lectures and meetings. Money is the engine that moves us down the track. Without it, we're stalled. And we *are* stalled."

"Why won't the Boston women come in with us? We should stand as one."

"They see us as too radical. They want a very nice movement." Elizabeth said "nice" as if the word stuck in her teeth.

"You infuriated them when you wrote that article about men assaulting women and said that every woman should get a large Newfoundland dog and her own pistol."

"They are ladies, Susan, fine ladies. You and I are no such animals." Elizabeth raked her hand through her curls. Her hair always soothed her. She still loved her hair; even at fifty-three when it was graying, it was still curly and abundant. One of her vanities was to have it done by a woman she trusted. Susan wore her hair raked back severely, but since she was a girl, Elizabeth had always been proud of her naturally curly mane. She envied Susan for the fact that her hair, no matter how plainly she wore it, was still a smooth glossy brown.

"We should have started our own group years ago." Susan removed her glasses and polished them carefully.

Elizabeth didn't want to argue, for there was a bond between them that she hoped would last as long as she did. There was no one's opinion she valued more or whom she trusted as she trusted Susan. "My dear, let's not be so testy with each other. We must put our good heads together and plan strategy. I've made mistakes. So have you. Don't try to walk forward looking over your shoulder. Please!"

Susan carefully fitted her glasses back on her nose. "Of course. We must woo the Boston women. They have the money and resources we lack."

"And the respectability." Elizabeth laughed. "Look, I'll offer to resign as president of the National."

"No! Don't sacrifice yourself to them!" Susan sat upright, frowning.

"It's no sacrifice. Office never meant a thing to me. It doesn't bother you that you aren't president. You always choose a lesser office when you could have any office you wish."

"I hate to see you immolate yourself for them."

She could never make Susan understand that resigning would mean liberation, time to write, time to read. "I'll make the offer. See if they want a symbolic rather than a real auto-da-fé." She stood, fanning herself. "I hear Amelia bringing Robbie and Harriot back from the beach."

Susan darted to the window. "You have sharp ears, Mrs. Stanton. Indeed, it's our children. I didn't hear a thing." They walked out onto the porch to greet Robbie along with his little shovel, Harriot with a beach umbrella and their wet towels hanging around their wet suits.

The women didn't have leisure to talk further until well after supper and evening games, when the children were at last in bed and the work of the household quieted. Susan was rocking in a chair she loved, out on the wide veranda. Fireflies winked on the lawn, a sight that made Elizabeth nostalgic for her childhood, when she had run about freely and when her father had seemed to approve of her intelligence and spirit. Later, he did not. All he wanted was a living son, and that he had been denied. Fireflies were the soul of hot summer evenings with her siblings, with her friends in the stately family home where they had played hide-and-seek or blindman's buff among the shrubbery while there was faint light in the sky. Their upbringing had been strict. They ate by a rigid regimen: breakfast at six, dinner at noon, supper at five and pie at eight. They were permitted horseback riding; let loose, she rode like a demon. There were fairs, parties, but she was forced to wear a cotton dress in red or blue with stiff neck ruffles, black alpaca aprons and, even in the hottest weather, knit stockings. She hated her clothes. They confined her. Her mother would announce, "If you think those are a hindrance, wait till you grow up and have to wear a corset and dresses that weigh half a ton." Elizabeth never wanted to come in on those warm summer nights to her stuffy bedroom where she lay in bed with her sister Tryphena sweating in her long nightgown until her hair and body were drenched.

She realized with a start that Susan was speaking, her voice low and thoughtful. ". . . also at the meeting was a young woman who makes collars. She gets twenty-two cents a collar. She can only make thirty a day."

"Susan, forgive me. I was woolgathering. What meeting is this?"

Susan frowned over her glasses. "Mrs. Stanton, the lives of these girls are very difficult!"

"I'm listening now. You know I'm interested."

"I've started Working Women's Association Number Two at a boardinghouse. I met with working girls—close to a hundred from the neighborhood. Their pay is so pitiful I don't know how any survive."

"Employers assume girls can live on air."

"They don't care how the girls live. They say there are always more where these came from. And of course there are." Susan clenched her hands in her lap. "Every day girls come to the city who've never been on their own. Get off the train, off the stage, and walk into what they cannot imagine. Every day girls land by boat or train and are dumped into a life for which they're pitifully unprepared. No one reaches out to them except madams and pimps and the proprietors of sweatshops."

"And you, Susan."

"I had a letter today about a young girl in Philadelphia, an English immigrant who went into domestic service. Her employer forced himself on her, then turned her into the street when she was expecting. She had her baby in an unheated garret, alone, and the baby died. She was close to starvation and had puerperal fever, but she has been tried for murder by a jury of men and is to be hanged. The judge outright said at sentencing he was making an example of her to scare other women."

Elizabeth stood. "Get me the name and the facts, and we'll take a delegation down to Philadelphia. We can't let her die. Get me the facts!"

That night she was working on a speech she had promised Susan about women workers when she got stuck for a phrase and began doodling. When she looked at what she had drawn, she saw she had made a big heart and inside it were two figures. One was all circles piled on circles including little curlicues for the hair. That was herself, obviously. A woman of curves and bulges, round face, breasts and belly and hips. Then next to it with joined hands was a stick figure, all straight lines. Susan was an arrow pointing to a target. Certainly they were Jack Sprat and his wife, Susan all lean and abstemious and herself plump and far more sensual and pleasure-loving. Susan had only the movement and her female friends. Elizabeth suspected Susan thought women simply shouldn't marry. At the same time, Susan believed marriage was eternal and continued in the afterlife, so not only did she disapprove of divorce, she frowned on widows or widowers marrying again. Elizabeth wanted marriage to be a legal contract, to be broken by the will of both parties or by any breach of the contract—excessive drunkenness, adultery, criminal behavior, wife-beating. When a marriage didn't work, the parties should be able to end it without great fuss and certainly without a church getting involved. Women were often stuck in hellish marriages that were sometimes fatal. On questions of love and sex and marriage, Susan and she could not find common ground.

However, it was certainly a great convenience that Susan had never married. It meant Susan was far more available to her as well as to other women. Furthermore, Susan alone among all the women of the New York contingent—and this was true of the Boston women as well—was unmarried and thus could sign contracts. Susan and she could never have started the *Revolution* if Susan were married. Married women, like idiots and children, could not sign contracts. Susan was the sole proprietor of the paper because Susan alone had the legal ability to sign for loans and arrange to contract out jobs. Everyone else on the editorial board was married, and so were most of their contributors. Susan was the only legal adult.

Susan and she had invited two of the Beecher sisters, Harriet Beecher Stowe, the famous novelist, and Isabella Beecher Hooker, who had just begun to involve herself in woman's rights, to join the *Revolution* as contributing editors. Both had said they would do so if the name of the paper was changed to something less controversial. Harriet let them know that Henry Ward Beecher, their brother, the charismatic preacher, disapproved of the name. Elizabeth and Susan refused to change it. They were trying to make a revolution, nothing less, so why lie about it? Harriet withdrew, but Isabella capitulated and began writing for them.

Elizabeth had frankly been surprised at Isabella's response. She had more independence from the Beecher clan than they had suspected. The Beechers were one of the most prominent American families, wielding great clout. Lincoln had called Harriet the little woman who started the big war. Catherine, the eldest sister, wrote books about education and running a household properly, although she, like Susan, had never married. She was equally famous as an educator and as a rule-maker for housewives. Isabella had always been under the shadow of her famous half sisters and half brother, Henry. She had married a successful lawyer, John Hooker, and raised two daughters. Sometimes a woman could seem in her domestic role meek and without gumption, then blossom when she was permitted a more public role.

Elizabeth had seen that with Lib Tilton. Susan and Elizabeth had begun talking with her away from Theo. Lib proved to have a keen intelligence. Lib was one of many women in the Plymouth congregation who adored Beecher. Elizabeth had gone to hear him, of course, and found him theatrical—a great performer but not much of a thinker. He was a stout man with flying gray hair around a central dome and an actor's voice and style. He strode up and down his platform waving his arms, stomping, acting out parts, bringing the audience to laughter and sometimes to tears. She did not quite trust him. She had heard rumors of his affairs with women of his congregation. She would not be surprised if the stories proved true. At any rate, Lib now acted as poetry editor of the *Revolution*. Theo was sarcastic about that, saying how could a woman who had never written a poem act as a poetry editor, but Elizabeth, who had seen Theo's verse, thought that Lib could prove to have better taste in poetry than her husband.

She tried to separate her disgust at the way Theo treated his wife from the man who worked hard for woman's rights as he had for the rights of Negroes, the staunch liberal who had not deserted her cause when so many had. She liked to talk politics with him, she enjoyed an occasional game of chess. He admired her and showed it, and she could not help basking a little, at a time when Susan and she were being vilified not only by their enemies but by their old allies in the Republican Party. After all, had her husband treated her with more respect than Theo showed to Lib? She was hard put to think of a man who actually took his wife's politics seriously. Perhaps Henry Blackwell, married to Lucy Stone, was the exception. They always seemed to be at one politically—but whose head gave the real direction? She was convinced that Blackwell was unfaithful. All those Boston women were so proper and so shocked when a woman brought up issues they considered controversial, anything to do with bodies, sex, marriage, divorce, childbirth, but their lives were not as conventional as they liked to pretend in public. Several of them had long-term serious relationships outside their marriages. These were times when the family was adored in public, when every preacher and public official and journalist praised fidelity and chastity and then in private did his best to escape the first and destroy the second.

Theo had become infatuated with Newport when he had stayed with

Paulina Wright Davis during a rights convention. Paulina had been a workhorse of the woman's rights movement since 1850, but because she was also a clotheshorse, she incurred disapproval. Susan was a bit uncomfortable around Paulina, who wore Paris gowns—her second husband was wealthy—and had several mansions to flit between. Paulina's answer to those who equated frumpiness with woman's rights was that she was a living rebuttal to the popular cartoon of suffragists with beards and mustaches smoking cigars. Theo had been even more impressed by Laura Bullard, a widow and patent medicine heiress. Elizabeth had heard from Paulina that he and Laura were having a passionate affair with a lot of high-toned rhetoric about spiritual affinities. Theo certainly cut a romantic figure with his flowing locks, and women pursued him.

She laid her cheek down on her arm and let herself doze. Then she snapped awake. An argument had formed in her mind. The assumption of employers and the government was that women's wages were supplemental, while men had to be paid a family wage. But that ignored how often women were the heads of families, because of desertion and death or injury. Susan would enjoy delivering that speech. Women had to be financially independent. Money squatted in the middle of Elizabeth's life like a troll with greedy jaws spread wide, all teeth and appetite. She wondered if she would ever be done driving herself to take yet another tour of speaking engagements to promote the movement, yes, but also for money, money, money.

Four days later, she and Susan were on the train to Philadelphia and thence to Harrisburg to confront the governor about Hester Vaughan, the woman to be hanged. They had written to a number of Pennsylvania women to meet them in Harrisburg. First they stopped to meet Hester in Moyamensing Prison, where she was confined. She stared at them when she met them, barely able to speak at first. Then she burst into tears and embraced them.

"I don't want to die! I want to go home. My mum wants me home. I didn't want to lose my baby, but I was so sick I couldn't crawl out of bed."

She told her story while Susan wrote down the account. She was thin as a piece of paper and as pale, only nineteen.

"We'll save you," Elizabeth promised. "I swear it on the heads of my children." She wrote up the story and sent it to the Working Women's Association in New York, urging them to get it into the papers. The more publicity they could stir up, the better. The *Revolution* would be coming out with a headline SHOULD HESTER HANG?

They worried and harassed the governor every day. They sent petitions, they harangued him wherever they could catch him. Elizabeth stood in front of his carriage and would not move. Susan waited in front of his house to buttonhole him. They called in the newspapers and gave them stories to make readers weep. Elizabeth cornered legislators and told the pitiful tale again and again. Susan pulled out troops of women. They held mass meetings in Philadelphia and New York where Elizabeth told Hester's sad history. Back and forth they went to the prison to cheer her up. The guards all knew them and Elizabeth did her best to charm them, hoping for better treatment for Hester.

"Ladies," the governor said, pulling on his beard, "don't you have anything to do but pester me? You're like a cloud of mosquitoes."

"Oh, we can bite worse than any mosquito." Elizabeth beamed at him. "Do you wish to be known in history as the man who hanged a sweet and wronged woman?"

Finally the governor pardoned Hester, and she was free. The governor insisted she be sent back to England, to her family. Hester wept with relief. Elizabeth, Susan and the contingent from the Working Women returned to New York with at least one little victory to warm them. The story had been carried in newspapers all over the country. Perhaps a judge somewhere else would think twice about killing a woman for her hard luck.

TWELVE

ICTORIA AND TENNIE were dining with the Commodore at Delmonico's. Dinner with Vanderbilt was always a long-drawn-out matter, not because of conversation or because he ate slowly—he didn't—but because he ate such an enormous amount. Tennie was working on his habits, but so far she had only managed to cut back his girth an inch at the waist. He put up with admonishments from her he would not accept from anyone else. He had already eaten a turbot and a tenderloin of beef. Tennie and Victoria were sticking to woodcock on toast. He was in a great mood tonight because Union Pacific had gone up—as Victoria and the spirits had advised him it would. Victoria sometimes wondered why an extra thirty thousand meant so much to him when he was worth a hundred million. Money to her meant freedom, power, the chance to fulfill the grand public destiny she had felt hovering before her since the time in her childhood when she began to experience visions and when the spirits began to talk with her. To him it seemed an entity in itself, far more real and potent in his life than his wife hidden away upstairs or his children, whom he despised. Money was his real lover and had certainly proved faithful. His other passion was winning. She doubted he had ever really loved a woman, but he was fond of Tennie. He preferred her company to just about everyone else's and she herself probably came in second. But the company of his money was more stimulating by far.

"There's a giant bim-bam-bang rally for Grant tomorrow," Tennie said. "Are you for him or Greeley or whoever the Democrats are running? I forget his name."

Victoria said, "The Democrats joined in with the radical Republicans and are for Greeley too. Before, they had somebody who dropped dead."

The Commodore grunted, waving a leg of turkey at them. "Whoever they got don't stand a chance. Even though the Congress didn't succeed in impeaching Johnson, no Democrat could get elected. They could run George Washington and he'd go down to defeat."

Victoria felt a gaze upon her, hard and determined. The man was perhaps thirty with a thick head of hair, lean, flashily dressed. Vanderbilt had noticed the whole thing. "That's Alfred Kumble giving you the eye. Don't bother with him. A minnow. One day he's rich and the next he's trying to rub two cents together to warm his mitts. Tries to corner stocks with no success. He used to follow Dan'l Drew around but now he's on his own. If he didn't have family money, he'd be sleeping in the street."

"I'm not interested. I was only curious who was staring at me." She was telling the truth; something predatory in the man's gaze chilled her. She did not need that kind of lover.

"Why, who wouldn't stare. I'm here with the two prettiest women in the place. Let them stare all they want. I won't charge them for looking."

"Old boy, you didn't answer me, who you're voting for." Tennie tapped his knuckles with her fan.

"I ain't voting. I don't give a damn. I can buy and sell politicians by the carload. I go up to Albany and I pay them off, and some other businessman goes up there and buys them off for more money. An honest politician is one who stays bought. That's all there is to it." He liked pie. He had already had two pieces, one of apple and one of cherry heaped with vanilla ice cream and whipped cream on top of that.

"How much does a legislator cost?" Victoria asked.

"No fixed price. Depends on the legislation and who's bidding against you. Most I ever paid was ten thousand."

"Still, you have to keep on eye on the laws they pass."

"What do I care for the law? Ain't I got the power?" He grinned and Victoria could see for a moment the handsome man he must have been in his prime. Tennie beamed warmly at him.

When they went off to the powder room to freshen up, Tennie said, "He's been hinting how his wife is sickly. He asked me this afternoon if I wanted to be the next Mrs. Vanderbilt."

Dropping her comb, Victoria turned to her sister. "Shhh. Don't talk about it in here. But what did you say?"

"That I'd think about it. I sure will. If I said yes and started jumping up and down, I'd be in real trouble with him."

Victoria turned back, meeting her sister's eyes in the baroque mirror. "You play it the way you see it, Tennie. You understand him. Just don't let his family get wind of this or they will do something to put an end to it."

"They'll blow up a hurricane, I know it. Besides, his wife's still kicking, and when I see her she doesn't look a bit frail to me."

Victoria felt a chill on the back of her neck, as if a spirit had caressed her. "You think he's capable of having something done to her?"

"He stuck her in an insane asylum at least once, didn't he? But I don't think he's the murdering type. He's too scared of ghosts."

"Put this in the back of the closet for now. It's too dangerous to talk about."

They trekked back to the table, all elegance and smiles. They were better dressed these days. They each had some good new gowns and a couple that looked new, obtained through the network of madams. Victoria had no more useful or more intimate friend than Annie Wood. Annie passed on tips to Victoria, who passed them on from the spirits to the Commodore. In return, Victoria gave Annie any information that might be useful. Victoria had little to invest yet—a few dollars.

The next morning she had brunch with Annie in the conservatory. They met at least four times a week to exchange information, gossip, speculation, or just to talk about their lives. After they had discussed the market, Annie said, "Stocks are all well and good, but I put most of my money into real estate."

Victoria was startled. "Why? There's plenty of land to be had cheap—dirt cheap, as they say."

"There's plenty of land out west, Victoria, but look at Manhattan. It's a fixed size. Over in Brooklyn, they can make more land when they need it from swamps and marshes, and the same with New Jersey. But Manhattan is rock and there's deep water on all sides. It can only grow north. So what's good enough for the Astors—buying land that isn't developed yet up by Central Park—is good enough for me."

"I've been up there with the Commodore when he's racing his horses. It's just barren country and shacks. A few farms, slaughterhouses, squatters' cabins." Nothing she could imagine getting excited about, but Annie's judgment in money matters was something to be respected.

"This city grows every year. The rich people keep trying to get away from the poor people, and north's the only direction they can go. Madame Restell saw that years ago and bought land on Fifth Avenue near the big cathedral that's going up." Annie fanned herself briskly, excitement quickening her. Annie had a whole assortment of fine painted fans, landscapes, flowers.

"Who's Madame Restell?"

"Ann Lohman. She's the best abortionist in all of New York. If you ever find yourself in the family way and you don't need another mouth to feed, you see Restell. She's saved the wives and daughters of the richest families in New York, the so-called better people. Made a fortune doing it. She built herself a mansion just below where the park starts. You should go look at it. It's enormous and every window has hangings that match. The rich people moving up there tried to get rid of her, tried to buy her out, but she wouldn't be moved. She drives in the park every day with her gorgeous horses and her fine phaeton and the respectable ladies pretend they don't see her."

Victoria was intrigued. Here was a woman who had gotten rich on her own, nobody's mistress, no wealthy family. "How can she be so bold? The regular physicians and their A.M.A. have made what she does illegal. When I was a girl, it wasn't. Until the baby quickened, it was just something women did if they had to. Nobody thought twice about it. Now it's against the law." She had suspected her first husband, Dr. Woodhull, of occasionally giving a woman some relief.

"She pays off the police and the chief is a friend. When she entertains, politicians and lawyers and men with money drop in. They say she's a fine lady with good manners and elegant taste—the finest food and wines and liquors. I've never had occasion to use her myself, but if any of my girls needs help, that's where I send them. She's reliable. She may lose a patient once in a while, but not often. They've tried to get her in court, but she has always escaped except once. I hear she did time years ago on Blackwell's Island. You keep her in mind if you have to have something taken care of. Although I suspect you have your ways."

"I do. I had my babies and now I take care of myself."

"Two. One able and one feeble."

Victoria drew herself up. Not even Annie was allowed to cast aspersions on Byron. "He's a sweet boy. There are many worse things that can happen to a mother than to have a boy who never grows up. He's a baby forever."

"A rather large baby."

"I love him, Annie. I would protect him with my life."

"But you love the girl better. You have to."

"She's a bright child." Victoria could remember her fear with Zulu, that there would be something wrong with her too. How obsessively she had watched over Zulu that first year, until she began to walk and talk. "She sees everything. She's wise beyond her age. I keep her close to me."

"Tennie's never had children?"

"Byron scared her. She's afraid, as I am, that there's something bad running in our family. Our mother's crazy at times. Buck is not to be trusted. I say this although I love both of them dearly. We all stick together. But I think we may have bad blood." She inched her chair a little closer to Annie's. "You never wanted to have children?" She wondered if Annie had a child stashed away someplace.

"I didn't think it a great idea to bring them into this life, darling, although plenty of whores do. I got pregnant once. Now there's no chance of it. The Virgin Mary is the only one on record who can do it alone. I hardly think I'm in her class."

VICTORIA WATCHED HER CHILDREN together. Zulu Maud was seven going on eight. She interpreted her brother's grunts and brought him water or a toy he liked or showed him some bright object that caught his attention so that he reached out toward it, making those strange noises that were all he had for speech. To her, what was he? More pet than brother. Byron felt safe and cared for with his sister and with her. He barely related to anyone else. James had about as much to do with him as he would with a goldfish in a bowl. Sometimes when he spoke of their immediate family, he would slip and refer to them as three—and she would have to remind him gently but firmly that they were four. His indifference to Byron bothered her, but she understood it. It was hard for anyone but herself and Zulu Maud to see him as a person. No other friend or lover seemed able to penetrate that barrier of strangeness to love her son, who could not speak or do any of the things the most ordinary child of paupers could perform. But he had a heart and feelings and probably inchoate thoughts. He reached out to her, his oversized head bobbing on his weak neck. Whenever he saw her, he burbled joy. He loved to be held in her arms. He was a being sent to her to be protected and loved, and she would never fail him. Actually there had been one other person who saw Byron as an individual and not a vegetable, and that had been his father, Canning Woodhull, when he was sober enough to notice anyone else. James's older brother George was sometimes kind and patient with Byron. George often visited them now that they were lodged in a comfortable house which was gradually being well furnished. George was a more emotional man than James, and he loved children. He had a special place in his big heart for those who had afflictions, even keeping as a pet a three-legged dog.

Zulu Maud was spinning a top while Byron swatted ineffectually at it, giggling and drooling. Zulu would very seriously wipe his mouth from time to time with a big white linen handkerchief with James's initials. Byron held still for these attentions. Other mothers with fourteen-year-old sons had to worry that they would be getting a maidservant pregnant or beginning to drink, to smoke, to gamble, to run with a bad crowd. Victoria was spared those worries. She could find something to be grateful for even in Byron's affliction. She had been thinking of Lord Byron's clubfoot when she named her son, for it was evident from birth he would not be a normal child.

Zulu Maud gritted her teeth and concentrated fiercely on the top Buck had given her. Victoria did her best to keep Buck and Roxanne away from the children, but it was hard, living under the same roof. She did not want them to have undue influence over Zulu, and she was afraid of Buck's cruel streak with Byron. They needed a bigger house than this narrow brownstone, but she did not have the money. Tennie and she could barely manage to support this establishment.

Zulu Maud's sausage curls bobbed and shook as she played. Her intense blue gaze was fixed upon the top as if to mesmerize it into spinning upright, not wobbling. Zulu had Victoria's eyes, that intense clear blue that people found fascinating or disturbing, depending on their temperaments. Perhaps the Gaelic strain from Buck, whose people came from northern Scotland, gave Victoria the beauty she found useful: black hair, pale perfect skin and intense blue eyes. Zulu had her bone structure, that chiseled look some admirers called aristocratic. That made Victoria smile. She came out of the dirt, yes, but she had known since the spirits began to single her out that she was indeed special and would, as they promised, achieve wealth and great things. She had finally come to a place where that was within her ken. It only remained to pursue those goals intelligently and without distraction.

Clearly, the first goal had to be wealth. Once she had the wherewithal to keep her extended family, she would be free to pursue the other goals. She was, the spirits said, to lead a great cause. Fame would follow. She could see her path as a golden road unfolding before her, as if she had only to shut her eyes, visualize it and step forward. But she knew better. There was a lot of work involved in paving that road with gold. The best place to start was to keep filling Vanderbilt's favor bank.

There was a final torchlight parade Sunday night for Grant. The election was Tuesday. Victoria thought she would probably vote for him, if she could. The fact that she couldn't annoyed her. She was surely the equal of any man. Her first husband had been a smart man but weak-willed. James was much stronger, but if he had never met her and been swept into a storm of passion, he would still be sitting in St. Louis writing secret essays about free love with his boring family closing him in and his boring business on his back. The passion was intermittent by now, but there was enough of it, and they had the bond of common ideas and a common destiny to fulfill.

She talked Tennie into going with her. They pinned their hair up under caps and put on men's jackets and trousers. It would have shocked just about everyone they knew, perhaps even Annie Wood, but the sisters had discovered several years ago that wearing men's attire enabled them to fade into crowds and go places ladies would never dare or be permitted, and women not considered ladies would be in danger. They simply passed as youths out together.

The parade was lively, raucous. The smell of the burning torches charred the air. Many of the men were drunk already, but the sisters knew how to handle themselves and nobody did more than jostle them. The parade streamed through the city, stopping traffic, filling Broadway from gutter to gutter. The rally was at Park Row where the newspapers were, so that they would be sure to carry word the next day of the huge turnout the Republicans had in this Democratic stronghold. Tennie wanted to leave, but Victoria didn't.

"I want to hear the speeches." She listened to them, not to be moved, not to be persuaded of anything, but to dissect their rhetorical devices, to see what kind of a speech worked and what fell flat. She studied each speaker's delivery. "I'll be giving speeches someday soon, Demosthenes told me so," she whispered to Tennie so that no one would overhear her voice. "I must study how it's done." They wormed their way toward the raised platform constructed of planks. GENERAL GRANT IN '68. HE WILL SET THE COUNTRY STRAIGHT.

She stood attentive through two and a half hours of speeches. The torches flared, the crowd roared and booed on cue. Half the audience were passing bottles around. The whores were working the crowd. They couldn't take the night off with so many men gathered. They would service as many as they could, one after the other, some in the cold alleys, some back in their own rooms in a nearby tenement or in a cheap hotel friendly to their trade. Victoria was glad she had brought only a dollar in a front pocket as she noticed pickpockets working the crowd, homeless boys probably. With so many men jostling each other, most of them drunk, distracted by the speeches and the excitement of the crowd, pickpockets would do well. She saw her reporter friend from the *Sun,* Charlie, but he did not recognize her dressed as a man. They were no longer lovers. Occasionally she would drop in on him at the newspaper, causing a stir when she walked past the desks. It was well that they came to know her, for one day she would need the help of newspapermen to become famous.

When they got home, she took out the notebook that stood beside her bed to make copious notes while she could still recall the various speakers. Women were not supposed to speak in public, but that taboo had been broken by women preachers, abolitionists and spiritualists. That was one of the things that had drawn her to spiritualism, although Roxanne had always had visions and premonitions and seen things other people thought were not there. Victoria had been brought up to expect the supernatural in daily life, and the spirits had not failed to manifest themselves when she was still a girl. It was the spirits that had first brought her in front of a crowd and banished fear, so that she enjoyed the attention instead of being immobilized by it.

There was a soft knock on the door. James's knock. "Come in." If she had not been alone, she would have gone to the door and opened it a crack to speak with him. That was their way. He had taught her the theory of free love, but she had put it into practice.

He was wearing a navy silk dressing gown, his bearing erect and foursquare as always, almost military. He looked quite handsome. His beard when she met him had been rather overgrown and scraggly, but now it was neatly trimmed—because she regularly trimmed it to save the cost of a barber. She felt a current between them this night. She smiled at him.

"How was the rally?"

"Exciting at first. Then boring. But I am trying to study rhetoric. The art of making speeches that actually move people."

"Would you like me to get you a book or two on the subject?"

James would know exactly what she should read. "I'd love that."

He looked toward the bed and then back toward her in silent question. She rose from her vanity and came toward him, letting her dressing gown fall to the floor in a slither of silk. She reached for the little box beside the bed with sponges soaked in boracic acid and inserted one. She spoke in a low, almost purring voice that she had observed worked well on James. "Put another log in the fireplace. Then put yourself next to me."

He did. She was always gentle with him, because of his war wounds. She had learned the places that pained him and the places he liked to be caressed. The skin around his mouth was sensitive to her tongue and so were his eyelids. If she reached under his balls, there was a spot between his balls and anus where pressure caused his prick to harden at once, magically. He would kiss and caress her breasts, but he got most excited when he squeezed her buttocks. He had told her she had a firm ass, something Woodhull had complained of, saying she had a behind like a boy's. They reached the point where she no longer had to be so careful not to bump against his six wounds, when his passion began to excite him beyond noticing. She closed her eyes then, giving over to the pressure of his hands and then his prick against her. He rubbed it back and forth against her seat of pleasure, as she had taught him, before thrusting in. He could keep at it for a goodly time once he was excited enough, more than enough time for her to push and push and push up the slope of sensation until her pleasure burst in her. He always knew that moment, and he began to thrust harder toward his own pleasure. In a minute he came and then subsided next to her. She held him for a time, making sure he felt loved, then rose to douche. She did not take chances with pregnancy. She could tell from James's breathing he had dozed off. She did not sleep well with him because of his thrashing nightmares, but once in a while after sex they spent the night in her bed. Carefully she slid in beside him, turning onto her side to study his face in the dying light of the fire. Love warmed her as she gazed. Her partner.

PREVIOUSLY

THIRTEEN

| *1862* |

SIX MONTHS EARLIER, Freydeh and Moishe had arrived in the clamor and confusion of Castle Garden. Now they were sleeping on the floor of a third-story flat on Essex with a German Jewish family, the Kuppersmiths. Mr. Kuppersmith was a butcher who hoped someday to have his own shop, but for now worked in a market. Mrs. Kuppersmith sold baskets in a shop run by her brother-in-law. The oldest boy curried horses in a stable. The daughter tried selling matches, but when the Kuppersmiths learned how many matchgirls were prostitutes, they sent her to make felt in a factory.

Freydeh and Moishe crossed to Brooklyn on the earliest ferry to buy bread half a cent cheaper. They would bring the bread back on the ferry in huge bundles on their backs and then set up curbside on Orchard Street. After three months, they bought an old cart from a retiring peddler. Then they could manage more bread. Most of their business was conducted in German, but they had a handful of Yiddish-speaking customers who sought them out to hear the *mamme loshen*. They were mostly Russian Jews, tailors by trade. Moishe tried to talk them into hiring him in some capacity, but they had families to supply them with all the workers they needed. They were a close-knit group for they had been alone without other Jews from Eastern Europe.

Here everything was different—everything. When she woke in the morning, lying on a pallet on the floor of the airless kitchen pressed against Moishe, she did not hear the noises of home—the children calling, her mother at the hearth, the cows lowing in the attached stable, the baaing of sheep and the cackling of the hens, the rooster with his high rasping call, the crows, the finches singing. Here the noise never ceased. Yes, horses neighed and she could hear a rooster, cats fighting in the courtyard where latrines poured their stinking overflow between the tenement facing the street and the rear house, dogs barking, cows lowing. Hooves on the paved cross street struck on the stones, the metal wheels roared. Hundreds of wagons were dragged through the narrow dusty streets. All day long, all night, wagons passed loaded with everything that must be shipped in and out of a great city. Always a murmur of voices, a huckster yelling, a beaten woman screaming, a gambler cursing, a mother calling out a window or up from the street. The dark stinking hallway shuddered with footsteps up and down every time water was needed, every time somebody decided to use the latrine in the courtyard, every time anyone went to work or came back, went out to buy or sell anything, needed some air. Factories stood on every cross street and toward the river, slaughterhouses and rendering shops made the air heavy with grease and blood. Herds of cows were driven through the wider streets toward their death. Peddlers hawked their wares all day as loudly as their hoarse voices could carry, hot corn, used clothes, hats, chickens, fruit, vegetables, used shoes and boots, knives or scissors to be sharpened. Sometimes she thought her head would burst. The first nights, she simply could not doze no matter how exhausted she was. She began to sleep with a rag tied around her head to muffle the sounds.

Everything overloaded her senses. Signs hung from every building—the tenements usually had a business or a store on the ground floor. Every fence, every building front and side, everything that could be printed upon demanded attention, yelled at her to look, to do, to buy whatever that sign was selling. It was a visual explosion of demands and claims. Their tenements were lit only by candles or oil lamps, but if they walked to the Bowery or Broadway, gaslights were everywhere, hissing and yellowish and far brighter than any lights she had known before.

She was used to prostitutes back home, but they kept to their house on the river. When they went out, they were dressed much like other women and did their business of shopping, praying in shul, seeing the wise woman who tended to bodily complaints. On the Bowery she stayed close to Moishe, clutching his arm in the crowd of people such as she had never seen—Irish, Italians, Hungarians, Negroes, an occasional Chinaman, the Yanks themselves—what the others called narrowbacks—all stirred together in a strange smelly bubbling soup of desires and fears and curiosity. Prostitutes were everywhere garishly got up, exposing half their breasts and ankles, painted and showy under the gaslights like the paper flowers women made here. She did not mean to stare, but she could not help it. Moishe always tried to look away. They embarrassed him. Maybe they reminded him that before they married, he had frequented that house on the river some Saturday nights, when Shabbos was over and the workweek not yet begun. Maybe he was embarrassed by so much exposed flesh. They made love passionately, but in the dark. They went up to the roof to make love when the weather permitted. There was no privacy in the apartment. They could hear the Kuppersmiths whenever they went at it, and so could the children and the other boarder, Herman. They could tell when Herman gave himself pleasure, usually when the Kuppersmiths were busy in bed with each other. Sometimes in the middle of the night when snoring assured them everyone else was asleep, silently they coupled on their pallet. A moan or movement from one of the many sleepers stilled them at once.

The Bowery B'hoys and their ladies were everywhere, thrusting confidently through the crowds as if others were just water and they were swimming along to shore, in this case a saloon, an oyster palace, a dance hall, a concert saloon, a peep show, a gambling hell, a pawnshop, a flophouse, a dime museum of freakish things or a theatrical presentation. Moishe and she had no money to waste, but they enjoyed staring at people and what they could see from the sidewalks. In a big window, mermaids swayed with paper seaweed around them—bare-breasted women got up as fish below the waist. In store windows, men were being tattooed. A fortune-teller called to them, saying she could see a great destiny for Moishe. Sailors on leave, Chinese in pigtails, even toffs from uptown wearing silk top hats sauntered past.

THE BREAD BUSINESS was not good—sometimes it rained on their bread before they got a tarpaulin to protect it. Some days they made a little, some days almost nothing. The river iced over in the middle of January and they could not get to Brooklyn to buy the bread. Moishe got a temporary job cleaning up in a slaughterhouse and came home reeking of death. He only got the job because so many had died of a strange high fever that swept the Lower East Side and killed the weak, the young, the old with a terrible racking cough you could hear even with the windows shut. She began peddling aprons a neighbor made and notions—ribbons, thread, yarn, needles, pins. It was slow but she began to develop a clientele. Women needed those things in every season, to make do, to repair clothing and make new clothing out of old. She called her wares from the street.

The job at the slaughterhouse ended in the spring, but Moishe got a better job hauling barrels. He was strong and he could lift and carry more than most men his size. A drayman who owned a heavy wagon pulled by two great bay horses hired him. They worked six days a week hauling beer barrels, nails, molasses, vinegar to groceries, grog shops, the docks, to and from railroad yards. Moishe began to build a map of the city in his head until he knew it like a native. They moved into their own flat and rented to three young men who slept on their floor. Moishe and she had a bedroom with a door that shut. It was dark and airless, only big enough for a bed and a chair, but they had privacy at last.

She got into trouble a couple of times with her peddling. Once she set up in a place by the curb on Orchard that a burly German told her was his own special spot.

"You got ownership papers? It looks like a public curb to me."

He whistled shrilly and within minutes a group of tough young men had gathered around her, all wearing the same kind of stiff black hats. They knocked her pushcart over, spilling her merchandise and trampling it underfoot. Two of them punched her in the face and arms. Her nose was bloody and she had a bruised and swollen eye and lip afterward. She could not raise her arm for days.

"You come here again and we'll break your arms and legs. You stay out of our territory, all along this block."

Another time, she got too far into the Irish neighborhood over by Corlears Hook and again she got beaten and her merchandise stolen. She was learning which streets and which blocks she must avoid. Gangs controlled some areas more tightly than others.

By the next winter, she was sure she was carrying. The baby had not quickened yet but her breasts were sore and her time had not come in two months. She had not told Moishe yet because she wanted to be positive.

She vomited occasionally and that was difficult to disguise. She thought Moishe must suspect something, but then men often didn't know enough about the ways of women to guess until the wife's belly stood out like a sack of potatoes. Neither of them spoke about it. She wondered if it were a superstition they held in common.

They sat in the front room the first night of Chanukah. Even though they didn't go to shul, she lit candles in the *chanukiyah* she had brought from Vilna. The little candle and the *shamesh* candle were burning as they sat in their two chairs. Their boarders were still out. It was six but already night, with the moon shining between the buildings on the snow on cornices and patches not yet rendered into ice and mud. They sat close to each other, just their knees touching.

"For two people who just arrived here a bit more than two years ago, I think we're doing not so badly after all," Moishe said in Yiddish. "*Nu,* are you satisfied, wife?"

"I am very satisfied, Moisheleh mine."

"Then is there something you want to tell me?"

"Can't keep anything from you, you old woodcutter. Yes. I'm carrying."

He gripped her hands. "Be careful now, be careful, Freydeleh. Don't go on those blocks where the Irish gangs rule. Stay in Germantown. The Hungarians are safe. Just watch yourself. I wish you didn't have to go out peddling."

"I can't sew a straight fine seam. I can't embroider or make lace. It's healthier than being stuck dawn till dark in a fetid factory bent over a machine or working at a table with men trying to paw you. I promise I'll be careful. This life in me is precious—our first child."

"First, but I hope not the last." He held her hands in his big callused hands, warm and dry and powerful.

IT WAS A GRAY DAY in early February, a sharp wind off the East River. It had snowed hard three days before, then thawed briefly, then frozen again. The streets were paved with dirty ice stained with horse urine and droppings. She had come home from her peddling to cook a stew of chicken necks, gizzards and hearts, with potatoes, turnips and onions. With bread that would make supper for Moishe, the two boarders and herself. She was cutting onions, the tears running freely down her face as she wiped it with an old handkerchief of Moishe's. She would have to wash it out afterward in the basin, for it was his only one. She wanted to tell him when he came home that she thought she had felt the baby quicken that afternoon as she was going along Mott Street with her cart. She wasn't sure—she had never been pregnant before—but she had felt *something.* She wished her mama were here beside her to advise her if there were any special precautions she should take now, if there were herbs or simples she should be taking to help her baby along. She had always imagined that, like her older sister, Sara, when she had her first baby, Mama would be at her side, whispering in her ear, singing to her.

She heard running up the steps. One of the street kids came banging on the door. "Missus, you got to come."

"What's wrong?" She clutched her apron in her hands.

"It's your old man. They're bringing him up."

Without even shutting the door she ran down the steps pell-mell in the dark of the staircase, round the first turn and down, round the second turn and down, round the third turn, and then she saw the men trying to carry Moishe up the steps. His head was all bloody. His arm hung at an angle and his leg was bleeding.

"Stop!" she yelled at them, and rushed forward. She missed a step and plummeted down toward them, banging on step after step to end up in a heap at the feet of the men dragging her battered and broken husband.

One of them helped her to her feet. "We bring him upstairs."

"He's hurt too bad. We have to take him to hospital."

They carried him through the streets to the Hebrew Hospital with her limping behind them and Moishe still dropping blood in a trail on the dirty ice. One of the men told her what had happened: the horse was startled by a loud noise as they were almost done loading barrels of beer. The horse reared in the shafts. The wagon tipped. The barrels cascaded down on Moishe.

She had felt herself begin to bleed as she sat beside him in the hospital, beside his unconscious broken body. Before morning, she had lost her husband and her unborn baby. She had nothing now, nothing.

FOURTEEN

| *1847* |

HEN ELIZABETH ELOPED with Henry, against her father's wishes, he was a well-known speaker and organizer for abolition but otherwise unemployed. After clerking for her father, the conservative judge, for almost two years in order to mend fences with the family, Henry decided they should move to Boston, where he joined a law firm. Judge Cady bought them a comfortable house in Chelsea. She had three children by then, all boys—Neil, Henry and Gerrit (called Gat). With her firstborn, Neil, she had hired a nurse who swaddled him in tight linen, shut the windows lest the air infect him, and kept him quiet when he cried with laudanum—an opium derivative. After the boy became sickly, Elizabeth fired the nurse and shocked her family by tearing off the linen bands to let his limbs move freely, opening the windows wide and throwing out the laudanum. Neil thrived, and so in turn did her other babies.

When Lucretia Mott came to Boston for a day, they spent it talking about woman's rights and fantasizing about a meeting of women to start a movement. Except for her short stature, Lucretia was unlike her in appearance, strict Quaker dress, a wrinkled, slightly desiccated face and hands, an expression of calm and sweetness, but her mind was lively and her political sense passionate and shrewd. They were both tiny women who had borne children—Elizabeth so far, three; Lucretia, six. Elizabeth both loved her as a friend and admired her as a mentor.

Lucretia was twenty-two years older than Elizabeth, but Elizabeth had never been bothered by age. After all, Henry was eleven years older. The other love of her life, Bayard, her brother-in-law, was older still. He had helped raise her. Most pleasures of her adolescence had been due to him—he taught her to jump fences on horseback, he took her sisters and her to dances her mother had forbidden. He taught them to read widely and critically. He made sure the girls had a good education, arguing that Elizabeth must go to a girls' school that was not a finishing school but something new, where real subjects were taught. But when she was twenty-one, he had proposed they run away together. He was madly in love with her.

She certainly had strong feelings for him, but not strong enough to betray her oldest sister, his wife, Tryphena. She refused, and never again did she permit him to be alone with her. She cared for him, and she could tell whenever she saw him at family gatherings that he still wanted to be with her. Temptations like that were useless. To give in to them would have ruined the lives of Tryphena and her family in widening circles of scandal and pain. Two years later, she met Henry at her cousin Gerrit's and fell in love. He seemed a dark hero to her, a knight of the abolitionist movement, addressing hostile crowds, persuading people to consider the Negro a fellow human, operating on the Underground Railroad that passed fugitive slaves to safety. Her cousin Gerrit's house was a station on the way to freedom.

Now she enjoyed Boston with its abundance of political and intellectual events. She met Emerson, Hawthorne, Frederick Douglass and Margaret Fuller. She felt at home among the abolitionists and reformers. But Henry grew dissatisfied. He said the climate gave him chronic lung congestion, but she could tell that what it gave him was the inability to run for public office in Massachusetts. Lacking connections and Brahmin background, he could not compete with local candidates. He felt he would do better in upstate New York, so he chose to move them to Seneca Falls. He was the husband; it was his decision to make and he made it.

Judge Cady seemed to think this move a good idea—they would be closer to him—and bought them a house on two acres overlooking the river, over a mile from the center of town. That is, theoretically it overlooked the river. The actual view from the front of the house was of tanneries, a mill, a foundry and workers' shacks. He warned them that the house had been empty for some years and was in bad repair. He challenged her to take charge of the work since she seemed to think women were so competent. She left her children and household effects—seventeen trunks' worth—with her family in Johnstown. She became a general commanding an expensive army of carpenters and workmen painting, repapering with light, pleasant wallpapers, repairing the dilapidated structure, turning a ramshackle porch into a solid columned structure, adding a kitchen wing off the back. It had a central hall with a steep staircase going up, a large front parlor and a back parlor in which she had French doors installed. She replaced the windows with larger ones to let in more light and air.

Stuck in a house needing constant work, she felt isolated with only her children, an Irish servant girl and few companions with whom she could discuss the subjects—political, intellectual—that she cared about. The road was unpaved. With no sidewalks, it was a trek through mud into town, where she could find only a few groceries, bars and billiard parlors. Seneca Falls was a rough river town with many taverns and many churches, not much else. She made friends with the neighbor women, although they found her forward and unconventional. She charmed them into liking her against their will, but she was lonely. Henry was gone more than he was there. He took the train to Albany and to Washington on a regular basis, to register patents for clients and to conduct business. He also traveled on political business—not so much abolitionist now as Republican Party politics. He wanted to run for some, any state office. He was intensely ambitious for himself but felt she should be satisfied being a mother and housewife. He had gradually lost interest in discussing ideas with her, and when he was home insisted she let him read the paper, smoke his pipe and that she keep the children from pestering him. Basically he came home to relax and be cosseted.

Everyone expected her to be absorbed by family life. What women did beyond that tended to be confined to church activities and perhaps a quilting bee or visits to sick neighbors. She missed the intellectual stimulation of Boston. She also missed all the support she had when they lived in her parents' home, with servants and relatives to take the children off her hands when she wanted to read or write. She was responsible for the sole running of a house and a farm her father had decided they should oversee a few miles outside of Seneca Falls.

Slowly she identified and gathered people who took an interest in ideas and she began to hold conversationals in the parlor. She collected a dozen regulars, instituting Saturday evening discussions of everything from slavery to women in history, from Sylvester Graham's ideas of the healthy regimen to the novels of Sir Walter Scott and Emerson's essays. She enforced a rule that no one could speak twice until everyone had spoken once. She was teaching the women and girls to voice their opinions, teaching them to be more articulate and forward.

One field where she had a free hand—since Henry took little interest—was the children's upbringing. She gave them freedom to run about, to climb trees, to go down to the river. She encouraged them to read and discuss with her. The neighbors regarded them as undisciplined hellions. She preferred energy to obedience. She made her own medicines. As for the conjugal embrace, they both enjoyed that a great deal. The only advantage she could find in Henry's constant, almost compulsive traveling was that when he came home they were new to each other and not at all an old married couple who might have lapsed into boredom. In the bedroom, Henry did not bore her, nor she him.

Otherwise, he was not the most stimulating companion these days. He still talked politics, but his were party machinations, who was running for what and who was supporting him, who controlled what committee in the legislature—not ideas and ideals. She listened and offered her comments, but it was a far cry from the excitement ignited by their days sharing anti-slavery activities. He confessed that he was considering changing his party affiliation. He had talked with Democratic politicians who had indicated they might support him if he ran for state senator on their ticket. She was shocked, as he had always derided the Democrats as pro-slavery. But she could feel the heat of his ambition for public office. He loved being in Albany. He liked speechmaking, the intrigue of the legislature, behind-the-scenes maneuvering, the constant courtship from lobbyists, the feeling of power and influence.

Sometimes after a day with the help of her maid, Kathleen, a day of mending torn clothes and washing linens and bleaching them, of making puddings and collecting eggs and hauling water to heat, a day of wiping runny noses and getting potions down Neil, who was sick in bed, of scrubbing the stairs and cleaning the windows and taking the horses out for exercise, of making bread, of replacing buttons, of knitting for fall, of reading stories to her sick boy, of spreading manure on what would be a bigger kitchen garden, of tidying behind the children and gluing a broken wooden soldier, she felt as if her head were both huge and empty, like an immense toy ball. Sometimes she wanted to pound the walls and scream. Sometimes she did. This was not living, this was picking up after living. Women of all classes came to her for medical advice, for comfort or help when their drunken husbands beat them or their children, for advice on finances—but what could she do to enlarge her own life?

She felt so depressed that she imagined simply going to sleep and never getting out of bed again. Women did that. Doctors had fancy names for it, neurasthenia, whatever, but she thought it was just that the drudgery became too much and they could not endure going on for the rest of their lives like a mule bound to a mill turning round and round pulling a heavy weight but never going anywhere. She looked into the faces of the women around her and she saw staring back at her the same bleak depression, the same exhaustion, the same sense of being imprisoned in a very tight place. She started to write an essay about women's dress, to keep her mind alive, when baby Gat fell down the steep narrow stairway that led from the boys' room. The doctor said he had brain fever and would not live, but she nursed him back to health. A daily, weekly, monthly, yearly round of repetitious, mind-numbing chores broken only by crises.

She loved her children, although she longed for a girl. She loved her children more than Henry and sometimes wondered if that should be so, but they did not fill her brain. She applied her intelligence to their upbringing, applied Graham's ideas of loose clothing, exercise, healthy foods, firm beds and lots of fresh air. Gat might have a cold this week, but no child of hers had died yet. Her mother had lost half her children and grown so depressed she had taken to her bed for years. Henry and Elizabeth had named their house Grasmere, after Wordsworth's house they had visited on their abolitionist honeymoon in England. But this Grasmere was not a place of high thought, lofty ambitions and excellent writing. It was a place of endless, tedious housework. Sometimes she muttered to herself in frustration, in rage that had to be contained: Was she not human too? Didn't she have a brain? A will? Ideas? At least she used to.

The second year in her drafty white clapboard house on the river overlooking the stinking tannery, Lucretia came to visit. Elizabeth poured out her frustrations. They talked about the lives of women. Although her father had given her the house, it was not hers. If Henry left her, he could take the children, and if she earned or inherited any money, it was his. Men owned their children. Women who gave birth to them and raised them had no right to custody. A woman's body belonged to her husband, no matter how brutal or syphilitic he might be. If a woman was raped, it was her disgrace. A woman giving birth out of wedlock could be imprisoned. She would certainly lose her job, even if her employer was the father and had forced himself on her. Few jobs were open to women—mostly domestic service, teaching children and prostitution. Churches preached obedience for women, no matter how stupid or how outrageous the behavior of the husband. Church and society demanded chastity from women. Men had sexual needs; women had children. The American Medical Association was conducting a war against women doctors and midwives, against women who provided contraception for other women or helped them abort unwanted pregnancies. The so-called regular doctors hated the alternative medical practitioners, like Graham, like almost every woman in medicine. She believed in natural medicine, in water cures, in exercise, in herbal remedies, in healthy diet. Her three boys had caught malaria in May and she had nursed them back to health without benefit of any "regular doctors," who would have bled them weak and purged them hollow.

Women were barred from almost all decent-paying professions. Women were exiled from society for missteps men committed with impunity and boasted about. No woman could vote, while any white male idiot had the right.

Lucretia folded her thin wrinkled hands together in her lap. "We have been talking about calling a meeting to discuss woman's rights for eight years, Elizabeth. Do thee not think it is time to cease talking and writing long letters to each other, and finally to call such a meeting? Where do thee think it should be? Boston? Philadelphia? New York?"

"If I'm to organize it, it'll have to be right here. I can't haul my children or my household to a city."

"Do thee think we could bring enough women to Seneca Falls to make such an event substantial?"

"The time is ripe. Women will come. You'll see. It need not be large to have an effect. Forty women would be quite ample."

Lucretia beamed at her. "Do thee know, Elizabeth, that thee are about the only female of my acquaintance who would not say, *I think* women will come, but who can make definite statements without waffling or blushing or hiding behind a man's opinion. Therefore I believe we will make it happen."

"But Lucretia, you have great confidence too. You have not lived an ordinary woman's life."

"I was born on Nantucket, where the men go to sea for years at a time chasing whales, and women run everything. Now let us fix a time for our meeting."

"When? In the fall?" Somehow she would find the time to write an appeal.

"Right now. Or the time and opportunity will slip away. I leave in ten days to go back to my family. We'll call it for next Saturday."

"Lucretia!" Elizabeth seized her friend's hands. "That's five days away! Are you mad?" She felt a surge of pure panic.

"People will certainly think so. But if there's sentiment among women to right our wrongs, then enough women will come. Perhaps not forty. Perhaps only twenty or twenty-five, but it will be a start—at long last, a start."

Elizabeth agreed to write a document to be presented to however few women were present. Five days! She began several documents and none of them struck her as strong enough, bold enough. Then, as she was drifting off to sleep, an idea struck her. Why invent a new format when there was a document celebrated every Fourth of July that provided a perfect framework? She got out of bed, lit a candle and began writing:

> When, in the course of human events, it becomes necessary for one portion of the family of man to assume among the people of the earth a position different from that which they have hitherto occupied, but one to which the laws of nature and of nature's God entitle them, a decent respect to the opinions of mankind requires that they should declare the causes that impel them to such a course.
>
> We hold these truths to be self-evident: that all men and women are created equal; that they are endowed by their Creator with certain inalienable rights, that among these are life, liberty, and the pursuit of happiness; that to secure these rights governments are instituted, deriving their just powers from the consent of the governed. . . .

The next day, she set up a work table in the nursery. She knew the Declaration of Independence by heart. There were many cross-outs, many interstitial scribblings on the pad of foolscap on which she was writing, but within an hour she had a good start on the document. She intended to append eighteen injuries, just as in the document she was using as a template for her Declaration.

> He has never permitted her to exercise her inalienable right to the elective franchise.
>
> He has compelled her to submit to laws, in the formation of which she had no voice.
>
> He has withheld from her rights which are given to the most ignorant and degraded men—both natives and foreigners.
>
> Having deprived her of this first right of a citizen, the elective franchise, thereby leaving her without representation in the halls of legislation, he has oppressed her on all sides.
>
> He has made her, if married, in the eye of the law, civilly dead.
>
> He has taken from her all rights in property, even to the wages she earns.

A wave of fatigue swept over her. She looked at the pages she had covered with her wild scrawl. Later she would continue until she had a sturdy eighteen clear grievances. Henry was due home the day after tomorrow. She hoped to finish by then so she could show him her writing—and also because there was always more work when he was home. Unpacking him. Larger meals. Tending to his clothes. Laundry and repairs and ironing. Starching his shirts. Sometimes entertaining colleagues with large formal meals till all hours. Cleaning up after same. It would be best if she finished her Declaration today. Lucretia could look it over before Henry saw it.

Lucretia liked it. Elizabeth was waiting for an opportunity now to show Henry. He was in good spirits because of a meeting with politicians who promised to back him if he ran for state office. He insisted she get the boys into bed early. As soon as the house was quiet, he came up behind her, slipping his hand under her skirts and hugging her against him. "Little wifey, my sweet Lizzie Lee. . . ."

"Oh, sweet am I now? I know what you want." But she swung around and embraced him. They clung together in the hall and then he urged her toward their bedroom. Bumping into the doorpost and then half tripping over his valise, they fell onto the bed together in a roil of tossed-up clothes.

"Wait. . . . Let's get properly undressed," she wheedled, her voice coming out huskier than usual.

"There's nothing proper about undress," he said in her ear, then got her petticoats untied, one after the other. She turned for him to undo her corset. If women wore less cumbersome clothes, how much easier and more convenient it would be for lovemaking, she thought, but forbore saying it. He did not like her to talk much in those moments.

She helped him out of his frock coat and waistcoat and trousers and then his long underwear, cotton for summer, his braces and stockings. He pulled off her drawers and silk stockings and they settled into the already stirred-up coverlets and face-to-face began to embrace. He was hard already. He came home eager for it unless he was ill. She loved that warm deep stirring in her, she couldn't help it, she didn't want to help it. "My dear, my dearest," she whispered, running her hands down his back. She loved the way his spine disappeared into his buttocks, like a tree going to ground. She loved the feel of him against her, so unlike her own body. They rolled back and forth as if wrestling till finally he put himself into her and they moved into a familiar rhythm. She knew from talking with other women that many husbands did not care if their wives enjoyed the conjugal embrace, but Henry did. He was more considerate in bed than out of it. He held off until she had her pleasure before he quickened his pace and moved high into her to spend.

She felt enormously close to him afterward. They had a little hard cider from her store in the basement—made from their orchard—neither wanting to sleep yet while he recounted stories of his travels and the legislature.

"There's something I want to show you." She bent over him to press her lips to the crown of his head where there was a bald spot the size of a nickel. She went to get her statement.

Henry read it, his face slowly contorting into a scowl. "You can't possibly mean to read this in public! You'll make a fool, a laughingstock out of me."

She was stung almost to tears, but angry also. She knew it was not badly written, not banal, not silly, not naïve: she knew it. "I do mean to read it. Your attempting to prevent me rather reinforces what I'm saying, doesn't it?" How could he come from bed with her and turn so cold and selfish?

"If you intend to stand up in public and make a spectacle of yourself reading this, this pack of nonsense, then I will leave town so I am not humiliated."

"If you so desire." She would not back down. She felt betrayed. He had been her hero, never afraid to stand against the crowd for his principles. Now he was cowering with fear. He had been her lover not half an hour before and now he was withdrawn and threatening.

"You can't stand up in public and read this manifesto of a termagant. You'll make both of us outcasts! And what arrogance! To imagine the public would care what a housewife in a small town thinks about anything."

So that was what he thought she had become: a small-town housewife. "There is nothing written there I don't stand behind, Henry. And I would have expected you to stand with me!"

"What do you expect to accomplish with this shameless nonsense?"

"I expect to have an impact, to count for something, yes!"

In the morning, Henry left. She was angered and shocked by his response, but it was easier with him gone. She could concentrate on preparations for the meeting. No matter how small it might turn out to be, there was much to arrange. She persuaded a neighbor to take her boys for the two days of the meeting—if it went for two days. Lucretia helped her polish the eighteen grievances, with a little more emphasis on economic hardships. In the middle of their work, Elizabeth's father, Judge Cady, arrived in his gig.

"Have you lost your mind!" he bellowed. "Henry told me what's going on."

Lucretia folded her hands together in her lap. "Thy daughter appears to be of sound mind to me and sound heart also."

"This is a farce! You'll be laughed at from one end of the county to the other."

"Then people will hear of what we are doing," Elizabeth said, although it was hard for her to keep up a façade of confidence and calm in the tempest of his anger.

The morning of July 19 arrived. Lucretia and Elizabeth with a few other women including her sister Mary, who had come with her son, went to the Methodist church reserved for the meeting. A crowd of women and some men were milling about outside. The streets were blocked with carriages. Elizabeth was astounded and almost frightened. They had placed only a small notice in the local paper. She had written the great Negro orator Frederick Douglass, since she'd gotten to know him in Boston and now he lived in Rochester, nor far away. She didn't expect him to come but wanted to tell him what she was doing.

Lucretia murmured at her ear, "We forgot to say women only. I think we assumed men would not be interested."

"Too late to think of that. We'll seat them." The church door was locked. Elizabeth was sure that someone had gotten to the minister and scared him. She boosted her nephew up to a window he could open. He slid into the church and a few minutes later let them in. By the time everyone filed in and those who could be accommodated were seated, they counted 267 women and 40 men. Elizabeth felt overwhelmed. Even Lucretia, who was used to making speeches, seemed reluctant to start. Her husband James took the podium, welcomed the overflow crowd and formally opened the meeting.

He called upon Elizabeth. Waves of hot blood and cold fear washed through her. When she stood, her knees trembled under her heavy skirts. Was she out of her mind, as Henry and her father thought? Questioning the roles of men and women was like questioning the rain. It just was. She began, "We gather here today to discuss our wrongs, civil and political." Then she began to read the Declaration of Sentiments. She felt faint with worry, remembering Henry's response. Would they laugh her out of the building? Would they rise and walk out? Her voice quavered at first. Her script shook in her hands till she could scarcely read it, but she knew what it said. She cleared her throat and continued. People were stirring in their pews, women fanning themselves in the heat of the humid July morning, people greeting each other, waving, women with babies on their laps jouncing them up and down. But before she had read halfway through her second paragraph, she felt something she had never experienced before, the intense mesmeric response of a crowd whose attention had been utterly captured. Between her sentences she could hear horses outside and a passing carriage, the cries of robins and sparrows in the trees, but inside the church, except for her strengthening voice, a silence received her words. When she looked up from her text, every gaze was intent upon her.

The battle came the second day, when she introduced the resolutions she had drawn up. Even Lucretia did not support her call for female suffrage, convinced she was asking too much, but the ex-slave Frederick Douglass rose to support votes for women. It was not the first time she had heard him speak and been impressed, but she was moved by his aid. Women and some men were looking to her as a leader—she who was the youngest woman who had spoken yesterday or today, she who her husband had feared would humiliate him by making a fool of herself. She made several speeches—something she had never done before—and began to enjoy it. She observed that when she spoke, people listened and appeared to be moved. Her brain had not died, as she had sometimes feared, shut up in a rickety house with a maidservant who could scarcely speak English and three little children, reciting nursery rhymes and boiling laundry and cooking puddings.

When she went home that night, she looked at herself in the mirror in her bedroom, meeting her eyes with a new bold confidence. She could not say she looked forward to the letdown that would come tomorrow when once again she was only a housewife with hampers of dirty linens, with bread and pies to bake and the boys to take berry-picking as she had promised. Then would come pies in the heat of the sweltering kitchen, stirring and stirring the preserves and jams that must be put up and the fruit for later pies. She would be back to the endless drudgery of the house, but she had tasted something else—a hint of freedom, of largeness of vision and vistas, of a world that included a public role as well as private unpaid work. Henry had called her just a small-town housewife, but she had proved to herself and an audience of women and men that she was more than that.

FIFTEEN

|1854|

AT TEN, TONY WAS big for his age. He could work as hard as his next older brother during haying season, and he was responsible for slopping the pigs, milking the cows and leading them to pasture and back. He helped his mother with the vegetable garden, carrying water, pouring manure tea on growing plants. Sometimes he was sent to take eggs warm from under the chickens, but usually his next younger brother was given that task. His father said that soon he'd drive the team and plow. Father was a strict taskmaster who never hesitated to take a strap or a stick to a lazy or disobedient child.

That fall Father said he would take him along hunting. They had little time for hunting during the most active season of the farm, but in the fall his father would often put his rifle on his shoulder and go shooting for birds or rabbits, accompanied by Samuel, the oldest boy. At times Father would travel with other farmers to hunt deer in the higher hills about two hours riding to the north in the buckboard so they could carry carcasses back, roughly butchered in the woods where the deer fell. Anthony worked to become a good marksman to please his father. Since he was nine, he had been trapping rabbits in a snare. At first he felt sorry for them, with their shiny eyes like black buttons and their soft fur, but Samuel said they were varmints who ate vegetables. Samuel said the more they struggled, the tighter grew the noose, like sinners in the hands of Satan—a phrase their preacher used that stuck in Tony's mind like a burr.

The soil of their farm was good, Father said. Generations of farmers had piled up stones for fences so that only a few heaved out every winter, humping from the soil like skulls rising from below. Sometimes local boys told each other scary stories about headless horsemen, bogeymen and witches. But when the evangelical preacher came that summer, his sermon was scarier, because hell was real and, as the preacher said, every one of them was in danger at all times of God's wrath raining down on them like on Sodom and Gomorrah in fire and brimstone. The true way was narrow; the way to sin and damnation, wide and heavily traveled.

His mother gripped his hand tight in the hard pew when she was not joining her hands together in prayer. His father listened and nodded and prayed when everyone did and sang the hymns loud and off-key. But his mother listened with a fervor that seemed to burn through her thin body. Her eyes would shine when she spoke of God at prayers every morning and night or when she beat him because he was wicked and broke the eggs he was carrying or used a bad word he did not know the meaning of, but repeated because another boy had said it. When she went to revivals, sometimes the spirit of God would shake her from head to foot until her light bones seemed to rattle. She had a true carrying voice that could sing the hymns loud and clear above all the people around them, as if only she were singing for God to hear. Tony was sure God would listen to her. He adored his mother. He feared his father, but his mother was his refuge.

The local Congregational church was plain white clapboard with no frippery, no stained glass windows. The Comstocks sat up front in the sixth row, because they were prosperous farmers, among the best in the township. Anthony was proud of his parents, his mother so pious and virtuous, his father hardworking and a good farmer recognized by all. The preacher was a short stout man with a red face and a shock of white hair, but when he launched into his sermons, he seemed a giant to Tony, who cowered before the righteous wrath of the Lord as delivered by his servant, his vessel, the Reverend Cole.

"It is the lust of the mind and the body of which you must beware. It is through lust that Eve brought sin into the world, it is through lust that Eve seduced Adam into evil and brought death into the world. Woe unto the woman who does not wrap herself in modesty and lower her eyes and go obediently under the yoke her Maker has placed on her and who refuses to give that compliance to God and to her husband which is her only virtue.

"Beware, beware of the fires of lust lest they burn your soul from you. Far hotter than the fires of lust are the fires of hell, where sinners burn eternally, while the flames lick the flesh from their bones, while their bones themselves blacken with flames, while their fat drips snapping from their bodies into the fire. Yet, O sinners, their flesh is never consumed but miraculously renewed to burn yet again and again and again, for God does not forgive the sins of the filthy body and filthy mind!

"None of us is free from evil, for we are born of woman. Evil can corrupt a child of five as easily as a man of forty. A man says to himself, it doesn't matter if I read this pamphlet about a woman's body. It can't do any harm to have another glass of whiskey with my friends in the saloon. What harm is there in dancing with neighbors, boys and girls together, to the saw of a fiddler? What harm is it to read a French book, or to go to the theater where half-naked women prance onstage and the word 'love' is bandied about—having nothing to do with the virtuous respectful love a woman bears her husband or with the love we all owe to our Maker. Well, my children, the harm is instantaneous and forever, for it is the harm of damnation. It is the harm of losing your soul for the sake of going to a circus and seeing elephants and tigers. It is the harm of losing your soul for all eternity for the sake of reading something you would be better off never setting your eyes upon. It is the harm of Judgment Day, when God shall save a few and damn the multitudes for the careless sins of their youth, their maturity and their old age. You are never too young nor ever too old to sin, and the price is high, men and women before me today, the price is terrifyingly high and it never stops. You will burn through eternity. Think how it hurts when you put your hand accidentally in the fire. Now imagine that not for a minute, not for an hour, not for a day, not for a week, not for a month, not for a year, not for a decade—but forever and ever and ever, that scorching pain you cannot stand, but you will stand it and you will stand it for all eternity. That is what awaits the sinner. Never forget hell's fire for a moment, because a moment is all it takes to damn yourself to that fire forever and ever."

Tony woke screaming that night and the next and the next, seeing devils around him grinning with big horns like bucks and pushing him into the fire. His father beat him; then his mother tucked him in. "You must feel you have been wicked, my Tony, to carry on so about the Word of God."

"I don't mean to be wicked, Mother. I want to be good."

"You must work hard, you must be vigilant to keep yourself pure. Then God will love you, and your purity will let you escape the Devil's snares." His mother kissed him on the brow and left him. He learned not to cry out when he had nightmares, for they went on tormenting him. If he did not cry, then Father would not punish him for waking the household and Mother would not worry that his thoughts were impure.

God tried him and the household sorely that August, for his mother came down with malaria. It had been a damp summer and hay rotted in the field. The corn had fungus. She seemed to fight the fever off; then it came back worse. She lay in her bed burning up, like the sinners the Reverend Cole had described, then she began to shake with cold. Her teeth chattered as she lay wrapped in a feather quilt she had made herself. She could not eat. At the end of ten days of the second siege, she died, with a neighbor at her side. All the older boys including Tony were out harvesting the field corn for the animals, the feed that would be stored in their tall silo. A neighbor woman came waving her kerchief, telling them they must come. They all ran toward the house, the boys, while their father unhooked the horse and rode back. His father got there in time to close her eyes. When the boys arrived panting, their mother was dead.

Tony missed her in the morning when he got up and there was no breakfast made, but the two eldest boys must make porridge for everybody and quick bread or griddle cakes. His older brother complained that they were doing women's work and must get a girl to come in. But their father said that would tempt the boys into wrongdoing, and besides, they could not afford it. The harvest had gone badly.

The next spring his brother Eben was killed, kicked and trampled by a horse that had bolted. His father seemed to lose heart. He looked different. More rumpled, grayer, thinner. Gradually the farm disintegrated around them. Still Anthony was able to go on from the local school to a church academy secondary school. There he was no longer son of one of the most prosperous farmers, but a poor boy whom the better-off looked down upon and who had to do chores to earn his keep. Every morning he rose before dawn to chop wood and stoke the stoves. Because he was big for his age and strong, if furniture needed to be hauled up or down or moved around, if trunks had to be carried to the dormitory and then to the trunk room, if a student was going home and his effects must be carried downstairs, there was Anthony the muscle, Anthony the poor boy who must do every job and do it willingly. Now there was no one to hold him and call him Tony and pray over him when she tucked him in. He was Anthony now, half an orphan.

He would remember when he was lying in his cot at night how life had been while his mother lived. His mother had been an angel, a heroine of virtue and temperance, one of the souls whom the Lord prized. She was in heaven as surely as sinners were roasting in hell. The Lord acted in mysterious ways, the Reverend Macdonald, who was headmaster, said frequently. The Lord had taken her for his own reasons, which Anthony would never understand and could not presume to judge, or he would be a sinner. But secretly at night, sometimes he almost wept and only kept himself from tears by biting hard on his lip, on the inside of his cheeks until they bled. He missed her terribly. She had been the only tenderness in his life, for his father was a stern taskmaster who put the work of the farm before anything on earth or in heaven. But his mother had loved him, he was sure of that, and he had loved her. Someday when he was grown and a successful man, he would marry a woman just like his mother. He would have sons and daughters and raise them in righteousness. But he would not be a farmer. No. He had wheedled his way into the secondary school because he was not going to spend his life wading in mud, dealing with sick cows and mad horses and stubborn chickens, shoveling manure, victimized by wind and hail and too much rain and drought and grasshoppers and vermin. His father had lost half his farm and was well on the way to losing the second half. The elder Comstock had been speculating to recoup his fortune, buying short, buying on margin; then he lost that money too.

No, Anthony would work at a desk or in a shop or in a bank or something of the sort. Perhaps he would apprentice himself to a lawyer. He had no interest in medicine, but the law seemed to him something almost as fine as religion. His mother, he knew, would have liked him to be a preacher, but he had no gift for oratory. He had a strong harsh voice, so that people cringed when he sang. He remembered his mother's clear voice rising like a bird from the congregation in their plain church. The chapel in this school was not plain. Their beds were hard, the rooms drafty, the books battered, the teachers careworn and often bored, but the chapel was almost luxurious. Some alumnus had given stained glass windows with figures of the prophets. The chapel even had an organ. The mathematics teacher played it clumsily, but it made a great loud sound that resonated up through the thin soles of his much-mended boots. He was not sure he approved of stained glass and walnut paneling, but it did show that one alumnus of this dreary school had made good. He was determined to make good himself, to do his duty but also to flourish.

The Reverend Macdonald could preach up a storm. He was aware he was teaching a school of boys verging on adolescence or well into it, and he spoke a great deal about the volcano of lust that could destroy a boy as well as a man and bring ruin and shame upon his family.

The passions of unregulated human nature, the preacher said, would burn through a family like a fire through a frame structure in dry windy weather and leave nothing behind but ashes and shame. Only true Christian marriage could atone for the sins of Adam and Eve, could prevent the lapse into our animal nature, could fulfill the only true purpose of the coming together of husband and wife—the production of offspring, to be fruitful and multiply as the Lord had commanded. Any other use for the conjugal bed was profane and harlotry, said the preacher, and Anthony felt those words engrave themselves upon his heart. Abominations abounded in the town around them and in the great cities of the land. Satan walked those streets, Satan called to boys and to men and to women too to cast aside their morality and go rolling in the mud of lust. That phrase particularly struck Anthony, for growing up on a working farm, he had a great deal of experience with mud. It was something he had more knowledge of than he had ever desired or wished to improve upon. Enough with mud and manure and rutting animals. The bodily part of man, said the Reverend Macdonald in a loud ringing voice, was that part of man belonging to Satan. It must be disciplined like a wicked child. Spare the rod and spoil the child. They used the rod a great deal in this school. Also a great stick with which the mathematics teacher would rap their knuckles or switch them across the buttocks over his desk. Anthony had been switched only once, when he had first come to the school and did not yet grasp all the rules. It would never happen again. He walked a narrow path, a poor boy here on sufferance, and made himself a good student who memorized everything stuck in front of him. There was a temperance meeting at the school as well as in town, and Anthony signed the pledge. Rum was of the devil. It corrupted men and wasted their goods.

Anthony was walking with the Reverend Macdonald back from the inn where the stagecoach stopped. They had just put a student on it, for at thirteen he still wet his bed and was suspected of abusing himself. He was being expelled in disgrace. He had sniveled all the way to the coach while Anthony struggled under the weight of his huge valise and the reverend puffed along with the boy gripped by the shoulder.

While the coach was loading, the reverend and Anthony sat on a bench to make sure the boy went off safely. A lady was mounting and she pulled up her heavy skirts to clamber in as the coach swayed. Anthony turned his face away so as not to see her nether limb, but he noticed out of the corner of his eye that the Reverend Macdonald did not avert his gaze but watched until she was seated inside. After the coach had left, he broached the matter. "Reverend, sir, you have said that we should avert our eyes when a lady inadvertently shows ankle or other distressing areas of her limbs. But you did not turn away, sir."

Macdonald looked annoyed. His face grew redder than usual, but his voice was mild. "I am a soldier of the Lord, boy. When you are enlisted in the army of God, you do not flee temptation but encounter it manfully. You may even test your resolve by permitting yourself to observe sin. The master may do what the apprentice should not attempt."

"I understand, Reverend." He was fascinated. He would enlist in the army of the Lord and he too would be strong and virtuous enough to look upon sin without wavering from his path of righteousness. There was something extraordinarily appealing and powerful-feeling in that idea.

He wrote home regularly, dutifully. Once upon a time he had automatically admired his father. His father was the best farmer, the most righteous man. But he no longer admired him, although he must remember the Fifth Commandment to honor his father—as best he could. After the death of his mother and his brother, his father allowed weakness to overcome him. He no longer behaved as the standard-bearer of the Lord, but wallowed in misfortune. In his heart Anthony no longer felt more than a dutiful love that he must bear a father who had begotten him. Then his father wrote that he had a business opportunity in England and was sailing the next fortnight. Anthony did not hear from him for three months. A brief note came. His father said he was doing well enough. He was working for a merchant in grain.

There was no farm to return to. His family was scattered. Anthony had nothing to call a home. Once he had made his fortune, he would collect his family and help them; until then, he would go his way and they would make what way they could. He pitied his youngest brother Abel, who had had the least time with their angelic mother and who was left to try to find the Lord and his own path of righteousness.

The following November, a letter came from his father saying that he had remarried, a pious widow whose merchant husband had left her a business to run. He did not invite any of his children to join him. Anthony prayed often by his cot although the other boys thought him overly pious. He prayed for his father's soul, remarried across the sea and forgetting his old family, and he prayed for each of his living brothers. But above all he prayed for little Abel, who now was only six but without guidance to avoid sin and damnation, and for his own soul, that he might do his duty and also make his way in the world. Anthony had no one, no one except the Lord, so he loved him and worshipped him with all the fervor of his growing adolescent body. If he worked hard and stayed pure, the Lord would provide.

SIXTEEN

| *1852* |

HEN VICTORIA WAS FOURTEEN, she took to her bed with pneumonia. Buck had exhausted her on the road with Tennie as spiritualist sisters, traveling in a caravan wagon. When she was silent, afterward Buck would beat her until she could not lie comfortably on her right side or her left or her back, but only on her stomach. If not enough money was taken in from a performance, he would eat and leave the girls hungry. Buck preferred Tennie, who was amenable and didn't take séances seriously. Buck found Victoria too reticent, too serious—unwilling to flirt with men who wanted their fortunes told. Now, shaking and drenched with sweat, she saw visions in her fever. An angel appeared to her as to Mary and announced she would be a great woman. The angel stood between the faded dirty curtains of the bedroom she shared with her siblings, shining too bright for her eyes to endure, speaking in a voice like organ music.

Buck finally called a doctor, Canning Woodhull, afraid she would die and he would lose a meal ticket. Dr. Woodhull sized up the situation, held her hand, mopped her forehead. He insisted she be fed properly and regularly. She must go back to school and have rest and sleep. She must walk in the fresh air to strengthen her body. He would walk with her. He was twice her age, but he began to court her. She found a protector in him, for he seemed far more gentle and educated than men she had known. He gave her books to read and advice on how to carry herself, how to behave, how to speak correctly. He lent her a book on grammar and one on deportment.

"You're being so good to me. Why do you bother?"

"I'm educating you to be my wife. Would you like that?"

"Oh yes!" She would escape Buck, Roxanne and the rest of the screaming, scheming, crazy clan. She would be a doctor's wife. He told her he came from a prominent family. Sometimes she smelled liquor on his breath, but Buck always smelled of liquor, as did most men she met on the road.

When Dr. Woodhull, as she thought of him still, asked Buck about marrying his daughter, Buck was furious. She was waiting at the head of the stairs in the drafty dirty house where they were living in Mount Gilead, Ohio, ready to rush down. Buck told Woodhull to get out of the house or he would empty a shotgun into him. Buck ran to the back porch where he kept his guns and the doctor fled via the front door.

She went back to her bed in despair, but Woodhull did not give up. He caught her at the stream as she was doing laundry, kissed her and said he still wanted to marry her. She must be true to him until they could run away together. She swore that she would wait. They worked out ways to meet and places to leave messages.

She turned fifteen before a good opportunity opened up. It was a mild November, although the rain had knocked most leaves from the maples and oaks. Buck had gone off to see a man about a horse. Roxanne had taken to her bed dead drunk. Utica, who'd become addicted to opium while helping their mother cook up the elixirs Buck sold, lay on her pallet dead to everything. Victoria sent a message.

They eloped and were married in Cleveland. Canning took her to bed in a hotel. The act itself was over in five minutes, her hymen broken and a little trickle of blood staining the bed. Then he passed out. She realized he was drunk. The next day they moved on and a week later found them in a cheap boardinghouse in Chicago, an iron gray city of smoke and the stench of blood from slaughterhouses. Most evenings she would have to go in search of her new husband from tavern to tavern. She began to wonder why he had been so persistent in the face of Buck's refusal, for now he seemed indifferent. Was she lacking in some female way? Her body had begun to fill out, but she wasn't fleshy. One night a bartender gave her an address, snickering. It was a brothel. She found Canning in bed with a woman even older than he was.

They had moved from a boardinghouse to a tiny top-floor room containing a bed, a basin, a chest of drawers and two straight chairs. She had only the dress she had eloped in, her cloak, a worn pair of boots. Winter was coming on rapidly. Far from having a thriving medical practice, Canning worked only occasionally in connection with local pharmacies. He was an educated man, and when he was sober he would teach her history or etiquette or grammar, but he was rarely sober long. He liked the company of whores, while he seemed to find little pleasure in hers. She was always having to beg him for money, to chase him from tavern to brothel, to turn out his pockets when he fell into bed and began to snore. From his wallet she learned he had a child—illegitimate perhaps?—in Indiana to whom he sent money, when he remembered, when he had any. She wondered if their marriage was legal, but she could not ask since she was not about to admit to searching his trousers.

She seemed to have married two men. Sober, Canning was intelligent, well spoken, well educated, a gentleman who seemed to care for her. When he was drunk, she was nothing to him. She was married to two men, but both were liars. There was no affluent family. There may or may not have been medical training. She turned to fortune-telling to survive. She never knew when he would come home or when he would vanish for a week. That summer she found herself pregnant. She was sixteen, with child and desperate. When she complained too much, Canning began punching her. He knocked her down several times. When he was sober, he did not remember hitting her and asked her how she had come by such bad bruises.

A bitter cold winter day she gave birth with Canning in attendance, a bottle of rye whiskey at his side. Her labor was long and several times she passed out. She believed she would die, but finally she gave birth to a boy with a misshapen and enlarged head. Canning left her and did not return for several days. Too weak to move, she lay in the bloody bed, her breasts dry, unable to nurse the baby, who seemed to have difficulty even finding the breast. A woman who lived down the hall cleaned her up, washed the baby and took him to a wet nurse. But the nurse must be paid and Victoria had no money. She was feverish and flat on her back. She had not eaten since she went into labor.

When she woke from an exhausted fever lying in her own sweat with Canning still gone, her mother was there. "I dreamed you was in trouble," Roxanne whispered. "A vision came to me. An angel appeared waving a fiery sword and told me where to find my poor girl."

Roxanne nursed her. She said something was wrong with the baby. The woman down the hall told her that Canning had come back, found her ill and left saying he was going to send a telegram. That explained Roxanne's miracle. Victoria was grateful to her mother, who fed her broth and eggs, cooing, "You're my daughter again. My sweet daughter who loves her mama. You're my beautifulest girl. Men are pigs, Vickie mine, just pigs rooting for their feed, for drink and dirtiness."

She held Byron tenderly. At last her milk had come down, a full week after the birth. Her mother was the rock she clung to as she slowly recovered. Roxanne said, "You see? Family comes through. Family is all you can count on, Vickie mine. We must always remember, we're one blood and that's what matters in the end. Whether you marry or you don't, you still got family. Blood counts."

"Mama, what's wrong with Byron?"

"I don't know, Vickie mine. But he's not right. Still he's a Claflin, you can see it in his black hair on his head and his black eyes. He's one of us, and we'll cleave to him and care for him, no matter what he is. Because family counts and he's family. You got blue eyes, but you're one of us through and through. So I come to bring you back from death's doorstep, by the will of the Almighty and my own powers."

Victoria had been raised to put blood before all. She had run off with Woodhull, so perhaps what was wrong with her son was punishment. Her mother had come to save her life when her husband had abandoned her to die in the tiny cold room of the dirty tenement. She would not forget.

Victoria slept with her mother instead of her husband. Gradually the whole Claflin clan appeared in Chicago, dribbling in. Utica, her next youngest sister, pretty but dim-witted, Buck, even Margaret Ann the eldest came to stay. She had been unfaithful to her husband, who had thrown her out. Tennie came with Buck. She was gorgeous now, no longer a child although only twelve. She had blossomed physically over the last two years. They moved into a boardinghouse together, all the Claflins and Canning. Buck had forgiven him, and often they went off drinking. Roxanne stuck close to Victoria, as if losing her once had determined she must keep a tight hold. Victoria was reading fortunes and consulting the spirits for those who wanted to speak with the departed. Almost every adult had lost a child or two or six; many wanted to be in touch with parents, grandparents, lost lovers. People died so often and easily. Most clients sought reassurance, and that she could give in plenty.

"Mama, I am in a bright place where the angels walk amongst us. I can see you and I know you're sad for me, but you shouldn't be. Brother Teddy and me, we're studying with the angels, things that you can't imagine on your plane of existence, Mama. I am not dead, Mama, but gone beyond. I am in a finer life where there is no disease, no pain, no poverty or hunger, no danger. There are other heavens beyond this one, but here is a fine place full of good souls. When you join us, Mama, we will be waiting for you."

Women wept with joy when their lost children spoke to them of their new lives. She made their souls lighter. That she was always willing to do, because even if she didn't sense that particular soul, after all, she had visions of the next existence and she could describe it perfectly to these mourners. Women spoke to her of beatings, of abuse, of cruelty and neglect, of husbands who sent them out to work, then took every penny and spent it on whores. She was a sponge who absorbed their pain and sorrow. Women had so much trouble. When she had power, she would change their lives.

Buck passed out flyers with pictures of both sisters. MORE RENOWNED THAN THE FOX SISTERS, THE MIRACLE SISTERS. The Fox sisters lived in upstate New York where they had started the craze for séances with spirit-rapping. When Tennie worked with Victoria, it was not the quiet meetings she conducted alone. Spirits rapped on tables, whooshed around the room, sometimes appeared sparkling, moaned or groaned or shrieked. Fellow boarders complained of the noise or of the Claflins usurping the parlor. When it got too bad in one boardinghouse, they moved to another. She was thankful to be eating regularly. Utica was seeing men in a room down the hall. The other boarders objected more to the séances than they did to the men visiting Utica. Buck brought them up and hung around to make sure they weren't brutal and that they paid. Usually he sat in the chair in the hall tilted against the wall smoking a cigar. Victoria was glad he had taken up cigars. Chewing tobacco was messier and he used to spit it all over the floor. She had become more squeamish. She felt embarrassed by her new attitudes.

Byron never learned to walk or talk. He could crawl so he had to be watched. Utica was good at that, and so was Tennie, when Victoria had clients who needed to commune with the spirits. Roxanne developed the habit of praying loudly over him, which scared the poor child so that he would begin to cry. Victoria noticed bruises on him. She did not know if Roxanne or Buck was responsible. She knew it was not Canning. In spite of his occasional drunken brutality with her, he had infinite patience with Byron. They were sinking deeper into Buck's scams and his willingness to make a living through the bodies of his daughters.

Gold had been discovered in California nine years before. She met men who were traveling there, following Horace Greeley's advice, Go west, young man. Maybe there Canning would straighten out. Whether he did or not, gold was supposed to have created an economy of easy money in San Francisco. Canning did not need much persuading, for he'd grown weary of the quarreling, screaming, praying Claflins.

The preferred way to travel was by boat, across Panama or Nicaragua, where Cornelius Vanderbilt had created a route, but they lacked the money. Then one day Canning came home with the amount. He would not answer her questions. She found blood on his trousers, on the cuffs of his shirt, splattered on his medical bag.

In San Francisco, she set herself up but people seemed uninterested in communing with spirits. The atmosphere was one where Canning felt right at home, with saloons and brothels everywhere and prostitutes on every busy corner. She got a job in a saloon but was fired when she refused to flirt with the customers and was not interested in sex with them. She tried sewing, but it paid miserably. They were living in the toughest part of town where men were shanghaied—knocked out by drugs in their booze to wake as crew on a steamer a day out to sea on the way to China.

Here in the land of gold, they had not enough money to pay next week's rent in the cheapest boardinghouse she could find. She made sure Byron had enough to eat, but frequently she had nothing but a little bread and maybe a few oysters or hot corn from a vender. A woman in the boardinghouse suggested she try out for the stage. She got a job as an actress in *The Country Cousin*. Her ability to memorize was useful, as was her beauty. She hated being strapped into a tight corset and low-cut dress to flounce around the stage while an audience of men ogled and roared. Still, she was making enough to move Byron and Canning out of the dreadful boardinghouse on the Barbary Coast and into a respectable one run by an Italian woman who could actually cook. The landlady pitied Byron and took him under her care. She did not think much of Canning, although she called on his medical services when necessary. Victoria got on with her. At twenty she often liked the women she met better than the men.

It was not an easy life on the stage, working behind the gaslights and then at parties afterward, where the actresses were expected to entertain men with deep pockets. At first the other actresses viewed her with suspicion, because she had developed fine manners and an air of quiet elegance. Canning had taught her that, building on her natural dignity. But she reached out to the other women; soon they were confiding their affairs, their miscarriages and abortions, their children, their lovers, their sugar daddies, their ambitions and fears. When she occasionally brought Byron with her, she could see the other women pitied her, which took the edge off envy they might otherwise feel. At the parties, for the first time she entered bourgeois space. Having grown up in poverty and simple, bare interiors, she was overwhelmed by the clutter, thick fabrics hanging and draping, velvet, paisley, multiple floor and wallpaper prints. Every surface was laden with bric-a-brac, vases, statuettes, curios. It gave her vertigo at first, this passion those with money had to occupy and decorate all available space.

She became friendly with another actress. Josie Mansfield had come out from the East Coast with her parents. After her father was killed in a duel, her mother remarried and her stepfather forced her into prostitution. He sounded a bit like Buck. Josie's mother was a hopeless drunk, much like Canning, who had also picked up a taste for opium. Canning was a millstone tied around Victoria's neck. Because of her job, she was no longer faithful, which made his indifference and shiftlessness hurt her less. He was a dependent, like Byron. Byron gave her more joy because he was an affectionate creature, sweet and passive.

Two years of obscene productions with men pawing her afterward kept her family in food and rent and clothing but made her feel she would lose her mind. She got a letter from her older sister Margaret Ann telling her the family was doing right fine these days with Tennie at fourteen selling Miss Tennessee's Magnetic Life Elixir. "How are you doing?" Margaret asked. "Bet you're panning gold for sure in California. I'm considering getting married again. How is your doctor? We think of you out in the golden West just rolling in dollars."

Victoria decided to return east. She had been on the stage long enough to know that her novelty was wearing off. She had to become a bigger star or be relegated to bit parts, and the way to bigger parts was to become the mistress of a producer. She didn't want any man to have that much control over her, for it would feel like Buck all over again. Prancing about partly dressed for an audience of goats in strung-together melodramas with the obligatory scene where her clothes such as they were would be half ripped off, was not the higher mission she had been promised would be hers.

One thing she would take away from San Francisco: confidence in her powers as a sexual being. She had learned she could satisfy men very well, and that she herself could enjoy the embrace. Once she overcame her reticence with a particular man, sexual response came easily, but she retained enough self-control always to know exactly how to apply pressure to the man at the proper time and place to effect intense pleasure. Sex was not simply something men visited upon helpless or compliant women. She could seduce. She would prefer to do so from a position of choice, but she found that sex gave her not only pleasure but strength. If she decided a particular man was the one she would prefer in a room, she had developed what she thought of as animal magnetism—a form of spiritual electricity—that would draw him to her. Once a man had met her gaze, she was sure she could have him. If women knew how to deal with sex more forthrightly, more intelligently, more aggressively, their lives would improve. Certainly they would enjoy them more. But it was a matter of power and choice.

Pregnant again, she took Canning and Byron to Indianapolis, where she worked as a spiritual healer and medium. She hoped she was carrying a girl this time, and that her daughter would be perfect. She wanted to bear her away from her family. In a dim and cold rented room, with the April rain striking the pane in torrents, a drunken and stupefied Canning delivered her of the baby girl she had been sure she would have. He left her and she woke to find the umbilical cord cut but untied and the baby bleeding to death. She grabbed the cord and tied it herself.

This time her milk came down. She named her baby Zulu Maud. The man in the white toga who had begun appearing suggested the name. "She will be a source of strength to you," the spirit told her. She clutched her baby to her breast that was oozing milk and watched the sweet little mouth suck eagerly. Outside through the window open now to benign spring breezes, she heard newsboys hawking papers about war. Confederate forces had fired on Fort Sumter in South Carolina. What would war mean? She held her sweet baby, worrying. One thing she knew: between her family and Canning, there was only one choice. She was done with him. She would go home to the Claflins and let Buck send her on the road with his tonics and elixirs, his cancer cures and his schemes for blackmailing. She would leave Canning wherever he lay. She would get back on her feet and then she would leave the Claflins also. She would set forth on her own with only her children, for the spirits would command and protect her. As soon as she was strong enough, she rose and began to pack her few belongings into an old satchel.

1869

SEVENTEEN

FREYDEH INSISTED SAMMY accompany her to shul. "Yes, so I don't go often. But it's polite since they invited us, we should both go. Maybe we'll find out something about Shaineh. It's like she vanished off the face of the earth."

"It happens," Sammy said glumly. "It happens here."

"I have faith we will find her." She tried to make her wild frizzy hair lie down nicely under a hat.

"I won't be with you anyhow. I'll be with the men."

"So you can learn something. Besides, they let children be with the women. At your age, it's your choice."

"I'll sit with the men, okay? I'm no child."

Giborah and Hetty's shul was a storefront on Orchard Street. They had made an ark for the Torah out of boards, and the women had stitched a curtain for it, a quilt of various pieces of cloth. The effect was attractive, Freydeh saw, peering out of the women's section from behind the *mehitzeh*. They had a real eternal lamp burning oil, wrought of silver and decorated with fine patterning like metal lace. Someone, maybe the rabbi, had brought it from the Pale, obviously. The rabbi was young, only in his middle twenties with a full dark beard and bushy head of hair.

Giborah poked her, pointing to a pregnant woman sitting in front of them. "That's the *rebbitzen*. It'll be their first child."

"When did he come over?"

"Only last year. Around the time we did, but he's from Minsk. We can't find nobody from Odessa around here excepting us. It's lonely here for us. You too?"

"Especially since my Moishe was killed. But Sammy is company."

"I wonder if I'll ever find a husband here. I need a *shadchen* who speaks Yiddish."

After the service, they had an Oneg Shabbos, with women bringing what they could to make nice—a kind of coffee cake with apples, some dried figs, as well as a loaf of fresh challah. They all tore off a piece for the *bracha* over the bread, then had a sip of the sweet wine. A wave of almost bitter nostalgia cut through her. Again it struck her afresh that she was an orphan with Mama and Papa dead and long buried. She could not regret that she had left, but she wished she had made money to send for them years ago so they would have taken passage, come to America and survived. If Moishe had not been killed, surely they could have sent her family money to cross the ocean.

Finally she got to ask the rabbi and members of the little congregation whether they had ever seen Shaineh. She pulled out the drawing carefully folded in her pocket.

Several of the men and the *rebbitzen* gathered around and stared solemnly at the picture. The rabbi's wife said, "I remember her. Such a pretty thing, and so alone. She was looking for work."

"I remember now," the rabbi said, plucking at his beard and frowning. "Yes. It was shortly after we began."

One of the men nodded. "I gave her the name of a man who hires seamstresses. She was going to apply to him."

"Do you remember who it was you sent her to?"

He gave her the name and address. She thanked him fervently. This was the first solid new piece of information she had gotten in two months. Sammy was eating figs and cake with both hands. She could hardly run and find the man tonight, so she stood to one side with Hetty and let Sammy eat whatever he wanted.

"We all need somebody," Hetty said. "You could marry again."

"I got no time. I want to set up in business for myself."

"Every Jew wants that, no? Except Giborah. She just wants a husband."

"May she find as good a one as I did, and may he live a lot longer. I had a good husband, the best. I lost him way too young." Standing at Hetty's elbow, she looked carefully at the woman's belly. "Hetty, are you with child?"

"Shhh! I don't like to say it till the quickening. You can never tell what will happen."

"You know it." Everything tonight conspired to remind her of her losses—husband, parents, unborn child. But she would hold fast to her hope of finding Shaineh.

SHE WAS STILL WORKING at the pharmacy, but Yonkelman's wife was recovering her health. Freydeh could tell her job wasn't going to last much longer. She wouldn't quit on him—he'd been good to her—but when he let her go, it would be a sign that it was time for her and Sammy to get going full-time. When she thought of being on her own without a job, she was excited but scared. Suppose they could not make the condoms fast enough? Suppose no one would buy them? Well, then she would look for another job, that was how it would be. In the meantime, they worked on rubber goods in what little spare time they had and tried to make them faster and faster.

Finally she begged off work early one Tuesday when business was slow. "I won't pay you the hours you don't work," Yonkelman said, tapping his finger on the counter. He liked to act stern. A truly stern boss would not have let her take off early with Sammy.

"I understand. But I have to try to find my sister."

The address was a loft where girls were stitching around tables. In September, the light was already gone by seven-thirty, but he had them working by kerosene lanterns on each table. The room was smoky and dark.

"I'm looking for my sister. A rabbi told me she had been referred here as a seamstress."

"Do you see her?"

Freydeh walked around each table while the exhausted girls squinted up at her. They were making coats of coarse wool. Their hands were bleeding from pushing the big needles through heavy fabric. She stared into each face with hope. "Is Shaineh Leibowitz here?"

"I remember her," one girl said. "From near Vilna, no? A pretty girl. She didn't last. She didn't work fast enough."

"How long ago was that?"

"He fired her after a month. That was in February, I think."

"Do you know where she went?"

"She was crying when he fired her. She said she had no place to go. She wasn't much of a seamstress, but she was a nice girl. I hope she made out okay."

"Do you know where she was living?"

The girl shook her head. "No idea. Someplace cheap."

The boss claimed to remember nothing. Another dead end. Freydeh's eyes burned with tears she kept from falling. How many tears she had held behind her eyes. How many tears she had not given herself permission to shed.

Another girl spoke up. "Give me your address. If I hear anything, I'll let you know."

That night the second girl came to their door, accompanied by her brother. "I had to tell you. She was in despair, your sister. She was so helpless. One of the other girls talked to her. Told her she could make a living in a house, you know? I don't know if she went, but I know where Lisa told her to go. That madam sometimes hires Jewish girls. You might not want to go there, or maybe you don't want to know her anymore if that's what happened. . . . But she was hungry and scared and she didn't have any idea how to survive in the city. Women get desperate, missus. You understand?"

"I understand. And she's still my sister even if she went to that house. So we'll go there too. Thank you!" She embraced the girl and then her brother took her back down the tenement steps.

"I don't like to take you to such places," she said to Sammy.

"So if they don't speak German or Yiddish or Russian, you think you can do okay? They won't understand you and they'll brush you off as a greenhorn. You won't understand everything they're saying either." He drew himself up, trying to look stern and adult. "You think I grew up down here and I don't know about whores and whorehouses? You think like it's something new to me?"

"I don't like exposing you."

"Shit, like I'm going to go get myself chained up like those schlemiels at the other brothel? Give me some credit. I don't have money for a pair of boots, I'm not going to waste it on sex when the street is full of girls who'll do it in the alley if I feel like it."

She buried her face in her hands. "Maybe it's good I never had a baby. Trying to keep you out of trouble is a full-time job."

"I don't steal no more. I don't beat up nobody unless they attack us in the street." Twice, they had to defend themselves on the way to the river.

"You have a good heart, Sammy. I just want to keep you safe."

"Nobody's safe around here, Freydeh. You know that."

"Nobody was safe in the Pale, either." She sighed heavily. "Someday we will get out of this neighborhood and live in a house with trees around us. I swear it."

"Trees?" He looked puzzled.

"They're nice. They clean the air. But now we got to get you winter boots."

"So far we been spending your money trying to make protectors, not getting any back. Maybe it's a bad idea."

"We'll make money. I believe in us."

Two days later, Yonkelman took her aside. "My wife is ready to come back to work, Mrs. Levin. I can't keep you on. But she can't make up the pills and powders the way you can. If you want to come in two days a week from eight till eight, I can use you. I do the serious stuff, but I haven't got time for what we sell so much of, the hair-raisers, the regulators, the tonics, the syrups."

"So when are you laying me off?"

"Next week. She'll be able to come in regular then."

It was a sign it was time to cut loose and start their business in earnest. She agreed to work for Yonkelman Sundays and Thursdays, at least through the fall and winter. Then they would have some money coming in, a trickle. Yonkelman was also letting Sammy go. They walked home in sober silence, thinking that everything they had planned and experimented with had become frighteningly real. They had been playing, but playtime was over. She felt as if she had been telling herself fairy tales. How could she, a woman and an immigrant, break into such a line of work? But she had to. It was the one thing she had thought of that might prove successful. All around them in her tenement and in the block and the neighborhood, women did piecework for so many cents a job, worked long hours like the girls in that coat factory and brought home less than they could survive on. She had to have the courage to do what she had imagined. Otherwise, how would they make it?

Besides, she could look harder for Shaineh. Working twelve hours a day six days a week left her little time to do anything besides the necessary household tasks she shared with Sammy, bringing up water, cooking, washing up, laundry, emptying chamber pots, the minimal housecleaning they had time to do. Shopping for the essentials—candles, bread, eggs, fish, sometimes chicken parts to make soup. Carrots, turnips, potatoes, some green vegetables, a piece fruit. Honey, vinegar, oil, flour, beans. Up and down the stairs fifty times a day. In September, it was still hot. Winters were hard with the cold wind off the river blowing through the tenements as if they were made of lace. But with the heat grinding them down and making their rubber-cooking hard to endure, with the heat baking them at night so they could not sleep, waking in the morning to the filthy air laden with every kind of bad smell on sheets damp with their sweat, it was difficult not to look forward to fall with its cleaner, cooler winds.

The day after Yonkelman let her go, they started for the brothel whose address they had been given by the young coat maker. It was across town in the Twenties, but since they were earning so little, they walked. They kept to the Bowery, then Third up to Fourteenth Street, where they stopped frequently to stare into shopwindows. The street was crowded, but not with the people they saw on the Bowery. This time of day, mostly women were about, lighting from carriages or cabs or strolling along the pavement together or with their servants just behind. The only place she saw lots of men was in carriages or in restaurants they passed—crowded, even the fancy ones. The scents that drifted onto the sidewalk made her mouth fill with saliva and her stomach growl. Roasting meat, roasting fowl, something spicy, something fried.

The shops were like a paradise of goods—shops that sold nothing but hats, hats with whole birds on them, hats laden with silk flowers, huge velvet cartwheels, hats like lacy towers. Other shops sold only scarves and shawls. Who were all the people who bought such extravagant things, and so many of them? She saw ladies swishing out of the shops followed by servants bearing mounds of packages.

"Now that we're not working regular, I sure would like to go up to Central Park, you know? I never been there. You were talking about trees? They got trees up there. That's where the rich folks live now." Sammy pointed north.

"We'll go some Saturday afternoon. I want to see it too. Where I grew up, Sammy, there were fields and trees. My papa was a woodcutter. My Moishe had been a woodcutter too, but he couldn't do that here."

"Not unless he went up to Central Park. I guess they don't let you do that. My pal Grubby says they don't let you do hardly anything unless you're rich and you have horses and a carriage. . . . But I'd still like to go. To see it."

They walked by the new dry goods stores, big as towns with women tripping in and out in bonnets and plumed hats and so many yards of material they could have rigged a ship with their skirts and underskirts. "Let's go inside," she said on impulse, unsure if they would let them in or not.

Sure enough, a gentleman standing by the door in a uniform looked sideways at them and began to follow them. Freydeh didn't care. This was like a palace. More clothes than she had ever seen, a high ceiling with a balcony, pneumatic tubes whizzing around or depositing their contents with a loud clunk. She smelled something wonderful. It came from a counter with many little bottles of colored liquor. A woman in fine white lawn and a big bustle was squirting herself with one little bottle. "No," she said to the salesman in black who was bowing to her, "I would prefer the first. I don't care for such a heavy perfume."

Freydeh had heard of perfume but never been near it. How could such a little bottle be too heavy? Then she sighed. "I'm a bad person. I'm getting distracted. Come, we'll continue on our way."

"You could live in here and there'd be everything you ever needed," Sammy said. "Did you see all those coats? Enough for everyone on our block." Downstairs she could see carpets, piles and piles of them up to a woman's shoulders.

They were both silent as they plodded on. Finally Freydeh said, "In shops at home, you have onions and you have yarn and you have vodka and wine and you have buttons and needles. Only what you need. Now I understand why everybody wants to be rich in America. There's so many things, you think you want to have them. You look and you think, Now why can't I have one of those? And two of those?"

"Did you really think the streets were paved with gold, like some greenhorns?"

She pulled off his cap and ruffled his hair. "I wasn't that ignorant. But I had no idea how crowded and filthy it would be. No one prepares you for that. But we go forward, Sammy, we go forward."

The brothel was an ordinary respectable-looking brownstone house in a row of them. Nothing set it off from its neighbors, no bare-breasted girls hanging out the windows, no drawings of curvaceous naked ladies. Freydeh wondered if they had the wrong address and this would be somebody's home. They rang the bell and had a longish wait. A Black man in livery answered. He seemed rather surprised at what he saw.

"She's looking for our sister," Sammy said. "We were told she might be working here. We've lost touch with her."

"Lost touch, huh? Probably threw her out."

"No," Freydeh said. "No! We don't care what she's done. She's our sister and we just want to see her."

He seemed to be making a decision. "Come into the parlor. I'll get Mrs. Baines, and she can talk with you. If she will."

"Thank you, thank you," Freydeh stammered. "We won't make no trouble. We just want to find her, to see her." She pulled the drawing from her bag and thrust it at him. "Maybe you recognize her? Shaineh?"

"Mrs. Baines, she'll let you know."

But she had seen a flicker of recognition in his eyes. No matter what they said, she knew that Shaineh had been here and maybe still was.

Mrs. Baines kept them waiting for half an hour. They sat together in the parlor on a plush sofa, gazing at the walls covered with red-striped wallpaper that looked like fabric, staring at the ceiling painted with floating half-naked nymphs. There was a whole bevy of them, blond, brunette, redhead, buxom and svelte, tall and short, all floating in draperies that bared a breast across a wishy-washy bluish sky studded with big-bosomed clouds. The effect was silly. The women looked unnatural swimming along in the sky with one tit hanging out and a good bit of leg exposed.

Two women dressed like ladies came out together, each carrying an empty basket. One was in black silk with white lace, her black hair in loose curls. The other—in a loose red jacket and serge walking skirt looped up to show yellow-and-black-striped petticoats, striped stockings and high heeled boots—had longer red hair. They nodded at Freydeh as the Negro butler showed them out. Freydeh wondered if they worked here. Somehow she didn't think so.

At last a tall lean woman wearing a pince-nez marched in. "Now what's this?"

"We're trying to find our sister," Sammy said, trying to sound respectful. Freydeh nodded fervently.

"Shaineh," she added. "Her name Shaineh Leibowitz."

"A Jewess?"

They both nodded and waited. Mrs. Baines took a seat in a high-backed chair somewhat like a mahogany throne upholstered in red pierced through with gold embroidery and eyed them, looking over both of them critically and carefully. "You're saying this woman you're talking about is your sister?"

Both nodded again and Freydeh repeated, "My sister, yeah, his aunt. Please?"

"What is it you want with her?"

"We lost her."

"Lost her?" The madam looked amused. "Ladies lose handkerchiefs, not sisters."

Freydeh turned to Sammy, for the explanation was too complicated for her rudimentary English. Sammy told the story, although he appeared in it as Freydeh's son. That seemed to be their new explanation to the world. They always seemed to be explaining themselves to strangers.

"So this man never gave you the letter? Why? Was he protecting this woman in some way?"

"Not him," Sammy said. "He wouldn't protect her if a brick was falling on her head. He was mad at Frey—Mother. He was mad at Mother because they had a fight about money."

"Isn't that what all fights are about?" Mrs. Baines yawned and lit a cigarette. "Money or jealousy. . . . So have you been looking for this young woman long?"

"Since Mama got the letter in her hands," Sammy said. He was getting good at this. She could understand most of what Sammy said. She was used to his accent. She was getting better at understanding spoken English, but putting a narrative together was still beyond her. What would she do without Sammy?

Freydeh could not contain herself any longer. She bounded up and handed the drawing to Mrs. Baines. "Please, do you know my Shaineh? Have you seen her? Is she here?"

The madam studied the drawing. At length she handed it back to Freydeh. "She was. Not any longer."

"Please how long ago and what happened to her?"

"Early last spring she came to us. She was starving and frostbitten. We took her in."

"She work as maid?"

"She was a virgin, as I'm sure you know. That was worth a reasonable amount of money."

Freydeh tried to keep her face still but her hands twitched in her lap. Poor Shaineh. It was *her* fault. If she had not quarreled with her old landlord Big Head, she would have received Shaineh's letter, met her, and everything would have been different. So different.

"You sold her cherry," Sammy said. "Did she get any of the money?"

"She got room, board and a percentage. We tried to train her to keep working here."

"But she left?" Sammy persisted. She could tell he disliked the madam.

"She wasn't cut out for the life. She was afraid of men. Some men like that, but mostly they like it if it's put on, not when it's real." Mrs. Baines grinned. She had a gold tooth that winked at them.

"So you threw her out?" Sammy was trying to control his anger.

"She found a man who liked it well enough so he promised to keep her. She went off with him, quite willingly, believe me. She was always nervous here."

"How long you keep her?" Freydeh asked. "How long?"

"Somewhat over three months. The end of June, she went off with her gentleman."

"Do you know his name?"

"Of course. He was a customer."

Freydeh found a piece of paper in her pocket. "Please to write man's name."

"I don't give out names of my customers."

"Lady, we don't care he's a gent that comes here for your girls," Sammy said. "We just want to find my aunt. Please, we've been trying to find her for months already. This isn't the first house we had to visit looking for her. My mama is a working woman and she don't have lots of time to run around looking and looking. This is the closest we come to her sister, so help us, please. We'd pay you, but we don't have any money."

Freydeh spoke up. "We make condoms now. We make good ones. We give you a sweet deal on them for your girls. You give us name, address if you got, and we sell you condoms, good right-made ones, for better price than anyplace."

Mrs. Baines smiled. They bargained back and forth. The bargaining seemed to make the woman more genial. Finally they settled on a price for three dozen as an experiment, payment on delivery and satisfactory testing. Then Mrs. Baines brought out a ledger. "I keep excellent books. Everything should be here."

"He paid you for her," Sammy said. It wasn't a question. "To take her away."

"The standard fee." She was licking her finger, turning the pages, scanning them.

"The books must be useful for a little extra money," Sammy said. Freydeh could tell he really disliked the woman. She was sure the woman could feel that too, but she was hardened against disapproval.

"I don't dabble in blackmail, boy. They're for the police captain, so he knows I'm not cheating him." Her finger paused. "Here it is. Oh, John Smith. We get a lot of those."

Freydeh turned to Sammy, puzzled. He explained, "It's like John Doe." Freydeh shrugged. Sammy went on, "It's not his real name."

"I can still help you," Mrs. Baines said. "He took her in a phaeton. I had my bouncer deliver her baggage. So I have the address. He had to pay Roscoe."

She wrote down an address on the Far West Side, not a neighborhood Freydeh knew. "Good luck. I expect delivery by next Wednesday."

"You get." Freydeh nodded, bobbing her head vehemently.

As they set out on their long trek to the address they had been given, Freydeh clapped Sammy on the bony shoulder. "So. We got our first order and we got an address. We are forging ahead, Sammy. Didn't I tell you? We're going to find my sister tonight and this week we're starting production."

"But we got to produce three dozen in a week."

"*Nu,* so, we'll do it. Starting tomorrow early."

They came wearily at last to the address—to where the address should have been. But there was nothing except a burned-out hulk. The block had endured a fierce fire, for three houses in a row were just outer walls and rubble. Freydeh stood in the street staring at the house whose address she had been given. Another dead end. She sat down on the ashy stoop and wept.

EIGHTEEN

NTHONY HAD CHANGED his job and now worked for Cochran, McLean and Company at the corner of Broadway and Grand. He was making a reasonable living on commissions, but he was not satisfied. Man was not created for a solitary life, and such a situation created temptation and improvident choices. A man needed a helpmate, so he began looking around to find a suitable candidate. He felt hollow. If a mighty wind picked him up and blew him out to sea, who besides his boss would miss him? Perhaps his mentor at the Y. Perhaps his pastor. He returned at night to his dismal room in the boardinghouse run by a respectable widow. Life was not supposed to be so empty for a virtuous man. He was entitled to marry. Marry or burn, Paul said in the Scriptures, and he did not wish to burn.

He courted a young woman he met at his church for a month of Sundays, but she was too forward. She expected attentions he considered inappropriate, constantly looping her arm through his and, the last time they saw each other, pressing into his side. She also giggled. She would not do. Someone more settled would be to his taste. He noticed a woman in one of the dry goods stores on his route. She was a well-spoken woman with a soft melodious voice that reminded him of his mother. He wondered if she sang as his mother had. She was rather pale, for she spent her days in the shop. Her father, who owned the store, had been a prosperous merchant in Stone Ridge near the Hudson, but he had lost his business due to the unscrupulousness of a partner. Mr. Hamilton was eager to tell Anthony all this, to explain he had not always stood behind the counter of a tiny shop that sold the cheaper sort of ladies' notions and sewing supplies. Once he had been a merchant to reckon with. His pew had been right in front of the altar, he told Anthony proudly. He had ridden in a fine brougham drawn by two white horses.

Anthony understood the plight of the woman, whose name he learned was Margaret. He too had been reared in a family that had been prosperous and then had come down in the world. It was a difficult burden, but Margaret bore it stoically. She had probably given up the hope of marrying, for she was already twenty-nine—past the age at which most women had any chance of finding a husband.

He liked her large pale blue eyes. Her hair was the lightest brown, straight and fine. She was tall and willowy. She had a slightly sad demeanor that touched him. He could make her happy, he knew it. As he considered over the next couple of months beginning to court her, he imagined her pleasure, her delight. He would carry her off from the dusty little dry goods store. The prospect was uplifting to contemplate. Why rush the matter? Finding a wife was almost as good as having one.

Then one fall day Margaret was not in the shop when he came by to show the newest merchandise—even though Mr. Hamilton would buy little of it—and take Hamilton's order for the same old. "Where's your daughter?"

"She could not shake a cough she had. It's kind of you to ask."

Anthony leaned forward. "She's at home then, recuperating?"

"We sent her to the country. We have a cousin, a prosperous farmer in Stone Ridge. We hope the clean country air will revive her."

Anthony felt as if the floor had given way beneath him. He was so accustomed to Margaret behind the high wooden counter, it had never occurred to him that someday she might not be there to smile shyly at him and then to cast her eyes down lest she seem forward. A modest woman, a demure woman, a proper woman. Now she had been sent off into the country where someone else might speak for her. She might decide to stay there. Anything could happen. She could be trampled by a horse. She could be bitten by a rattlesnake, for venomous snakes, he had been told, were common in the mountains.

He prayed for her on his knees beside his narrow bed in the boardinghouse, hearing the sounds of dishwashing from below and the chatter of the maid and the boardinghouse keeper, hearing the raucous laughter of the men in the parlor smoking and telling stories and lies to each other. This was the life he had determined to put behind him; yet he had hesitated. He was a fool to have risked losing a good woman who seemed to have every virtue he desired in a wife.

He gave short shrift to his salesmanship the next day and rushed to Mr. Hamilton's shop immediately afterward, to catch him while the shop was still open. He knew they stayed open late in order to catch the last business that might conceivably come to them.

"Mr. Comstock," Mr. Hamilton greeted him. "We aren't ready for a new order yet. You aren't due back to us for another three and a half weeks."

"It's not for Cochran, McLean I've come. It's for myself."

Behind the counter where Margaret usually stood was a much older woman, white-haired but with a strong resemblance to his Margaret, who might be her mother. He greeted the woman and then turned back to Mr. Hamilton.

"I have had the pleasure of studying your daughter's behavior and demeanor for some months now, and I am much impressed with her modesty and her hard work for you and her gentleness."

"She's a good worker," Mr. Hamilton said, clearly puzzled. "Did you want to hire her?"

But the mother had a better idea of what was afoot. She came out from behind the counter, patting at her hair, her eyes glittering. She beamed at him.

"I want to ask for Margaret's hand in marriage."

"But you're years younger than she is."

"We are suited, I believe. Age differences matter little when a husband and wife have similar values. I believe I can keep her in a reasonable manner—not the lap of luxury, but well enough." He was afraid that Mr. Hamilton was going to refuse him. It occurred to him that although he doubted the father could possibly find him an unworthy suitor, perhaps he wanted to keep Margaret working in the shop. "You must think first of the happiness of your daughter, Mr. Hamilton."

"Oh yes, Edmund. It's a wonderful chance for Margaret. She can marry at last and have a family. I wanted that so badly for her, all these years. You must say yes."

"I suppose. But you must consult Margaret. She will be back within ten days."

"Do I have your permission to speak with her then, to propose matrimony?"

Mr. Hamilton sighed. Anthony, who was skilled at reading expressions, decided his suspicions were correct. The father did not so much mind losing a daughter as losing a shop clerk. "What religion are you, Mr. Comstock?"

"I'm a Congregationalist."

"We're Presbyterian."

"Close enough," Mrs. Hamilton said. "Close enough." She accompanied him to the door and stepped outside with him. "Don't mind my husband," she said in a low voice, almost a whisper. "I know Margaret likes you. She has spoken of your visits to the store in a manner that shows a favorable impression. Press your suit as soon as she returns, and I believe this marriage will go forward."

"Thank you, Mrs. Hamilton." He took her hand and squeezed it. "I look forward to your being my mother-in-law. My own mother died when I was ten, and never have I stopped missing her."

He allowed two weeks to pass before he returned to the store. This time Margaret was behind the counter. She had more color in her face than usual, from the country sun, but he could see that she blushed at the sight of him. She was not wearing the usual shop apron but had on a dress of blue dimity, with a blue ribbon in her fine light brown hair. "Mr. Comstock," she said softly, then looked down.

"You've been in the country."

"Yes, with a cousin."

A long awkward silence spread between them. The father was frowning, banging drawers open and shut. "Miss Hamilton," he began, "may I return when you are done with work here? Might we take a short walk together?"

Margaret glanced at her father before replying—a dutiful daughter. When, after a minute, her father nodded, she turned back to Anthony. "I should be pleased to accompany you on a short walk."

At seven-thirty, he returned to the shop. She was waiting for him already in her cloak and bonnet. She dressed in an old-fashioned style, a bonnet instead of the large plumed hats of the current style. She wore a simple woolen cloak over her blue dress, but her gloves were new white kid. She was neat and simple, something he felt comfortable with. After they were married, he could provide her with many little items of finery that women enjoyed, for he knew all about ladies' fashions from his job.

They walked in silence for two blocks, his arm holding hers. He must speak. They were both nervous. She tripped twice on a curb. She was so slight that although she was fairly tall for a woman, her bones felt like those of a little bird, one of those warblers he used to see in the spring and fall on his father's farm. "Miss Hamilton, I have come to admire you greatly over the time we have been acquainted."

"Thank you, Mr. Comstock." She lowered her chin to her chest.

Nothing forward about her. All proper. He must act. "Miss Hamilton, it would make me extremely proud and happy if you would permit me to court you with the aim of persuading you to marry me."

Her breath came out in a long hiss. She did not speak for a minute and he was afraid she had some objection to his suit. But she said only, "Yes, Mr. Comstock, I'd be pleased if you were to court me with the intention of proceeding toward marriage."

He clasped her hand in his. Hers was quite cold. So for that matter was his. "I don't want to rush you, to push you too hard."

She smiled slightly. "I have no objection to speed, myself, but I suspect my parents will insist on a proper length of time for the engagement."

He wished for a selfish moment that they could run off, marry and be together. But everything must be done with decorum and in the proper manner befitting the social position he intended to achieve for himself and now for Margaret too.

It proved to be a long and sometimes tedious courtship under the gaze of her watchful parents, but they moved inexorably toward marriage. The date was set for the following June. As May whittled down on his calendar, he began to think about marriage in the physical sense. He had no clear idea what to do. On the farm, he had seen the rooster servicing his hens, but that did not help. When the cows had been freshened by the bull, he had been forbidden to watch and sent inside with his younger brothers. He had heard the farm cats yowling. His mother said they were fighting, but his older brother told him they were mating. He had no idea why they screamed. Perhaps the act was painful. Was it necessary to remove all clothing?

He did not wish to appear a fool or to risk injuring his delicate Margaret. He must find out what to do. He took time on his lunch break to visit one of those nasty bookshops that catered to young men and corrupted them. It was a simple matter to find the shelf of marriage manuals, so called, that gave explicit descriptions of the male and female body, inflaming whoever read them, and described the act as well as methods for avoiding God's purpose for that act. He was disgusted, but he purchased one of the manuals and carried it off, along with *The Lustful Turk* and *Venus's Miscellany*. He read it overnight, containing his outraged feelings. Now at least he knew what to expect. Then he perused the two other obscene volumes. If he were weaker in his Christian values, such books might have corrupted him, but since he read them and viewed the obscene illustrations only to acquaint himself with the kind of literature to be destroyed, he emerged unscathed.

The next day he went to the same captain of police who had assisted him before. He showed him the vile books and once again they proceeded to the shop in question with two patrolmen, confiscating all the dirty books they could find as well as a stash of French postcards he simply could not believe as he looked through them. He studied them carefully to know what he was dealing with. These bookshops were dens of iniquity indeed. Someday he would close every one of them. He would wipe them off the face of God's earth. The two novels were rife with women who behaved without morals, shameless whores who wriggled and screamed with lust. He was confident his wife would never behave so, for she was a thoroughly virtuous woman. She would do her duty and nothing more.

Now he knew what he must do to his precious Margaret. It would be difficult for them both, but he would be man enough to perform the act. Soon they would have children to carry on the Comstock name, children to gather around him in wonderful family evenings in the parlor of the home they would soon share. Children to rear in Christian values and to protect from all the vicious snares of the city.

He began to look for a house in earnest. After two weeks, he decided it would be much better for Margaret and for their children to come if he looked in Brooklyn. Ferries crossed the river regularly and many gentlemen traveled to their offices from homes in the city of Brooklyn, which struck him as far more respectable than Manhattan. Trees shaded the streets of family homes and solid brick and brownstone row houses, some quite fine. He had set aside five hundred dollars, free and clear, to put down on a house when he found one that pleased him.

Over the next three weeks, he looked at fourteen houses without being satisfied by any. Finally, just six days before the wedding, he saw a large two-story yellow house with a porch around three sides, nice carpentry work, a corner tower that included on the second floor a spacious master bedroom. He put his five hundred down on impulse, realizing only afterward that he had not consulted Margaret. Well, it was a bargain, a large and commodious house with excellent wood paneling and wallpaper they would not have to change. They would have to live in a boardinghouse for the first weeks, until they had it furnished, but then they would be in their own home. He told Margaret about it that evening. "It has indoor plumbing—water closets and bathtubs and running water in the kitchen sink. It has central heating, three bedrooms and a maid's room."

"I'm sure it's perfect, Mr. Comstock. I look forward to seeing our new home."

He had the most agreeable wife in the world, he was convinced. He brought her to the house and she admired it. "I will leave the furnishing of it largely to you, my Margaret, so long as you stay within the budget I have established." It was only recently he had begun to use her given name. He constantly begged her to use his, but she demurred.

"After we are married. Before then, it wouldn't be proper."

At last the day of their wedding approached. They joined the Clinton Avenue Congregational Church, within easy walking distance of their new house—which should be ready for them in a month.

Anthony took off three days for a brief honeymoon, all he felt they could afford with their new house and the necessity of furnishing it. Margaret's uncle in Stone Ridge had helped with the cost of the wedding. They took the steamer to Cape May in New Jersey, where people of influence often went in the summers. A gentleman on the board of the YMCA lent them a cottage on his estate for their honeymoon. Their first night together they were both exhausted and Anthony was content to sleep beside his bride. He did not believe she knew what to expect, for she said nothing and made no untoward gestures.

The next night he prepared to consummate the marriage. They walked on the beach and briefly bathed, separately, in the areas set up for men and for women. Then they ate supper in a fine restaurant in a local hotel, where they began with oysters, then roast beef, and finished with strawberry pudding. The hotelier, who seemed to guess that they were newlyweds, tried to push alcohol upon them in the form of champagne, but they stuck to water. Finally it was time to go back to the cottage and the four-poster double bed they were to share again tonight.

"Margaret, do you understand your wifely duty in bed?"

"I know I am to sleep with you. Didn't we do so last night?"

"We slept together side by side, but marriage entails something more. If we don't carry through on that, we shall have no children."

"My mother told me they came from sleeping together."

"Not quite." Her innocence thrilled him. She looked at him with her large pale blue eyes—eyes almost gray—with trust and adoration. He stroked her fine hair from her forehead. "I'll take care of everything. You must lift up your nightgown, close your eyes and part your limbs."

It was difficult to push into her. She cried out in pain. "Patience, my Margaret. We must persist."

She bit her hand and turned her face to the side while tears rolled slowly from her eyes. This was true womanhood. He was so proud of her, enduring his onslaught without a word of reproach. He kept hammering at the opening and finally something tore and he could force himself in. He had to rest for several minutes and wait to recover his manhood. He was fearful he would not be able to continue, for the pounding had been painful for him also. He had entirely wilted. Margaret did not move but lay patiently enduring. An image flashed through his mind, an illustration from *The Lustful Turk* in which a buxom wench was being had by the Turk himself. She clung to a bedpost entirely naked, her voluptuous buttocks outthrust while the Turk, wearing a nightshirt, his member exposed, pushed into her from behind.

Now he was firm again and could proceed. It was a matter of seconds before he discharged with a groan and withdrew. He kissed her brow, then lay back down beside her, taking her hand in his own. Her hand was chilly in spite of the warmth of the night. "You were very brave, my Maggie." He felt the need to give her a pet name, now that she was entirely his.

"Is that it?" she asked. "Or need we do more?"

"That was sufficient."

"Good," she said, then gently disengaged her hand.

NINETEEN

THE COMMODORE WENT off to Saratoga Springs in August, as was his habit, but this time he took Tennie with him to his suite in the so-called cottage wing of the United States Hotel. Its north porch was called the millionaires' piazza. Tennie cajoled him into inviting Victoria and the Colonel up for a week. The United States Hotel was built around a large garden with a tall plume of fountain in the center, every bench and promenade crowded with ladies in fine muslins or pale lawn carrying parasols among the elm trees. The men lounged about in top hats, some in white velvet or silk suits. Victoria had never seen so much extravagant finery. The ladies seemed to change their dresses on the hour: the morning promenade in one outfit, lunch in another, change for tea, again for dinner, then for an evening concert or dance, plus special outfits for picnics, the races, day excursions. Even strolling under the elms, even taking the waters, ladies wore rubies, diamonds, sapphires, pearls. They glittered as they flitted, daughters on display to make good matches, bored wives hoping for a discreet affair while their husbands were in the city tending to business, rich men's mistresses almost accepted here and certainly highly visible. Tennie told her women arrived with twenty trunks of clothing. The sisters could not hope to match that elegance, but men did not seem to look at them any the less for their simple attire as they promenaded on Broadway. Every morning, there were open-air concerts where people paid far more attention to each other than to the music. It was a popular time for discussing the horses that were to run in the afternoon, for flirting and arranging assignations.

James disappeared into the casino, where she could not follow him since women were not permitted past the ornate parlors. However, nothing kept the women from betting on the races every afternoon. Victoria had a sixth sense about horses. She rarely lost. James had off-and-on luck at roulette, but Victoria made money every day at the track. If they were careful, they could return from this vacation with cash they desperately needed. The races were the high point of her day. It was a dusty walk to the track, the road jammed with four-in-hands, phaetons, farouches and every conceivable type of fancy carriage. Often James bought local popcorn for them to nibble on. She liked to watch the thoroughbreds run, but more she liked collecting her winnings and tucking them away. Suppers in the hotel were long and hectic, the dining rooms deafening and overcrowded. Victoria and James ate heartily, for the food was good; even better, it was free: beef à la mode, Cobb ham, turkey with oysters, striped bass with anchovy sauce, ham glacé with champagne sauce, salamis of grouse aux olives, roast partridge with celery sauce, ragout of oxtail with small turnips. They were Vanderbilt's guests and accorded deferential treatment by the staff.

Vanderbilt enjoyed racing his own horses on Bloomingdale Road back in Manhattan better than betting on other men's horses at the track. He took the healing waters regularly and spent a lot of time sending telegrams to his New York office—the hotel had a telegraph line and a ticker-tape machine on which he could keep track of his holdings and the market. It was the first she had ever seen, and he was happy to explain its workings. He found her interest in stocks amusing. "Never met a woman who took an interest. Got one motto, Vickie. Don't buy what you don't want and don't sell what you ain't got. That sums up my Wall Street strategy." She doubted his plans were that simple. She apprenticed herself to him, for stocks seemed to be one way to make a lot of money fast in the galloping bull market of the immediate postwar.

She understood he was advising her against the short selling that Fisk and Gould had as their strategy so often. She saw Jim Fisk with Josie on his arm on Broadway, promenading. It was the first time she had actually laid eyes on Josie's keeper, Vanderbilt's nemesis, although as she had advised him through spirit messages, Fisk and Gould had shown up suddenly at his home offering a truce. Jim Fisk was a huge man, as was the Commodore, equally florid, but Fisk was a dandy. He was wearing a fancy officer's army uniform dripping with gold braid. A diamond stickpin sparkled on his chest. Diamonds glinted on the fob of his gold watch, while Vanderbilt dressed always in the style of thirty years ago, prim and severe and a bit rumpled. Fisk was several decades younger. Women stared from behind fluttering fans as he passed. He was not the sort of man Victoria found attractive, but obviously that was not the case with many of the women eyeing him. He was flamboyant and strutted along the pavement, seeking the attention that surrounded him, followed by a buzz of voices. The world was his stage and he was the principal actor, hero in his own drama. She could understand why Josie thought him a bit of a fool. Yet he did very well for himself. It was said that his father was a simple New England peddler, and that was how he had begun, before the Civil War made his fortune.

Josie and she exchanged glances without speaking. Their connection was mutually advantageous but not for public consumption. Josie was dressed in magenta silk with a larger than usual bustle and a magenta parasol to match; her underskirt was emerald green. He carried a gold-tipped cane he swung jauntily. They were a procession, followed by men in business attire, some in fancy army uniforms.

Beside Victoria under the shade of an elm tree, holding her arm in his, James sneered. "Fisk bought himself a regiment of the National Guard, the Ninth. He loves to dress up like an officer, but he's simply a pig in gold braid," he muttered in her ear. "I heard he's brought the whole band here and is treating them to a weekend of drinking, gambling and womanizing. He loves playing soldier. On board his steamships, he wears an admiral's uniform. What a pretender!"

She was sorry to return to the heat and filth of Manhattan. She envied Tennie staying in the pleasant tree-filled patio of the hotel, in the large dim rooms Vanderbilt rented or sitting on the porch watching fashionable ladies pass in their gowns of the hour, watching the men watch the ladies. She especially missed the races, and the money she had won at them. Back in New York, she went shopping and improved her wardrobe.

However, Tennie did not remain long in Saratoga. A week after James and Victoria returned, the Commodore's wife died. Vanderbilt promptly rushed back to the city to bury her, with his children and their spouses and offspring in attendance, as well as cronies from the Union Club, the stock market, his various railroad and steamship enterprises. He did not encourage the sisters to attend. No matter, Tennie said, sure he would ask her to marry him again, and this time she would accept.

Victoria was not convinced. True, the Commodore was not overly nice about social matters. She doubted that any of the scandalous doings that could be dug up about Tennie, the Claflins or herself would ruffle Vanderbilt, but she doubted that his family would feel the same way about a young wife they must regard as a fortune-hunter.

Tennie had met William, his oldest son, whom he had recently decided was not the idiot he had always judged him. The old man was using William now to run one of his railroads and to sit on boards he wanted to keep a sharp eye on. William, in turn, kept a hard watch on what the old man did. Victoria did not think the Commodore was aware how carefully his presumably well-controlled heirs monitored his activities, but she was conscious of their scrutiny. They worried more about Tennie than about her; after all, her relations with Vanderbilt were limited to giving him messages from the spirits. Vanderbilt had bedded governesses for years, but he had never had an official mistress. Tennie was widely seen in that role. He dined with her most nights at Delmonico's or Niblo's Garden in the Metropolitan Hotel, with its live shrubs, its statues of nymphs and shepherdesses, its arches illuminated by gaslight. Never had the Commodore dined out so frequently and never with the same woman. Yet it was known that Tennie lived with Victoria, Colonel Blood and Victoria's family, so it did not seem that the Commodore was keeping her. There was a good deal of gossip about what their arrangement might be. Some said he had already married her, but to Victoria's regret, that was hardly the case. Tennie reported he was talking marriage again, but not in a pressing way. She was careful not to seem eager. She played the old boy along. "Don't play him too long," Victoria warned.

"Listen, if I seem the slightest bit eager, he'll toss me off. The less eager I seem, the hotter he is. I have to stay something of a prize, something to be won." They were dressing to go to the theater with James.

"I hope you're right. But we need a second-tier plan, in case he doesn't marry you."

"Maybe he can set us up in some business? I'd just as soon make my own money." Tennie's hair crackled as she brushed it, lush and electric. "He was a brute to his wife. He's a tyrant in his family. I get on with him swimmingly, but he's no prize aside from the money. If he asks me, I'll marry the old goat, but I have no illusions as to what he is."

"You think he'll treat you as badly as he did her?"

"No. She was a breeding machine. He never had much respect for her. He respected his mother. He considered her a shrewd woman with the resources she had available. I strike him as smart and shrewd like his mother.

But believe me, if I annoyed him or crossed him, I'd be on the chopping block fast."

Victoria and Tennie were playing a difficult game, keeping the rest of the Claflin clan away from the Commodore. Utica was clamoring to meet him, convinced her charms would brush Tennie aside. Roxanne was simply jealous. She had never forgiven James for marrying her daughter, and she thought the sisters spent far too much time with Vanderbilt. She was not the sharpest, but she was loyal and passionate in her devotion to them. Victoria would never hurt or offend her mother if she could avoid it.

One advantage of her marriage to Canning had been that he had schooled her in the demeanor and voice patterns of a lady. She had taught Tennie. Tennie's style was more colorful than her own—more in the direction of a successful courtesan perhaps—but Victoria used her own charm and beauty carefully, creating an image of power and reticence. She might appear wellborn—but any public appearance of the Claflins would destroy the impression she painstakingly cultivated.

The winter passed much as the summer and fall had. They spent a great deal of time with the Commodore, but Victoria was also pursuing acquaintances among writers, both literary and political, among artists. She was slowly coming to know and mingle with a variety of interesting men and women. She was studying the political and intellectual life of New York, always asking questions, always interested, charming whomever she could and collecting information and ideas. She practiced speaking clearly and movingly. After all, as a child she had fascinated audiences with her messages from the spirit world. New York represented a more cynical and sophisticated audience, but one she could impress with her eloquence and passion—when the time came. A few women had learned to capture an audience. She heard Susan B. Anthony speak and also Elizabeth Cady Stanton, who was magnificent and compelling. Both worked the Lyceum circuit, lecturing. There was money to be made there.

She had the gift of memorization that had stood her so well on the stage, where she had learned to project her voice to an audience. She had learned to endure and even to enjoy all those gazes fixed upon her. She had learned to handle herself before a crowd and to win them over. She studied rhetoric and delivery, standing before the pier mirror in her room. She tried various gestures, noting which seemed fluid and natural and which appeared stagy. All through the winter and spring locked in her room, she practiced her new art.

James and she had taken separate rooms, for he was troubled by nightmares and often cried aloud or struck out wildly in his sleep. It was also convenient for her, since she could practice oratory without waking him, and when she took a lover she could see him privately. She had the gift for taking lovers and letting them go without injuring their pride. A woman trying to make her way to fame and fortune could never have too many friends. She was attracted not by flash or wealth or power, but by knowledge. Every lover was also her mentor, her educator. Her lack of education took a great deal of energy and discipline to overcome. That most women were also ill educated was of no import. She had a role to play in history. She felt a particular interest in politics and economics, fields that she had been told were foreign to women. She had a reform mission she was born for. Sometimes of late she thought it might have to do with women. Stanton's speeches moved her. Stanton had spoken not only of votes for women but of women's role in the family, in marriage, in childbearing, in child-rearing, spoken about divorce and contraception. Stanton had spoken sympathetically and movingly about working women; had not Victoria been working since she was little? She would like to meet Stanton, but she did not yet know anyone in her circle. She must make that meeting happen, but there was time. The first step was still money.

If Tennie was in charge of the Commodore's body, Victoria was the only woman with whom he talked finance. He took quite seriously the advice and information the spirits passed on. Victoria never told him anything without a discussion afterward of what it might mean for his holdings and his strategy in the market. Every conversation taught her more about finance. He obviously found it exciting to talk with an attractive woman about what meant the most to him—a novelty he enjoyed. She was educating herself for investment at the same time that she was making him dependent on her tips.

The next summer, the Commodore went off to Saratoga, but he did not take Tennie. His son William insisted on accompanying him, claiming family business. Tennie was put out, but there was little she could do. The Commodore had been talking marriage again. "We should get hitched in the fall," he said. "I got to deal with my family and the upshot of the Erie business, but when I get back to New York we'll do it. Okay?"

Tennie felt the time was ripe. It was a year since his wife had died. "Yes, old boy, yes. I have thought about it long and hard, and I think I'd make a good wife for you. I'm willing to devote myself body and soul to keeping you happy and healthy."

"Good girl. I'll see you as soon as my namby-pamby son gets off my back. For a weak-minded dolt, he can be a real mule. He's bringing his wife and kids and half my idiot relatives. Even my drunken wastrel son Corny." Vanderbilt began to pace in his sunny bedroom, the best room in the mansion on Washington Place. He strode up and down, puffing and roaring like one of his steam locomotives. "Corny drives me crazy. Runs up bills and expects me to pay them. When I won't, he uses the Vanderbilt name to borrow money. That publisher Horace Greeley bails him out every time. I told Greeley I don't give a hoot, I'll be damned if I'll pay Corny's bills. But Greeley says he doesn't expect to be paid back, and then he goes on doling out money to Corny as if the fool isn't going to spend it on high living and be broke again by the following Monday."

"No use getting so upset, old boy. Every family has a black sheep. Corny is yours, but at least he hasn't shot anybody. Be thankful he's just a ne'er-do-well and not an outlaw or something worse."

So Vanderbilt went off to Saratoga grumbling about William spoiling his vacation. They did not hear from him until they read in the papers that Cornelius Vanderbilt Sr. had eloped to Canada with his second cousin called Frankie and married her.

Tennie threw the newspaper across the room, cursing like a sailor. "Shhh!" Victoria shook her head. "We can still use him. Don't yell or Buck will get involved."

"He promised to marry *me*! How could he do this? I never heard of this damned cousin."

"I suspect his son William was behind it. Found her acceptable and sicced her on the Commodore."

Tennie paced, tearing at her hair. "He asked me to marry him and I accepted. How could he run off with another woman?"

"I suggest as soon as he returns to New York, you go to his office and ask him. Politely but firmly. No scenes but straight-up questions. I'll go with you, if that would help. We don't want him to dump us. It's too late to scream about him getting married—it's done. We have to keep up a good relationship and wish him the best."

Tennie picked up a chinoiserie vase Utica had bought and threw it into the fireplace, where it exploded into shards. "I'd like to break his neck. But I won't, I'll be treacle. Maybe we can turn this to our advantage. At least I don't have to be a wife. I'm not real keen on wifehood, you know."

Victoria picked up the pieces of china and put them into a folded paper. "We'll see what this wife is like, how hard she tries to push us out of his life. And his pockets. If we can make him feel just moderately guilty, I have an idea how he might help us. And make us rich into the bargain. And that's what we really want, isn't it?"

TWENTY

ELIZABETH AND SUSAN sat side by side in a train that was not moving, although it was still belching black smoke and soot back on them. It was too hot to shut the window, so they sat there half choked and getting filthier by the minute. Word came back that the engine had hit a horse. "Poor thing!" Elizabeth said, for she loved horses still. "It's not fair to them. What do they know of trains?"

Susan took out her pocket watch and looked at it with a resigned sigh. "We're going to be late. We won't have time to eat."

"The food we've been getting on this trip, it's healthier to go hungry." Elizabeth wiped her forehead with a handkerchief no longer clean or white.

"I only hope the audience waits for us. The agent said we were sold out."

"Ah!" Elizabeth cried out in pleasure as the train lurched forward. But then it stopped again. "Enough of this sitting about." She rose and made her way along the railroad car. She spied a mother with a baby, and at once engaged her. The baby, a girl, was cranky in the heat. Elizabeth talked the mother into loosening the swaddling bands. Soon she had the little girl bouncing in her arms and chortling. Then, standing in the aisle with the baby, she talked with the woman about raising a daughter. She next got into conversation with a federal land agent about homesteading. Finally she chatted with an ex-soldier who had lost an arm at Manassas. All the other women were huddled in their seats fanning themselves, but she never saw any reason not to get to know fellow travelers.

With a great lurch the train finally got under way and they were once again rushing across the cornfields at a great clip, perhaps twenty-five miles an hour. It was too noisy to talk, so she went over her speech, one of three she had given in town after town all over Missouri and Ohio and now would give again and again in Wisconsin, each time tweaking it a little. It kept things fresh. A local reference. A little anecdote. A new joke.

The train pulled into Beloit an hour and forty minutes late. A committee of three women and five men was waiting for them in the station. By the time everyone had been introduced—Elizabeth had a method of remembering names for a few hours that consisted of picking out one physical characteristic of each person (mole on chin; bushy eyebrows that meet; red hair that looks dyed; sparrow mannerisms) and fixing the name to that—it was time to go directly to the opera house. One of the women handed her a sandwich of homemade bread and ham which she ate in the open wagon as they rattled and bumped along.

"We have a good crowd." Elizabeth peeked out from behind the dusty plush curtain. "I do prefer it when the seats are full."

"It's the same amount of work for forty people as it is for four hundred." Susan was polishing her glasses.

Susan spoke first. When Elizabeth came out from behind the curtain, she beamed at the audience as if she were about to give them a treat. Excitement, controversy, humor, warmth and practical advice. As she stood at the podium with the gaslights glaring on her, she loved the heat of the crowd beating back. It was electrifying, no matter how many times she gave a speech ninety percent the same from town to town. That feeling of the crowd stirred up, excited, even at times angry: it was like nothing else. That had been Henry's vice too, but now he had cut himself off because of his chicanery in office when he had been given the plum of customs official. He was jealous of the attention paid to her, as once she had envied him his freedom.

THE UNION AND CENTRAL PACIFIC railroads had met at Promontory Point and the continent was crossed, joined east to west by railroad and telegraph. All over the States, there were parades and fireworks. Elizabeth and Amelia traveled into Manhattan with Harriot and Robbie to see the celebration. They would spend the night in the flat where Henry lived, for this was too momentous an occasion for the children to miss. After the parade, there were hours of oratory while the kids grew cranky. At last after sunset the fireworks filled the sky over the harbor and although Harriot covered her ears at the detonations, she oohed and aahed along with Robbie at the bright exploding flowers zooming toward them. Henry had been holding forth on how important this link across the continent was to business. It was a relief to have the blasts drown him out. All that seemed left of their great love affair—besides the children, of course—was his capacity to annoy her.

BACK IN TENAFLY the next day, Elizabeth sat at the dining room table with Amelia answering letters piled up over the past two months. Elizabeth was never sure whom she would count as her closest companion, Amelia or Susan. Susan was her intellectual and political companion, but Amelia shared everything that went on in the household.

Amelia picked up the letters waiting to be put into envelopes and stamped. The recipients were on their own translating Elizabeth's scrawl, but in order to be sure the letters could pass through the post office, Amelia wrote the addresses in her neat sloping hand. A hundred times, Elizabeth thought she should dictate her correspondence to Amelia, whose handwriting was so legible Elizabeth could read it upside down. "Julius," Amelia said—it was a nickname out of adolescence. Only her oldest friends called her that—"why do thee sign thy full name on every single letter even to thine own sisters? Elizabeth Cady Stanton—as if they wouldn't know."

"I fight constantly to keep my square foot of ground. You're Amelia Willard in the morning, at noon and in the night. But if you married tomorrow, Amelia, say you married John Brown—"

"He was a good man in his heart but a violent one. And he was married. He had several sons—"

"All right, tomorrow morning you marry John Smith—"

"Didn't he marry Priscilla Alden? I'll not be committing bigamy, Julius, not even for thee."

"Stop it!" She made a mock slap at Amelia. "Now you marry John Smith and five minutes later you're no longer Amelia Willard. You vanish from the face of the earth. You're Mrs. John Smith—a mere appendage. He's swollen and you've shrunk."

"But Lucy Stone is still Lucy Stone, as she was born."

"That's one of the strongest things she ever did. Nowadays she fears to cross a single Republican politician or a single husband who's worried what will happen if the divorce or property laws change. . . ." Elizabeth drew a deep breath and smiled at Amelia. Amelia was neither plump like herself nor lean and bony like Susan, but a middle-of-the-weight, middle-of-the-road woman, strong-backed, strong-armed but of a sweet disposition—even if a little too inclined to tease her. "That's why I sign my full name. Only my enemies call me Mrs. Henry Stanton—to make me not exist."

"Thee hast many first names, however. Elizabeth. Julius. Two of thy school friends call thee Johnston after thy hometown. Thy sisters call thee Libby, as does Lucretia Mott. Thy husband used to call thee Lizzie Lee—"

"In the days when we were truly man and wife." Elizabeth sighed heavily, signing another letter and passing it to Amelia. "That's to Lucretia. I hope to see her again in a couple of weeks."

"Thee wrote her just the day before yesterday."

"I keep her apprised of all that's going on. Philadelphia is just too far away. I want her in the next room." She stood and walked to the windows, open on the warm October day. The maples were beginning to turn golden in the yard. Blue and lavender New England asters were blooming in beds she could see from the window, as were the hundreds of tiny flowers of white boltonia. "In another life, I would have time to garden. I'd grow beds and beds of flowers."

"In another life, thee might be a fierce tiger and leap upon the men who frustrate thee so. That I can see before Julius in her rose garden."

"I wouldn't mind rending a few limb from limb. Back to the correspondence." Next a group wanting to be part of the National Woman Suffrage Association. Elizabeth wrote the same letter she did to all such, Welcome. Any group that wanted to join had only to let them know. She scrawled a reply and went on to the next. Susan usually handled the correspondence—for one thing, her handwriting was legible—but she was on the road lecturing.

"Why do thy old friends call thee Julius? I've always wondered about that."

"In a school play, I was Julius Caesar and they all got to stab me. My friend Mary said I had his temperament and would make a great general." Elizabeth scribbled another reply. "Susan and I are generals. Although lately we're losing every battle. When they passed that damned Fifteenth Amendment that brought the word 'male' into the Constitution for the first time, I knew it would take us fifty years to get it out. I won't live to see that."

"Perhaps like Moses on Pisgah Mountain, thee will see the land of equality even if thee fears not to live in it."

She put down the pen. "The matter of a woman's name is not trivial, Amelia. Slaves have no names but what their masters give them. Sambo McNaught signifies the Negro belonging to Master McNaught. Similarly, a woman's name disappears upon marriage because she becomes property too. So it matters what a woman is called."

Ever since the meeting of the National Woman Suffrage Association in January in Washington, groups had been asking to join. That did not include the Boston women. Lucy Stone had aligned with Julia Ward Howe to organize their own association. Lucretia had been invited but had refused. Susan and Elizabeth had pointedly not been asked. The New England women were going to organize a new national suffrage organization this winter, to rival the National. They would include men and would take great care to do nothing that went against the Republican Party's agenda. Elizabeth propped her head on her hand. "Do these letters never end? Susan does so well with this. I'll be glad when she's back. Three more weeks!"

SUSAN RETURNED FROM her lecture tour and slept in her room for eighteen hours straight. When she finally woke, Elizabeth had Amelia bring up breakfast. Susan sat up in bed staring at the tray, reaching for her glasses on the bedside table. Elizabeth took a seat in a rocking chair by the window and grinned at her. "You're having breakfast in bed, Susan dear. Let me coddle you a bit."

"We can't afford to get soft, Mrs. Stanton. We must keep our backs straight and our heads high."

"Outside the house. Today and tomorrow, you put your feet up, you relax for once and I'll make you chocolate pudding. We have strategy to discuss. We have a war to plan. I have news from Boston. Lucy Stone refuses to share leadership with me. I offered to resign—"

"Mrs. Stanton, you cannot!"

"She didn't care. She won't participate in any organization in which her husband cannot vote. Apparently she's worried about male suffrage. Perhaps that will be their new plank."

"Who else is involved besides Lucy and Julia? And Lucy's hubby, Henry."

"Chalk up another Henry—Henry Ward Beecher, the passionate preacher."

"Is Tilton involved? Has he turned against us?"

"He's trying to negotiate a truce. No, he hasn't deserted us. Yet, anyhow. He has some bone to pick with Beecher. Therefore, though Beecher may be the dog who wags the tail, Tilton will not wag this time."

"We should go see him this week."

"Agreed. Now, Lucy has lined up Abby Kelly and a bunch of other New Englanders, that's it so far. They've called a convention in Cleveland in two weeks."

Susan climbed out of bed, setting the tray aside. "I'll bathe and make plans to attend."

"We've very purposely not been invited, my dear."

"I'd like to see them keep me out. I intend to march in as if I expected a welcome, and I intend to give a speech. Tomorrow, write it for me. They shall not hold their convention without me unless they carry me out bodily."

Amelia came to collect the tray. "Thee has little to worry about on that score. I can't imagine the women's convention that would oust Susan B. Anthony."

Elizabeth patted Susan's hand. "I find these endless conventions boring as tea parties. I'm going to abstain from them."

"Mrs. Stanton, you cannot do that! You can't abandon the movement."

"Conventions aren't the movement. We want to reach women all over the States, on the frontier, in Western towns. The women who go to these conventions are already for suffrage even if they don't see eye to eye with you and me."

"But you cannot give over the movement to the New England caucus overloaded with husbands and male preachers."

"Oh, I'll go now and then. But I'm finished attending every single convention ten women in Knoxville decide to hold."

"I'll go to Cleveland and assume they'll let me speak. I'll be meek and mild but state our position unwaveringly."

Amelia laughed. "Thee will march in with banners flying, oh Susan, angels of fire in thy hair. Thee has still thy Quaker meekness with all the stubbornness underneath we conceal in our little gray dresses like so many Protestant nuns. Ah, but don't we know how to make ourselves heard when that small still voice speaks through us? If I were a gambling woman, I would bet upon thee, Susan."

Elizabeth stood on her lawn under the trees whose leaves had mostly fallen, except for a few parched remnants clinging to the oaks. She drew her coat about her and tucked her hands into her old muff. She was not dressed for going out in public, wearing an old serge dress much mended and scruffy boots, for the grass was damp. A dank wind picked at her but the air felt clean, unlike the city air she would be breathing this time tomorrow. Susan would leave in the morning early, then she would get herself organized to go into the city to the *Revolution* office.

She was happiest in Tenafly, where sometimes when Susan was here with Amelia present and her favorite daughter Harriot she felt as if she had created a little paradise of women. In her house they could be free together. In her house they could govern themselves. In her house, their ideas were listened to, taken seriously, discussed, improved upon. The rest of their lives was war, but here she found peace and a reasonable amount of plenty. It revived her. It fed her. It enabled her to go on.

TWENTY-ONE

OVER THE NEXT MONTH and a half, Freydeh and Sam canvassed the neighbors of the house where Shaineh was said to have lived. Most of them had never met her; some were new to the area; some spoke no language Freydeh or Sam understood. An old man told them the body of a woman had been found in the building by the team of firemen who had won the battle with another firehouse to squirt water on the fire and then loot the ruins. Freydeh refused to believe that was Shaineh. It could have been any woman living in the three burned houses.

Freydeh's English had been improving under Sam's tutelage. In the fall, she had sent him to school. When he came home, they worked together or he ran errands, getting supplies or distributing to their customers. They cut their prices to a bare profit to compete with those already established in the business, and they were not yet as fast as they needed to be. Still, they paid their rent, they had enough to eat. Gradually she was improving Sam's wardrobe as well as her own. He had difficulty learning to wear shoes, for he had been barefoot in all weather for years. He complained that boots hurt his feet. He developed bleeding blisters, but she would not let him go shoeless any longer. "Long as you're barefoot, you mark yourself a street kid. Nobody will trust you with orders. You don't live in a box in an alley any longer."

She had new wool mittens she had knitted from good yarn, and when she crawled into her bed at night her stomach no longer growled with emptiness. Sam had his own cot in the front room. They had slowly acquired a skillet, glasses and cups and a pillow apiece, a better kerosene lamp. The vision that Moishe and she had brought with them to the New World of a better and more ample life was slowly coming to pass. She had written to Sara, her older sister married and with three children already, to tell her what had happened with Shaineh and ask if she knew where Shaineh was. At last Sara wrote back a bitter letter, not understanding how big a city Manhattan was, berating Freydeh and saying she had heard from Shaineh, who was working as a seamstress and living on Varick Street. That was the burned-out house.

Finally, in December, they found a woman who had known Shaineh, an Irishwoman of maybe twenty and wary with them. She asked them as many questions as they asked her. Freydeh said she worked in a pharmacy and Sammy kept his mouth shut. Finally the woman sat them down and gave them some tea.

"How could you speak with her? She didn't know English," Sammy said.

"Sure and she did. She had an accent thicker than a brick, but she could talk with me fine as you."

"Do you know what happened? Was she hurt in the fire?" Freydeh wrung her hands in frustration. She wanted to shake the answers from the woman.

The woman scrutinized her carefully, squinting a little. Then she seemed to come to a decision. "She ran away."

"From the fire, you mean?"

"From that scummy Yankee who was keeping her. He was a brute. He locked her in. Sometimes she'd be hungry, poor thing, and my brother would get money from her through the window, then bring her food. It was nailed so she couldn't get out the window, just open it a mite."

"She didn't get burned in the fire?"

"One of the men broke in the door and let her out and she ran with just the clothes on her back and what she could carry in her wee hand. But she was in the female way."

"With child?" Freydeh asked.

The woman nodded. "She ran to get away from him. That's all I know."

"Do you know his name?"

"I only saw him coming and going. He called her Samantha, but she told my brother that wasn't her name. She said her name meant pretty. And for sure, she's a pretty little thing. Tiny hands and feet and golden hair."

Freydeh was a little surprised. Shaineh had dainty hands and feet but her hair was a light brown. "I thank you, Mrs. Connor. You've been a big help. I knew she wasn't dead. I knew it."

"Well, you keep looking for her, 'cause a lot of bad things can happen to a pretty little thing like her in this place."

"That man sounds like one of the bad things."

Mrs. Connor nodded. "The saints be with you. Keep looking. Don't ye lose heart."

"Now what?" Sammy said when they trudged off down the street. A light snow had begun to fall again. Even horse piss froze almost as soon as it dropped in the street, and the patties of manure steamed in the frigid air. In winter, the air felt cleaner in the city, but the streets were almost impassible, with heaps of filthy snow and ice mixed with what didn't bear thinking about. Still the traffic of carts kept clattering and clanking past all day and all night. They dodged them as they crossed each street.

"If she's with child, she probably can't afford to have it. So she'll have to seek a remedy. Madame Restell is the best. I'll start with her. She knows me, if she remembers—and that woman has a memory that files every face and name away in its crevices. I used to buy remedies from her when I worked for Yonkelman."

With Sammy in school during the days and orders beginning to come in as fast as they could fill them, it was several weeks before Freydeh could go to see Madame Restell, the most famous abortionist in New York City. Finally she trotted off to Chambers Street, near Greenwich Street, where Madame lived and practiced. Chambers was a fashionable street lined with brick houses not nearly so tall as the tenements Freydeh was used to. It was paved and obviously the garbage was picked up here. Someone had cleared most of the sidewalks of snow and offal. The house was next door to a station house of the police, but Madame had remarked to her that she got on perfectly well with them, and unless some politician or clergyman was making a momentary fuss, they were friendly and peaceable together. However, the neighborhood was obviously not as fine as it had been. There were businesses moving in and signs for professionals appeared in parlor-story windows. But the worst intrusion was a depot for the Hudson Railroad, whose trains she could plainly hear, causing the windows along the street to rattle.

The fine brick house in which she had been accustomed to find Madame Restell was still there, still well kept, but Madame was no longer using it for business. Her husband, Charles Lohman (now calling himself Dr. E. Melreau, although so far as she knew his background was as a printer), had an office there where he made up patent medicines. His receptionist informed her that the family was living and Madame was operating in a new mansion way uptown on Fifth Avenue.

That was a trip that required more time off than Freydeh could manage for several weeks. She was a little nervous about going all the way up there, where the rich people lived. She didn't want to keep Sammy out of school when he had so much catching up to do, but she didn't want to venture into that foreign territory without him and his good speaking. She could make herself understood to Yankees now, but she had a thick accent and anybody could tell she was an immigrant. With other immigrants, so what? But traveling up where the fancy people lived and spoke so fine, she wanted Sammy with her. He was a smart lad, she had always known that, and he could write now and do sums. It was good for him to get an education, but it did take up lots of his time.

Christmas came and went. The Yankees made a fuss about it and so did the Germans who weren't Jewish. She had heard that even some of the German Jews celebrated it. So what was to celebrate? They were worse fools than she had thought. Not all the goyim made such a fuss. She didn't see the Hungarians or the Italians making much of it. Still, the holiday decorations made her uneasy. Meanwhile, the market for the condoms they were manufacturing grew. They were beginning to get a reputation for good quality and cheap price that kept their customers buying and brought them new ones. Every week a new pharmacy or bookstore or rubber goods store would start ordering from them.

January came in with fierce weather and one storm after another. It was February before they could set out to locate Madame Restell's mansion. The rich were building up near the new Central Park. What was it central to? It was miles uptown. A German couple in their building had gone ice-skating there. It was a new fad. People put metal things like knives on their feet and went scooting around on the ice. Sammy was intrigued. She had gone in a sleigh on the ice of the river near her shtetl many times, but she was sure she would fall on her face if she tried those weird shoes with knives on the bottom. Her neighbors hadn't felt comfortable in the new park. They said there were nothing but swells and ladies dressed up in furs who gave them the evil eye as they skated around. It was a nice park, but only the rich belonged there. There were so many rules of what a person could and couldn't do that it was pointless to go all that way, for ordinary folk just couldn't enjoy themselves or be at their ease.

During a February thaw, she waited for Sammy at his school, grabbed his arm and they were off by horsecar to find Madame Restell. They were heading for Fifth Avenue and Fifty-second Street. She was not sure that Madame Restell, who had always been genial and friendly in the past while she was conducting her business on Chambers Street, would be glad to see her uptown. That Freydeh was a Jew had never seemed to bother Madame, who appeared to lack the common social snobberies and prejudices. But now it might be different. They might spend an hour getting up to Fifty-second Street only to have Madame or more likely a servant slam the door in their faces. Still she had to try. If Madame would talk with her and it turned out she had never seen Shaineh, still Madame would know the other abortionists Freydeh could visit.

After the horsecar deposited them by the unfinished great cathedral the local Catholics were building, they made their way over ridges of frozen mud and slicks of ice, threading past piles of lumber and bricks, great blocks of sandstone and limestone. Everywhere buildings were going up, mostly fine mansions. Madame already had hers. Across from a Catholic orphanage with grounds of stately trees, she had an imposing pile, almost, to Freydeh's eyes, a castle. It was built of brownstone, four stories tall with expansive gardens, now sere and bleak, a fountain shut off for the winter, stables, a carriage house. Madame had done well for herself, obviously, and she was willing to proclaim it to the world, in the same way that she advertised her trade openly in the newspapers. She was a woman who did not believe she had anything to be ashamed of, and she would not hide herself or her good fortune.

"Are we really going in there?" For once, Sammy's confidence was quelled.

Freydeh too was intimidated by the front door, framed with balconies and approached by a flight of wide shallow steps with balustrades on either side. All the windows had identical flowered satin draperies and fancy shades. She kept walking around to the side. There it was: another entrance, not a servants' entrance but for clients. It bore a silver plate saying APPOINTMENTS. Behind the iron fence through the gate that stood open, a path led to an elegant door with a bell pull. Grinding her teeth with anxiety, Freydeh marched toward the door. "Maybe you should wait outside." She pointed to a bench that sat beside the flagstone walk.

"You don't want me to come in?"

"Wait. I know Madame, if she remembers me."

She was let in by a servant in livery and led to a fancy reception room, all walnut-paneled with bronze statuary, a Persian carpet, leather and plush chairs. Madame's circulars were on every little table. A female assistant of late middle age whom she remembered from the Chambers office greeted her and asked her what she wanted.

She explained that she knew Madame and that she had come not for help for herself but in an effort to find her sister, whom she had lost track of and whom she thought Madame may well have helped when she was in the family way. She needed to find her, and she hoped that Madame would be willing to help her.

"Madame isn't here."

"Will she be back soon?"

"Every day at this time, weather permitting, she takes her team and rides in the park."

"Central Park."

The woman nodded. "It has miles of fine carriageways. Madame loves riding in an open carriage and taking the air."

"Should I wait for her?"

"We don't schedule any more appointments until five. Why don't you return then? Or you could simply wait. It's only half an hour."

"I'll return in just a little tiny while."

She hastened outside and found a very cold Sammy huddled on the bench. She brought him up to date and they walked briskly along Fifth Avenue. Near the entrance to the park, a vendor was selling hot coffee and corn cakes. Freydeh treated Sammy to both, to warm him up, and then they strolled on. Much of the neighborhood was still raw building sites, some thick with scrub, some with foundations or walls going up, some with finished mansions. Horses were dragging drays piled high with building supplies and the noise of hammer and saw, of cursing and singing and yelling rang in their ears. There was a sharp smell of horse urine and sawdust.

As they were returning, Sammy said, "Wow, look at that!"

She recognized Madame, riding in an open carriage being driven by a very large light Negro gentleman in full livery who held the reins on a snow white horse and a shiny black horse, stepping along in perfect symmetry, hoof by hoof. Silver bells jangled on their harnesses. Madame was wearing white fur with her hands in a fur muff and an elaborate hat covered with white plumes on her head. She passed them without looking and the carriage turned into Fifty-second Street. They followed behind, walking slowly so as to give her time to get inside and change if she needed to.

As the sun began to set, it got colder. Freydeh did not think she could leave Sammy outside. The waiting room was warm although she did not see a fireplace. How was it heated? Every part of the room seemed warm. She muttered a question to Sammy in Yiddish and he pointed to a metal object. "The heat's coming from there."

A young and attractive woman entered. "Madame can see you now. But the boy will have to wait."

Sammy shrugged and took one of the plush seats. He looked content to wait in the warm well-furnished room. She followed the woman into the next office and took the chair pointed out to her, across from a large mahogany desk. The room had medical textbooks and anatomy charts here and there. It was even more luxurious than the outer office. The carpet was a fine Oriental and there was a painting of swans on a pond. She was admiring the room when Madame bustled in. She was still a fine-looking woman with black hair, a striking face and a full figure held erect, although she had begun to age a little. Her abundant dark hair had one streak of white. She wore a mauve flowered moiré silk and an orchid on her bosom. Madame was living like the rich lady she presumably was.

"You have perhaps a problem that brings you to me? Why don't you tell me about it?"

Freydeh began to talk about her sister when Madame interrupted her. "I remember you. Yes, I'm sure of it. Didn't you used to come to me to buy pills and potions for a pharmacy? You didn't speak much English but you always had a note from the pharmacist and you did the sums quickly in your head. I remember that."

"Yeah, that was me, Madame."

"Do you still work for that pharmacy?"

"No, I work on my own. I make male protectors—condoms. Four different kinds, I make now. Good quality and cheap."

Madame laughed. "That's a good line for a woman. You'll make money. Keep at it, and you may be doing as well as I am someday." She propped her hands on the desk. "Do you have a sample of your work?"

Freydeh dug in her carryall and pulled out a packet.

Madame Restell carefully unwrapped a condom and tested it on her hand. She examined the workmanship carefully. "You do an excellent job. Good for you. And why are you carrying them with you?"

Freydeh laughed. "Not for use by me. If I see a rubber goods store or a pharmacy, I stop and show them my wares to see if I can make a sale."

"Good business practice. You have a head for it."

"I want to make enough for a little house and my sister to live with me—and my nephew Sammy, who's waiting outside."

"You have no children?"

"My husband died five years ago. I'm a widow. And when he was killed, I lost my baby."

"I have one daughter."

"Is that her I met? She has a resemblance to you."

"You've learned to speak well since we last met. Good for you. When I arrived here, I had an English country accent—hardly anyone could understand me. So I learned to speak the way the New Yorkers do, and now nobody knows I wasn't born here. . . . No, that's my granddaughter. I do think there's a resemblance, more than with my own daughter. She lives with me—she and my grandson, Charlie. They are precious to me. Caroline helps me with the practice."

"You're lucky, Madame."

"Well, I can afford them. Thousands of women who come to me can't feed another mouth. But you know, what you do and what I do are against the law now."

"Madame, you must have protection? You advertise. You don't live under a rock."

"Far from it!" Madame Restell laughed. She had a full melodious laugh that shook her shoulders and made her eyes gleam. "I shock them down to their bootheels. When I drive in the park in my carriage, the fine ladies look away. They come to me heavily veiled, but they come. And they pay dearly. But their husbands come to me socially—the judges, the police commissioner, the politicians, the lawyers, they come to my at-homes, they come to my parties. You and I, Mrs. Levin, we have our use to society. They pretend otherwise, but they need us as much as they need their policemen and their cooks and butlers. They scorn us, but they can't live without us. The society would be overrun with shame, with unwanted children, with bastards, with even more homeless children wandering the streets starving. Women would be thrown out into the street by their parents, by their husbands. We save them in our different ways, but we both save their lives and their honor and their futures."

"Back in the little village where I grew up, midwives did what you do, and the men never knew of it. It was our business, the women, when to have children, when not to have children."

Madame nodded. "It used to be that way. But young women come to the city now and they don't know how to protect themselves. They get into trouble and they don't know what to do. The world has changed, Mrs. Levin, maybe not for the better."

"The world here's so different. I can't make my older sister understand this isn't some little place where I can find my missing sister."

"So that's what you came to me for. You believe she was with child and needed to get rid of her troubles."

"I don't know if she came to you, but I got to find her." She told Restell the whole story. Restell did not hurry her along but listened carefully. Then she examined the drawing Freydeh always carried.

"I recognize her. She called herself Samantha. Let me check my records." She rang a bell under her desk and the young woman appeared. "Caroline, find me the records of a Samantha I think it was Leibowitz?"

Freydeh nodded.

Caroline bobbed a little curtsy and disappeared behind a massive door. She was gone for some minutes.

"You keep records of every woman you help?"

"I do. Carefully hidden. No one searching this house would find them. But I view them as a kind of insurance. Not the names and records of women like your sister. She had little money, as I recall. I charge poor women twenty dollars and rich women a hundred or more. Nowadays, up here, I get mostly the hundred-dollar trade. But I still help women who most need it. I was not born to money, you understand. I earned it the hard way. I was born in poverty and worked as a domestic servant. I'm not ashamed of that any more than I feel shame for how I made my money."

"We all get by how we can, Madame."

Caroline at last returned with some papers. Madame took them from her and through a pince-nez read them. "Your sister was four and a half months along. I could not help her. I begged her not to try to lose the baby—it was too late. She wept but I think she understood me."

"Do you know where she is?"

"She gave me an address. Caroline, would you write it down for Mrs. Levin?"

The young woman wrote carefully in an ornate hand and then gave her the piece of paper. She smiled shyly as she handed it over. She did look like a younger, slighter version of Restell.

"Madame, thank you. I hope I find my sister. And maybe a new child."

"She should have delivered this month or very soon. She's a pretty young woman, but her hair is lighter than in your drawing."

"It didn't used to be."

Madame smiled. "Many things are not what they used to be, Mrs. Levin. Be well and I hope you find your sister. You're a rarely sensible woman. It was a pleasure seeing you again."

Caroline rose and showed Freydeh out. They picked up Sammy on the way, rousing him, for he had fallen asleep in the overstuffed plush chair near the metal object that gave off so much heat. "What makes this house so warm?" Freydeh asked Madame's granddaughter.

"We have a furnace."

"A furnace?"

"Central heating. . . . I remember when we had only a Franklin stove." Caroline smiled at her. "Madame must think a great deal of you to give you such an interview. She is all business with most of the women who come. She doesn't have many women friends these days."

"She is kind. We understand each other."

"Well, good luck to you. Should you need her again, I imagine my grandmother would be glad to see you."

"Thank you, sweet one." Freydeh touched her cheek. "You're as pretty as my Shaineh, my little sister. It's her I'm looking for."

TWENTY-TWO

THROUGHOUT LATE SUMMER and early fall of 1869, Victoria and Tennessee continued to see the Commodore regularly. Except for the fact that he was married and his new wife wanted them to move uptown where other rich people lived, only the frequency with which they saw Vanderbilt changed. He now dined with his new wife some evenings, but he also dined with the two of them often enough. He continued his liaison with Tennie, who acquiesced for the possible advantages.

"I doubt I would have been comfortable as Mrs. Vanderbilt. The old boy is something mad about bossing his people around. And I'd like a younger husband, frankly, if I have to have one. One I wouldn't have to spend half an hour getting hard." They were working on hats. Women wore extravagant big hats with dead birds, plumes, whole gardens of artificial flowers bedecking them. The basic hats they had bought cheap downtown from a pushcart, but the decorations were up to them, as neither was about to spend a lot of money at a milliner's. Upstairs, Roxanne was praying in loud singsong to protect her dear children from the dreadful snares of this wicked city and return them all safely to Ohio. In the next room, Buck was playing whist with two men Utica had brought by while Zulu watched. She was an observant little girl, a trait Victoria encouraged.

"It's all water under the bridge now. We need him. Something big is happening with the gold market and I'm trying to pump Josie about exactly what it is."

"Fisk is behind it? The old boy has a bee up his rump about Fisk and Gould." Tennie put on the hat she had finished, sashaying into the next room to twirl in front of the men. They applauded and Zulu followed her back in.

"Gould is playing some complicated game with gold. Trying to get the facts out of Josie without appearing to pump her is taking forever. Fisk just bought her a brownstone on Twenty-third Street, right near Castle Erie—the Pike Opera House where Gould and Fisk have offices. If Josie used her brains, she'd be rich in her own right." She patted Zulu on the cheek. "Be smart, my darling, whatever else you become."

"Well, Vickie, you have brains enough for the two of us."

"You're not stupid. Don't ever let anyone tell you that you are. You're just a little careless and overly loquacious at times. It's part of your charm."

"What is lo . . . loquashus?" Zulu asked.

Victoria explained. She had endless patience with her daughter. "Where's Byron?"

"He's sleeping on the couch." Zulu pointed to the next room.

"Thank you, precious." Victoria ruffled her hair, dark as her own now. "You should always keep on eye on him, because unlike you and me, he can't take care of himself. He's helpless as a newborn kitten."

"Not really," Zulu said, looking her mother in the eye. "He's strong. He grabbed my arm and left a bruise."

"Let me see. Oh, precious, he didn't mean to hurt you. But I'll try to teach him to be more careful. Sometimes, you know, he does understand. He wants to please."

"I know, Mommy. Don't worry." Zulu came and laid her head in Victoria's lap, next to the feathers she was attaching to a swoopy black hat.

Victoria stroked her hair. From the next room came loud voices arguing about a play. Buck was cursing and there was a clatter as he knocked his chair to the floor. Victoria sighed. They were bored. She must think of something for them to do before her family caused trouble.

"Papa," she said when things had calmed down. "It would be ever so helpful if you'd go down to Wall Street and listen to the sidewalk brokers. Hear what they're talking about. Sometimes you pick up good information. Would you mind doing that?"

"I'll get on my finery." Buck liked acting the part of investor. Sometimes she gave him a twenty to play with. The streets around the Exchange were crowded with the lesser fish of Wall Street, the fly-by-night brokers, the men who had gambled and lost and wanted to gamble again, the little operators who had no office or even a desk to call their own. Sometimes Buck came back with useful rumors, who was buying, who was selling what, who was said to be trying to corner something. Victoria believed she could never have too much information. Josie was a better source, when she paid attention, but Buck was more reliable in transmitting what he heard. She had bought him a fine frock coat, shirts and boots in which he looked respectable; by now, many sidewalk brokers recognized him. They thought him one of them or a possible investor. Victoria had begun quietly playing the market through the Commodore. Sometimes she followed his advice, but occasionally she took a flier on her own. She had a fortune to make. Vanderbilt already had his.

Jubilee Jim Fisk and the little ferret Gould were planning something, Vanderbilt knew it, she knew it, and half Wall Street knew it. Buck came home to supper with rumors that Gould was trying to corner gold. Gold was central to finance in every country that operated in the capital markets, a currency recognized worldwide. Merchants doing business abroad had to pay in gold, for paper money was no good in Europe or in the far-flung European empires. Once the United States had been on the gold standard, but the Civil War had thrown that out. The government was minting twenty-dollar gold coins, but it had proclaimed that all debts could be paid in paper money, of which it issued four hundred million. Paper money was generally regarded as worth only about two-thirds of gold specie. There was a regular trade in gold and greenbacks carried out in the Gold Room just off Wall Street. It was big business, often conducted on the slimmest of margins. Gould said a man with a hundred thousand in cash could do business for twenty million in gold if his credit was good. She had been listening to Vanderbilt for the last year and a half, gently grilling him about the market and investments until she felt she had begun to grasp finance.

She reported what she had learned to the Commodore Thursday at Delmonico's, where he had brought the sisters for an unfashionably early supper. "I keep hearing that Gould is buying gold, trying to corner it. How can he do that?"

The Commodore chuckled. "I'm betting he can't."

"Why does he think he can? Fisk is in on it too."

"Let's say I sell some locomotives in Birmingham, England. The sale is in gold, but I don't get it right away. They can't telegraph me gold. So if the price of gold drops while I'm twiddling my thumbs waiting for the payment to arrive, I'm screwed. So I cover my ass by selling short in gold. If the price of gold drops, I'll make my profit on the short selling—buying gold I don't have on speculation that people will be dumping it. If the price of gold rises, I'll be beaten on my short, but I'll be covered by the increased worth of the payment coming my way. See? Either way, the merchant makes his profit."

Victoria picked at her lamb. She was far more interested in the conversation than in the food. Tennie was eating roast beef with zest, paying little heed to the conversation, but careful to beam and make eyes at the Commodore while she dined at his expense. "How do Gould and Fisk fit into this picture?"

"They plan to buy up all the gold they can, and then when the merchants who have plenty of money short the gold, they can squeeze the bejesus out of them. They hope to fleece them like so many little lambs."

"So will you join them in the attempt to corner gold?"

"The government has a hundred million in gold in the vaults in this city. If Grant wants to, he can throw a spanner in their engine and it will blow up in their faces. It's sticky and tricky. I plan to keep an eye on those dogs, but I won't jump in until I see how the wind blows."

She was not satisfied with Vanderbilt's take on the situation. She decided to lay out her knowledge before Annie Wood. Together they would figure out what they needed to know. If Fisk and Gould were going to make a killing, so was she. According to the Commodore, not a lot of capital was needed to make money if the scheme worked. That was perfect for her.

Annie listened carefully, drinking more of her dark coffee than she normally did and pouring it liberally for Victoria. Sun streamed into the conservatory where they sat by the statue of Daphne. It was September, no hint of fall in the air but the heat and the humidity of full summer lay like a sodden carpet on the city. A servant girl fanned them as they sat mulling over what Victoria had pieced together.

"One of my clients, a judge in the Tammany machine, let something drop about Gould buying himself a bank along with Fisk and a bunch of the Tweed cronies. Tenth National Bank. It's a small bank as banks go, but they must have a reason for wanting it. Gould always has deep reasons. He never buys for the sake of acquisition."

Victoria felt as if she were on castors, going back and forth, back and forth between her sources of information and the Commodore, who snapped to attention. "A bank? I didn't notice that. It's a small unimportant bank, but this is interesting. The little weasel is smarter than I thought."

"In what way?"

"Okay, he wants to corner gold. Now a bank can issue certified checks. Everybody treats them as good as cash. So he has an unlimited supply of fake cash, don't you see? It's a variation on the old Erie Railroad swindle where he did me in by printing stock as fast as his damned presses could slosh it out. He's going to do the same with certified checks for buying gold."

"The man is brilliant, you must admit."

"He's a scoundrel and he can crash the market single-handed—or two-handed, him and Jubilee Jim with the five-carat stickpin flashing. They're crooks. But they're able crooks, I'll give them that."

Victoria understood that the Commodore considered this game of Gould and Fisk a dirty one, but to her that could not matter, as this looked to be her only chance. She made a great fuss over Josie, who was always hungry for flattery, and she and Annie bided their time, trying to understand the game. Victoria took all the money she had to buy gold. Everyone knew that she was a favorite of the Commodore, and she was extended credit beyond reason. The gold traders and brokers either thought she was a front for Vanderbilt or suspected he was backing her. As a married woman, she had to carry out her transactions in Colonel Blood's name. He was caught up by her gold fever and borrowed from his brother in New Jersey. It was a dangerous strategy. Usually such opportunities and such information were kept from women, or spilled only to frivolous women like Josie who could not comprehend what was at stake.

In a rare sign of confidence, Buck gave her his winnings at whist, poker and faro to invest. Every day she woke more on edge. Josie remarked that the president was in the bag because Gould and Fisk were thick with Grant's brother-in-law, Abel Corbin, a speculator and lawyer to whom Grant was grateful because he had married his middle-aged spinster sister. Corbin was living just off Madison Square, quite near Erie Castle, and Gould and Fisk dropped in on him daily. The president and Mrs. Grant had been guests of the Corbins several times since the marriage, at which it was said Grant had told Corbin, Ask me for anything! Now apparently he was getting his wish, for Corbin was up to his neck in gold-buying, along with Gould and Fisk. They had to be sure that Grant would not release a flood of gold from the government's vaults and thus drive the price of gold back down. Every day it edged upward. Grant had let Fisk give him passage on his steamship *The Narragansett,* putting the president and his wife up in the sumptuous bridal suite. Everyone in New York thought Gould and Fisk had the president in their pocket, for he had sat in Fisk's box at the Opera House and Fisk and Gould had called on him while he was visiting the Corbins.

The Commodore was not so sure. He thought Grant was suspicious of Gould, although he didn't seem to mind Fisk. "But what could a real general make of Jubilee Jim in his fake admiral's uniform? He'd judge him a blustery faking fool, Vickie. We'll see, we'll see."

Still, when the spirits through Victoria advised Vanderbilt that it was time to buy gold, he bought. Victoria was more nervous than ever, but if she was right, she could not leave the Commodore out. If she made money, so must he, or he would not forgive her. If they lost, her own money and her source of patronage would vanish at once.

Victoria felt as if she were wearing a path between Annie's and the Commodore's. She also began to call on Josie in the brownstone Fisk had bought her. She came with flowers or bonbons or little china dogs for Josie. Josie had a live yappy little Pomeranian and miniature dogs on every table and in a special glass curio cabinet. Josie was not the most stimulating company, but Victoria could not do without her inside track. Josie was flattered by Victoria's attentions. She had admired Victoria since San Francisco. She was lonely in the house with its satin chaise lounges, its huge dreadful oil paintings of naked nymphs as fleshy as Josie alternating with sentimental portraits of children in gossamer finery, its stuffed birds and doggy bric-a-brac on every surface, bronze satyrs, vases and Moorish footstools and peacock feathers in still more vases, mirror-backed shelves covered with china dogs of every size and breed. With half this money, Victoria knew she could create a luxurious but livable domicile.

First she had to make that money, and to succeed in her enormous flier in gold, she had to keep abreast of exactly what was happening with Gould and Fisk. She had briefly considered trying to get close to one or the other, but she could not encroach on Josie's territory—she was scrupulous with her women friends, always, even ones as silly as Josie. Gould, she had learned, was a family man with no vices besides his total lack of morals in the marketplace. He rushed home to his wife and daughters without fail. He had never taken a mistress or even flirted with another woman to anyone's knowledge.

The price of gold had sunk as the harvest came in, and she bought whatever she could. But she had nothing to back up most of what she had bought on the slimmest of margins, and if the plan fell apart, she could do nothing but flee. She would have to collect her family and abscond in the night, as they had so many times after the failure of one bad scheme or another. This was her one big opportunity; where could she go if she failed in New York? Europe?

Annie was buying too. They were gambling together, so they could not save each other if they foundered. It was dangerous. Victoria had no leisure to pursue culture or even to read a new and interesting book. Her days were spent running from source to source. She was having trouble sleeping. She would wake soaked with sweat or freezing in spite of the heat of the season.

The president once again passed through New York and stayed with the Corbins. Gould lent Grant's party a private railroad car to Pennsylvania. Everyone said that Grant was in Gould's pocket and that he was in on the gold manipulation. Vanderbilt invested nine million. She was in for two million herself, on scant assets. Now Gould had Fisk play the bull and conspicuously buy gold, to pump up the price daily.

Then the president wrote Corbin an angry letter telling him to stop his speculations and leave him out of it. Grant had had enough scandal and didn't crave more. He was, Victoria thought, a naïve man politically, but he wasn't an idiot and he had finally guessed what had occasioned Fisk and Gould's presents and favors. Wednesday morning, September 22,

Corbin called Gould and Fisk to him to give them the bad news, and it was reported, by Josie who had it all secondhand from Jim Fisk, that Corbin had wept and pleaded with them to take the gold off his hands. Gould refused, but offered him a compromise if he would keep the president's rebuff a secret. That he did, but it was no secret to Josie, who heard it all in bed, and thus no secret to Victoria. Thursday morning Gould and Fisk met at Josie's, where they felt no one would overhear them, to plan a strategy to sell off the bulk of their gold secretly, while pretending to bull up the gold market further.

Victoria came by in the afternoon with a great bouquet of the pink roses Josie liked, a bottle of Boal Madeira and a honey cake. Over the course of the wine and cake, Josie told her of all the excitement and speculation swirling around the two men.

She sent a note to the Commodore saying that the spirits had an urgent message for him. His own mother had appeared before her in the daytime to relay it, so she felt it must be important. He sent her back a scrawled note saying to come at seven-thirty to his house. So far his wife had not objected to the visits of either of the sisters. Victoria considered that Frankie might be a very bright woman indeed. She seemed to possess a keen grasp of what was dangerous and what was to her advantage. Victoria wished Frankie nothing but the best.

His revered mother, Victoria told him in trance, said that he must sell when gold reached $150 and not wait a penny more, even though it might momentarily go higher. Vanderbilt seemed startled and thoughtful when she came out of her induced trance. "Was the news bad?" she asked, careful to maintain the illusion.

"Could be good. We'll see tomorrow. I got to move carefully, on eggshells, so's nobody gets wind of what I'm doing. If you've taken a flurry in gold, I advise you to sell slowly and by various hands. Spread it around, but get out now."

Friday, Victoria drove down to the Exchange with James in a rented carriage. If all went well today, soon she would buy her own. When gold opened at $150, James left her in the carriage and went to carry out the selling. She had orders with a couple of brokers to do the same. The price continued to rise. She had never seen such excitement in the crowds of men pushing each other off the sidewalks and into the street, speculators gone mad with excitement, some desperate to cover their shorts, others madly buying on the assumption that gold was being cornered and would soon rise to $200. Men rushed about in the clear hot September morning, gesticulating, yelling, grimly silent. She saw Josie in sky blue and mauve sitting with Fisk in his carriage. He seemed calm. He was on top of the action. He appeared to be buying, but she was sure he was secretly selling too. Then at one point he entered the Gold Room and sent the carriage away with Josie.

The frenzy continued past noon. Then, shortly after one, the local representative of the U.S. Treasury announced that Grant had ordered the government to sell four million in gold. The price began to drop. It dropped and it dropped and it dropped. Victoria tried to figure out how they had done. When James joined her in the carriage and they began to work their way out of the mob of angry, hysterical speculators, James brought out a small pad and did the arithmetic. If their sums were correct, they had cleared over seven hundred thousand dollars. Vanderbilt too should be grateful.

This was only the beginning. She had an idea that she had been waiting to suggest to him, waiting until he was properly in her debt for her advice and she could claim a great favor. She held James's hand as the carriage struggled through the pond of men pushing each other and shoving and screaming in their frustration and rage. Many speculators had been ruined today, and not a few fine merchants. Gould and Fisk had much to answer for, but she was for the moment well satisfied. The spirits had told her years ago that she would be rich. Now she was. The next step was to be famous, and then to change the world. She held James's gloved hand in hers and smiled at him. They were both feeling wonderful, she could tell, and they would go home, drink champagne and go to bed together. Then they would make plans—a fine house, a carriage, appropriate furniture and furnishings, a tutor for Zulu Maud, a caretaker for Byron who would be kind to him and keep him from getting in trouble when she was out. And an office from which she could carry out her plans, her new project that she intended to confide in James that evening before she approached the Commodore. The papers were full of "Black Friday" and the resulting panic, the ruin of banks, brokerage houses and merchants, the suicides of some. The newsboys were crying themselves hoarse in the streets. She wondered how Fisk and Gould had done. Josie would tell her soon enough.

1870

TWENTY-THREE

ELIZABETH HELD OUT a crisp white envelope of heavy paper that had come in the morning mail. "Look what the mailman brought."

Susan put on her spectacles to examine the writing. "Paula, it seems. Why are you looking like a cat in cream?"

"The youngest of the Beecher sisters, Isabella Beecher Hooker, has shown some interest lately in woman's rights. . . ."

Susan frowned. "I'd rather get hold of Harriet Beecher Stowe."

"Paula's Isabella's friend. She wants Isabella to be ours too."

"It's fine to make friends, but she's been buried in domesticity for years. *Harriet* is world-famous. I suspect the American group made Henry Ward Beecher their president in order to rope her in, for she adores her brother."

"Isabella is supposed to be a bit more independent. Paula thinks she'd be an asset if we could wean her away from the Boston ladies." Isabella had written for the *Revolution,* but Elizabeth had never met her. Until recently, nobody had known Isabella, one of two nondescript Beecher sisters, as opposed to Harriet, the famous author, and Catherine, who wrote books of advice Elizabeth could not abide. If a woman did everything in the household as Catherine laid out her duties, she'd never read a book, never hear a piece of music, never have a thought that did not pertain to the correct method of bleaching muslin or laying out the silverware for an important dinner. Harriet was harder to pin down—a strong abolitionist with some interest in suffrage, but pride in being a Beecher, daughter of a prominent minister, sister of seven prominent ministers, with a lot of the lady nonsense that vitiated so many wellborn women. Elizabeth was not sure how she had escaped it herself, but she was too strongly opinionated, too sensual perhaps, to fit into the rigid mold of the proper lady. Harriet probably was too, but she expected propriety of other women. However, she had recently broken every rule when she decided to champion Lord Byron's wife and to reveal Byron's incest with his half sister. A lady was never supposed to think of such things, to know about them, and certainly if she had the misfortune of doing so, never to reveal such unseemly facts in public.

Paula wanted to bring them together with Isabella in her palatial house in Providence. Elizabeth never begrudged Paula the fortune she had married, for she used her money for the cause. Whether Isabella Beecher Hooker turned out to be as interesting as Paula claimed or whether she proved to be too timid to be of use, Elizabeth felt she owed it to Paula to get on the train and chug off to Providence.

Paula had an Italianate mansion on College Hill, near the grave of Roger Williams, for whom Elizabeth had a great deal of respect. She felt in his tolerance of all beliefs and his unwillingness to have any religion declared the established one of the settlement he founded, he had been far ahead of his time and perhaps well ahead of hers, in which there was a strong movement to have Christianity declared the official religion and God introduced into all manner of legislation.

It was relaxing to visit Paula, to have fine meals served on Limoges china and spotless linen tablecloths, to have baths drawn for them and their clothes taken away, cleaned, mended, ironed, all invisibly, silently as if the labor of a household which she had worn herself out doing for so many years were here carried out by elves. Such labor could never be truly invisible to her, but Paula was used to luxury. Isabella was there when they arrived, a woman of small stature with well-coiffed brown hair, just a trace of gray at forty-six, large slightly fixed gray eyes, thin and bony in spite of having borne three children. Elizabeth rather envied Isabella, because with each of her own seven children, she had put on weight she had never taken off.

Isabella was obviously wary of them, no doubt having been fed tales of how they were man-hating fiends wearing trousers and smoking cigars, as suffragists were always pictured in newspapers. Elizabeth had no idea if Isabella might become a friend, but she would try to neutralize her. They talked of their children, their upbringing, their schooling, their health problems, their marriages and families. Two of Isabella's children were married. One boy was still at home. Isabella spoke lovingly of her husband, John Hooker, a successful lawyer. Elizabeth could tell from Isabella's questions that she did not know that Elizabeth and her husband were separated. Unlike Elizabeth, Isabella had never supported herself or her children, so she had little interest in the economic problems of poor or working women. She did, however, exhibit a keen grasp of constitutional law and the arguments for women's right to vote. Her mind was sharp and well organized. Elizabeth compared notes with Susan.

"She's able," Susan said. "She could be a good speaker. She doesn't seem to have the timidity that makes so many of our sisters unable to speak in public and say what they mean outright and powerfully."

"Paula says she's gushing over you. You tell me you have no charm, Susan, but women are always getting crushes on you. You disarm and then you mesmerize."

"Nonsense! I'm approachable and friendly. I'm like a comfortable chair. That's all, Mrs. Stanton. You're the one who sparkles."

"Well, we've both been working on her, and we may be getting someplace."

Susan gave her a certain smile that made Elizabeth feel the world had promise after all. "I think we may win her."

INDEED, WHEN THEY RETURNED to Tenafly, an affectionate letter from Isabella arrived with a note from Paula shortly thereafter telling them, "Isabella won't break with the Boston faction, for some are old friends, but she will not hear slander of either of you from them."

Within a month, Isabella organized a woman's rights convention in Hartford. Elizabeth was heartily sick of conventions, but she went with Susan, as Isabella was inviting both the Boston and the New York factions, hoping to reconcile them. Within an hour of their arrival, it was clear that Lucy Stone could scarcely bear the sight of them. William Lloyd Garrison called Elizabeth an ingrate to her face. He was accustomed to being the grand old man of the abolitionist movement and he expected deference, even reverence. Elizabeth remembered how badly he had treated Frederick Douglass years before, when Douglass had started a newspaper Garrison considered a rival to his own. "Abolitionists," she said sotto voce to Susan, "want us to remain in chains of gratitude. They think they created us." Elizabeth looked over at Garrison, who had come because Isabella had called this convention and she was a Beecher, the same reason the Boston contingent attended. Garrison was glaring at them from under his impressive brows. Lucy Stone, wearing a plain black dress with a white bodice, with her hair pulled back as Susan wore hers, pretended she did not see them. Lucy's husband, Henry Blackwell, brushed past them without a glance. Isabella sped about from one group to the other trying to bring them together.

Isabella obviously adored Susan, but she confided in Elizabeth that she thought Susan's problem was lacking a husband. Elizabeth felt like laughing, but she controlled herself. "Don't you think her spinsterhood frees her? Enables her to travel and choose without coercion what she will or will not put her energies into?"

"Motherhood is our strength," Isabella said. "It is the basis of our potentiality. It is because we are mothers that we care for others, for the world, for the future as we care for our own offspring. We are finer than men because we are more connected to the generative power. Susan has relinquished that power. It's noble of her. A more dignified, more authentic woman I do not know, but she hasn't experienced her own power because of her spinsterhood."

Elizabeth thought of her children, beloved consumers of her time, her energy, her intelligence. They had almost eaten her alive. Motherhood had given her joy and pain, sweetness and sorrow, but she could not see how motherhood had given her power. Perhaps women had power in the sense that a woman could harm her babies, could turn into Medea and kill—but fathers did so as often or oftener. She considered Isabella's glorification of motherhood a fantasy, but she was not going to fight about it. If Isabella wanted to feel superior to Susan because she had a husband and Susan had none, let Isabella enjoy her opinions.

Husbands had many overt and subtle ways of influencing their wives: getting them pregnant, controlling how much money was doled out for household expenses, giving or withdrawing their presence, moving a woman out of a comfortable and stimulating situation into a small town where she seemed weird for having a notion in her head, making fun of the wife's projects, making sure she lacked time to carry them out, playing on her weaknesses. Isabella had a supportive husband in John Hooker, who seemed to encourage her feminist activities, but he was one in ten thousand.

Still, she was grateful to Isabella for trying to make peace, for the cause would be better served if they all pulled together. Isabella reminded Elizabeth of herself when she had begun to be active outside the round of drudgery in the house, but John Hooker had provided far more abundantly than Henry had been able to. Elizabeth noticed that Isabella had the full range of complaints that better-off women seemed prone to suffer. Prone was the word, Elizabeth thought as she surveyed Isabella across the room full of attentive women dwelling on Isabella's speech about the constitutional basis of woman's rights. Isabella suffered from excessive menstrual flow, a displaced uterus, headaches, back pains, dyspepsia, constipation, nasal polyps, a diseased nervous system. The excessive menstrual flow was probably one of those common symptoms of menopause that Elizabeth had endured for a year or two. She herself had been healthy until her last child, dropping her babies with hardly a pause. Henry had said she was like a peasant woman, who had her child and went out to plow the field an hour later. He had not said that with admiration. Her hardiness shocked him. Ladies were not so vigorous. But Isabella, all that neurasthenia aside, seemed to have plenty of energy for what she really wanted to do. Perhaps Isabella's problems were due to tight corseting. Boredom was the lot of many women kept by well-off husbands and confined to the home.

Isabella was drawn to Susan and to her because they were radical, because they championed causes that shocked other women. Isabella could not resist the excitement of breaking taboos. The American had a hierarchical structure based on delegates. Members had to be elected from local organizations, turned into auxiliaries of the American. Elizabeth privately thought this structure represented the influence of the many men involved in running the American. The National was intentionally much looser. Anyone who paid a dollar to join and attended meetings had a vote. The National had minimal structure, all women from bottom to top. Elizabeth overheard Henry Ward Beecher telling Isabella that her Connecticut organization must join the American. Isabella's brows drew together as she stretched her long aristocratic neck and narrowed her eyes at her half brother. "I do not consider such affiliation necessary. Our organization's growing. We don't need to be anyone's auxiliary."

"If you affiliate with the National, you'll be tarred with the brush of radicalism. Cady Stanton and Anthony are dangerous women." Henry tossed his head, letting his long hair swirl. He was going bald on top but made up for it with extra length all around. He had a strong build and a strong face. Elizabeth noticed several women gazing at him over their fans with passionate interest. She viewed him with a strong splash of skepticism, but he was catnip to many women. He exuded a kind of animal magnetism and energy.

"They were friends of yours not long ago. They used to dine with you."

"They have plunged into dangerous waters. Their demands are scandalous."

"More scandalous than our sister's publication of Byron's sins? Really! I hardly think so." Isabella was smiling sweetly but her foot tapped under the outermost petticoat of striped blue and silver silk.

"I don't approve. Harriet makes wild mistakes at times. But she's writing for my paper now, not for the *Revolution*. Such a violent name."

"The revolution whose benefits we enjoy daily was fought with guns, Henry, not with lace handkerchiefs." Isabella turned on her dainty heel and with a swishing of multiple petticoats under her overskirt of fine blue velvet, swept away, looking flushed and proud of herself.

"We have a convert in Isabella," Elizabeth said to Susan.

"There is fire in her soul, Mrs. Stanton. You will see."

"You may be right. If she'll help us with our bills, I'll adore her too."

The American shortly brought out its own periodical, the *Women's Journal,* dealing only with suffrage and printed on fine paper with a heft to it that reeked respectability. It was well financed, well distributed and designed to appeal to professional women—doctors, lawyers, educators, teachers, women running businesses—and to club women. It said with every inch of print, suffrage is nice, suffrage is safe, you can be a lady and support suffrage. Elizabeth ground her teeth. The American would draw most of the money available. The Republican Party would be satisfied with it, the men married to suffragists would be satisfied with it, they would hold endless meetings debating who to let in and who to keep out. It would be a long tea party and club meeting. She would have merged the groups if she could, but not at the price of becoming respectable and banging away at one issue only and letting all the other problems and concerns of women go hang.

TWENTY-FOUR

NTHONY WAS PROUD of their fine house in Brooklyn. One of their neighbors was H. B. Spelman, whose son-in-law John Rockefeller was in the oil business. Anthony had already made Mr. Spelman's acquaintance. Although he was a Baptist, not a Congregationalist, Spelman did seem an honest Christian gentleman and should prove a good neighbor.

Maggie ran the household perfectly with the help of an Irish maid. Anthony did not like her being a papist, but they could not afford to pay much. Although he was a good salesman, the job had begun to bore him. Nor did he see how he could rise in Cochran, McLean. Every morning he caught the ferry across the East River and made his way to Broadway and Grand, then out into the field to sell notions. Every evening he came home on the ferry and rushed to Maggie. She cooked the simple, ample meals that pleased him: roasts, chops, hams, New England boiled dinner, potatoes boiled or mashed, roast turkey or chicken or duck, venison when the butcher had it, boiled cabbage or turnips.

Domesticity was everything he had hoped for. He had a neat clean obedient Christian wife, almost a saint. Twice a month she endured the marital embrace without complaint. He felt calm now, in control of his body and his mind even if his ability to succeed financially was proving a disappointment. He felt destined for far more than being a salesman of ribbons and buttons and laces, but what?

In the meantime, they enjoyed the Clinton Congregational Church, within walking distance of their house. Anthony, who always sought counsel from older, wiser men, had established a deep connection with the pastor, William Ives Budington, a tall lean New Englander with black side-whiskers peppered with white. They understood each other, for they had a similar commitment to rigorous Christianity, to high morality, to fighting Satan in whatever form he appeared to corrupt men and women but especially youth. Budington had been educated at Yale and Andover

Seminary; during the war he had been a delegate in the Christian Commission, another bond between them. Sometimes they talked of the war and its dangers for troops beyond the bullets, grapeshot and cannonballs—the moral dangers. Budington called him "son" and allowed him to visit at night if he was troubled so that they might pray together, kneeling on the floor beside Budington's narrow bed—for the minister was a widower whose wife had died years before in childbirth.

Every Sunday Anthony and Maggie went to church. Then Anthony stayed on to teach a Sunday school class for boys while Maggie prepared Sunday dinner for him and often for Budington. After dinner, Anthony gathered a group to hold a Sunday prayer meeting at a nearby jail while Maggie cleaned up. The lost souls there were sometimes open to the Lord and sometimes obdurate, hardened to a life of crime. His weekends were filled with the Lord's work; his workdays felt trivial by comparison. Still, he must work to keep his wife and support their sweet tidy home. Whenever he walked into the homely parlor Maggie had created, he felt a sense of possession that filled him like a good warm meal. His wife, his piano, his sofa, his heavy draperies, his fine flowered wallpaper, his chandelier. He could sink into the horsehair sofa and close his eyes knowing that Maggie would come shortly and ask him what he needed—a powder for his headache, a glass of lemonade or a cup of tea or to have his forehead or shoulders rubbed. How he loved those attentions. He had been wise to persist in his courtship, for home life was all he had imagined in dreary boardinghouses, in the cold drafty dormitory of the boys' school, in the run-down farmhouse after his mother passed on. He could tell Maggie was happy too, for she often sang while she worked, and sometimes played hymns on the upright piano.

Maggie was naturally maternal. He was sure that soon they would be fruitful and multiply. All that their house lacked was a baby. He was patient. He prayed for a boy to call son, as Budington called him son, to continue his line, to instruct in the proper way to be a man. Soon Maggie would be that way, and out of their true marriage of souls, a child would be born.

Except for the stagnation of his work life, Anthony considered himself truly happy. However, as he was walking back from the prayer meeting at the jailhouse, he passed two saloons open in spite of the Sunday blue laws. This was inexcusable on the Lord's day. The reek of beer and whiskey choked him. Men and women were in there together laughing, singing ribald songs, playing cards. One old salt had a concertina. Two couples were dancing, rubbing their bodies together. He went in search of a policeman and eventually found one, sitting on a bench overlooking the East River. A forty-five-minute search had not put Anthony in a better mood.

"There are two saloons open today against the Sunday laws. It's your duty to close them. Here are the addresses." He handed the policeman, a burly blond man with a scar across his left hand as if from a knife attack, one of his order slips with the addresses of the offending saloons on the back. "I'll go with you, if you need me."

"What would I need you for? You'd be best off not meddling in working people's business. So you want to go to church, go. There's folks that want to go to the saloon on their one day of rest, and I for one am not about to roust them out."

"You refuse to enforce the laws you are sworn to uphold."

"Stick it up your snout. I enforce the real laws—murder, rape, burglary, robbery. Working stiffs having a couple of beers do nobody harm."

"Give me your name, please." Comstock wrote that down on the same receipt that the policeman refused to take. Then he set off for the precinct. He made a complaint against the offensive policeman and also reported the open saloons. He walked briskly home through the spring air, moist and busy with little breezes, the leaves just opening on the trees that lined his street.

The next Sunday, the same two saloons were still wide open, their doors ajar leaking boozy stench from within. Drink weakened the strength and stamina of a man, but worse, it sapped his will to duty. It led him into vile acts his sane self would never sink to. Edward had been led astray by drink, by dives like these, by the company of unclean women, unto his untimely death. He could close his eyes and see those couples rubbing against each other to the wheezing of the concertina, the woman's bosom swinging loosely against the man's chest as she gyrated her hips.

Obviously the police were not inclined to act. The next time he saw his neighbor Mr. Spelman in the street, he stopped him and asked if he might have a moment of his time to discuss a local problem. Mr. Spelman seemed surprised but invited him in. He sat in Mr. Spelman's luxurious parlor, with a grand piano instead of the upright in his own parlor, furnished sumptuously with plush sofas, a brocade fainting lounge, oil paintings of hunting dogs and horses leaping fences. He described the problem succinctly, for he had learned not to waste the time of important men.

"They have obviously corrupted the constabulary." Spelman frowned.

"You'll go to the mayor. I was a heavy contributor to his last election. If I give you a note of introduction stating I'm one hundred percent behind your crusade, I'm confident he will act."

Spelman gave him the letter in a fine envelope sealed with wax and they shook hands. Anthony would steal the time from his salesmanship this very week to make an appointment with the mayor of Brooklyn. That policeman, whose name he still had handy, and that precinct riddled with corruption would soon feel the heat, a foretaste of what was in store for them in the afterlife, where they would burn like living torches. Thinking of hell always made him feel better.

The mayor, a heavyset man with a bald head he must polish like a doorknob, received Anthony cordially, read the letter and said he would do something forthwith about the problem. Anthony was pleased but not convinced. He next went to the Board of Excise. They seemed to take the matter more seriously than the mayor and promised by a unanimous vote that they would shut down the offending saloons.

On Friday, he was walking briskly from the ferry and had just turned onto his street when a short well-muscled man waylaid him. "Anthony Comstock?"

"I am he. And who are you?"

"Randolph Parsons, proprietor and owner of the Lucky Monkey. You're trying to shut me down and take my livelihood, you son of a bitch." The man shook his fist.

Anthony assumed a defensive stance. He knew how to fight and he had forty or fifty pounds and at least six inches on the brute. "You were breaking the law. Lawbreakers deserve to be shut down."

"Sunday's the only day poor folks get to enjoy themselves. What would you know of that?" The man had withdrawn a pace. He reached into his coat and drew out a large nasty pistol. "You lay off me or I'll blow your brains out. You hear me? I pay my protection regular and I deserve to be left in peace to make a decent living for my wife and eight kids. Meddle with me, it's the last stupid thing you'll ever do."

The man returned his pistol to his coat and strode off. Anthony could fight. He was strong and fast, fearing the fists of no man, but a pistol could kill him and then what would happen to Maggie and who would protect this neighborhood? It was full of men like Spelman who would give him verbal support, write a note, shake his hand and perhaps even contribute a dollar or two, but who would never put themselves in danger to protect women and children and the susceptible. He would not walk in fear. In the morning, he went to the mayor to report the threat to his life.

The mayor took it calmly. "Buy yourself a revolver. You may need it for protection if you continue your crusade."

"That's all you have to say? I should descend to the level of the animal who threatened me?"

"You can't expect a police guard, Mr. Comstock. After all, you're trying to take his livelihood. I don't imagine you expect congratulations."

"From him, perhaps not. But from decent citizens."

The mayor sighed, wiping his shiny head with a handkerchief marked with his initials. "You'll find that decent citizens by and large prefer to let others enjoy their vices so long as it doesn't bother them. Even when they like what you're doing, they don't look out for their champions the way that the wicked certainly do."

Anthony bought himself a revolver. He did not wish to start carrying it through the streets like a ruffian, but he had seen the saloon keeper hanging about. Although he had managed to avoid him by circling around and coming through the yard in the next street, he could not keep hiding. The one person who took the threat seriously was Maggie, who wept and clutched him. Tears were rare for her—she was a woman of admirable self-control—but in this case he felt they were justified.

The next week, the man caught him again in the next block. "I warned you to leave me alone, but you keep trying to put me out of business!"

Anthony looked around. Two men were walking along chatting as they carried their briefcases home. He signaled to them, but they immediately turned and retreated up the street. He saw curtains on the houses stir, but no one came out to support him. "I'm obeying the law, as you should."

"You're meddling in my business. You're trying to force my family to starve." The man pulled out his pistol and stuck it into Anthony's face.

Anthony drew out his own revolver. "Back off, lowlife. I was in the army and I know how to use this. Understand?"

They stood with their weapons trained on each other. Finally the man turned and trudged away. "You haven't seen the last of me, you priggy son of a bitch."

"If you malign my mother again, I'll shoot you like a rabid dog," Anthony called after the man. Then he walked on home.

Still, the man could not be left to wave a gun around the streets of Brooklyn. Anthony had moved here, like many of his neighbors, for a quieter, more respectable ambience than Manhattan offered. Anthony again went before the Board of Excise and into the courts in pursuit of justice. He was lucky in his judge, as he found himself facing one who was sympathetic, a Baptist like Mr. Spelman and a teetotaler who despised drunkards. The saloonkeepers were hauled into court.

Anthony was happy to testify. One of the men died of a heart attack during the trial, but the other—his attacker—lost his license. Anthony was pleased. One dead, the other defanged. He was disappointed, however, to see nothing but a three-line summary in the report on the docket of the court. He began to keep a diary to record his triumphs. He took far more satisfaction in his victory over the two merchants of vice than in his daytime job. His boss, however, at Cochran, McLean was not so pleased with him. He called Anthony into his office.

"Your performance this last month leaves much to be desired, Mr. Comstock. You were one of our star salesman, but of late you are fulfilling old customers' orders, not finding new ones. We can't remain stagnant. Other companies are out there competing. If we don't grow, we shrink."

"I have been a little distracted of late," Anthony began. "I have recently married—"

"You married last June. Surely you don't expect me to believe you're still on honeymoon?"

"I've been trying to clean up my neighborhood, to rid it of vice and lawbreaking saloons."

"On your own time. If it interferes with your work for us, then we'll no longer require your services. Dozens of young men are begging for a good job with us. Do I make myself clear?"

"Perfectly. I'll try to give better satisfaction." Anthony sounded meek, but he was angry. Doing the Lord's work was surely more important than selling ribbons and laces. Still, he could not afford to lose this job.

If only he could find some way to support himself and Maggie doing the right thing. That would be a destiny to satisfy him—upholding the law, fighting evildoers, protecting innocent children and young people from the filth of the streets and the temptations that could corrode that innocence quickly enough. He could not sacrifice his family to carry out what Spelman had been kind enough to refer to as his crusade. Surely the Lord would show him how to do both at once without skimping on either duty. The Lord, if he had faith, would provide.

TWENTY-FIVE

REYDEH FOLLOWED UP on the address Madame Restell had given her. Yes, the landlady said, a young pregnant woman had stayed there, claiming her husband was in the West looking for work, but she had grown suspicious and asked her to leave. No, she didn't have a forwarding address.

Every few weeks, Freydeh visited one of the few shuls people from the Pale attended—Polish, Russian or Lithuanian Jews—to ask about Shaineh. Winter passed into spring, spring into summer, summer into fall, and now winter was closing in again. Sammy was doing all right in school. He could write English and do sums and even long division, although the teacher said his spelling was weak. It was hard to dress him as he kept growing. He was taller than Freydeh and his voice was breaking. She redoubled her watch on him, for puberty was a time when the street might call to him again and seduce him from her. He was the only family she had, and she poured out her affection on him.

In January of 1870 at a storefront shul on Clinton she found someone who recognized Shaineh. "Yes, she comes here sometimes with her little girl. She says she's a widow, but maybe her husband deserted her." The rabbi was as young as Freydeh—if she could be called young any longer. "She uses the name Samantha Leibowitz but she told me her name at home was Shaineh." He had a scar running through his brown beard—a scar such as a whip or a saber might leave. She could guess how he had gotten it and why he had left the Pale.

"How old is the little girl?"

"Just a babe in arms. Six months? A pretty little *pisherkeh.*"

"Do you know where I can find my sister?"

"She has a job in a German bakery. Not Jews. She comes so irregularly, I can't tell you more."

She thanked him fervently, again and again. She put a little in the *tsedakah* box. Once she could have used charity herself, but now they were eating enough, with warm coats for the winter. They had quilts, each with a nice little bed. They even hung curtains on the windows so no one from the street could look in. They had decent secondhand boots to keep their feet dry. If only she could find Shaineh and her little girl, she would be happy as a widow could be.

Sammy did most deliveries, fulfilling orders at pharmacies, rubber goods places, the occasional bookstore. But while he was in school, sometimes she had to carry an order over herself. One of those times she ran into her old admirer Izzy White, wizened as a finger left in water too long, a small man with a huge voice booming at her. "So this is my thanks being so nice to you? You go into business as my rival? And what kind of business is this for a woman?"

"A good one, believe me. Yonkelman let me go."

He pointed to the pharmacist. "Old Abey here, he says you undersell me. Well, I got a family to support. I need the money more than you."

"I got a family to support too. My adopted son, my sister, her baby. And how come you said you wasn't married, Izzy, tell me that? Carrying on flirting with me."

"So I find you attractive, sue me."

"So now I undersell you and I make better merchandise." She put her bundle down on the counter and turned to Abe, the pharmacist. "Isn't that so, Mr. Berger?" To him she spoke German. It seemed to her she switched languages every five minutes all day, from Yiddish to German to Russian to English and back to Yiddish again.

"She delivers good product, Izzy," Abe Berger said. "My customers like her stuff. A woman, a man, what do I care? Just so I make my little profit."

She collected her money and swept out of the store. Izzy was right behind her. "I never expected you would end up this way, Freydeleh."

"I ain't ending up yet. I'm still kicking and I'm kicking your behind right now, Izzy. So lay off me."

"You're still a fine-built woman, Freydeleh. I wouldn't mind trying out your merchandise with you."

"I would mind, Izzy. Don't lean on me. I'm a good woman and I don't take no guff from you or anybody else."

"Who is this Sammy Abe says delivers your merchandise?"

"He's my adopted son—an orphan, the child of a woman from my shtetl." How many stories she had told about Sammy already.

She wanted to get rid of Izzy because there was a bakery three blocks from the pharmacy, a German bakery she wanted to visit to ask about Shaineh. Remember to call her Samantha, she told herself.

"You're a user, Freydeh," Izzy said. "You pumped me for information and now you're trying to put me out of business, underselling me. You used me and I wonder how many others!"

She walked fast and Izzy didn't keep up. He turned and left her, muttering to himself. A user. That made her uncomfortable. She could see herself flirting with Izzy to get him to feed her the details of manufacture. She had taken advantage of her job with Yonkelman to learn how the pharmacy business worked. Did she pick Sammy off the streets to use him in her business? It made her dizzy. She could see her whole life one way and then the other. Certainly she wanted a better life for herself, but for Sammy too. Had she taken advantage of Izzy? In a way, yes, but he had tried to take advantage of her. Did that make it better?

In the bakery several women, a man and a dirty little girl were ahead of her. After the woman behind the counter had waited on everyone except Freydeh, she said to the little girl, "Get out of here, you pest."

"Just gimme old bread. Old bread you give to the rats."

"Get out of here. Go beg in the street, you worthless dirty little beast."

"I'm hungry. I'm starving." The girl had a way of wheedling. She was Jewish, Freydeh knew. She was also absolutely filthy. "Just give me some old bread."

The girl had black hair, not dark brown but black, dark eyes of Oriental cast like Jews from Kazan, but her skin, as far as Freydeh could see through the dirt, was milky pale. Freydeh plunked down four cents on the counter. "Give her a roll and give me a roll too." It wouldn't be kosher in here, but she had to buy something.

The girl took the roll and ran out. Freydeh made her usual fruitless inquiry. Nobody worked here but family, the woman said, and never had. She didn't believe in hiring outsiders. And, she said pointedly, looking Freydeh up and down, she certainly wouldn't hire a Jew.

When Freydeh emerged from the shop, about to toss the roll in the gutter, she saw the child licking her fingers as she sat on the curb. "Here, little one." She handed her the other roll.

The girl took it and ate it quickly and totally. "What do you want?"

"What makes you think I want anything?"

She nodded at a group of boys at the end of the street. "They buy me a roll if I let them poke me."

"Poke you?" Suddenly she got the girl's meaning. "How old are you?"

"I dunno. Eight, nine I think?"

"How long have you been on the street?"

The little girl held up two fingers. "It was the summer with the cholera."

"That killed your family?"

"My mama died having a baby. The cholera got my papa. So the landlord put me out and I live in Thieves' Alley."

"Where were your parents from?"

The girl shrugged. "I don't remember. I was born on the boat."

"What's your name?"

"Katie, they call me. My name in school was Katerina but my mama called me Kezia."

"That's your Hebrew name."

The girl looked at her sideways, mistrustful. "That's not true."

Leaning over the girl, Freydeh could see her bruises—on her arms, on her legs, exposed by the torn and too small dress. A bruise on her forehead her long hair almost hid. "Don't be afraid. I'm a Yid too."

Suddenly tears ran from the corners of the girl's eyes. "Everybody hates me. . . . Do you have another roll?"

Freydeh sighed. Sammy was going to kill her, she was an idiot, but she could not leave this child here on the street to be used sexually by the street thugs and beaten and starved. "Come. I'll feed you."

"Do you run a house?"

"What do you mean?"

"Helena, she was on the street with me. She was bigger than me and getting her tits and her hair was red. A woman came and put her in a house where men paid for her. But she got clothes and food. The woman didn't want me. She said I was damaged goods, but I'm stronger than I look."

"I just work making things and selling them. I'm not taking you to do things that are dirty with boys or men who hurt you. Come along, Kezia, if you want to eat and sleep in a bed."

Kezia stared at her, frightened. She made Freydeh think of an alley cat being offered food, ready to grab and run. "What for?"

Freydeh shrugged. "Because a little girl shouldn't be alone and hungry on the streets."

The girl jumped up from the curb. Her eyes were still mistrustful, but Freydeh understood the poor child would follow anybody who offered food and a little warmth. It was lucky she had not been led down to the river to be raped and her throat slit—yet. Freydeh couldn't take in the thousands of children starving on every street, but she could save who she could. That was why Hashem had not given her a baby of her own body with her love Moishe: so she could save Sammy. She would keep trying to find her sister Shaineh, but in the meantime maybe she should take in this little girl. She had money enough to feed Sammy and herself and now Kezia—if she stayed. At least the child could have a meal to fill her belly and be cleaned up.

She would watch the child carefully. Sometimes street life made even a young child bad so that she would steal from someone trying to help her or would harbor a streak of violence so that you could never turn your back. Sometimes the street life was all a child knew, and they would return to what made them feel that that was how things were and would always be. She would have to see if Kezia was able to leave the street behind. In the meantime, the little girl stank of urine and shit and surely had lice. It would be a project to clean her up, for Freydeh would not wash her in the yard but in the privacy of their little flat. She would have to find her clothes. The ones Kezia wore were far too small for her, scarcely decent. She took Kezia's filthy paw in her hand and led her along. The child was barefoot, of course. The temperature was mild today, a fine late October day, but the nights had been chilly. She could imagine the child curled up in her scanty rags in an alley full of rats and human and animal feces, the garbage of years of neglect. Kezia followed her willingly to whatever fate Freydeh intended, probably figuring that anything was an improvement. She had an old scar on her foot and a livid purple bruise on her cheek. Freydeh matched her footsteps to the little girl's and pulled her along gently, never letting go her grip of the small, almost fleshless hand lest Kezia change her mind and bolt as they moved into what had to be foreign territory. "Do you remember where you lived when your papa was alive?"

Kezia pointed with her free hand. "That way."

"You don't have any relatives?"

"I had a brother. He ran away after Papa died."

No help there. "We have five more blocks to go to where I live."

Sammy was home already, studying with a book at the table near the window light. "What's that?"

"A surprise." Freydeh laughed. "This is Kezia. I found her begging at a bakery."

"And you brought her home?"

"Am I for him?" Kezia asked, sucking her dirty thumb.

"No. Maybe he'll be your brother."

"Like hell I will. . . . You took a year and a half knowing me to take me in, and you pick up this thing on the street?"

"I had to decide at once. Now, go get me some water and we'll heat it and clean her up."

She left Kezia and went into the hall with Sammy. "You're special to me. But I couldn't leave her there. I just couldn't. She's been beaten and ravished and starved. I felt it was my destiny to save her."

"Just don't leave any coins lying around."

"It will take a while to tame her, of that I'm sure. She'll have to be taught to be a little girl again."

"She's damaged goods."

"She's a little girl who had a hard life. If it works out, we can make it better. Only the truly evil are damaged beyond repair. Little girls aren't." But she had no idea if Kezia could adapt to life with them.

Kezia was standing in the middle of the floor as if in awe, turning slowly around and staring at everything. "You live here? Just you and him? Nobody else?"

"And now you. Who did you used to live with?"

"My mama and papa and me lived in the kitchen with a family and two other boarders. One of them slept in the kitchen too." Kezia made a face. "I didn't like him. After my mama died, he hurt me."

"No one here is going to hurt you."

"That boy doesn't like me."

"That's Sammy. He will. You'll be a good girl, and everyone will like you just fine, Kezia. I promise you. We all try to help each other here." Why should Kezia trust her? Only desperation held her there while Freydeh boiled water in a kettle on the two-ring coal stove, sent Sammy down for more, stripped Kezia to her waist and began scrubbing the months of dirt. The more she scrubbed, the more bruises and scarring she found. She felt like weeping as she surveyed Kezia's tiny thin body. Besides the bruise on her forehead and the ones on her arms and legs Freydeh had noticed earlier, a scar ran along her back where she had been struck with something sharp and the scab had healed into a long welt. Her thighs were bruised all along the inside, probably from being used sexually.

"Kezia, you have head lice. I'm going to shave your head. You'll look funny for a couple of weeks, but then your beautiful hair will grow back and you won't have lice."

"You have to cut off all my hair?"

"Look." Freydeh caught one of the lice between her nails and showed it to Kezia. "Your head is covered with these. They've been biting you."

Kezia nodded, tears in her eyes. "All my hair?"

"Just this once. Otherwise we'll all have head lice before the week is up." She wanted to hug the poor child, but she did not want to frighten Kezia, and it was also necessary to clean and delouse the girl before she was huggable. She wrapped Kezia in an old dress of her own—one she would have to boil afterward. Eventually Kezia was clean and her head shaven. Freydeh dressed the wounds she could and rubbed salve on the bruises. Then she fed Kezia bread and cheese and put on a stew to cook.

"I'll go to the market tomorrow and find you some clothes. Yours will have to go." She had Sammy carry them down to the street and discard them, for the seams were full of lice and fleas. She cut part of her old dress into a sort of shift, pinned under the girl's arms.

"What's all that for?" Kezia was pointing at the rack of rubber sheets, the metal table, the vat for vulcanizing and the forms for making condoms.

"We make rubber goods for a living. We make them here and we sell them to pharmacies and other stores. . . . Have you ever gone to school, Kezia?"

She nodded. "When Papa was alive."

"Can you read and write?"

"I read a little bit. I know the alphabet. But I don't know how to write. . . . Are you mad at me?"

"No! But we'll try to get you into school."

Sammy frowned. "She has to do some work. She's no good to us."

"I can do things!" Kezia shouted at him. "I can fetch water. I can cut up things. I used to help my mama cook."

"It will all work out," Freydeh promised, looking at the bone-thin waif with her body covered with old and new bruises and her head shaven like a clay bowl. She did not know how it would work out, but Hashem had put this little one in her path, and she accepted responsibility. If Kezia would try, she would try and they would make it work. After a while, Sammy would come round. He had a good heart. He would have to make room in it for this raw little *pisherkeh*.

After supper, she put Kezia to sleep in her bed and occupied herself sewing her old dress into a little one for Kezia. The spare material could be bindings to wrap her legs. She had to find a used dress and a shawl—that would be a start. They didn't let barefoot children into school. She would measure Kezia's feet with a stick and then find shoes to make do.

Everything was make do, yes, but Freydeh could remember when she had no bed to call her own, not a coat or boots for winter. She looked at Sammy, still studying at the table with the kerosene lamp at the head of his book, and she remembered when he was little bigger than Kezia and just as thin and battered. Now he was tall and filling out. She had bought him a pair of glasses he used sometimes, never in the street. He was a bit nearsighted. That meant he didn't need glasses for reading. He was a lot healthier than he used to be, although he still got sore throats too often. It was the bad air, she was sure. He was a good boy, tempted sometimes by the street, but loyal to her. What would Kezia turn out to be? She had no idea. Sammy was right, she had leapt into action without knowing the child, but again, she felt she had no choice. So she had chosen life for Kezia, and life it would be.

TWENTY-SIX

ICTORIA WAS ECSTATIC. Presenting the Commodore with an opportunity to make a huge profit in gold and get out unscathed when half the brokers on Wall Street and two-thirds of the investors were stripped clean and left to drown in debt should make him generous. She approached him with her idea and he considered it, mulling it over long enough to unnerve her—enjoying his power, of course. He loved power almost as much as money. She could not sleep all week. She scarcely ate. She had been so sure he would support her scheme. The next week, he agreed.

Now Woodhull, Claflin and Company was a brokerage firm with offices and their first clients. Victoria had laboriously written out a script for Tennie so she would not make a mistake with a customer if Victoria was occupied. Tennie was not as quick as Victoria at memorizing, but during the weeks the office was being set up, legally and physically, Victoria rehearsed with her sister. They visited a tailor and had business suits made up, men's jackets with straight severe skirts ending at the ankles—no hoops, bustles or trains. If they were going to make a success of their business, they couldn't dress like tarts or superior courtesans or even like ladies. They were the first female brokers ever, and the newspapers covered their opening. The journalists were treated to good wine, good beer and better bourbon to warm their copy. It worked. They were declared a great success within days after their doors opened to the public, long before they actually turned a profit.

The Commodore did not abandon them. Between him and the financial tidbits Annie Wood shared and Josie let drop, they were able to offer their clients good information. Victoria did not pretend to knowledge she lacked. She intended to be honest in her business practices—aside from letting anyone know where the information came from. Everyone thought her source was Vanderbilt. She was careful never to affirm his influence or to deny it, but she also gave credit to the spirits. Anyone put off by spiritualism would probably not come to women to do business.

Victoria was well off, as Demosthenes had promised long ago. Had she not brought her ragtag family to a fine house on East Thirty-eighth Street? The offices were located in Hoffman House, a fine hotel on fashionable Madison Square, famous for its paintings, statuary, seventy-foot-long bar, ornate banquet hall with a ceiling decorated in gold, silver and allegorical paintings of nymphs and goddesses, and for being the hangout of Boss Tweed. The parlor of their office was ladylike, with bucolic oils on the walls in ornate frames, a piano, green velvet sofa and chairs. Vases of fresh flowers stood on tables shaped like pillars of Greek temples. A portrait of the Commodore hung prominently, where it would be seen by anyone entering. No point in hiding their assets. The Commodore had a Wall Street reputation as honest, firm in his word and shrewd beyond imagining. That he had made money in gold when everyone else, including probably Fisk and Gould in the end, had been losing it by the bushel only increased his reputation for financial wisdom.

After the first week, when hordes of men came to gawk, Victoria hired a butler who greeted all comers and pointed them toward a sign that said "All Gentlemen will state their business and then retire at once." Victoria did not want to give the impression that the brokerage office was the anteroom to a brothel, or that men could lounge around playing cards or chatting.

Their offices were furnished with walnut desks, cabinets and a teletype and ticker-tape machine, which only the best brokerage houses had.

Everything, Victoria felt, reeked of quality. *Here you may invest your money with confidence and here you may be sure of discreet and intelligent advice. Here you will find quick and efficient service.* The newspapers called them "The Bewitching Brokers," "The Queens of Finance," "the Female Sovereigns of Wall Street," but Victoria aspired to success rather than fame for their novelty.

Some women had money: widows, but also an increasing number of professionals like herself—an untapped market. It was assumed by male brokers that they could not possibly invest for themselves or manage their own money, yet they did. Victoria intended to encourage women to invest with her.

Within a month, they had too many clients for the small suite in the Hoffman. They could not handle everything themselves, and there was no room for anyone else. They moved into larger offices at 44 Broad Street. Colonel Blood sat at a huge desk in the front office—no more sofas and pianos, but the portrait of the Commodore moved with them—with the stock ticker and a large imposing safe. James had been a successful businessman in St. Louis before the war had alienated him from his previous bourgeois life, so she trusted him to run the office. The first person he hired was his own brother, for whom he had worked when they first came to New York. George commuted every day from New Jersey to keep the firm's books. Victoria insisted that all be done legally and cleanly. She could trust no Claflin to do that, but George Blood would keep the books to the penny.

Their opening here was an even greater event than the previous opening at the hotel. The street outside was so blocked with carriages, the police had to intervene. Of course the Commodore came, taking center stage and beaming at the sisters. Fortunately he had left by the time Josie brought in Jim Fisk. "So this is the little lady who outdid us in gold," he said, patting Victoria's arm.

She removed herself slightly, smiling but keeping a distance. "The spirits gave me counsel, Mr. Fisk."

"Good spirits own lots of railroads too."

"No, Mr. Fisk. It was I who advised our patron to sell—not vice versa."

Even Boss Tweed came. She greeted him effusively, although he made her nervous. He was a gross man—obese, looking as if he were rolled in oil—but immensely powerful. He had gangs of thugs at his command; he controlled the Irish vote and the mayoralty, all public works in the city and many private contractors as well. He bought and sold politicians as another man might buy up a carload of overshoes. She knew little about his private life except that he had put on a lavish wedding for his daughter, fit for a princess. The rooms were mobbed now. Actresses came, actors and producers, opera singers, lawyers, journalists, editors, merchants, they came to drink and eat the pastries set out, both savory and sweet that Tennie had arranged, and to gape, yes, to gape.

Her office and Tennie's were much as they had been in the Hoffman House, except that instead of the hotel furniture, Victoria had desks made for them with Greek key details, to honor her spirit guide. Another difference was a special entrance for women, who could skip the front office with Colonel Blood and the clerk who screened callers. In a parlor by Victoria's office, women could feel comfortable and private. No men were allowed into this part of the office, not even James.

That device was an immediate success. The professional women Victoria had hoped to attract came, not only singly but often in pairs or small groups to give each other confidence. Women felt that this firm had been created for their benefit. Not only proper ladies came: madams spread the word through their grapevine that Tennie and Victoria would receive them graciously and treat them and their money with respect. Victoria's web of informants now extended through a number of the better brothels. She reduced her commission for any madam who passed on useful information from her girls and their clients. That too pleased the madams, who recognized a good deal.

One afternoon, Josie swept in, resplendent in a scarlet satin overskirt partly covering a gold brocaded underskirt, all arranged over an extra large bustle, under a fur cloak against the cold of a snowy day in late February. She threw back a hood lined with ermine. On her large bosom, a great emerald brooch sparkled, echoed by her earrings, gifts from Jim Fisk.

"What brings you by, Josie? I'm delighted to see you. Would you care for some sherry?"

"Don't mind if I do. . . . But this is a business call. You've been telling me for years I ought to invest. I'm not going to let Jim keep me in a cage the rest of my life, so I'm taking your advice. I mean to have my own money now. I want you to make it happen. I'll give you some money and you make it grow like Jack's beanstalk."

"This is a wise move, Josie. Every woman needs her own money, her own independence. Then you can choose whom you will love and whom you will not."

"Exactly!" Josie squeezed her hand through fine kid gloves, dyed green. "You'll set me free."

"I will. Now would you prefer champagne or sherry? And we have some delicious chocolates from Belgium."

Most days the Commodore dropped by to offer advice and collect their information. Whenever he appeared, Victoria and Tennie stopped whatever they were doing and saw him in Tennie's office, where Victoria could leave them alone together in case the Commodore had something more than stocks in mind. Tennie was always ready to roll up her sleeves and give him one of her special massages. She confided in Victoria that he needed release less often, as his new wife Frankie was giving it to him once a week. He was thrilled with his marriage. He had been hangdog with Tennie at first, but now he was assured she bore him no ill will.

When he left, Tennie smoothed down her newly shorn locks. They had both decided to wear their hair shorter. Perhaps they would start a new fashion. It was part of looking more severe for business. "It's more work than it used to be."

In addition to the brokerage business, Victoria was busy furnishing the new house leased just off Fifth Avenue in a fashionable section, Murray Hill. She could not trust Roxanne, Utica or Buck to get involved with decorating the house, as their taste was lurid. Roxanne loved religious pictures, the more lugubrious the better. Buck liked large florid nudes. He would have been crazy about Josie, but Victoria had taken care never to let him meet her. Her family spent money amazingly fast. Buck liked horses and he liked to gamble, two ways of making piles of greenbacks disappear.

The house must be impressive without being gauche. She was going to have a salon. Now that she was rich and becoming famous, she needed men and women of advanced political ideas to stimulate her mind and teach her about history and politics and economics, as James had begun to do many years ago. Now she wanted more stimulation, vaster vistas than James could provide, new European notions. She longed for intellectual excitement after all the time she spent with the Commodore, who had never met an idea he had noticed.

She filled the house with mirrors that multiplied the light and scattered it. The salon had a colored glass dome through which the light beamed down prismatically, bathing the room and its occupants in magical hues. She loved velvet. Purple velvet downstairs, green velvet in her bedroom. Tennie chose lilac velvet for hers. Victoria had blue wallpaper hung in Byron's room, where his new caretaker slept. Zulu Maud, nine now, got warm pink. Occasionally Victoria brought Zulu along to the brokerage offices, to see what her mother did for a living and be inspired. She kept her daughter close. Zulu was going to have the kind of sheltered, pampered childhood she had not even been able to dream of as a young girl. No one was going to exploit her. Ever!

Her whole family moved in, not only Roxanne, Utica and Buck but their oldest sister Margaret Ann with her three children, sister Polly, her daughter Rosa and Polly's brand-new husband Dr. Sparr, who did mesmeric healing in the parlor downstairs two afternoons a week. Utica and Roxanne spent most days getting drunk or wheedling money to buy clothes. Fashion magazines lay all around the salon until Victoria gathered them up and dumped them in Utica's room. She did not want her house to appear frivolous to the visitors she was beginning to invite. She wanted them to take her seriously. Not "The Bewitching Brokers" but someone with ideas, heft, destiny.

She was choosing her lovers carefully. She had become involved with an older freethinker, Stephen Pearl Andrews, an extremely intelligent man, lean and still in good shape. He had been a follower of Fourier and had started a phalanx, a small utopian community, on Long Island, but it had not lasted long. He knew many of the leaders in woman's rights and promised to introduce her. Their relationship was occasionally sexual but primarily intellectual. She was the student and he the teacher, but they argued frequently. They enjoyed debating. He critiqued her writing and encouraged her plan to start a paper with Tennie.

Her other new lover had been a general in the Civil War and now was a senator from Massachusetts, Benjamin Butler. She had met him when she went to Washington to sit quietly in the woman's rights convention, to size up the leaders and study the lay of the land. She did not attempt to meet any of them yet, but she liked what she heard. She set out to learn from Butler how government worked. He indicated he would mentor her if she was willing to become his lover. She did not hesitate. He was a dynamic, almost flamboyant man, brave and well connected in Washington although resembling a pug. He was sympathetic to woman's rights and willing to champion her. By and by, she would need his influence if she was to accomplish something great and good. After her early experiences, sex came easily to her. She took precautions—the same ones they sold to the madams. She saw no reason to discontinue that business, although she had passed on some of the deliveries to Utica and Buck. The way they spent money, they might as well make a little for the household. She still went in person to take the orders, as madams were a precious source of financial information. When she was with one of her lovers, she thought only of him. She focused on him exclusively. She never spoke of the others. James welcomed the good connections she was making. He especially liked Stephen, who often stayed in the household overnight, sometimes with her, sometimes in the guest room.

She was still casting about for the right way to stake a claim to her new proposed identity when one evening of penetrating cold in late February, a gentleman appeared at the door and was announced by the downstairs maid. "Dr. Canning Woodhull, Esquire."

He stumbled into the salon where Victoria was hearing Zulu's lessons. He was emaciated, his scraggly beard unkempt, his hair matted. He stuttered when he spoke and it took several minutes for him to address her coherently. She sent Zulu upstairs. He had not even looked at his daughter, perhaps had not guessed who she was.

"What is it, Canning?" She could not bring herself to address him in a more distant way. After all, he was the father of her children.

"I . . . I think I'm dying. . . ."

"Of what?" She had a moment of fear that he might be contagious, might infect her daughter.

"Look at my hands." He held out both bony hands before him. They were shaking so violently he could not unbutton his tattered coat.

"You've been drinking."

"It's the curse I bear."

His pupils were dilated. He was on some drug as well. He sank to the floor and knelt there. "Wait." She rang for the butler. Tennie and she had a staff of twelve, including the coachman, the cook, Byron's caretaker, various maids. "Tell cook to prepare some broth. Then help me get this gentleman upstairs into the third-floor guest room."

"Where's my son?" Canning asked as they half carried him up the stairs between them.

"He's in his bedroom playing with blocks. He can't read the letters on them, but he likes to pile them up and knock them down."

"Can I see him?"

"In the morning. We'll get you cleaned up and into bed." She called Tennie.

"Is that Canning? Oh my god. He's a bum."

"Drugs and drink. But I can't turn him out. He'll die in the street."

"But he can't stay here!"

"Why not? Everybody else in the world does."

They got him bathed, then into bed. Victoria felt false modesty was ridiculous. After all, she had been married to the man for years. Hard years, yes, but once she had loved him. She felt little more toward him than as if he had been a dog she had owned for a pet who had run away and then been found starving and injured in the road. She would see he got proper care. She spooned broth into him.

"My darling Vickie," he mumbled. "You've always been so good and kind. My wife. . . ."

"I'm not your wife and I'm not your darling. I'm with Colonel Blood and you would do well to remember that if you wish my help and my protection. You're the father of my two children—"

"Two?"

"The little girl who was doing her multiplication tables when you arrived—she's Zulu Maud, your daughter as well as mine."

"Is she . . . slow?"

"She's bright and lively and sweet." She stood. "She calls Colonel Blood 'Father' and you should leave well enough alone. Claim Byron, but you may not claim Zulu Maud."

Over the next week, Canning began slowly to regain his health. Soon he was out finding opium and morphine again, shutting himself in his room, but he made himself useful with Byron. Byron didn't care who this ragged man was. He was happy as a puppy with the attention. Canning had little else to do but take care of Byron and play simple games with him, as one would with a child who had not yet learned to speak. She let one of the caretakers go, the one she did not trust, for she had found bruises on Byron recently that she did not believe came from clumsiness, as the man insisted. Canning could share the care of Byron with the stout lady of late middle age who came in every day but Sunday to be with him.

When Zulu Maud asked her who the funny old man was, she said he was Byron's father. "I was married to him many years ago—but you can see why I left him. Your father is a great improvement, don't you think?"

"Daddy is smart and handsome and he goes to work every day."

"Absolutely." Victoria ruffled Zulu's hair. "And we like all that. We like it very much. We wouldn't mind if everybody in the house did the same—like your Aunt Tennie and me."

"When I grow up, I'll go to work every day too."

Victoria kissed the top of her daughter's head. "Perhaps you'll work with me. That way, we'll always be together."

TWENTY-SEVEN

ELIZABETH WAS ASTONISHED and pleased by how efficient Isabella was proving to be. She put on the Washington convention, sparing Susan a lot of hard work. She had the same organizational gifts Susan had—the ability to stage an event, keeping the details that must be delegated on some vast list in her head and checking them off as they were done or reassigning them if a problem or delay arose. Just as Elizabeth appreciated Susan's abilities, she was delighted with Isabella, although that delight did not prompt her to go to Washington.

Today Elizabeth was working on a speech about raising daughters, for even committed suffragists seemed uncertain what they should tell their daughters and what they should permit or urge upon them. She had raised two, which gave her credentials. She was grappling with the organization of the talk when Susan came in, breathless from walking from the train. Obviously she had been in a hurry, rushing over the icy sidewalks. It was March but still wintry. Susan cast her simple bonnet and gloves on a chair, where Amelia promptly seized them and stashed them away. Amelia stood in the doorway then, as eager as Elizabeth to find what had given the flush to Susan's cheeks and caused her to rush from the station to the Tenafly house.

Susan knew she had an audience, so with a glint of mischief she proceeded to say how much she needed a bit of tea to warm her.

"Thee don't look cold to me," Amelia muttered, but she went to make tea while Susan patted her hair into its bun and then had her tea with a buttery scone Amelia had baked. Elizabeth was ready to pour the tea on Susan's head by the time she relented. "You will never guess where I went today."

"To hell, if you don't stop playing with us," Elizabeth snapped.

"I visited the offices of those women brokers the papers have been full of, Woodhull and Claflin. I met Victoria Woodhull."

"What do you think of her? They say she and her sister are both Vanderbilt's mistresses."

"She struck me as intelligent, charming. She isn't a floozy, Mrs. Stanton."

"How would thee know?" Amelia snorted and turned half away but did not leave.

"The offices are well appointed but businesslike. She has a separate entrance for women—"

"Like a concert saloon," Elizabeth said.

"No, Mrs. Stanton. Hear me out. It leads directly into a cozy parlor right by the sisters' offices. Tennie, the younger, was with a client when I arrived, but Victoria joined me. Men have to enter through the front and are grilled by Victoria's husband, Colonel James Blood, who was wounded six times in the Civil War on the Northern side. After our tête-à-tête in the women's parlor, Mrs. Woodhull introduced me to him and his brother. There's even one of those machines that spits out prices of stocks minute by minute."

"Is Vanderbilt behind them? I dislike that man. He runs his railroads efficiently by squeezing his workers."

"Mrs. Woodhull told me that the money behind the brokerage is hers and her sister's, money they made on Wall Street. Vanderbilt has accepted stock advice from her and gives them tips in return. She says she has served as his financial adviser. She comes from poverty, a large family in Ohio. She was blunt and open with me. She has brought her entire family to New York to keep them in comfort. She said she and her sister already made seven hundred fifty thousand dollars and were prepared to help other women invest as successfully as they have."

"Seven hundred fifty thousand dollars? I can't imagine that much money. Did you believe her?"

"I did. I want you to meet her, Mrs. Stanton."

"To what end? With my children in college, I have little to spare and nothing to invest."

"I spoke to her about woman's rights, and I found not only was she fascinated but she's been thinking about the situation of women. She believes that ours is the cause she was born to serve, and that once she has established herself in business, she can aid our movement."

"Oh, we could use an angel, we surely could. A woman who made her own money and wants to give us some! Susan, I share your excitement."

"Be careful with this woman," Amelia said. "She may be no better than she should be. They say she has been divorced."

"If she makes a commitment to our cause, I don't care if she's had twelve husbands. Every woman is entitled to a few mistakes in that line," Elizabeth said with a wince. "If women were free to have affairs as men do, many foolish marriages would be avoided, and the sum of pain in the world would diminish."

"Mrs. Stanton! You don't really mean that." But Susan was amused, Elizabeth could tell from the crinkles at the corners of her eyes.

"We'll never know, will we? I'm past the age of more than polite flirtation."

THEODORE TILTON HAD BEGUN a new suffrage party aimed at uniting the two organizations, the American and the National, over the spring and summer of 1870, but it fizzled out. The distance between the groups widened. But Theo had at least tried to make peace, and Elizabeth thought he deserved credit. With so much more money behind them, the American was outshining their National. The American had a slick well-financed journal focused only on suffrage, while the *Revolution* got deeper in debt every month. The American had the money to do a huge mailing campaign and were affiliating chapters all over the country. Their recent convention had been large.

This evening she and Susan had been invited by Tilton to dine with him and Lib. Lib would probably always feel more at home with Susan, but she had warmed to Elizabeth. In their presence, she was vivacious, full of ideas, quite different from the subdued wife. Susan and she were to meet with Theo that afternoon at Laura Bullard's to discuss the possible transfer of their journal, too far into debt to continue. It was a sad decision, but one forced on them by their creditors. Susan was not persuaded they should let go.

Lib had seemed more confident lately, blooming. Tiny as she was, her beauty and newfound energy lit up a room. She had confided in Susan that her marriage had changed but provided no details. She said only that it had become more equal. Elizabeth wondered what that meant. Theodore had been enjoying a long affair with Laura Bullard, a widow and heir through her father to a large patent medicine fortune. A sophisticated lady who had lived in France for many years, she was an ardent believer in progressive ideas, including free love. It was one of the many clandestine affairs that percolated through the woman's rights movement. For all the Boston contingent's squeamishness about discussing marriage, divorce or,

God help them, sex, they were just as apt to have "affinities" as anybody in New York. Elizabeth wondered what Lib meant when she spoke of a new equality. She didn't mean that Theodore was home more or that he had given up the lecture circuit or his affairs. Still, Lib was obviously happy. The death of her little son years before had thrown her into a depression Elizabeth felt the woman had only fully emerged from that summer.

Elizabeth herself was suffering the sense of being embattled on all sides. Susan and she had been effectively thrust aside in the woman's movement by the Boston-led American with their alignment with the Republican Party, more favorable notice in the press, their slick journal. Elizabeth was making a living and supporting her younger children through lectures. She was also subsidizing the New York apartment where Henry lived. He had a journalistic sinecure that did not begin to cover his expenses. With every issue, the *Revolution* was leaking money they did not have. She did not want to see it die, but they simply could not continue. "Susan, we must find someone with money to buy it, or at least to put money into the paper."

"Does Theo have any money?"

"His special friend Laura Bullard does. Theo turned down a hefty bribe to support a railroad stock scheme that Henry Ward Beecher and most of the Republican establishment in Brooklyn went heartily into. Theo said his principles were worth more than could be bought. So I doubt he has money to spare. These days, you have money or you have principles."

"I'd trust Theo more than most with the paper, if it comes to that."

"Susan, it has come to that. We have no money to put out another issue and no one will extend us more credit. Either we pass on the *Revolution* to someone who can afford it, or it will simply cease. Do you want that?"

Susan pushed her face into her hands. "No," she said in a muffled voice, "but to me it's like giving away my own child."

They took the train to the ferry, the ferry to Manhattan, a cab across and then the ferry to Brooklyn. "Look, Susan, the caisson," Elizabeth said, standing at the rail with the wind blowing her curls so they whipped her cheeks, "They've started building the bridge. Perhaps when they finish, even more will come over to hear Beecher. He can preach in a stadium." Beecher was close to President Grant and the Republican cabal that ran Brooklyn. His congregation included many of the richest and most powerful men in Brooklyn and some in Manhattan who journeyed over to Plymouth Church for his sermons on the power of love and how God had ordained the order of things, where the deserving enjoyed riches like spreading chestnut trees, protecting the less fortunate beneath their leafy branches.

"He got rid of the articles of faith. Now all the Republican Party pooh-bahs have joined and turned Plymouth Church into their clubhouse." Susan snorted.

"It is also said he preaches to twenty of his mistresses every Sunday."

"Mrs. Stanton, that's just gossip. We shouldn't repeat such nonsense."

Elizabeth pursed her lips. "I'm not convinced it's gossip."

She had never seen a building project such as this bridge. The caisson was made of lumber. Men were lowered in it down to the bottom of the East River and below. The bridge was to stand upon bedrock. It was cruel, dangerous work and several men had died already, falling, swept away in the violent currents or of the painful seizures they called caisson disease. Why did every bit of progress have to be paid for by the deaths of the workers who made it happen?

They joined the crowd rushing off the ferry, always a little dangerous in the press of bodies. The boat hook hanging on the dock was a reminder how often passengers fell into the East River and were drowned or crushed. Still she could not resist taking a last glance back at Manhattan. The steeple of Trinity stuck out above all other buildings. Masts of sailing ships bristled like so many enormous toothpicks.

That afternoon, at Laura Bullard's house, the deal was closed with great rapidity and the *Revolution* passed to Laura Bullard and Theodore Tilton, the new editors. Theo and his mistress had papers already drawn up. Elizabeth had quietly broached the matter with Theo a few weeks before, to feel out his interest. She had not expected such a rapid response. Susan looked as if she would weep, then put on her stoical face. Dinner, it turned out, was to be at Laura Bullard's. Lib was nowhere to be seen. Where was she, Elizabeth wondered. Laura's house was larger and more sumptuous than Theo's or Elizabeth's, with a staff of servants, including a cook. The rooms were furnished with heavy draperies, a large tapestry imitating a medieval hanging with ladies and knights, fine Oriental carpets and chandeliers gaudy with gaslight. The furniture was oversized and ornately carved. Bronze statuary of shepherds and savages stood everywhere in an almost jungle confusion of bric-a-brac.

Dinner felt stiff. The food was fine and the wine excellent and free-flowing. Even Susan sipped a glass of tawny port, as letting the *Revolution* go had been upsetting for her even more than for Elizabeth. Theo was drinking heavily and seemed to be undergoing some inner turmoil. He did not look his usual tousled handsome self, but drawn, off-color, as if he had been sleeping badly. Laura tried to soothe him, without much effect. Finally Theo exploded. "Henry Ward Beecher, who was supposed to be my true friend, my brother, has destroyed my life."

"You mean those shenanigans with the president, the regular Republicans cutting you out of the loop?" Elizabeth was surprised he should take that so seriously, since he hadn't been supporting Grant.

"Beecher has defiled my bed while professing friendship. And now he has made my own wife. . . . She is carrying his child!"

Elizabeth frowned. "How can you be sure?"

"She confessed it."

"Theo, how can you speak of defiling the marriage bed when you've had intimate friends for years? Here we sit in Laura's house eating her food and drinking her wine. Can you possibly feel you are defiling Lib?" Elizabeth shook her head wearily. Men were a joke sometimes. It was fine for Theodore to have passionate relationships, but Lib was to be punished for probably the only affair of her life.

"When she first confessed her affair with Beecher, I tried to forgive him for seducing her while I was off giving lectures to pay for our home. I thought we'd all have our relationships and be friends together. . . . But he's a snake. He impregnated her. He lied to me, he played me false." Theodore was tearing at his hair.

Elizabeth had never seen him so distraught. Laura and she tried to calm him. Susan stood. "I must speak with Lib." Hurrying from the room, she went to get her cloak. It was only a matter of blocks to the Tilton residence.

Theo was ranting about how he had received Beecher into his house, tried to restore their full friendship, tried to make everything good between them, then this! His wife carrying another man's child. It was not to be endured. Hadn't he supported Beecher in every way, ghostwritten his articles, held his hand, edited his work?

At eleven, Theo announced he was going home. Elizabeth was not about to walk, especially so late, so Laura sent them in her carriage. When they entered the Tilton home, Susan and Lib were sitting up in the parlor. Lib ran up to him, furious. She was a full foot shorter than her husband, pregnancy thickening her waist. "You were supposed to pick me up to go to dinner with Laura. You promised!"

"Did I? I don't think so."

Lib screamed at him, "Liar! Liar!"

Theo stared down at her. He was a little drunk but not enough to explain his reaction. "Your child is not my child!" He pointed at her belly with an expression of deep revulsion scoring his face. "Are any of the children mine? How can I ever know?" Then he struck Lib hard across the face. Elizabeth was shocked.

Lib ran upstairs to her bedroom, with Susan on her heels. Elizabeth paused to say to Theo, "You're behaving like an idiot! Some supporter of woman's rights you are." Then more slowly she climbed the steps, holding on to the banister, and followed them into Lib's bedroom. She dropped into the overstuffed chair by the window, sighing. She did not enjoy domestic tantrums. She was exhausted. Giving over the *Revolution* had depressed her, even though the money drain had kept her awake nights for the last few months. Susan was locking the door—a response Elizabeth thought overdramatic. Susan had never been married and thus had no idea what storms could blow up between a husband and wife and how noisy it could get.

She changed her mind when Theo began banging on the door screaming to be let in. Lib was shouting at him and he was shouting back. The door rattled at his thumping but did not give way, although he was threatening to break it down.

Susan stood just inside the door. "I will not turn this key. You're out of control. Get hold of yourself!"

"No woman can come between me and my wife."

"You'll get at Lib only through my dead body," Susan said grimly, leaning against the shaking door.

Elizabeth was on her feet now. "Theodore Tilton, you must calm down. Your wife has committed no act you did not carry out before her. Are you drunk or crazy?"

A long silence followed. Theo stopped banging on the door. Finally they heard his footsteps receding. Probably he would return to Laura to spend the night.

"Come," Susan said. "We must barricade the door lest he come back and break it open."

Elizabeth joined them in pushing the bed against the door. Exhausted, all three of them climbed into the bed half undressed and put out the light. Lib had stopped crying but was overwrought and snuggled against Susan, holding her thin body as if to a spar after an ocean wreck. Lib began to talk about how she had become involved with Henry Ward

Beecher. Elizabeth feigned sleep, knowing that Lib would never confide in her as she did in Susan. The relationship had begun when Beecher started bringing her his sermons and his writing to critique, praising her intelligence and insight, as Theo never did. Henry and she had become closer and closer. His wife was a cold, materialistic and distant woman who could not give him the kind of attentive love the great man needed. They had become soul mates.

She had never intended their relationship to go beyond the platonic. But Theo was gone so often giving lectures, attending conferences, or simply gallivanting off to his other women that she was deeply lonely and often depressed. Theo had never, she thought, been faithful, although she had been too naïve in the first decade of her marriage to guess. She genuinely liked Laura Bullard, considering her a friend. Laura had explained that she had no desire for a husband. A passionate friendship was just what she wanted, nothing more. She wished only to work with Theo and sleep with him sometimes and exchange ideas. She had no intention of threatening their marriage, she said, and Lib believed her. Laura was wealthy and did not want to lose her independence to any man. A husband would be an impediment.

"Did Beecher force himself upon you?" Susan asked.

"Oh, no! Never. He was the gentlest lover a woman could ever have. I experienced such joy with him. He made me feel cherished, Susan."

Exhausted as she was, Elizabeth was too interested to doze off. All this business of free love was exciting in its way. Why shouldn't women too have adventures? She had not been tempted, because her Henry had been a good lover, however lacking as a husband. She had been deeply and passionately in love with him for a long time. She had changed, he had changed, and all the childbearing and -rearing had dimmed her sexual nature; but when she wanted to be embraced, it had been Henry she desired. Other men might flirt with her and she with them. She had found the great Negro abolitionist Frederick Douglass attractive, but affairs took time she never had. She preferred to put her energy into her writing, her speaking, her political work, her children, her friends. She had a brief moment of wondering if men named Henry were better lovers than others, since she suspected from Lib's roundabout descriptions that she experienced pleasure with Henry and none with Theo. She could hear Theo moving about downstairs. So he had not gone to Laura. The morning, if they ever got through this night, would be interesting, if likely to prove melodramatic.

"So when you confessed to Theo, he stormed out of the house."

"He was gone for three days. I was crazy with worrying. Then he returned and he wasn't angry. He said we'd have a better, more honest marriage with both of us enjoying our passionate affinities. That's what he said."

"Did you tell Beecher that Theo knew about the affair?" Susan asked.

Lib moaned. "I meant to. Theo made me promise to tell. Somehow I never could. Things seemed to be going along so well I didn't want to upset Henry."

"Then you told Theo you were with child."

"He figured it out. I never told him."

Elizabeth sighed. What a mess. No wonder she'd never had the energy for such complications, and no wonder Susan hadn't bothered with the whole untidy business of sexual love. In the morning they would coerce, cajole, embarrass Theo into behaving better toward his wife, if he would listen. She was not convinced he would. This night might have shattered several friendships. Now she regretted they had given over the *Revolution* to Theo and Laura. But who else wanted it? She was fighting on so many fronts she felt overwhelmed. That was why she had let go of the *Revolution,* although they could not get rid of the debts they had incurred. But she felt far less sure of the wisdom of that decision than she had in the so distant morning of what must by now be yesterday.

TWENTY-EIGHT

THE FIRST COUPLE of months with Kezia were bumpy. Freydeh noticed a bad smell in the bedroom, and found that Kezia was hiding bits of food under the bed, where they had attracted mice and soon would bring rats. Kezia cried when brought to task, but she did it again the next week. She would pick up things she found in the street, a lost glove, a piece of half-rotten melon, a pin that had rusted. She had to be taught again and again to clean herself properly with a basin of water. If not watched, she would soon be dirty again. She seemed afraid of soap and water.

Once Kezia was cleaned up and started school, they learned she could draw. She could see a picture of a racehorse or a tiger and catch the essence in a few lines. They were making several types of condoms and labeling them according to some animal that might inspire the buyer. They had the elephant type (for those massively endowed). Men liked to buy them, even if she suspected that not all of them needed the extra large. They had the tiger—brightly striped. They had the rooster with a little tickler on it. Kezia drew pictures they had printed on the boxes. Madams liked the fancy ones for their clients.

She delivered to the brothels herself, so as not to put Sammy in the way of temptation. That morning she took Annie Wood her supply for the next two weeks. Annie was entertaining another woman in the conservatory, a room Freydeh loved, where they were drinking coffee. The other woman was as dark as Annie was fair, at least in hair color—black hair like Kezia's, but her eyes were blue and her complexion ivory. She was beautiful, not dressed like a whore but severely, in black silk with a white rose—a real rose, not a cloth rose—at her throat. They had been talking about railroads when the colored servant led Freydeh between the potted palms to the table. Freydeh was a little nervous as this was obviously a Yankee lady, whatever she was doing in a brothel, although she had a strange feeling she'd seen the woman before.

Annie waved her to a seat. Sometimes Annie treated her as an equal, sometimes as a servant. "This is Freydeh Levin. She manufactures the line of condoms we supply. A businesswoman like us."

"What do you do?" Freydeh asked the lady. She could be a madam who dressed to distinguish herself from her girls. Freydeh had learned a lot about brothels since she had gone into condoms—and since she had been searching for her sister.

"I'm a stockbroker. Have you heard of me?"

"I'm sorry," Freydeh said. "How would I have?"

The lady smiled, more amused than annoyed. "The papers got a lot of copy out of my sister and myself."

"I'm working on my English, but mostly I read German papers." They had news of things back in Europe, where the remnants of her people were. She had recently sent money urging Sara to take her family and come. She had not heard back yet.

"What made you go into your line of work?" the woman asked.

"It's a way I can make money as a woman. I figured that out when I worked in a pharmacy. Now I work for myself and my children."

"How many children do you have?" the lady asked, leaning on her elbow.

"An older boy and a younger girl."

"It's the same with me," the lady said. "An older boy and a younger girl. They're the reason I work at the trade I've chosen. Before that, I was a spirit medium."

Freydeh wasn't sure what that was, but she thought spirits were a lot of superstitious nonsense. You lived and then you died, that was the end of it. She didn't imagine a heaven of clouds and white light. She didn't imagine being born as a cow or a crow. But she kept her opinions to herself, as she so often had to in a world riddled with imagination and superstition. She was working on Kezia's weird set of beliefs.

Annie laughed, shaking her curls. "A woman has to have her own money. My business has been good to me. I pay off the men I have to. If they finally close me down, I have enough saved to live on comfortably. Thanks in part to my friend here. If you care to invest any money, she's the one you want."

"Here." The woman handed her a card. Her hands were well kept, manicured, soft, but there was a little scar on the back of her left hand that spoke of days that had not always been so easy. Freydeh's hands were callused and spotted with burns. "If you want to invest, just come see me."

Freydeh thanked the woman, peering at the card. Woodhull, Claflin and Company, stockbrokers. Nice, but if she got ahead with money, she would move them to a safer neighborhood. If she had money like Annie and this lady—Woodhull or Claflin?—there were things she'd do, rather than gamble in the stock market. Land. A house. She believed in owning something solid, something you could live in or grow food on, not pieces of paper that could lose their value overnight.

That afternoon, Kezia came home late. Freydeh surveyed her. She had bruises on her face and her arm, a scratch on her cheek. This would have been normal for the girl Freydeh had rescued from the streets, but the new improved Kezia usually had skin clear as good china. Her hair had grown out black and straight and her posture was no longer that of someone expecting to be hit.

"Why did you get into a fight like a common street arab?" Freydeh was not pleased. She stood glaring, arms folded across her bosom.

"They said bad things. Elizaveta and Karla."

"You have to learn not to take insults to heart."

"They weren't talking about me."

"Who, then?"

"You, Mamaleh."

"Me? What do they know about me?"

"They said because you make condoms, you're a whore. So I hit them."

"I hope you won." Freydeh sighed. "They're envious because you have new clothes. You have two dresses and a pinafore and a woolen shawl. That's enough to fire up the envy of most girls in that school."

"I know you're a good woman, Mamaleh, far better than their mothers. I just can't stand for them to say evil about you."

"It don't hurt me, Kezia, my honey. My little piece of heaven." She knew she was growing attached to the girl. A daughter of her own. "I chose this work because a woman can do it, we can work on our own right here and make a good living. All the women wearing their fingers to the bone making paper or cloth flowers, seamstresses stitching coats, jackets, dresses, pants, knitting socks. They work so hard and they make not enough to live on, hungry all the time and in mended rags. Lots of married couples use them, Kezia, to keep from having what they'd be forced to get rid of, what they can't afford to feed. How many dead babies have you seen in the alleys?"

"I know, I know. They're stupid mean girls. They pick on me."

"Defend yourself when you must, but don't worry about my good name. The rabbi likes it just fine when I put some money in. He always greets me—not as warmly as a successful businessman, a successful shop owner, but next in line." With two children to raise, she had begun going to shul now and then. Freethinking was not for kids. They needed rules. And in shul, they met other good Jewish kids. Kezia had been shy and nervous at first, but then she had made friends with a little girl there.

"Where's Sammy?" Kezia was looking around for her hero. Over the past four months, she had come to admire Sammy.

"Delivering. He'll be back soon. Go get yourself cleaned up. I want you to draw me a panther."

When Sammy arrived, he saw the bruise at once. "What happened? Did somebody beat you up?"

Kezia told him. Sammy was scornful but protective. They fought often, screaming at each other over the last chunk of bread or bit of potato.

Now that she was no longer hiding food, Kezia still ate as if the meal could vanish from the table. Sammy was growing fast, filling out, and they both wanted more food than she could provide. This was the third year with Shaineh somewhere in the city but nowhere she could find her. Freydeh judged herself a bad woman for preferring to make money and collect children that could be hers instead of finding her sister. Maybe if she had quit everything else and just looked for Shaineh, she would have found her a year ago. If Moishe had lived, no doubt she would be a better person, because she would not have to make every decision alone. What did she know about raising an American girl or boy? She could not even speak correctly. Who could she turn to for advice? Nobody. She went to lectures when she could to make herself smarter, but she worked most evenings and weekends. No Shabbos for her except for shul.

Sometimes she went alone to bakeries. Sometimes Sammy or Kezia came along. Always she bought something for them, a roll, a cookie. Sometimes it was hard for her to remember that Sammy and Kezia had never met Shaineh, for they talked about her together, second-guessing what might have happened. By now, she knew her adopted children far better than she knew her own sister. Sammy, who had been in on the search since the beginning, was determined to find Shaineh. However, she suspected Kezia just liked to go along to get a poppy seed roll, cookie or little tart. Kezia ate whatever she could lay her hands on, but she especially appreciated sweets. She was still too thin, for she had grown taller more than sideways. Sammy was taller than Freydeh, gangly but beginning to fill out. His voice had deepened. His face was still boyish, but his manner was growing stronger. It was he who challenged the baker in the second bakery they went to that Saturday.

"No, never seen her," the man said, gingery mustache and sideburns dusted with flour, a heavy man almost as broad as he was tall. That was what every baker they asked said, as they handed back the much-thumbed tattered drawing the street artist had made of Shaineh. He shook his head but did not bother to look up. He did not even ask them if they wanted to buy anything besides two sugar cookies. Kezia had eaten hers at once, a bite at a time around the edge and then into the center. Sammy ate his more casually, staring at the man, frowning.

The man said again, "Can't help you. Never saw her. Goodbye."

Something in his voice bothered Sammy. "You do know. You just aren't saying. That could get you in trouble."

"I don't want trouble," the man said. "Just leave me alone."

Freydeh stepped nearer. "Believe me, we aren't going anyplace till you tell us what you know." She turned and addressed the women waiting for bread. "Best shop someplace else. This man has urgent business with us, and we're not getting out of the way." She repeated that in German.

The man turned, squinting as if he had something in his eye. "You got no right to hold up my customers. They'll go someplace else."

"We got every right," Sammy said. "You know something about our sister."

The man, square as a pavement stone, chewed on his mustache. Then he finally muttered, "Okay, she did work here."

"What happened? Where is she?"

"One day this man come."

"What man? When was this?" Sammy was leaning half over the counter now.

"Just before Christmas. Four weeks ago. This man came in and Samantha stared at him like she was going to faint dead away."

"What did he look like?" Freydeh asked.

"He was maybe thirty. He was a toff, well dressed, with a diamond stickpin in his cravat. His nails was clean and he was wearing fine boots and a beaver hat. He was close to six feet tall."

"Did he speak to her?"

"He yelled at all of us. He said she was his wife what had run away from him and he was there to bring her back. And we better not get in between a man and his lawful wedded wife."

"What did Samantha do?"

"She said she wasn't his wife and she didn't want to go with him, but he grabbed her. He had a heavy weighted cane, one of those things you see the better-off thugs wielding. He wasn't no river rat."

"So you let him take her away?"

"If she was his wife, he was entitled. She started screaming she had a child—she did. She had her little girl tied up in the back room so she wouldn't get burned—tied to a table leg. She could crawl around the table but she couldn't burn herself. A cute little bugger. Samantha called her Reba—"

"That was our mother's name. . . . She's dead. Do you have her still?"

"He yelled at her, 'Whose is it?' And she said, 'She's yours but you didn't want her so she's all mine.' When I heard that, I knew she was his, and I told her to get out with her kid and go home with her man and leave us alone. So he took them both."

Freydeh said nothing, biting her tongue. She wanted to punch the ginger man in the face, but first she wanted to shake every bit of information he had out of him. "Did you get a name?"

"I didn't ask. Not my business."

Sammy leaned closer, fingering the knife in his pocket. "The name?"

"Al something she called him. Alfred or Albert, that's all I know. So she picked up the baby and he took hold of her and dragged her out, and that was the end of that. I don't want no trouble. She was crying and begging, but he was the father of her child, so she had to go with him. He had rights."

"And she had none? Oh, never mind."

"And you don't know anything else?" Sammy was still leaning over the counter. He was taller than the baker and could make himself look mean. "You know something, I can tell."

"Just he got into a spider phaeton and started whipping the horse and they were off. That's all I saw."

"Anything about the phaeton? Color?"

"I was scared of the guy. He wasn't no B'hoy like we see around here. He was a plug-ugly but highfalutin and wrathy."

"Try to remember."

"I only saw it was dark-colored like maroon and the horse was gray. That was it. And he had a serving man with him in those fancy suits they wear—livery."

"Again, what color?"

"Two colors. I didn't get a good look. It was like blue and white or blue and silver. Light blue. Believe me, I didn't see nothing more."

Kezia was eyeing the cakes through the glass. Not only was that an extravagance Freydeh would not commit, but she disliked the baker. He had lied to them. He had not protected Shaineh from the man, obviously the one who had kept her locked in a room until she escaped in the fire. Her captor was the father of her child. It was more important than ever that they find Shaineh, quickly, and her little girl too.

As they were walking home, Freydeh clapped Sammy on the shoulder. "You were great, Sammy, you did just what was needed. I can't believe how mean you sounded. Without you, I would have left him and learned not one thing."

"But what did we learn? Not much that helps us find her."

She stopped at a fish market. "We can have fresh whitefish. I love whitefish. I can't bake it like we did at home, but I can make it good on the burner. This is a treat for all of us, but especially for Sammy."

At supper Sammy enjoyed the fish, certainly, for it was a big treat, but he seemed preoccupied. After they had hauled up water from the pump and washed dishes in the basin, he perched by the window, motioning her to come sit by him.

"I have to stay out of school this week. I'll help you write a note how sick I am."

"Why do you want to stay out of school? Education is important, Sammy. I want you to make something of yourself."

"I need to go around to the stables. So he has some money. He has a fancy carriage and fancy clothes and a footman in livery, but I bet he doesn't have his own stables. I bet he keeps his horse and carriage in a stable near where he lives."

"But how will you find it?"

"I bet he don't live up on Fifth Avenue by Madame Restell's. I'll start in the Twenties and Thirties."

"You stay in school. I'll look."

"Freydeh, you can't go around to stables. I can hang around pretending I'm looking for a job and find out where he keeps his maroon spider phaeton and his gray horse. Then I can find out who he is and where he lives."

"He may have Shaineh locked up some other place."

"Once we find him, we can follow him. We're only four weeks behind now."

She was torn. She desperately wanted to find Shaineh, but she was afraid of the temptations that would beset Sammy if he stayed out of school. She doubted if stableboys were a good influence. It was hard to keep a young man from getting into trouble, and Sammy was growing into a fine young man. But he was right: if they did not follow up on what they had been told quickly, they would lose their only shot at finding her lost sister. She had to trust him. She had to. Slowly she nodded.

1871

TWENTY-NINE

ANTHONY WAS DEEPLY satisfied with his personal life. His dear wife was in the family way at last. He cosseted her. Sometimes he even cooked, to keep her from tiring herself by standing too long on her feet, for her ankles were swollen and her back often ached. He knew most men refused to do what was regarded as women's work and thus demeaning, but he felt himself too securely a man to worry. He carried out all his church duties, Sunday school, prayer meetings at the jail, special meetings at the Y, but always he hastened home to his Maggie. He was proud of their house with its comfortable furnishings, the piano in the parlor that even now she often played for him, old favorite songs and hymns. He liked the neighborhood, where many prosperous Christian families lived. He could walk to church, although now that Maggie was so far along, he had a cab take them. He would have liked to have a carriage, but he was not advancing in the dry goods trade.

He was bored with his toil of fancy and fashion. He tried to do the Lord's business on his own time for these were wicked days, when depravity was spewed out by countless presses, flaunted on the stage, sold from shop after shop. Newspapers carried open advertisements for the prevention of children and the killing of them once fecundated. The sporting papers for men spoke openly of so-called star courtesans, filthy women with the gates of hell between their legs. Brothels were corrupting youth on every other block in Manhattan. Streetwalkers roamed alone or in packs even on Broadway; in the theaters they filled the balconies. Wicked upper-class women disposed of potential offspring as if they were tossing out spoiled fruit. All they cared about was pleasure and fancy clothes, jewels, hats, gloves, boots. Maggie was nothing like that. She made her own dresses and she kept a tight budget—as they had to. Success was eluding him, and here he was starting a family. He was frustrated into impotent rages in which he strode the streets of Brooklyn until he had worn out his temper lest he carry it home.

The city was rotten, like Nineveh in the Good Book that Jonah was sent to warn, and a strong man was needed to set things right. He attended meetings of the National Reform Association, full of devout men and clergy. They wanted the nation to pass a constitutional amendment to place the United States firmly under God, to declare God and Jesus Christ the rulers and the Bible the supreme authority. A Presbyterian who had been president was now a justice of the Supreme Court. Anthony did not think much of Presbyterians, for he did not find them evangelical enough, but certainly they were supporting this fine project. After all, his wife had been raised Presbyterian, and her father, the shopkeeper, had been an elder of his church. They had a certain strictness that was appropriate. The proposed amendment would settle the nation once again on the way of virtue and restore Bible teaching to schools. There would be no room for freethinkers or freelusters, for radicals with dangerous ideas. But the movement was not making the headway the founders had expected. Some of them were moving into reforming morals, fighting obscenity that destroyed the bodies and minds of so many young growing boys, leading to enervation and insanity.

In his Connecticut village, if someone was doing something bad, everybody shortly knew and could punish that person, drive him out of town. Here in the city, a boy could go astray and no one pay heed. Young men's lives, like poor Edward's, were wasted. Now that Anthony was about to be a father, his duty to fight evil was clearer than ever. Budington encouraged him, something he needed these days when his job oppressed him.

He pondered the YMCA. They had money, for many important men of business belonged, some even serving on their board, like J. Pierpont Morgan. Such men cared deeply about the generation growing up, that they learn to cultivate good habits and avoid evil ones. If only he could demonstrate to these rich and powerful men his usefulness, his ability to serve as their strong arm in the war against those who would corrupt and enervate youth, he could carry out the Lord's work and support his family at the same time. The Y had recently limited membership to evangelical Christians. They had been responsible for passage of the state law against obscenity. Surely if he could reach the men in charge, he could persuade them of his zeal.

He had been studying the YMCA structure. William E. Dodge was one of the leaders, young and wealthy, son of the man who had led the New York Tract Society that proselytized widely. The father had poured money into evangelical causes, and the son was following in his footsteps. Another leader was Cephas Brainerd, a prominent lawyer and active in Republican inner circles. Then there was Morris Jesup, who had lost his father at twelve, as Anthony had lost his mother. He knew about hard work and scrabbling his way to the top. Only a decade older than Anthony, he was a banker and railroad financier everyone said was worth millions upon millions. Yet he too had been raised in a devout Congregationalist family in Connecticut. Anthony was particularly avid to make personal contact with Jesup. He knew in his bones that they would speak the same language, would understand the world in a similar way.

The great day arrived when Maggie was taken abed to deliver his first child. He rushed home but the doctor threw him out. He paced the streets, then took refuge at the Clinton Avenue Church, where Budington consoled him and they prayed together. After several hours, Anthony went home, where Maggie's mother had arrived, but the doctor again shooed him away. Maggie was still in labor. He could hear her screaming. He was terrified and knelt on the porch begging the Lord to deliver her. Then he rushed back to the church and Budington joined him in a prayer vigil through the night. In the morning, Budington sent a boy to see what was happening. Nothing. Maggie was still in labor. The doctor feared for her life. She had been trying to deliver the child for more than thirty hours.

Budington bid the boy stay on the porch of the house until there was news. Finally, at noon, the boy came. Maggie had given birth to a baby girl. Anthony got to his feet shakily. He had been kneeling for so long he could scarcely stand, but he stomped his feet and then set out for the house, after tipping the boy.

Maggie lay pale and listless. He was afraid, for she looked like his mother as she was dying, but the doctor slapped his back. "It's just the way of women. She's narrow in the hips. It was a hard birth, but I got the baby out safely. She needs a long rest and she'll be as good as ever."

Mrs. Hamilton, his mother-in-law, was muttering to herself. "Should have had a midwife, not a doctor. They know what to do. Look at the marks on the poor baby from his nasty devices, yanking her out."

He ignored the old woman. Doctors were the modern way. Midwives he did not trust. It was said they could help women avoid pregnancy and even to abort. Doctors were on the side of the father. He thanked Mrs. Hamilton politely for having attended his wife and tried to pack her off, but she resisted. Maggie begged him in a tiny voice to let her mother stay. He agreed reluctantly. Gingerly he touched the baby. Her head was creased and she was red and blue and bruised, but she had everything, little fingers, little toes, a little nose, a rosebud mouth. Lillie, he would call her, after his own mother. She was an angel come to earth to be his sweet child. "Lillie," he said aloud. "Our dear Lillie. My first child."

The doctor took him aside. "I wouldn't be in any hurry for a second. Your wife is very weak. Childbirth is taxing for her. Give her time to recover."

Anthony agreed. He would sleep in the child's room for a period of weeks while his dear Maggie recovered her strength. Maggie must not die. He would protect her. Maggie had the same long face and long-fingered hands as his mother. Her hair was even the same light brown with a slight curl. They were both such good women, but unlike his father, who had made his mother bear ten children, five of whom died too young for him to remember them, he would not force Maggie to bear more than another couple of children. A Christian man should be able to control his base appetites. Although they were bidden to be fruitful and multiply, the Scriptures did not say a man must force his wife to bear more children than she had the strength for. In the meantime, he had an adorable little baby daughter.

Outside the door, he had to be hard, to compete. Outside the oak door of his narrow but ample house, he fought for a living and to create a world fit for his children and other people's—the clean upstanding people who counted. The city was flooded with dirty noisy immigrants who let their children run in the streets like packs of wild dogs. They cursed, they drank, they brought unhealthy and primitive customs with them like their smelly ill-cooked food. They brought diseases that flourished in their filthy slums, whose pestilence crept like a sewer fog through the city, into the houses of those who tried to live upright, virtuous lives.

He closed his eyes, sitting at the bedside of his precious Maggie, who loosely held the baby in her arms as she dozed, her mouth fallen open, her cheeks pale and sunken from loss of blood. The room still reeked of blood, but he did not want to open a window for fear she would become chilled. He wondered if she would mind if he removed his black suit coat. He hung it carefully on the back of the chair, for she told him he was always rumpling his clothes. He was a big man and a strong one. Strong enough for both of them. Strong enough to fight the fight for Jesus every day. He closed his eyes again, perhaps he dozed too, sitting in the chair keeping vigil. Perhaps he dozed or perhaps he didn't, but he saw a vision.

It was like something from the Apocalypse of St. John the Apostle. It was a great red beast with the face of a swarthy man with black shining eyes and many long pointed teeth, a huge beast like a bull. One of its horns was red and one of its horns was black. It was trampling through fields of young corn that were really young boys growing up green and straight, but now trampled into the muck beneath the cloven hooves of this great red beast. A voice like that of an angel spoke loudly to him and said, "And the one horn was Drink and the second horn was Smut." The beast was thundering toward him trampling the fine boys under its hooves, and it was chanting about freedom and free love and free lust and bad women as it stomped the youth, their blood mixing with the mud. He rose up and stood to meet it. He was going to stop the beast, to wrestle it to the ground like Samson. The beast rushed toward him snorting. Anthony stood his ground, then woke with a start, staring around him.

Maggie was still sleeping, but she looked better. He touched her forehead. It was clammy. He would make broth. He knew perfectly well how to make beef broth. He had many good household skills acquired growing up in a motherless house, before he went away to school. He would cook a healthy digestive broth for her and bring it to her on a tray. In all ways, he was a much better husband than his father had been. He would have kept his mother alive if he had been her husband. He would have coddled and cosseted her as he did his Maggie.

There was a case in the papers of a young fair-haired woman whose naked body had been found in a trunk shipped railway express from New York to Chicago. It was a sensational murder, for she had clearly bled to death from an abortion. Her body was put on ice at Bellevue. Hundreds of men filed by to look at her, the picture of tragedy, purity defiled and then vilely killed by a dirty abortionist. It was the moral outrage of the entire metropolitan area, on the front page of every paper. MAIDEN BETRAYED.

The police soon arrested a Polish Jew named Rosenzweig, although he called himself Dr. Franklin to disguise his origins. His family all lined up in court and insisted he had been with them and had never done such a thing. He just dispensed pills and powders and in Poland he had been a doctor, they said. Anthony followed the case and one day he stole away from his sales rounds and went to court. He had to arrive very early because crowds of men attended the trial every day. It was the sensation of the month.

The men's sporting papers ran huge stories clamoring for the Jew to be hanged. Anthony despised the sporting papers because they played to the young men who came to the city, ignorant of what could happen to them. They lauded prostitution and ran lascivious ads, but they did oppose abortionists and called for their prosecution. They got one thing right with all the evil they did.

Anthony watched the prosecutor carefully. He was earnest but not forceful enough. He used too much legal language and didn't make the jury feel outrage. Anthony could do a better job. It should be him going after the scum of the city. It should be him shouldering the weight of justice. That was what he had been born for. A destiny awaited him, but how to break through to it? Not by selling notions.

The murdered girl was Alyce Bowlsby. Her murderer spoke with a strong accent that the newspapers made fun of. He kept saying Alyce had threatened to kill herself. A handkerchief with her initials had been found in his office. The defense tried to call a woman friend of Alyce's. However the judge would not let the witness be sworn in. The judge exhibited, Anthony felt, an appropriate sense of decency. No female ears should hear of such a subject.

The miscreant was found guilty and taken away to prison. But still, Anthony did not feel satisfied. He wanted to punish Rosenzweig in a way that would crush him and deter others. He should be publicly flogged; he should be hanged in Union Square. Anthony could have handled everything more powerfully. He ought to be up there prosecuting evildoers. He ought to be out catching them.

Maggie finally recovered enough to get out of bed. They had to use a wet nurse, as she hadn't enough milk. However, she was her cheerful self and once again providing him with a home that was a haven from all the ugly things in the city and the hardness of the commercial world. She was the angel in his house, frail still. He wondered if it was time to move back into their shared bedroom. The baby cried sometimes at night and woke him. That also woke Maggie, who would carry the baby to bed with her. After a week of this, she simply took Lillie into her bed for the entire night. Anthony began to sleep through again. Perhaps it was a little soon to return to Maggie's bed.

Budington, who kept up on everything important going on in the causes they were both passionate about, told him that Jesup was appointing a committee on Obscene Literature. Anthony was burning to be part of this new crusade of the YMCA. Who knew more about that subject than himself? He needed to reach these men and offer himself to their cause. The time was ripe. He had to prove to them that he was the man to prune the tree of evil and protect the young men from their worst enemies, the forces that summoned them into vice. He had only to reach these important and wealthy men to get them to make him their deputy.

THIRTY

THE TIME HAD COME, Victoria was sure, for her to move into the larger world and accomplish the great tasks Demosthenes and her spirits had long promised would be her destiny. Society needed her. She knew what it was to grow up ignorant of her own body, to bleed her menses and think she was dying because her crazy hyperreligious mother could not bring herself to discuss sex. She knew what it was to be exploited as a child, helpless as a woman, to be forced into sex without her consent. She knew what it was to be yoked with a drunkard in a hideous travesty of love, to bear a child alone in a tenement and almost bleed to death. She knew what it was to have to support not only herself but a child, and then a drunken drug-addicted husband, and then, with Tennie, the entire Claflin clan plus Canning again. She could not be cruel to him, although she kept him at a distance from herself and from Zulu Maud. Canning spent most of his days taking care of the boy, seeing he ate, got cleaned up, dressed and had some exercise. Canning and Byron seemed able to communicate, both broken souls but hardly devoid of feeling.

Tennie and she had started *Woodhull & Claflin's Weekly* to promote their ideas about woman's rights, labor rights, economic reform, whatever struck them as important, and whatever Stephen Pearl Andrews and James wanted to write. It was smartly done, sixteen pages with easy-to-read type—unlike most papers—good layout and clear writing. Tennie had a sense of style, and their paper looked like quality but with a certain raciness. Victoria strongly supported women's education and equal pay for equal work. She ran a Washington column every issue and solicited reports on movements in Europe. She herself wrote a story about a nursing home in Brooklyn where alcoholism was being appropriately treated as a disease. They covered the stock market and financial news, as well as the arts. They always had a couple of poems and book reviews. They even covered sports, fashion and yachting. In the first issue, they began serializing a translation of a novel by George Sand, with whom Victoria felt a kinship. From the beginning, they had plenty of advertising, and every issue afterward brought more. Tennie had taken it upon herself to rope in advertisers before they started, but soon no persuasion was needed. Then they handed off subscriptions and ads to an agent, who did it all professionally.

It was time to go to Washington again. Tennie and James could run the brokerage firm in her absence. Victoria was careful to stroke their clients and make sure they felt personally cared for before she packed up three trunks and left on the train. Benjamin Butler was delighted to see her. He came to her hotel, and before and after their lovemaking, brought her up to date on what was going on in Congress. Victoria and Tennie had been supporting the Sixteenth Amendment to give the vote to women, but Benjamin told her it was a dead horse. Voting it into committee was a way to kill it. She should seek a different path to victory. He suggested that she focus on an argument that the Constitution gave the right to vote to all citizens, and women were citizens. She wrote an essay to that effect for the *Weekly,* and then followed it up two weeks later with a closely argued document based on constitutional law which Butler wrote and she went over, changing some of the language, then signed and sent on to New York.

He was a man who liked nudity. He liked her to leave her robe off while they were talking. Victoria viewed modesty as hypocrisy. If she was intimate with a man, why pretend to shudder if he wanted to look at her body as well as touch or enter it? The sight of a man's naked body meant little to her. Mostly she was attracted to a man's personality, his knowledge, his ability. A dynamic man who could teach her something fascinating and useful excited her. Such a man was worth knowing on every level.

Butler was almost bald, but he had lush whiskers. His eyes were dark and piercing in their gaze. No one would ever call him handsome—he was short and resembled a pug—yet when he walked into a room, everyone knew he had arrived, men and women alike, and they turned to him. He exuded an energy that was electric.

Returning briefly to New York, she worked on a memorial—a petition by a private citizen to Congress. Butler would know how to approach that body. She would argue as she had in her articles that the Constitution already gave women the right to vote as citizens, and no further legislation was needed to assure that right. She would petition Congress to pass an act declaring that women were citizens and thus had suffrage. She carefully prepared her speech, consulting James and especially Stephen. She went over it again and again, strengthening the legal arguments. She worked on the memorial until she thought she had something Congress would have to listen to—if she got the chance to stand before the lawmakers. For a woman to do this would be most unusual, and she would need every bit of Senator Butler's influence and power to bring it off. Telegraphing Butler, she set off again.

The better hotels of Washington were watering holes for members of Congress, their wives and mistresses, the lobbyists who swarmed around them. The public rooms were thick with smoke while the men drank mint juleps and whiskey skins. Before each introduction, Benjamin would prepare her, feeding her information so that she could charm them. "He's prouder of his hunting dogs than of his office or his children." "He's a fanatical operagoer. Adores Italian opera." "He likes to think himself a great gourmet and an expert on wines." "He loves to talk about his exploits in the Civil War—which were negligible. Flatter him." "He imagines himself a great orator. Tell him you heard his last speech from the gallery and were moved to tears."

She listened, she memorized, and she performed. Quickly her fame spread among the politicians: intelligent, beautiful and charming and unusually knowledgeable for a woman. She grew a little weary of Washington, where gossip was an obsession, a job, an amusement and a tool. She was spending more time with Butler than she had anticipated. As a winning general, he had occupied New Orleans, where he had been called "Beast Butler" because he ordered that New Orleans ladies who spat upon or insulted his soldiers in the streets would be arrested as prostitutes. He also ordered that every escaped slave under his jurisdiction was to be considered "contraband of war" and therefore immediately free. In the Senate, he was powerful and respected among the radical Republicans. He had led the unsuccessful attempt to impeach Johnson. He took her memorial in hand and went over it, reworking parts and making suggestions for other passages.

Benjamin told her that many women suffragists were in town for a convention Isabella Beecher Hooker was organizing. Susan B. Anthony had pleaded with one of the congressmen on the House Judiciary Committee to move the Sixteenth Amendment granting the vote to women out of committee and onto the floor of the House. He told her Congress had more important questions to consider than such silliness. She responded that when women had the vote, their questions would gain importance at once. But Susan and Isabella were stymied, she heard from Benjamin, who knew them all.

"Never you mind, Vickie darling," Benjamin said, squeezing her shoulder. "You shall address the Joint House and Senate Judiciary Committees the day after tomorrow."

"Really? Are you serious? You've done it!" She hugged him hard. He was not a tall man, but he was solidly built, like a bull on hind legs. He had some other characteristics imputed to bulls. She could feel his erection. For the miracle he had created for her, he deserved to have it used. "Here," she said, unbuttoning him. "Come and let's see what we can do with this."

Benjamin would only have sex with him on top. For a short man, he was heavy. Sometimes she felt as if he would squeeze the breath out of her. He was a rough lover, heavy-handed, passionate, impulsive. Once they were launched, the bed could have caught fire and she did not think he would notice. She was more accustomed to men like James and Stephen, whom she must take in hand and excite, whom she led through the act. With Benjamin, it was as if she stepped into a swiftly moving river and the current took her. She enjoyed letting go. Once he entered her, he went on and on. She had no trouble reaching orgasm once, sometimes twice with him. His prick was thick, like the rest of him. It was more like rutting than making love, but quite satisfying. She did not have to flatter him, to cajole or sweet-talk. He was about as sentimental as a spittoon. He did not speak of making love or joining; he simply called it fucking. He liked her body and praised it. He liked her without pretending more. She trusted him and his advice. They were allies.

That evening, Victoria was chatting with a congressional aide in the lounge of her hotel who told her that not only was the press coming in force, but the woman's rights convention had postponed its opening for a day so that they could hear her. She owed Benjamin a tremendous boon. She could not have asked for better timing or publicity for her entrée into the woman's rights movement, a possible political base for her.

She was frightened when the time came for her to go to Capitol Hill. Although Benjamin, James and Stephen had all had a hand in the philosophical, legal and constitutional arguments, if she had not understood it, she would never have signed it and she would never go up to Congress to deliver it in person, as requested by the joint committees. She knew that she had mastered the memorial and the arguments behind it, but still her hands were shaking. The joint committees were meeting in a room big enough to hold them and the press and the audience that had collected, including many women who were probably leaders of the convention that had been postponed so they could see and hear her. She recognized Susan B. Anthony from attending her lectures, but could not find Elizabeth Cady Stanton, the woman she most wanted to meet.

Benjamin saw that her hands were trembling. He grasped her arm. "You must be strong! Now is no time for feminine modesty. You must speak up so they can hear you and sound competent and confident. Make me proud."

"I'm more nervous about the women hearing me than the congressmen and the senators. I know the ladies have heard rumors about me."

"Well, Isabella Beecher Hooker may snub you—her family are great snobs who think most highly of themselves and each other next to God."

A congressman standing next to them overheard and turned. "It would ill become a Beecher to cast any smirch on Mrs. Woodhull. I am told that Henry Ward Beecher preaches to twenty of his mistresses every Sunday."

Victoria smiled at him. At least he seemed to be on her side. She wanted to ask Benjamin who he was, but she was ushered into the hearing room. She drew deep breaths. Spirits be with me, Demosthenes, be with me. I may not be meek, I may not show my fear. I must be bold, as Benjamin has chided me. For a moment, her teeth chattered although the room was overheated.

Her hands trembled for a moment longer. She felt cold and then hot. The woman finely dressed sitting next to Susan B. Anthony, who was all in black like Victoria, must be Isabella. I must conquer you, I must win you to my side, Victoria thought, and looked straight into Isabella's eyes. She kept her gaze fixed there for several minutes. Isabella blushed. Victoria touched the white rose she always wore at her neck.

Benjamin took charge. He got everyone seated, passed out copies of the memorial, spoke to this one and that one, then called the meeting to order. When she was introduced, she rose and the room swam around her. She held tight to the edge of the table. Her voice caught in her throat and once again she trembled, not just her hands but her entire body. This was her grand moment, and she was failing. She was too weak a woman. The men were looking at each other, out the window, one was reading something—a letter? A note? Another was rolling his eyes. Another yawned and scratched himself. Her voice died in the center of the room. Two of the journalists against the wall were chatting. Another was aiming at a spittoon and missing.

No! She pulled herself upright. I am on the stage. This is a part. I am playing a role I have learned by heart. I have done it many times before. By the fourth sentence her voice rang out as it had when she was acting in silly plays in San Francisco, a strong melodious voice low for a woman and a little husky that could carry up to the second balcony. She breathed from the diaphragm and poured out her words.

Now their eyes were on her. The man with the note put it down. They had stopped smirking, stopped looking out the window. They were listening. Victoria glanced at Isabella. She was sitting with her mouth slightly open, her eyes glistening. Victoria knew she could win her. She gave her entire speech with passion, with clarity. When she had finished, she stood a moment more and then she collapsed into her chair, the breath gone out of her with her inspiration. Her mind felt empty.

One of the congressmen seized her hand. "That was amazing."

"Do you agree with my arguments?"

"Can't say I remember a word you said, but you're a pretty creature if ever I saw one."

She was led out to Benjamin's office, where Susan and Isabella joined them. Susan was beaming. She had a wonderful warm smile, clasping Victoria's hands.

"My dear Woodhull," Susan said, "you have breathed new life into our movement. You have brought to me hope as strong and energetic as yourself. In two decades of fighting this good fight, I've never felt so energized."

Victoria kissed Susan on the cheek. "Your faith means the world to me. I long to be of use to our great cause."

Isabella was approaching. She had a high forehead and the Beecher jaw, her hair in long curls. Victoria had years of experience sizing up men and women. Isabella was an enthusiast, probably also a devotee of spiritualism, like herself. That was the way to approach her.

Isabella started to speak, but Victoria got in first. "We have met before." She held Isabella's gaze, having discovered already that the woman was susceptible to that kind of mesmerizing eye lock.

"No . . . I don't think so," Isabella stammered.

"Not in this life," Victoria said. "But I sense that we knew each other before. . . . On another plane of existence."

Isabella seized her hand and wrung it. "Oh, dear Mrs. Woodhull. You are the savior of our movement. You will lead us like Moses out of bondage."

Victoria kept her gaze locked with Isabella's. "I will try. I have a vision of the grandest revolution this nation has ever seen. And the three of us here will play a great role in this. I know it."

Benjamin marched in from the hall. "Your memorial is being set in type. I'll use my franking and we can send out thousands of copies, also a petition we should draw up directly, to present to Congress after we have enough—impressive numbers—of signatures. We need thousands."

Susan wrung Benjamin's hand. "I can't wait to tell Mrs. Stanton."

"Where is Mrs. Stanton?" Victoria still hoped to meet her, disappointed that the philosopher, the greatest brain of woman's rights, had not come to hear her.

"She's back in New Jersey writing. She's tired of conventions—she says they don't move things forward but just act as social events and occasions for infighting. She'll be furious with herself when she hears what she missed!" Susan did not sound at all unhappy. "She'll see that important events do occur when women come together determined to act."

Victoria met with the women the next day at their convention, gave them money and pledged more for a delegation to remain in Washington to lobby Congress. Isabella offered to head the group. Victoria felt reasonably sure of her now. She was smitten. Victoria was familiar with the looks that Isabella gave her, the doting glances, the fervent handclasps. When they were alone, Victoria was effusive and spoke much of the spirits. When she was with Susan, she spoke of political tactics and how they might proceed with Congress while the fire was still lit.

Victoria received a note from the president's wife, Julia Grant, complimenting her on the memorial. Susan told her that Mrs. Grant was sympathetic to the movement. Then an invitation came from President and Mrs.

Grant inviting her to tea at the White House. No one in woman's rights had ever been invited to meet with the president, Susan said in great excitement, hugging her. She liked Susan's forthright manner. Susan might be an aging virgin, but she had a shrewd mind and she was not a prude. She kept her eye on the goal. Isabella was flightier, more emotional, more prone to enthusiasms and visions and extravagance. Susan would stand by her as long as she was useful. Isabella was a little in love with her, although she would never have phrased it that way to herself. As long as Victoria kept Isabella feeling special, the Beecher woman would never waver.

The visit to the White House was formal and stiff. But for Victoria, the supreme moment came when the president showed her the Oval Office, shook his finger at her and, pointing to the presidential chair, said, "Someday you will occupy this chair, no doubt, the way you've been playing the politician here."

When Victoria repeated that to Susan, Susan laughed. "He was teasing you."

Victoria shook her head. She knew it was the spirits speaking through the president. "Nonetheless, I think I'll run for president."

Isabella clutched herself in excitement. "What a truly excellent idea!"

"Why on earth would you do that?" Susan asked. "We need the right to vote long before we can elect a woman to any office."

Victoria smiled serenely. She knew she was called on to lead a mighty crusade. "It's a way to raise issues and force the other candidates to discuss woman's rights."

"That's quite clever," Susan said. "It should garner publicity for our cause."

Victoria rode back on the train to New York with Susan while Isabella remained in Washington to head the small delegation of women who would lobby Congress. Susan was eager to introduce her to Cady Stanton. She must make a favorable impression on Stanton or she would not have the leverage in the movement that she needed.

That week, *Woodhull & Claflin's Weekly* carried her memorial in full, and the week after, it bannered her intention to run for president. The idea of running was all her own. Had not the spirits promised her that she would be a great leader and had they not spoken through Grant? Everything was working out according to plan. They had come to New York, Tennie and she, and snared Vanderbilt. They had made enough money to feel rich. She had encountered men and women of ideas who educated and stimulated her. She had become famous. Reporters wrote up everything she did. She had entered the woman's rights movement with a great splash and now she was counted among its leaders. All was happening as the spirits had instructed her so many years before, that she would be rich and famous and lead a great cause.

"Running for president is fine, so long as you don't take it too seriously or waste time electioneering," James said. "It gets your name in the papers. It could provide you a springboard for the lecture circuit. But otherwise, best to treat it as a publicity stunt."

She felt an unusual anger toward him, but she concealed it. He did not believe in her as she believed in herself. His attitude belittled her. She decided she would not open herself and her plans to him as fully as she always had. She felt just a sliver of distance between them. She said nothing and she did not act any differently toward him, but in her heart she knew he did not believe in her as fully as she had always hoped.

She had to return to Washington again briefly, because Isabella, Benjamin and she had been invited to lecture at Lincoln Hall on constitutional equality. Isabella came to her—Victoria was staying with Benjamin, as his family was out of town—almost in tears. "I have never spoken to a large audience before. How can I? I just cannot do it, Victoria."

"Do you remember how frightened I was when I first began to speak before the joint committees of Congress? I know you saw how I was trembling. Call on the spirits, Isabella. They will aid you. The spirits are inspiring and protecting you! You need only feel their presence, draw upon their aid, and you will succeed."

Victoria was far more confident this time. Her ability to memorize stood her in good stead, because she could speak without a written text, apparently extemporaneously. Audiences liked that. They felt that a speaker who did not read her speech knew her stuff.

Benjamin was powerful, as always, a master of rhetoric. The surprise was Isabella. Victoria was sure that Isabella had been asked because of her connection with the powerful, famous and respected Beecher clan. But Isabella spoke well. Her voice was higher-pitched than Victoria's but carried well and sounded convincing. She understood what she was discussing—she had a kind of legal mind, in spite of her effusiveness and her romantic side. She made an elegant presentation, dressed in mauve velvet and white satin with a huge bustle that emphasized her tiny waist, amethysts plaited into her hair and at her throat. The audience was silent and engrossed. She lacked Butler's rhetorical flair or Victoria's ability to fascinate, but she was coherent, logical and persuasive. Isabella was thrilled with her own success.

"This is what I was born for. I could never draw or paint, never write like Harriet, I have no gift for educating girls like Catherine—but I have discovered at last my own true gifts. I have found my métier at last—because of you, dear Victoria. Because of you!"

Victoria was growing accustomed to women developing crushes on her. Her charm worked on women as well as men. She had always had women friends, but these new conquests were a more accomplished type than she had encountered before. It was all going very well indeed.

THIRTY-ONE

ELIZABETH KNEW ONLY what she read in the papers, accounts of Victoria Woodhull addressing the joint committees of Congress, apparently triumphantly. There were, of course, cartoons—Woodhull as a schoolmarm lecturing Congress, Woodhull as a circus performer riding an elephant labeled Benjamin Butler. But most of the coverage was surprisingly respectful. Susan was going to gloat over her that she had missed the most spectacular and meaningful advance of their movement in several years. She could hardly endure waiting till Susan appeared. She considered going off by train to Washington, but that would be too abject—to arrive after everything important had happened, as a sort of caboose to the powerful engine Mrs. Woodhull seemed to embody.

Finally Susan appeared, rosy-cheeked and scarcely able to take the time to throw aside her cloak and gloves before launching into an account of the Washington adventure, as Elizabeth had been calling it to herself.

"So Isabella stayed in Washington?"

"She's heading our delegation. Woodhull is paying. Also Senator Butler has sent out thousands upon thousands of copies of Woodhull's memorial along with petitions requesting that Congress make a declaration of our right to vote according to the Constitution."

"Is she paying for all this?"

"It's free, Mrs. Stanton. The petitions are going out on Senator Butler's franking privilege. We could never have afforded this."

Elizabeth asked Amelia to make coffee. "We certainly couldn't. Now I'm sorry we let go of the *Revolution*. Perhaps Woodhull would have helped us with our debts."

"We still have them. I don't know how I'll ever pay them off. . . . If you could manage to contribute something?"

"Susan, I have my younger children still to support. I have this house, where you are a member of the household whenever you wish. I live off the lecture circuit, the same as you. I have no money to spare. Nothing!"

"I wish we could ask Woodhull to pay off a creditor or two, but she has her own paper." Susan pulled a copy from her reticule.

Elizabeth poured them both big mugs of coffee with hot milk. "It's pretty progressive. She seems bright. Is she?"

"You can judge for yourself, Mrs. Stanton." Susan drank her coffee, holding the cup in both hands to warm them. "I've invited her for luncheon next Sunday. Here."

"Will she come?" Elizabeth turned to Amelia. "Bring Susan some soup."

"She's eager to make your acquaintance. She was bitterly disappointed that you weren't in Washington."

"All right, Susan, admitted: I'm sorry I didn't go. But I've been to so many of these conventions, I'm heartily sick of them."

"It was a most hopeful and stimulating experience, Mrs. Stanton. I'm convinced Woodhull will be a great asset for our movement."

In the papers the next morning was an account of President Grant receiving Woodhull at the White House. Elizabeth shook her head in wonder. In a couple of weeks, Woodhull had accomplished more for the cause than they had been able to do in the last year. Sunday she would meet this marvel. All that buildup and probably she would meet someone flashy, arrogant or just a pawn in a male game. There were always rumors circulating that the *Weekly* was written by various men, from Woodhull's husband to Stephen Pearl Andrews. Pearlo was an old friend of hers; she could ask him directly. She dashed off a note at once.

The first issue of the *Revolution* was out. Susan looked at it and threw it across the room in a rare fit of anger. Elizabeth read it, sighing and muttering over the watered-down paper full of homilies and arguments that women and men had common interests and should all just get along. She was not overly fond of Tilton these days, but what could they do? She and Susan had sold it to Laura Bullard for a dollar so that it would continue—but what a pallid continuation. She felt as if they had given away a child and now that child was being turned into a simpering fool. Certainly this paper would anger no one, inspire no one. Isabella was upset with the change and quit as literary editor. Besides, she was immensely busy in Washington carrying out the great work that her dear Queen, as she called Victoria, had given her. Now "Queen" was a common term of endearment among women Elizabeth knew, but this particular usage made her wince. Isabella was enamored, there could be no other word for it. Isabella had that enthusiastic side, a dither of spiritualism.

Elizabeth liked the spiritualists well enough—they were a far gentler less doctrinaire religious group than most, and more egalitarian. The Quakers and the spiritualists were the only religions that gave women a strong role—and among spiritualists, many leaders and prominent mediums were women. Elizabeth had seen how comforting spiritualism was to mothers who had lost children, which included most women. A mother could feel her beloved son or daughter had simply passed onto a higher plane of being where they were still evolving and from which they could communicate. It was marvelously comforting to the bereft, and most Americans were often enough in mourning. After all, just about every family had a son or brother or husband killed in the Civil War.

She had lost her faith years before—no, she did not like that phrasing, suggesting she had misplaced it absentmindedly like a glove. She had fought her way free. She had wrestled with it like Jacob with the angel, and she had scars to prove the battle. She was not done yet. At some point in her life, she would take on religion and its role in denigrating women and keeping them subservient and compliant. It was a great task she promised herself she would tackle in her elder years.

Sunday arrived and Elizabeth was impatient to finally meet this Woodhull, who had so enraptured Susan and Isabella. To prepare a proper lunch for the woman who had been asked to address a joint committee of Congress and invited to the White House and lauded as a successful stockbroker, she needed to put out a meal that was elegant. She joined Amelia and the maid Maureen in the kitchen to assist in the complicated preparations.

At eleven-thirty, she put on one of her better dresses, a blue and green and gold taffeta walking dress. Susan was dressed in a gray walking suit with a fine garnet pendant one of her young admirers had pressed on her.

Amelia wore Quaker gray and white as she set out vases of camellias from the conservatory.

Just before twelve, they heard a knocking. Amelia opened the door and ushered in a young woman, taking her fur-lined cape. The woman was dressed in black, an unusually simple dress but finely tailored and of the best silk. She wore a single white rose at her throat. The startling thing about her, besides the simplicity of her dress, was her beauty. Elizabeth had been pretty in her day, certainly, and Isabella had been considered so, but Victoria Woodhull was simply and outstandingly beautiful. Her eyes were the most striking feature, being a singularly bright and piercing blue that seemed to gather light in their direct, forceful gaze.

Woodhull greeted Susan warmly, hugging her. Then she approached Elizabeth where she sat, seizing her hand. Woodhull's grasp was strong. "To meet you at last fulfills one of my ambitions," she said. Her voice was also striking, low-pitched but quite carrying, a little huskiness never affecting its clarity. "I've admired you for years. You're a unique and powerful voice of liberation. The breadth of your interests and your erudition are extraordinary. You stand head and shoulders above us all."

"You flatter me," Elizabeth said, but did not really think so. She had been so embattled in the last couple of years that praise was like balm ladled over her sore ego. "You're a very striking woman. Everyone in the press and in the movement has been talking about nothing but you."

"If it's useful to the movement, good," Woodhull said.

They sat almost knee to knee, Woodhull having dragged an overstuffed chair almost effortlessly near the rocker. Susan brought a straight chair up to them and all three sat tête-à-tête. Amelia was unnecessarily fussing with the vases and papers scattered about. "Amelia, don't stand there. Take a seat. I know you're as curious about Mrs. Woodhull as I am," Elizabeth said dryly.

Amelia took a seat on a davenport, sitting dead center on the edge of the cushion lest she be thought to be taking liberties in the salon.

"I am prepared to offer ten thousand to your association. Some of it can be in the form of printing. We have female typographers working for us at the *Weekly*."

"Ten thousand would be of great assistance to us," Elizabeth said, a wide smile spreading across her face.

Susan added, "I suppose it's too late to get the *Revolution* back."

Woodhull smiled. "We already have a weekly paper. You would both be most welcome in its pages."

They thanked her, although in truth Elizabeth had no idea when she could write anything she had not already pledged to do. "You had a great success in Washington."

"I hope my ideas were persuasive. I was so happy when your association asked me to repeat my memorial to your convention."

"You were the star of the convention," Susan said fervently.

Woodhull waved that away. She had fine long-fingered pale hands. "We managed, all of us, to stir things up in Washington."

"Amelia, perhaps we could eat?" Amelia and Elizabeth stood. Amelia went off to serve, with the help of Maureen, and Elizabeth led the way into the dining room. She was pleased to see Amelia had placed lilies as a centerpiece. Having a conservatory was a luxury she passionately appreciated. It was small, not a place she could sit and read among the plants, but it sufficed to fill vases in the house.

Amelia and the maid had prepared a rich and buttery terrapin soup. It was a lot of work, but Amelia had been willing to undertake it since this was an occasion. Elizabeth had left the disgusting part of the terrapin preparation to them, cooking beet and rice soubise and a pie from dried apples that would end the meal. Amelia and she had gutted squabs the night before and hung them. They were the main course.

Woodhull was a dainty eater but put it away. She complimented Amelia, who answered, "Maureen and Elizabeth did part of the work. Elizabeth is a fine cook, thee should realize. 'Tis one of her many gifts. She has a touch with pastry that equals any woman's."

Over the soup, Woodhull said, "You should be aware that the Boston women don't trust me. I am not a lady in their eyes."

"We have too many ladies, and too few useful women," Elizabeth said. "I'm not interested in gossip about your past or your lovers. I'm interested in your ideas and your abilities." And your money, Elizabeth added with sour honesty to herself. It was dreadful to be so mercenary, but as she was always reminding Susan, movements ran on money and theirs had run out. "The Boston ladies find me a bit rank too. I write and lecture upon topics they consider unmentionable—divorce, childbirth, sexuality, contraception, abortion. They think it shocking to discuss such things in public. But I'm old enough to remember when it was shocking for a woman to lecture about anything. If the Grimke sisters had listened to their critics, we might have had slavery for another twenty years. They spoke powerfully and moved audiences." Elizabeth frowned. "I have a question for you. What does it mean that you've announced that you're running for president?"

"Consider this. If a woman comes into a city and gives a speech on woman's rights, perhaps the papers will cover it and perhaps not." Victoria put down her spoon and leaned slightly forward. "But if a woman bold enough to run for president comes into that same city and gives a speech, it will be in every newspaper."

"Very shrewd," Elizabeth said.

There was a calm certainty in this woman that Elizabeth found attractive. Woodhull was much less fussy than Isabella. She focused attention on herself without seeming to try. Her beauty certainly helped, but Elizabeth had met beauties whom people admired when they entered a room and then ignored. They were lovely wallpaper. Woodhull was a presence. She did not play with her dress or her gloves or her necklace, she did not fidget with her hair or the folds of her gown. She sat quite still and radiated power and certainty.

"I believe, and I know Isabella does also, that it's our time at last." Woodhull leaned forward again, staring into Elizabeth's eyes. "We must strike at the core of resistance. Push onward in every way. The more publicity we arouse for our cause, the more chance we have to succeed."

"Is your sister—the Claflin part of Woodhull and Claflin—also interested in woman's rights?"

"She surely is. She too had a disastrous marriage and a difficult childhood. Our father took her on the road to tell fortunes and sell patent medicines—the scandalous past to which the Boston ladies refer. We were exploited as children. Our special powers were abused. But I forgive my parents—they were poor and needy. Tennie and I still support them. We're not ashamed of coming from poverty. Stephen Pearl Andrews has met all my family and he can tell you exactly what stock we sprang from. They're crude and uncultured, yes, but we refuse to disown them, as I find so many young people who come to New York do. Our parents were hardly saints, but they did their best to feed us.

"I was only able to attend school spottily. I had to work. I've educated myself. I read history, economics, literature, philosophy. I never stop trying to improve my grasp of the forces that have shaped and will shape society. If I'm no longer ignorant, I owe it to my own efforts and finding mentors who help me with choosing books to read and subjects to study."

Elizabeth suspected that Woodhull had heard the rumors that she did not write the articles signed with her name, that she had not written the memorial. She was answering that accusation obliquely. Elizabeth was sorry she had written to Pearlo with her query about Woodhull.

"What do you consider the most important reforms for women?" Susan asked her. "In your own opinion."

Woodhull frowned, considering. "Of course the vote is extremely important. With the vote, we can tackle other problems facing women. We know from the case of Wyoming that we will vote in large numbers as soon as we're able. But working women survive on miserable pittances. The current situation of marriage makes a woman a chattel. Child-rearing is absurd for girls who grow up ignorant of everything real and of their own bodies and desires."

"So you are for divorce reform?"

"Of course. I'm a divorced woman. Someone must have told you that already."

Susan nodded. "The Boston ladies have been writing me missives."

Elizabeth waited until Amelia had cleared the course and was about to bring in the pie, fruit and cheese. "Mrs. Woodhull, what do you need from us?"

Woodhull cocked her head to the side on her swanlike neck. "I need your advice and wisdom. I need to find a reliable biographer, not a scandalmonger, to write up a biography of me for my campaign. Perhaps it can replace all those wild rumors floating about."

Susan and Elizabeth conferred. Finally Elizabeth said, "I believe Theodore Tilton could do it. He writes vividly and swiftly. For years, he wrote Henry Ward Beecher's essays and articles for the *Independent*. Beecher is famous for missing deadlines."

"If you approach him, it would be better not to mention my name," Susan said. "He threw me out of his house recently, when I attempted to see his wife, Lib. I was worried about her."

"Threw you out of his house? What occasioned such violence?"

Elizabeth told the story of their night in Brooklyn with Laura Bullard, Theo and Lib Tilton. Woodhull listened, fascinated. "That explains what rumors I heard about Beecher in Washington. But if his affairs are known, are they accepted by the members of his church?"

"It is 'known' as a rumor," Susan said primly, "but such a rumor that anyone who needs to dismiss it can. He's the most popular preacher in the States. His sermons are printed in the papers. He mints money by lecturing. A whole publishing house depends on him. He's the engine behind the God is Love movement in Protestant churches, the liberalizing of Calvinist dogma—"

"He has no theology or philosophy," Elizabeth said, "Only sentimentality. But he's all the more popular for that. His congregation numbers three thousand and includes the most powerful and influential men in politics and commerce in Brooklyn and even in Manhattan."

"Perhaps we are all doomed to be gossiped about on this plane of existence. In any event, you both agree that Theodore Tilton would be the first author to speak to about my biography?"

Elizabeth nodded. "I no longer completely trust him, but he's a fast and competent writer and won't be shocked by whatever you tell him."

"Good," Woodhull said. "I've heard about him. I'm eager to meet him. He sounds quite . . . interesting."

THIRTY-TWO

FREYDEH FELT GUILTY keeping Sammy out of school, but if they did not follow up on their lead quickly, it would vanish as all the others had. She would make it up to Sammy, she would see he got back in school when they had found Shaineh and her little girl. She could not go on sacrificing Sammy to Shaineh.

He was making his way from stable to stable, slowly. She had to keep buying him cigarettes all the lads were smoking so he could offer them to the stableboys to befriend them. Sometimes beer was necessary. She did not have to worry about Sammy getting drunk, as he despised drunkards—men who had often beaten him in his street urchin days. She worried more about his being tempted to join one of the gangs that preyed lucratively on neighborhoods. They offered a step up to boys from the streets and the blocks—a social network, an identity, a means of making money, a way of advancing. As they grew, they might move into firefighting and then into politics. Many of the Tweed men had started in local gangs. If she had not taken him in and he had survived those vulnerable years, he would probably have joined a gang and would now be a full member of the Sheeny mob or the Whyos or the River Pirates. His hero would be a bank robber, locally famous and much admired.

"Do you envy those stableboys?" she asked him at supper, after a day he had spent in five different stables, hanging around the guys who worked there.

"Being around horses and horse shit all day and all night? Nah. I don't like horses . . . they're too big. I don't want to climb up on one, and I sure don't want one of them stepping on me. They can cripple you for life."

Lacking Sammy's help, she was up early and up late fulfilling orders. She pressed Kezia into service with the packing. At night she was almost too exhausted to sleep. There were a hundred stables to check out in their target area, more if it turned out that they were wrong about the probable location. Every family who could afford it kept a horse. Every time Sammy appeared at the end of a day of plying stableboys with cigarettes or beer, she greeted him with the same question, "Did you learn anything?" and every day she got the same answer as he stumbled in, worn out, reeking of tobacco and sometimes of beer.

The sketch of Shaineh had grown worn and greasy and was tearing along its folds, so Kezia copied it and made new pictures for each of them to carry, with lighter hair. When she was working with Kezia, Freydeh taught her songs she had heard her own mother sing—Yiddish songs, songs from services in the shul, an occasional Russian or Polish ditty that had passed into shtetl culture. Kezia had a reedy voice but singing made her happy as they worked together by candlelight. How many years it had been since Freydeh sang as she worked. Her mother sang constantly. Freydeh's father teased her mother, saying she was half finch and he would get some seeds to feed her instead of human food.

She told Kezia stories about her mother and father, her sisters and brothers, telling Kezia that they were her kin now. When she introduced a new name to Kezia, Kezia always asked the same thing, "Would they like me?" Always Freydeh assured the girl that they would indeed love her.

She was sending money to Sara so that soon her sister and brother-in-law and their three children could come over. Sara's husband Asher wanted to bring his father too, but she told him he would have to earn that money here and send it back. They had changed their minds about emigrating, for they wrote that things were getting worse. They were afraid. The money orders Freydeh sent when she could were their lifeline, Sara wrote. She had stopped berating Freydeh for having lost Shaineh and now mostly wrote how she wanted to come to the *goldeneh medina*. Freydeh replied it wasn't so golden over here, believe her, but that if everyone in the family worked, they could get ahead. The letters took so long that often they crossed in the mails. She always read Sara's letters to Sammy and to Kezia.

"What do they do in the Pale?" Sammy asked.

"Sara took over my mother's vodka business. Her husband Asher works for a miller. Here they'll have to do whatever they can."

"Is Sara strong like you or tiny like Shaineh?"

"She's a good-sized woman. She's not as strong as me—I got Papa's strength—but she's no fragile flower. I scarcely know Asher or their children. The oldest was just four when Moishe and I left. She had a kid crawling around who died. The two others weren't even in her belly yet."

Sunday afternoon she was working on the vulcanization and Kezia was sitting singing monotonously to herself a song she had learned in school about a farmer—a Yankee song that Kezia did not understand. When Freydeh, always trying to improve her English, asked Kezia what a "dell" was, Kezia had no idea. She said it maybe was a cottage? Maybe where the family lived?

When Sammy burst in, Freydeh turned from her molding. "Is something wrong?"

"I think I found that toff." Sammy threw himself down in a chair. He must have run for blocks. She brought him a glass of water from the pitcherful she had boiled. The water had been making people sick lately. A man from Hungary who had been a doctor told her to boil it before drinking it. She could not see what good that would do, but she obeyed, and none of them had gotten sick.

"Where is he? Tell me everything! Had they ever seen Shaineh?"

"They don't know where the family lives, but it has to be nearby. The stables are behind a row of houses on Twenty-ninth Street, between Broadway and Sixth—not far from that toff restaurant Delmonico's. There are at least three men who use the phaeton. Their last name is Kumble. The stableboys say they're rolling in money."

"What does their money come from?"

"They don't know."

"At last we have a name. Alfred or Albert Kumble. But how can we find him?"

"Easy. We go to Billyboy Hanrahan and look at a city directory. Just bring him a donation and he'll let you look up Kumble."

She kissed Sammy on the brow. "You are a good, good boy. Now you go back to school."

"No! Once we have his address, I watch his house. None of them ever seen Shaineh, so I doubt he keeps her there. If we want to find her, we have to follow him. He must have her in a room in a boardinghouse or a brothel."

She set out with Sammy for the ward boss, who held open house Sunday afternoons when he wasn't putting on a picnic or a dance. She had never met him, but of course she knew him on sight. The Twelfth Ward boss was an Irish fellow married to a German woman, thus combining the two biggest blocks of voters in the ward. Billyboy Hanrahan was a bald man with enormous hands and broad shoulders and a lopsided nose, a remnant of days when he had led turf battles in the streets. He was a shrewd, jovial man with a reputation for being a good family type, faithful to his wife and loving to his eight surviving children. His attitude in the ward was paternal but tough. He laid down the law and he expected to be obeyed, but he also discharged largesse in the form of putting pressure on landlords now and then to prevent evictions, getting some money to widows and their children, feeding the hungry in hard times, keeping the criminal element within accepted bounds. He expected the vote to be delivered unanimously for Tammany, and he paid for extra votes. Generally if people had not been on the wrong side of his temper, they liked him. When the city outlawed pigs, he helped distribute lumber so people could pen them in their privy yards instead of letting them run loose in the streets to eat offal and garbage, as had been the rule for decades. He knew people needed their pigs, so he helped them keep them under cover. The police weren't about to chase pigs unless they were in the street, in which case there would be a big police barbeque, but the poor family would lose their pork.

She was nervous going to him, even with Sammy at her side. She wore her good dress—the least mended and bedraggled—and pinned her hair up and put on her only hat. They took him a present of five dollars.

He was holding forth in a saloon named the Belching Cow, at a table at the back with henchmen in attendance and his son at his side, a boy of sixteen or seventeen, a smaller version of his father except for an enormous shock of dark brown hair. They stood in the line waiting for his attention, as mothers described daughters in trouble, sons needing work, as workmen who hadn't been paid complained, as a dispute between a laundress and a client over a torn shirt was settled.

The henchman to his left took the offerings of money or occasionally meat, a chicken, a pair of shoes, a gold chain. The gold chain was left by a tough who simply laid it down and left. Then at last it was their turn. She let Sammy do the talking. The boss was glad to let them look at the directory, and wished them luck in finding the lost sister. "These filthy rich toffs, they come and take our women and use them like rags. I hope you deal with him when you find her." He made a quick motion across his throat. "Do it careful-like and nobody the wiser."

Sammy nodded. They looked into the directory and there he was, Alfred Benedict Kumble, merchant. He was listed with a Josiah Francis Kumble, also a merchant, Benjamin Augustus Kumble and Abigail Fielding Kumble, widow. His mother? Sammy wrote the address on an old numbers tab he found on the floor. Somebody had played the numbers, lost and tossed away his receipt.

They had Kumble's address, but Freydeh could not let Sammy spend his days and nights watching the house. She insisted he return to school. They did not yet even know which of the young men who came and went was Alfred. There were three brothers, Josiah, Benjamin and Alfred. Twice they saw an old lady venture out, probably Abigail. A much younger woman also appeared with one of the young men—the bearded one—and once with the old lady. A nurse appeared with a perambulator with a baby inside and they saw a little boy looking out a window.

They discussed whether to dismiss the man who had appeared with the presumed mother of the baby and the young boy.

"That he's married don't mean he can't have a mistress," Sammy argued.

"Who could afford two households?"

"He's probably only keeping Shaineh in one room. And there's at least three incomes going into that house, right? Plus maybe the dead father left them well fixed. I say there's money there. I've counted four servants besides the nurse with the baby. There may be more."

"They have the whole house to themselves, that's true." Freydeh rubbed her hands together. "I feel like we're getting close."

They took turns occasionally following the men. Two of them—the heavyset one and the one with chin whiskers—went off to an establishment on the East River waterfront, a Federal-style building of brick four stories high. Sammy found a sign: Upham and Kumble, merchants. Apparently they dealt with imports or exports, although of what Freydeh had no idea. The third young man, the tallest of the brothers, was a broker who operated out of a small office near Gold Street. He spent much of his time on the street talking intently with one or another man, and some of it eating or drinking with other men in the establishments that clustered around the Exchange. He was a snappier dresser than the other two, but they were obviously brothers and the brief description the baker had given could fit any of them.

Sammy got excited the first evening he saw the spider phaeton go out from the stable, and he trotted quickly to follow it as best he could through the crowded streets. However, it turned out to contain the mother of the young children and one of the export-import brothers. They stopped at a private club where some gala was being held. Obviously the phaeton was shared by all the brothers. They also had a runabout used for family outings.

Sometimes Freydeh imagined confronting the brothers, one at a time, and demanding she be taken to her sister. But they were Yankees and she was a Jew, they were rich and she was barely out of poverty, they were native-born and she was an immigrant with an accent as thick as a slice of liverwurst. She would only get into trouble, and whichever brother had Shaineh locked up would simply move her. They attempted to keep their surveillance unobtrusive. Indeed, there were always loiterers on the street, men out of work, servants stealing a little time off, couples making an assignation, boys delivering meat or milk or bread. Once a telegram was delivered and the brother who was a broker went rushing off in a cab to his little office.

They argued about which brother was the likely one and came to the conclusion that it was the broker, since he was the least conservative dresser of the brothers. Then one evening Freydeh was lurking outside when she saw the married couple arguing upstairs, exchanging heated words until the husband—the bearded brother—stormed out of the room and then out of the house. She followed him at a discreet distance until he went into a brothel two blocks down. Could Shaineh be there?

It was a couple of days before Freydeh could approach the madam, presumably to offer her a sample of their condoms to try. The woman had no one in the house who resembled Shaineh. She said taking in someone who wasn't willing was more trouble than she needed. She waved her hand heavy with rings. "I have girls trying to get into my house every week. They know it's safe and lucrative here and I take care of my girls. I pity the poor streetwalkers with no one to look out for their health or safety, any man's prey, and the ones with a pimp are worse off than those without. I'll try your product. I don't want disease spread in my house. Word gets around and then you lose the carriage trade."

After that they took the married brother off their list. If he went to a brothel, he wasn't keeping Shaineh. They concentrated on the other two.

If only one of them would call the other by name in the street, they would be settled. The boys in the stable only knew the men as Kumbles.

Then Sammy had an idea. They got him into the most respectable clothes they could find and he waited outside the export-import office, then strolled up to the fat one. "Why, aren't you Alfred Kumble?"

The man swung around to stare at him. "You've mistaken me for my younger brother. Do you know him?"

"Surely I do," Sammy said. "Sorry. I'm a bit weak-eyed and you look so much like him."

"Everybody says so. Shall I tell him you sent him greetings?"

"Noah Braithwaite," Sammy said, a name he had seen in an adventure story he had been reading about bank robbers, a little yellow-backed book. Noah Braithwaite was the owner of the bank in the story. Sammy hoped the dim light concealed the shabbiness of his clothes, a simulation of businessman's attire fifth-hand from a pushcart.

"Now we've found the momser, we can follow him to Shaineh." Freydeh wrung Sammy's hand. "Take more chicken. Please! You are my sweet darling boy. Who else could have found this out? Nobody! Take more chicken. We'll sell those clothes back and get you a good hat to cover your head. Someday we'll dress you just as good as that *momser* and not even secondhand. Someday we will all live in a house in Brooklyn and spit on people like Alfred Kumble."

Sammy cocked an eye at her and shrugged. "Do you believe that?"

"When I took you off the street, did you think we would have our own place? Be able to eat chicken every Shabbos? Wear boots on our feet?"

"And me," Kezia said. "I go to school. I have clothes. We eat three times every day. I have my own name back."

He grinned. "Okay. I'll start packing for Brooklyn."

1872

THIRTY-THREE

NTHONY KNELT ON THE FLOOR of Reverend Budington's cold bedroom with his minister at his side. They both fervently prayed for Anthony to achieve acceptance of the Lord's will. "Heavenly Father," Budington prayed, "as thou art a father whose son died grievously even though he returned to you in his Ascension, bring comfort to our good brother Anthony and lead him to an understanding of thy ways and acceptance of the passing over of his beloved baby daughter . . . Lillie Comstock."

"Lord, I want to accept thy will, to bow my too proud neck before thy mighty sword, but I love my little daughter with my whole heart . . . ."

"Heavenly Father, our brother Anthony's grief is extreme and profound. Help to ease his mourning. Help him into thy blessed light. Strengthen his faith for he feels sorely tried."

They prayed together for two hours until Anthony was hoarse. He knew he had to leave, walk home through the dark deserted streets of Brooklyn where snow was lightly falling. There Maggie would be lying awake staring at the ceiling, sometimes with slow tears coursing down her cheeks unheeded, still as a stone and as unresponsive. He used to hurry home every evening impatient to arrive in his sweet family, striding along and cutting corners so as to be with Maggie and Lillie even five minutes sooner. They'd had one year of joy.

Now he dreaded walking into his house where a mourning wreath marked the door, where his wife all in black would be lying as if in state, where even the Irish maid no longer sang at her work but scuttled about like a wraith. The death of little Lillie had sucked all the joy and energy from his household. The doctor said his wife was neurasthenic and must have a complete rest cure or she might suffer a permanent collapse. They could not seem to comfort each other. There was no one to blame for Lillie's sudden fever no medicines the doctor gave could lower. Her poor tiny body was bled with leeches and she was given emetics to draw the ills from her system until she was so weak she could no longer lift her head off the pillow. She sank into a stupor from which she never revived. Anthony understood that the doctor had tried every heroic remedy available to modern medicine. Maggie and he, sitting by her crib, had held hands, praying together. That was the last time they had been so close. After that, Maggie withdrew. Her mother was the only soul she related to. Her mother still mourned her three lost sons; all they could speak about together was the death of little children. It could not be good for Maggie to dwell upon their loss night and day, to the exclusion of every other interest, including himself.

Yet he grieved too, violently sometimes. He clung to his faith in the maelstrom, feeling himself in imminent danger of being sucked under into despair. Budington held him from drowning. More than ever, the tedious trivial business of selling notions seemed a vapid work to occupy an able man when there was so much evil in the city to fight against. If he could throw himself full-time into the fray, he might recover his sense of purpose. More even than before, the life of precious children needed protection. If he had lost his own Lillie, he could save the lilies of the gardens around him, preserve them clean of mind and body in their respectable houses. Death might enter in a thousand forms, not just as disease that wasted the body and carried off the soul, but in a fever stoked by filthy books—not only pornography but penny dreadfuls, the yellow books that fascinated young men, susceptible to overexcitation of mind and body. Vulnerable young men could gaze at whorish women on French postcards and even view naked women, their breasts and rear ends and sometimes even their nether regions on display, causing moral and ultimately physical and mental enfeeblement. It led to the solitary vice, the mental institution and the graveyard. He could fight this social evil if only he had backing so that he could leave his petty toils.

He moved against a book dealer, William Simpson. He went to the police and informed them of Simpson's den, producing two books he had purchased there and the receipt as proof, in his usual manner. The precinct captain said he would take care of the matter, but the next time Anthony checked the store, it was wide open. The captain said the following Friday he would send a man along with Anthony to make an arrest. Anthony stopped by the precinct at five-thirty on Friday and the constable went with him to Simpson's. When they entered the bookstore to make the arrest, the dirty books had vanished. In their place was a wall of inspiring booklets from the Tract Society. Anthony was furious.

The constable seemed to think it was funny. "You really think these fine Christian tracts are obscene? Mr. Simpson is doing a right brisk business in saving souls, far as I can see."

They were in cahoots. The police had warned Simpson and might even have helped him move his dirty wares under cover. Someone had also tipped off a reporter, who appeared smirking and tried to interview Anthony. The following Sunday, the *Mercury* ran a sarcastic story about the meddling Mr. Comstock and his effort to arrest a book dealer selling religious material from the Tract Society.

The article, however, was informative in spite of the snide tone. The reporter referred to Ann and Nassau Streets in Manhattan as places where such books were commonly sold. That was a call to action for Anthony and he decided to explore the area. He had noticed ads in men's sporting papers like the *Police Gazette* and *Day's Doings*—ads for smut and illicit objects to prevent conception or interrupt it. These murderers openly solicited business. He remembered a series of exposés in the *Tribune* about abortionists by a reporter who seemed to have some notions of morality. He had clipped them at the time. Yes, here they were, signed by Robert Griffith. He set out to find Griffith, taking along his lists of advertisers for smut and obscene rubber goods, and also the *Mercury* article attacking him.

Griffith, who turned out to be a fine Christian gentleman near Anthony's age and with a family of his own, was sympathetic. Anthony succeeded in getting Griffith fired up about the idea of exposing smut peddlers, so much so that Griffith agreed to go out on an expedition with Anthony. Griffith treated him with respect, and even introduced him to his publisher, Horace Greeley, who was genial. "You're doing a real public service, Mr. Comstock. So the police won't act? I'll put in a word in the right places. Then I want the two of you to accompany the arresting officers on an expedition to destroy these men. The *Tribune*'s behind you one hundred percent, Comstock. We'll make you famous." Greeley was a strange lank man with a feeble shake who laid a cold hand on Anthony's shoulder, where it rested like a fallen leaf on a granite ledge. "I have heard you recently lost a daughter, Mr. Comstock. You have my sympathy and understanding. I have lost six children, Mr. Comstock—six!"

Anthony could not imagine the pain of so much loss—or was it numbing after the third or fourth death? He experienced a great desire to get out of the presence of Horace Greeley, as if so much bad parental luck could rub off. He had read that Greeley was going to run for president, but Anthony could not imagine it. The man had the aspect of a cold-blooded creature, perhaps a salamander. He thanked Greeley profusely for his support, finding himself sweating although the office was quite chilly—no fire in the fireplace and a window partly open in spite of the temperature outside.

"He must believe in saving on coal for heating," Anthony said to Griffith as they walked down the long corridor from Greeley's office.

"He's one of those Sylvester Graham believers—sex twelve times a year, keep the windows open so lots of fresh air chills you to the bone, wear loose clothing and eat no meat or fowl and lots of whole grains. No beer, no wine, no liquor, no fun."

"I hold with the no booze, but if he's on such a healthy routine, what happened to kill off his children?"

"There's war between his wife and himself, that's all I know."

"Do you have children?"

"Two and a third on the way. I want a big family. How about you?"

"I'd like a large family." But he did not think he was going to get one. The doctor kept telling him that Maggie was fragile and he should not impose upon her. Something of the desire to live had gone out of her with Lillie. He could understand that, but he was her husband and she must cleave to him, as the Lord instructed. Surely the Lord would grant them another child to replace the lost soul he had taken to be with him. He decided he was going to move back into Maggie's bed that night, no matter what the doctor said. A new pregnancy would buck up her spirits. She would have something to live for. "Well," he said, clapping Griffith on the back, "at least Greeley is against smut."

"He has political ambitions. He wants to be known as a defender of the family."

"So much the better." If Greeley wanted to use him, Anthony wanted to use the *Tribune.*

THEY GATHERED FIRST in an oyster bar near Ann Street, Griffith, two policemen, a sketch artist for the *Tribune* and himself. These two policemen behaved entirely differently, serious, respectful. This was Greeley's doing. Anthony went in each time with the sketch artist and purchased an obscene book or a rubber object. Then he carried it outside, it was recorded in his pocket notebook, and then the police and Griffith returned with him—the artist having remained in place—and the purveyor of obscenity was arrested. The two policemen confiscated the stock, loading it into a wagon waiting outside. They carried through five raids. The dray they had brought along was heaped high with obscene books, postcards and rubber goods—French protectors, womb veils, all the paraphernalia of deceit and interference with the Lord's will. The cart followed them to the station house.

The following day, the entire adventure was written up at length in the *Tribune,* with drawings of himself brandishing a cane over the head of a cowering bookseller, drawn in caricature as a swarthy small man with a huge potbelly and long nose. Actually none of the booksellers looked anything like that caricature of a Jew—they were all native-born. But it gave an impression Anthony found perfect. The article was extremely favorable, treating him as a hero. He was grateful to Griffith. He would not forget the reporter, but would slip him information when he was planning an action. They made an excellent partnership. Griffith told him that an editorial praising his work to protect the youth of the city was being written even as they spoke. Griffith told the truth, because two days later there it was: A CRUSADER IN OUR MIDST.

He was sleeping with Maggie again. She had not been enthusiastic about the idea—he would have been shocked if she had shown undue passion. He loved her with his entire being. She was devout, frugal, conscientious and a soldier at housekeeping. Always when he came home, there was a good hot meal waiting. His clothes were perfectly kept, although she told him he must roll around in them to get them so messy. If he had any criticism, it would be that she did not work the maid hard enough. She formed too ready an attachment, not always keeping the requisite distance. But even that fault was due to her gentle disposition and kind heart. She was a thoroughly good woman; in his visits to the dark side of the city, he was beginning to understand how rare and wonderful that was. Women were weak and easily corrupted, except for those like his mother and Maggie who were armored by religion. Without that armor, women rotted from within and brought down any man who came near them.

Soon he guessed she might be pregnant again, for she was vomiting her breakfast. She said nothing. Of course, it was too delicate a matter to discuss. He noticed her mother was about more than usual. He never discouraged those visits unless she stayed around when he came home. He did not like sharing his wife with anyone. Her attention was balm to him after the tedium of his job or the darkness of his exertions on behalf of the Lord.

Soon the trial opened of the purveyors of filth he had raided with Griffith. He was a star prosecution witness and once again the papers noted him, this time with almost universal approval. The Lord had called him and he had answered, like Joshua at the battle of Jericho. His next target was Williams Haynes, who had been publishing obscene books since well before the Civil War. His wife worked with him, a coarse foul woman no doubt. Haynes had a henchman who operated a store on Nassau Street in the heart of the filth district, and another who distributed Haynes's output from his sporting goods store. Anthony was closing in on all of them, having alerted Griffith to his plans, when Haynes up and died of a heart attack. Anthony was grimly satisfied. A dead pornographer was as good as one in jail. He added Haynes to the list in his ledger book: "W. Haynes, ob. book and plate publisher, dead."

He took the ferry to New Jersey to visit the Widow Haynes. She was a tiny white-haired woman with a sweet tinkling voice, dressed in a black dimity gown. She received him in her parlor, which seemed respectable enough. She did not invite him to sit but stood before him quivering with rage. "You drove my husband to the grave!"

"Perhaps his conscience did him in."

"His books were fine erotica. There was nothing vulgar or disgusting in them, including the beautiful etchings."

"They were obscene, madam, and they must be destroyed." Beautiful! They were foul. He remembered endless naked women lying upon beds in all manner of shameless poses, rumps in the air, breasts hanging down, men with their members rigid and exposed, naked men leaning on pillars as if waiting for an omnibus.

"They are my only income, now that you have hounded my husband to his death. I will fight you to my dying day."

"Suppose I buy out your inventory. I don't imagine you intend to go on publishing by yourself."

She glared, but they began to haggle price. Finally she invited him to sit down on a horsehair couch. Anthony wrote a check which would wipe out his account at the Brooklyn bank while removing an entire source of filth from the market forever.

He noted in his book "24 cases Ob. Stereotype Plates, 182 Ob. Steel and Cooper Plate engravings for 22 different books, 500 assorted Ob. books." He went through it all carefully, making a detailed inventory. The $650 left him broke. He would not be able to pay his mortgage if he did not secure backing. It was time to approach the Y.

He wrote a letter to Robert McBurney to request help and delivered it to him in person. McBurney looked at the letter and grimaced. "This is a pencil scrawl. How do you expect me to carry something like this to the board? Really. Make a fair copy in ink, please, before I even consider what if anything to do with it."

Anthony stormed out, leaving the note. What an appalling and effeminate reaction to his plea for assistance.

But the Lord was looking out for Anthony. He received a note from the president of the YMCA, Morris Jesup. It turned out that Jesup had come into McBurney's office to ask about some other matter, noticed Anthony's note and read it. Anthony learned this because Jesup actually came to see him. Anthony was in his study, where he had the books and plates. One by one he was examining them. He had worked his way through about a third of his take. A novel had been open to a plate of a naked woman copulating with two men at once, one man in the usual place and the other in her rump. Quickly he stuffed it into a drawer and invited Jesup to sit.

"Rewrite the letter. Attach a description of everything you've done on your own from the beginning, with arrest records and outcomes. I will hand-carry it to our board and support your request."

Anthony wrung Jesup's hand. "I would desperately appreciate your support. I put my family in hock to seize these plates. I need help in destroying them."

"We'll take that up. In the meantime, I'll cover your costs myself." On the spot, Jesup wrote him a check for his expenses in the Haynes case and added $150.

"That's more than the Widow Haynes charged me."

"The extra is for your efforts."

"Mr. Jesup, sir, I can scarcely believe you're doing this!"

"Anthony—you don't mind if I call you that?—so many of us have worked our lives away making a fortune for our families, and then we see our sons, who should inherit and run our affairs, seduced by corruption, by what they see as good times. The city is being swamped by dirty foreigners with corrupt customs, creating slums—breeding grounds of crime and vice. Tammany uses them and protects them. We men of substance must clean up our cities or society will rot and young men will gamble and waste the resources their fathers and grandfathers slaved to create."

"Mr. Jesup, believe it, I am the man to head the effort."

"I'm going to set up a meeting with the members of our Committee to Suppress Vice. You'll find a great many of the most prominent men of business and finance are ready to support an effort to contain this contagion. Not only are our sons in danger, but our workers are sloughing off responsibilities in pursuit of low pleasures. They rush from the office to the brothel, from the bureau to the gambling hell. You'll meet with my committee as soon as I can arrange it, and we'll work out a formal arrangement of cooperation with your work."

"That would be a big help. I've been exhausting my own resources."

Jesup patted him on the shoulder. "I'm one hundred percent behind you. I have been looking for a strong able man to lead this fight. What's your background?"

Anthony almost said, Similar to yours, but realized that would tip his hand, that he had scouted out the leadership of the YMCA. Better to let Jesup draw that conclusion himself. Anthony sketched out his religious and family antecedents, his Civil War experiences. When he finished, Jesup said. "You're our man, I'm convinced. Now you must prepare carefully for the meeting I'll host. Don't be timid. Be forthright. Be bold. You want to persuade them you can do the job. Come with press clippings, come with lists of what you've accomplished as specific as possible—dates, names, outcomes. You need to show them you're strong, responsible, and that you can head this crusade."

"I shall, Mr. Jesup. And I am!" Anthony saw Jesup out and felt like leaping into the air and shouting to the Lord like a Baptist.

"Maggie," he called out. "Maggie! We're saved. The Lord has provided. We have money again. We have friends in high places!"

THIRTY-FOUR

VICTORIA AND STEPHEN PEARL Andrews—whom she had begun calling Pearlo after Cady Stanton's usage—were reading an amazing document by a German named Karl Marx entitled *The Communist Manifesto*. Pearlo discovered that it had never been printed in the States. He was determined to share it with as many people as possible. "It hit me like a thunderclap," he said to Victoria.

They often read in bed together, discussing ideas and debating. The physical intimacy was quite secondary. Pearlo was not what she would consider a great lover—he was well over sixty and rather fragile—but she needed his mind to test her own against. He was widely read, with several languages at his disposal including Chinese. "We can publish it in the *Weekly* in its entirety," she suggested.

"Brilliant! I'll go over the translation and improve it. The German is more powerful."

She particularly appreciated Pearlo these days because he encouraged her campaign for the presidency. Nobody else around her took it seriously, not even James. But she had been promised by her spirits she would be a great leader, and Pearlo believed in her.

They were seeing Vanderbilt less frequently. Victoria had little time to spend these days in the brokerage offices, leaving it mostly to James. Tennie went in oftener, but the *Weekly* used up much of their energy. If a client made an appointment or needed her special stroking, Victoria would rush to the offices. Until Pearlo asked her what Vanderbilt thought of the *Manifesto,* she had not considered his reaction. Indeed, he paid no attention to its appearance, for ideas he viewed as unimportant as the horse manure he stepped over in the street.

Further, he was around less because of his Frankie. She had moved him uptown into a splendid new mansion on Fifth Avenue near Central Park. She refurbished his wardrobe and kept him home several nights a week—something new and exotic to the Commodore. He did not need Tennie's ministrations as often, and his health—which he claimed Frankie was watching over with a keen eye—began to deteriorate. He was unaccustomed to physical weakness and tried to ignore it, but he was slowing down. Still, they met at least once a week for the Commodore to pass on information on stocks and for her to pass on in séance what she learned from her network of madams and from Josie and thus from Fisk.

Josie was happy with how her stocks had done under Victoria and James's guidance. She had her own little nest egg, which made her less dependent on Fisk. She was flirting with other men and obviously looking around. Victoria and Annie Wood tried to tell her that she could scarcely do better, for Fisk was rich, generous and crazy about her.

"But I don't love him. Never have. Never will."

Victoria—who felt that if she concentrated on any man long enough, providing he was equipped with intellect and knowledge, she could love him sufficiently—found such fastidiousness of the emotions rather silly. It wasn't hard to love somebody. Many things in life were hard, but that wasn't one of them. And it was important for a woman to stay on good terms with all her lovers—she thought it mean-spirited to discard someone you had been in bed with and behave as if there were no connection.

Josie was suddenly giggling. "But I've met him! The man of my dreams."

Victoria groaned. "A dream is an illusion."

"He ain't!" Josie tossed her dark curls. "He's a gentleman and a real looker. He's handsome, only twenty-eight and athletic—used to be a gymnast. From an old Philadelphia family. He has dark hair, the darlingest little mustache. He can dance. Oh, if you'd meet him, you'd fall in love with him too."

"What does he do?" Annie asked.

"He's got an oil business—the Brooklyn Oil Refinery."

"Edward Stiles Stokes," Annie said. "Oh dear. He's a terrible businessman. Fisk is keeping him afloat. Does Fisk know you're having an affair?"

"Eddie comes from money and he may be lousy at business, but he's great in bed. And when you wake up next to him, you don't wonder how you got into bed with a beached whale!"

"This could be a real mess," Annie said. "When Fisk finds out, and he will—Josie, you have the discretion of an alley cat caterwauling on a fence—he can ruin Stokes, and you with him."

She flicked her gloved hand at them. "He hasn't found out and I have all his letters, so he'd better behave!"

"Blackmail?" Victoria asked. "Do you think he'll actually pay you for the return of his letters? He loves the spotlight."

"But no man wants to parade the broken heart of a cuckold in public," Annie said, fanning herself slowly with a new ostrich fan.

"I'm counting on that," Josie said. "I have the man I want now, and Fisk can go to hell." She toasted both of them with a big café au lait cup.

"Don't push him, Josie. He might take revenge."

"He's all wrapped up in being an impresario. He has a new production called *Temptations* with long chorus lines, all blondes on odd dates and all brunettes on even dates. They juggle balls of fire. There's a giant waterfall onstage. It's a hit and he's ecstatic. Plus he's putting it to the chorines, a different one every night. He doesn't even notice what I'm doing."

"May it stay that way," Victoria said.

"Amen," said Annie.

"I can tell you one thing I heard him and the weasel talking about." That was how Josie referred to Fisk's partner, Jay Gould. "The price of Erie is rising because there's rumors the British investors are going to drive Fisk and Gould out. So expect Erie to climb."

"Thank you," said Annie and Victoria in chorus.

ELIZABETH CADY STANTON had told her to call her Julius as her Quaker companion did, the woman introduced simply as Amelia. Julius was affectionate with Victoria. They gossiped about personalities in the movement for hours. Julius knew Pearlo from their abolitionist days and was fond of him. If she guessed the nature of their relationship, she said nothing. When Beecher's name came up one day, Julius vented about him. They had once been friends, but with him assuming the chairmanship of the rival American organization, she was angry. "Woman's rights indeed," she said. "He thinks most of the women he knows have a right to his passionate attentions."

Victoria's memory was jolted. She remembered the tale Susan had told about Tilton and his wife. It was a most interesting story, and she filed it away mentally. The next time she saw Theo Tilton, she would probe him about the matter.

Julius lacked the front, the pretense and hypocrisy she had come to expect from ladies—women who had been raised by respectable and comfortable families and had married into more of the same. Julius confided that she was separated from her husband. She certainly had enough children of various ages—there were usually at least of couple of them about—but they did not define her. It seemed to Victoria that she was more of a mother on the side, almost as a hobby. She dressed well but simply, with a preference for blue.

Victoria was waiting for an opportunity to bring up the Beecher story with Theo. He had begun work on her biography. He sat across from her in a parlor at home—the little one she used for talking with friends and writing—while she recounted a period in her life and he took notes. He was writing her life as they proceeded, for he was, as Julius had suggested, facile. Tonight she was describing her marriage with Dr. Woodhull, to whom she had briefly introduced him.

He looked up, brushing a lock of his long wavy light brown hair from his eyes. "Are you still . . . close?"

"Sexually intimate, you mean?" She disliked euphemisms.

"Are you?" His gaze met hers and broke away.

"No. We were barely intimate when we were married. I let him live here out of charity, frankly. He's frail and too far gone to support himself." Something more than usual was on Theo's mind. "Is something bothering you tonight?"

He sat silent for a moment, his gaze on her. "May I show you a small piece I've written?"

"You mean, other than my campaign biography?"

"Quite other. . . . It's a poem."

"Certainly, if you wish." She didn't know much about poetry. Literature had been neglected in her education by her various mentors, but she liked to read it on occasion and always published some in the *Weekly.* She did like George Sand's novels, peopled by passionate and active women she could identify with.

He took out of the bosom pocket of his waistcoat a folded sheet of foolscap and laid it on the table in front of her. She took it up at once. He retreated to his armchair across the room.

How beautiful thou art and darkly radiant,
As if the fulsome moon could burn the eyes
As does the sun, but thou art of the night,
Bright within dark as if in a disguise.

How dark thy hair and thy eyes, how bright
Blue as the overarching firmament.
Ah, lady who hast taken away my heart,
Do clasp me to thee and make me not depart!

"It's written to you," he said softly.

No one had ever written her a poem. It made her feel cherished. She met his gaze and smiled at him, not quite sure what her response should be. Should she try to critique the poem? Probably not. That was not the purpose for which he had composed it. She simply waited, smiling.

He rose, the armchair tipping over, and rushed across the room, throwing himself on his knees and clasping hers, his head landing on her thigh. "Darling Victoria, precious Victoria!"

She stroked his fine flyaway hair. "Theo, what is it?"

"I've fallen in love with you. The more I know you, the more I must know of you. To be near you is driving me half mad."

"I don't need you to go mad, Theo. Do you want me?"

In answer he rose and pulled her into his arms and began to kiss her. His mouth was full and soft. His tongue was agile in her mouth. He pushed her back onto the love seat that stood next to her chair and fell upon her, his mouth still pressed against hers, one hand clutching her left breast through the stuff of her gown. She kissed him back, enjoying his passion, enjoying the skill of his mouth. But the door stood open and any of the members of her family or her staff could pass by.

She freed her mouth. "Patience, Theo, patience a moment."

He was contrite. "I'm sorry. Forgive me. I didn't mean to force you."

"No force needed." She smiled, looking at him. He was indeed handsome. She had not thought of him in that way, but now she was interested. "We need some privacy. This way."

She led him to a linen closet where she handed him a couple of pillows and took out a feather bed. Told him to wait a moment in the hall. She slipped into her bedroom and prepared herself. Then she motioned him to follow her up a steep flight of steps to the roof. It was a warm night and the stars were huge overhead. They spread the feather bed on the flat tar roof, where they lay together kissing, rolling to and fro, touching what was bare to touch until they were both seething. He stepped out of his trousers, peeled off his loose shirt and then helped her out of her dress, crinoline, and with practiced fingers undid her corset. After all, he was a married man. He had to be quite used to undoing women's clothing. As he bared her shoulders and then her breasts and lastly, letting her drawers drop to the roof, her buttocks and legs, her whole body bare at last to him, he kissed what he uncovered.

His body was lean and almost hairless, excitingly smooth. She could feel his muscles, not huge but firm. He was well made. She would like to see him in gaslight, but not now. Not right now. She could feel him hard against her, not a thick penis but long and slightly canted to the right with a full hood. His hands were strong but long-fingered. One of those long fingers slipped into her. Ah, he knew something about exciting a woman, he did. Two fingers now probed her, sliding in and out. She parted her thighs wide for him, to indicate she was ready. He slid his weight over her and pushed in. Slowly he moved at first, then picked up the tempo. He was keeping himself high against her, so that she got maximum pressure against the seat of her pleasure. He was good, this poet, he was exactly what she wanted.

"I want you, I have you," he was blurting out as he pumped into her. "We're bad, we're bad, Victoria. I want you, bad, bad Victoria."

She did not consider herself bad in the least, but who cared what nonsense he muttered when he was riding her into such excitement that she bit his shoulder and plunged up to meet him, her ass banging on the roof through the feather bed. Then she was up and over, and a moment later she felt him gush into her.

They lay on the roof in the balmy night air, sleeping in each other's arms until something woke him and he rolled over onto her and began again. Then they both slept. She woke to the sun already burning down on their bare skin. She opened her eyes, yawned and tried to slip from his arms. He woke. He was amazingly handsome in the orange light of the morning sun, his hair loose and wild, his eyes half closed, his lips swollen. He pulled her down on him, kissing her passionately and keeping her on top. He was firm again. This time she rode him, rode him hard with her hair swishing, her breasts bouncing. She was a little sore by now but she wanted him too badly for that to matter. Finally they descended the steep stairs from the roof and she went off to draw a bath. They bathed together, facing, the water scented lavender. In the tub he played with her, sliding his fingers into her as she faced him and she came again.

When he had finally left and she put herself together, she reflected on the night. He was an amazingly resilient lover. She felt enthralled. She could not wait to see him again. She felt as if she had met the lover she had always craved. He was sensitive, he was a fine writer everyone said, he had good politics, he was helping her in her campaign for president, and most importantly, the sex was unparalleled.

She forgot all about her intention to quiz him, but after their third night of passionate sex on the roof, he told her the story of Beecher and his wife over breakfast. He still felt overly sorry for himself.

"You must have a passionate relationship with your wife. Why become furious if she supplements your pleasure with a close friend?"

"Lib is, Lib was a good woman. She was pure. She was my angel."

"No women are angels, Theo. We all have our own needs. Surely you tried to awaken her?"

"I would never have corrupted her. Only that traitor Beecher would dare."

She began to understand he believed in good and bad women. The bad women were sexually responsive; the good women were cold. She knew herself on the verge of falling in love with him; surely she could teach him what she knew about men and women. Theo was passionate but not that intelligent. He knew a great deal about local and national politics, but ideologically he was naïve. She could fix that; she would. He was patient with Zulu Maud, making her laugh until she fell out of her chair. His ego was a bit fragile and he needed frequent praise. But he was an energetic and tireless lover. Their summer nights on the roof or in her bed were sensual and exhausting in the best way. He had the ability to make love several times a night; she had never felt so satisfied. She felt bound to him sexually to the point where she did not really desire even her husband or Pearlo. He stirred her to the point of obsession. When she looked at him she felt her spirit yearning toward him. Did he love her? Or did he only crave her? The sex and her campaign biography marched on together. When he spoke of himself and her as bad, she withdrew emotionally. Yet when he touched her, she burned. She had only to look at his long-fingered sensitive hands and she grew hungry all over again. If only she could educate him out of his nonsense about women, he would be a perfect mate.

In the meantime, he introduced her to other sorts of pleasure. They did silly things, a kind of playing she had never experienced. They went rowing in Central Park, they went to the seaside and picnicked at Coney Island, they went riding together. Victoria loved riding, as fast as possible. It thrilled her. Never had she done so many things with a lover that were not either directly sexual or intellectual. He took her to see P. T. Barnum's lions and tigers and midgets and bought her cotton candy. They went to the horse races together, as she had in Saratoga that wonderful week. They watched a game of baseball and yelled for the team he chose as theirs. She had never had a childhood, but Theo was giving her one. She was besotted with him.

Theo had gone off to Washington when a parade was scheduled. The Orangemen had got a permit to march on July 12 to celebrate the Battle of the Boyne when they had defeated the Catholics in Ireland. Since the Catholic Irish far outnumbered them and both sides hated each other, not only were the police ordered to protect the march, but the National Guard was called up. It sounded exciting, so Tennie and she put on men's clothing to go watch it. They told no one where they were going except for James, who quickly took his heaviest cane and accompanied them.

The Orangemen had gathered in midtown and now they were marching down Eighth Avenue to Twenty-third, then to turn east and down Broadway to Union Square. Only seventy Orangemen braved the heat and the hostile crowds, but thousands of soldiers were in full gear to protect them, with mounted policemen ahead, platoons of policemen on foot, the Seventh Regiment deployed behind them, the Twenty-seventh to the right, and behind them, the Eighty fourth and Sixth Regiments, and then still more police. Victoria thought it a ridiculous sight, that handful of marchers and all those escorts, rank upon rank. She was surprised to see the Ninth Regiment flanking and protecting the marchers on their left, Fisk in his resplendent colonel's uniform marching at their head. The Ninth was famous for its band, but most of the men had as much fighting experience as Fisk himself. Still, Fisk was there to lead them in his glittering white uniform, waving his sword like a baton. The day was hot, in a hot summer. The sun drummed on their heads. The masses along the sidewalks and crowding the rooftops were in an ugly mood and threw rocks and garbage at the marchers. Marchers and hecklers shouted insults at each other.

"Don't you think we should go?" James suggested.

Tennie said, "Oh, just a little longer. Let's see what's going to happen." They were standing on the corner of Twenty-seventh and Eighth. The Orangemen had passed them, all seventy, and the rear regiments went clumping past with rifles on their shoulders. "It's fine to see a parade," Tennie said, "no matter how stupid the pretext. I do like men in uniform—to look at, anyhow."

"I've seen rather too many of them," James said. "Living and dead, whole and in pieces."

Victoria squeezed his hand. "We can go. Just wait till the parade passes us."

A loud noise startled them. James said, "Now! That was a shot."

They turned to make their way home, but they could not buck the crowd, which was swarming toward the noise.

"I think it came from the roof," James said, and that was all he had time to say before a great fusillade of shots rang out. James grabbed both of their arms and began to fight against the current of the mob pressing toward the battle. It seemed to be one-sided now, as every regiment began to fire at will, wildly into the crowds on the sidewalk, at folks leaning out windows, at the rooftops. Now people were screaming and running away from the firing instead of toward it. James yanked them both bodily up onto a stoop where they could see what was happening. Bodies lay on the sidewalks, a man with his head half blown off, his brain exposed; a little girl lying facedown in a pool of blood; a woman dragging herself along with her thigh smashed. The bodies lay faceup, facedown, faceless, blood pooling on the cobblestones and the planks. A woman passed screaming, carrying a baby crushed by the fleeing mob.

It was over as they watched. The soldiers drew back into their columns, the band commenced playing "The Battle Hymn of the Republic," and the parade resumed. As the soldiers marched on and the entire parade turned the corner of Twenty-third Street, people poured back into the street to carry off the dead and wounded. A great sound of keening arose.

"Let's get out of here"—James wiped his forehead—"before worse happens. The next time you two get it into your heads to attend a riot, I'll lock you in the cellar."

Tennie was white with shock and stumbled as she went. Her auburn hair had come loose. Victoria told her to shove it under her cap lest they cause another riot. Women in men's clothing were likely to be stoned in the street. It broke all of society's rules—as, Victoria thought, did so many of the things Tennie and she enjoyed. Tennie had not said a word since the shooting. She stepped in a puddle of blood and kept stopping to try to rub her boots on the curb.

When they were two blocks away and out of the press of bodies—although people were still running toward or away from Eighth Avenue and a horse ambulance clattered by—she stopped James for a moment. "Thank you, my dear. Thank you for getting us safely out of there. You have, as always, a cool head, and I want you to know how much I value that." The smell of gunpowder still hung in the air and the wounded were screaming where they lay.

At Annie's the next day, Josie filled them in. Fisk's ankle was trampled by a horse. He was caught flat-footed in the riot. He hopped into a bakery. When he was spied through the bakery window, people began to call for him to come out and be hanged from a streetlamp, for his regiment shooting down unarmed civilians in cold blood. He went out the back, over a fence and then into a basement window and up on the next street. He fled through basements, between buildings, through yards and alleyways until a piece of amazing luck—or, Josie said, because the devil had informed his friend—he found Jay Gould in a hansom cab, who took him in and carried him to safety. "Imagine that fat hog leaping over fences!"

The papers reported forty-seven civilians dead, two soldiers and one policeman, and eighty-three wounded, many seriously. The papers played up the heroism of the soldiers in the face of the unruly and violent Irish. Most newspapers also published caricatures of Jim Fisk trundling his bulk through yards, running for dear life in his fancy uniform, fake medals and bright buttons flying.

"Frankly," Josie said, "I'm ashamed to be seen with him. The time has come to end this farce. I'm going to live with Edward openly. He wants to, I want to. Jim Fisk can eat his epaulets."

When Josie had gone, Victoria and Annie consulted. "I can try to fix him up with another mistress," Annie said, "but he has a whole theater company to run through first, and I've heard he's made a good start."

"Perhaps he won't even notice Josie's defection."

"No luck there. The chorines are just sex. He loves Josie. Don't ask me why. Sometimes a man fixates on a woman, and the less she loves him, the more he wants her. He keeps her and beds her, but she's aloof and he must realize she doesn't love him. He's hooked on making her love him. He always thinks it's about to happen."

Victoria sighed. "We will miss him."

ISABELLA WAS AT JULIUS'S in Tenafly when next Victoria visited. She was depressed because Congress had refused to agree that women already had the right to vote. Victoria said, "Never mind. We will bypass them and claim the White House ourselves."

"It was only the first step with Congress," Julius said. Victoria was pleased that Isabella had never been treated to a nickname for Elizabeth, and in Isabella's presence she used the more formal "Elizabeth." It showed that Cady Stanton had accorded her a degree of intimacy beyond that given to Isabella, in spite of her social position.

"I really had my ears burned off by my sisters at Nook Farm." Isabella flung herself on a chaise lounge. She was wearing a white satin dress with large check weave, trimmed with emerald green satin ribbons, with a double row of little satin bows down the front and at the wrists. On a chair lay a huge pale green silk crepe hat with mauve artificial lilies and a real dead bird. Julius, by contrast, wore a blue serge walking dress and no bustle. Isabella complained, "Catherine knows so much, of course. She writes at length about proper motherhood, who has never borne nor raised a child. She writes about marriage and the complete satisfaction that housekeeping should bring to a woman, who has never married and never had to care for a house. Harriet and she attack you constantly, Vickie, my dear Queen. They don't know you and they refuse to meet you. I will not give up, however. I am convinced that if Harriet or Catherine were to meet you face-to-face, you would win them over completely!"

"I'd appreciate the opportunity. I'm aware the Boston contingent gossip about me constantly. You know that I am a free lover, that I espouse the doctrine of affinities. That shocks them."

"It shocks a great many people," Elizabeth said. "You have to stick to your guns. You can't trim your ideas to suit anyone else. I never do. I won't lie out of cowardice or to please the hypocrites and the mealymouthed. It doesn't work in the long run to conceal your ideas, because they will out."

"Do you believe that, Isabella?" Victoria caught her gaze and held it. She was thinking of what she had heard about Henry, Isabella's brother, who practiced free love but refused to acknowledge it. He simply preached a mushy gospel of Love, careful never to define what he meant. Out of curiosity, she had gone with Theo to hear the great man in Plymouth Church. It was a rather plain brick building, looking more like a gymnasium or a theater than a church, but it held three thousand. He was certainly a dynamic speaker, highly theatrical, acting out parts, causing his audience to laugh, to weep, to groan. As Roxanne would say, a lot of froth but not much milk.

"I believe we must speak out for what we believe in. The spirits come to me also, Vickie, and I—like you—take instructions from them and attempt to carry out their advice. My mother appears to me whenever I am in crisis and gives me counsel." Isabella's mood changed in an instant and she laughed. "Better now than when she was alive, I mean when she was on this plane of existence."

VICTORIA WAS PREPARING for the weeklong National Woman Suffrage Association meeting at Apollo Hall to formally launch her campaign. Pearlo had been helping her—until his wife died suddenly and he retreated into mourning. Julius took his place, moving into the Woodhull house for convenience until the convention. However, a disgusting commotion developed.

Tennie came running to her, her hair loose and wild, her face flushed so that a spot as if she wore rouge stood out on her cheeks. "Vickie, we're undone!" Buck, Mama Roxanne, Polly and her husband, Dr. Sparr, had decided to blackmail Vanderbilt, claiming he had corrupted Tennie. Mama had come to her only after the letter had been sent but no reply received. Tennie was hysterical. "He'll cut us off completely. He's proud of never paying a penny of blackmail. He'll never forgive us."

"Why did they do such a thing? We've given them everything they wanted." Victoria clutched her heart.

Tennie collapsed in a chair. Two large tears rolled down her cheeks and she blew her nose loudly into a handkerchief. "Mama has this notion of taking us back to Ohio and beginning our old life again. Vickie, I don't care if we lose every last penny. I will not go back there! I won't be hauled from town to town selling patent medicine that can half kill people. I will not go to bed with random men so Buck can tear ass into the room and blackmail them."

Victoria took her sister in her arms. "We'll never return to that life, I promise. But they must leave the house at once. We'll set them up on their own. We must get them packed and out of here before worse damage is done."

Protesting, screaming, weeping, Roxanne along with Buck, Polly and her husband and children were all packed off to a good boardinghouse a few blocks away. Roxanne kept shouting that Colonel Blood had stolen both her loving daughters away from her. She swore she would go to the police, she would go to court, but she would never, never let go of her own flesh and blood.

Victoria then took Tennie and they headed for Vanderbilt's. He would not see them. He had his butler close the door in their faces. Victoria sat down on the steps with her head in her hands. They were losing their best sources of information on stocks. How could they continue the business?

"He has to forgive us. We didn't do anything! I wrote him a note, but it was returned unopened," Tennie said. "How can the old boy just dump us?"

"He won't forgive. When he gets disgusted with someone, he writes them off. We've seen him do that time after time." Victoria sighed, getting to her feet, shaking down her dress and reaching for Tennie's hand. "It's who we are, Tennie, Claflins. We can't disown them, but they're as destructive as a pack of wild dogs. They rip up everything."

There was nothing to do but go home and get ready for the convention in three more days. Maybe if they could not be brokers any longer, she could find another source of money. She must not despair. The spirits would come through for her. She kept telling that to Tennie.

THE HALL FILLED RAPIDLY to overflowing. Some of the National women demurred at Victoria sitting on the platform with them, but Julius seated Victoria between herself and the eminently respectable grandmother of the movement, Lucretia Mott. Mott whispered something in Julius's ear. Stanton said firmly, "Victoria has the courage to say openly what people like Henry Ward Beecher and several of the Boston women practice secretly. Let us honor her honesty, Lucretia."

When the time came for Victoria to speak, she knew she faced many skeptics. She began quietly as she always did, and then the spirit filled her, adrenaline coursed through her veins igniting her brain and tongue, and she spoke ringingly of a woman's rights. "I ask for equality, nothing more. Sexual freedom means the abolition of prostitution both in and out of marriage, means the emancipation of woman from sexual slavery and her coming into ownership and control of her own body. . . ." She spoke for half an hour until the audience erupted into cheers. When she returned to her seat, Lucretia Mott hugged her.

It was not until she went home that she learned from James that Roxanne had sworn out a complaint against him for alienating her children from her, for forcing them into prostitution and using them for blackmail—exactly what Buck had tried to do. She was claiming that the house was filled with communists, free lovers and woman's rights people brought there by Colonel Blood and Stephen Pearl Andrews. The newspapers picked up on the scandal at once, bannered across front pages. Victoria's triumph was yanked out from under her. She was loyal to her family, but oh, the cost. Roxanne was crazy, Victoria knew it, but still her mother.

The court case commenced immediately. Roxanne made wild accusations. Tennie, in defending herself, blabbed far too freely about their upbringing and previous life. The reporters were amused and titillated. Rumors were reported from all the places the Claflins had lived, stories of houses of prostitution supposedly run by Victoria, of Victoria scandalous on the stage in San Francisco. The irregular living arrangements were the subject of lurid testimony, although both Victoria and James conducted themselves coolly on the stand. Nobody else did. Tennie had to be removed from the courtroom to shut her up, she became so emotional talking about her life as a fortune-teller traveling from town to town and fleecing people. Under cross-examination, the presence of Victoria's ex-husband Dr. Woodhull was revealed, and that seemed to shock the reporters and the public more than anything, even though James explained that Woodhull was there to care for his brain-damaged son.

The judge dismissed the charges but the papers exploited the story, sensing Victoria's new vulnerability. From the bewitching broker and the female politician, she became the notorious Woodhull, free lover and communist. When Victoria returned from court, Annie sent her a message to come at once. She was bubbling over with news. Josie had given her boyfriend Eddie Stokes all of Jim Fisk's letters for publication. Since Stokes had lost his position in the oil company, he was desperate for money. "Jim paid them fifteen thousand in cash for the letters back," Annie said. "I'm sure it was worth it to him not to be made a complete fool of in public. But he hates being taken as much as the Commodore does. So he immediately charged them with blackmail. They're countersuing for libel and perjury. It'll drag everyone connected with it through the muck."

Every day the papers linked woman's rights with the scandalous Claflin family and the notorious Victoria Woodhull. Horace Greeley was writing editorials defaming her as a woman with two husbands under the same roof, a fallen woman whom the National had embraced, making them an organization of free lovers. Many women in the National were threatening to quit unless Victoria was removed from the leadership. They attacked to distance the organization from her—the same women who had cheered and embraced her five days before. Only Elizabeth and Isabella stood by her. Susan had withdrawn. She knew that Elizabeth and Susan quarreled about her. Then she turned to Theo, asking him to introduce her at the next rally.

He glared at her coldly. "I can't do that. Don't ask me again."

"But why?" She was genuinely shocked. "Because of your wife?" It had never occurred to her he would refuse her request.

"Don't be absurd. Because I've promised to support Horace Greeley."

She stared. "How can you? After writing my campaign bio. You make me look like a fool. And Greeley—he hates woman's rights."

Theo grimaced. "You can't win. He could. And then I'd be able to ask for a position in the government and get out of Brooklyn and away from Beecher."

His defection shocked and wounded her. How could he have lain in her arms, making wild love countless times, how could he have said he loved her again and again, then just stroll off and forget her? She felt used. He, whom she had adored, was the one lover with whom she was not going to maintain a friendship. She was left almost without defenders on what she had expected to be the launch of her campaign. Theo's desertion scalded her. He had never loved her, she knew that now.

She saw Josie from time to time. Josie was unabashedly infatuated with Eddie Stokes, who was slim and wiry where Jim Fisk was fat, who was from an old rich Philadelphia family as opposed to Fisk's New England peddler roots. Stokes dressed like a gentleman while Fisk dressed like a mountebank. Stokes had a reputation for temper, but Josie did not believe he would ever hurt her.

In January, the grand jury returned an indictment against Stokes for blackmail. Josie was beside herself and ran to Victoria and to Annie to ask their advice, which she promptly ignored. Victoria was arguing with Roxanne in the boardinghouse where she had moved them when she heard newsboys crying headlines in the street, "Jim Fisk Shot Down," "Fisk Murdered in Cold Blood over Actress."

Victoria went down to the street and bought several papers, taking them home to read away from her mother's hectoring. Stokes had walked into the Grand Central Hotel and caught Fisk walking up the stairway. He was on his way to see a widow he had installed there with her children to help her out—one of his many charity cases. Fisk could ruin ten thousand men and reach out to a needy family. Stokes pulled out a pistol and shot Fisk twice, once in the arm and once in the abdomen. He tossed the pistol under a sofa and ran off toward the barbershop on the ground level. There he was seized and taken upstairs to the room where Fisk lay slowly dying. Fisk identified Stokes as the man who had shot him.

The papers printed special editions every two hours, reporting on

Fisk's condition. His wife took the train from Boston and attended him, as did his little partner Gould. No one had ever seen Gould weep before. It was duly reported in the papers. Fisk spoke calmly with everyone present, dictating his will. He was given morphine for the pain, passed out and never regained consciousness.

Victoria and Tennie joined the immense procession passing by his lying in state at the Opera House, in an open casket in his colonel's uniform. Thousands waited in line, women throwing flowers at the casket. The next day, the cortege crept up Fifth Avenue to the depot with military bands, soldiers in uniform, troops of policemen, a hearse drawn by six matched white horses.

Erie stock rose abruptly on Fisk's death. Popular sentiment turned him into a hero, and ballads were sung on street corners and penny sheets sold. His generosity in sending railroad cars of food and clothing to Chicago after the Great Fire was retold. He left an estate of considerably less than a million, for he had spent almost all he made. Henry Ward Beecher gave sermons on Fisk as a bad example, but the masses mourned him. He was the kind of rich man they approved of, because he was irrationally generous and spread around what he made. They could understand his keeping of actresses and chorus girls far better than they understood Gould, the dour family man true to his wife. Fisk's diamonds and his carriages and his canaries were auctioned off to pay for the funeral. Victoria was sorry he was gone, and for what? Jealousy was an evil that caused great damage. It was important never to allow herself to feel it. Fortunately, James was free from its vise. Those who believed in free love, so defamed in the papers and from the pulpit, did not go about gunning each other down in cold blood. Perhaps she should incorporate that into one of her speeches.

In the meantime, she had the damage caused by the Claflin clan to contain, if only she could. Everything had been almost within her grasp—money, the fame, the power—and now it all was slipping away.

THIRTY-FIVE

IT WAS NOT THAT Elizabeth and Susan had never quarreled, but their disagreement over Victoria was deeper and more painful. Elizabeth felt close to Victoria. Her charm and wit were delightful. Like Susan, Victoria had a quick mind, but one less rigid, more innovative in her thinking. Her analysis leapt over the entire suffrage question, of which Elizabeth was at times heartily sick—such a one-string harp, as if everything that kept women down would be erased if they could walk into polling places.

Elizabeth enjoyed Victoria's salon, especially now that the cruder family members had been exiled. Elizabeth came from an old, respected and well-off family in Johnstown, New York. She should have been more of a snob, and in some ways she was, but she saw Victoria as a truly brilliant woman and gave her credit for raising herself out of the muck into which she had been born. She admired self-made heroic figures like Frederick Douglass—and like Victoria. She missed Pearlo at Victoria's—he had withdrawn, cooped up in his house withering away waiting for his wife to contact him from the afterlife. Although Elizabeth knew he had been Victoria's lover, she assumed from his age and fragility that this had been an affair more of minds than the obviously mismatched bodies. Elizabeth did not share Susan's horrified disdain of Victoria's free love ideas and her expression of them in the lecture hall and in her bedroom. She had no desire for lovers herself, but she rather liked seeing a woman behave just as she wished, taking lovers and not so much discarding them as turning them into friends if they did not continue to please her. She liked Victoria's daring and her total lack of shame in proclaiming how she lived. Her ideas and her actions were seamless.

Elizabeth was perfectly well aware of liaisons in the woman's rights movement, as there had been in abolitionist groups. Anna Dickinson and Wendell Phillips had been lovers for years. Lucy Stone's husband Henry

Blackwell had long enjoyed a passionate affair with a married woman, Abby Patton. The only difference Elizabeth could see was that others concealed their adventures and Victoria did not bother, since she did not believe what she did was wrong. Elizabeth and Susan fought bitterly about Victoria until it tore them apart.

Theo had brought out his short laudatory biography of Victoria. Now he was going to Cleveland to nominate Horace Greeley, the *Tribune* editor, abuser of his wife Mary and opponent of woman's rights, as the candidate of the Democrats and breakaway Liberal Republicans—who repudiated the graft in government under Grant. After all that had gone on between them, he would not support Victoria, who was insulted to tears; the breach appeared permanent. Theo was disillusioned with liberal politics, unsuccessful in his career moves—mostly because of Beecher and the scandal—but determined to reach a position of power where he would overshadow his onetime mentor, now his enemy. Elizabeth, who liked Theo but had always seen him as a bit of a mental lightweight, was not as shocked as Victoria or Isabella. Isabella had drawn the story of the Beecher-Tilton romance out of Victoria and come to Elizabeth for confirmation. Elizabeth told her of the melodramatic night in Brooklyn.

Isabella wrote her brother to come forward and be truthful. He begged her to remain silent, hinting at suicide. Isabella was naïve to believe Beecher would abandon his extremely well-paid position as head of the influential Plymouth Church to appear on a platform at Victoria's side proclaiming publicly what he practiced privately—the implications of his gospel of Love. Beecher had just brought out the first volume of his life of Jesus and had never been more famous. He was not about to sacrifice book sales or lecture fees. He was even recommending soap and liniment in advertisements for a handsome price.

The National's convention was fast approaching. Victoria announced that it would be a joint convention of the National and her People's Party, infuriating Susan. At the planning meeting the day before the convention was to open, Susan attacked Victoria and Elizabeth protested. How dare Susan try to impose her notions of morality on everyone? She was behaving like that fanatic Comstock who was running around New York arresting free thought people for daring to have ideas different from his small-town background. Everything he disagreed with was obscene. Susan was being just as narrow-minded; she did not approve of the truly radical platform of the People's Party and thus she wanted to deny Victoria and her supporters the use of Steinway Hall.

Elizabeth rose to her feet. "Susan, if you ram this through, I will resign!"

"I will not let the National be corrupted by the ideas and practices of Woodhull!"

They glared at each other, as angry as either ever had been. Elizabeth felt as if part of her heart were being torn out of her breast. "Then I resign."

"So be it," Susan said, her face a mask of disdain.

Elizabeth was not about to stay away. Although Susan was presiding in her place, Elizabeth still gave the keynote address and boldly proclaimed that everyone who could should vote the People's Party. Victoria stepped forward, seized the lectern and moved that the two conventions join as one. Still presiding, Susan refused to put the motion. Elizabeth knew why. She could sense that the majority in the hall were moved by Victoria and wanted to support her. Elizabeth was delighted when Victoria refused to relinquish the podium and began speaking in her impassioned oratory about how beautiful the world could be if they would join to overcome corruption, inequality and oppression. Elizabeth noticed after a few minutes that Susan had left the platform. Was she going to walk out of her own convention? Elizabeth shook her head sadly. Susan would not share the platform with Victoria. Suddenly the lights went out. Someone had turned off the gaslights, leaving the hall completely dark. Women were screaming in fear.

Victoria went on speaking extemporaneously for several minutes, but no one was listening. Women were trying to escape, bumping into each other, occasionally shrieking, pushing, trying to force their way toward the doors, which opened wide. Victoria stopped and turned to Elizabeth, as if she could see in the dark. "What has happened? Is it a fire?"

"It's Susan," Elizabeth said.

Victoria took her arm. "Come. I'll get you out of here. She's a strong woman in her way, isn't she?"

The next day Victoria was nominated at Apollo Hall by the group calling itself the Equal Rights Party. Frederick Douglass was chosen as her vice presidential running mate—without his permission, but when he was notified the next day, he did not repudiate them. He seemed amused but not affronted. In spite of their disagreements about the Fifteenth Amendment, in spite of some of the inflammatory and racist things Elizabeth had said when she was infuriated by giving the vote to Negro men and denying it to all women, they remained friends.

Victoria launched her campaign and Susan retired to gather her forces.

Isabella was buoyant. She was writing regularly for the *Weekly* under a variety of pseudonyms, praising Victoria's campaign. Susan decided to support Grant for a second term. Elizabeth was disgusted. The Grant administration was corrupt to the core. One scandal followed another until it seemed there was no one in the White House, the Cabinet or Congress untainted by bribery. The Union Pacific Railroad had distributed shares of Crédit Mobilier among Congress like party favors to buy their votes.

Now Theo was promoting a Southern strategy for Horace Greeley, that white-coated worm, promising an end to Reconstruction, while the papers were ignoring Victoria's campaign—except for Thomas Nast, the acid cartoonist of *Harper's,* who had helped bring down Boss Tweed. He was attacking Victoria as Mrs. Satan.

Victoria came to Elizabeth extremely upset. "I am being pilloried. My lecture engagements are canceled in city after city. And to add to everything else, my first husband, Dr. Woodhull, died in our home."

"I'm sorry to hear that. What did he die of?"

As usual, Victoria was blunt. "We have been trying various doctors to get him off morphine. This new doctor cut his dosage too quickly. I've been so busy I didn't see what was happening. He died overnight. Now my idiot sister Utica is swearing to the police that he was murdered—as if I haven't done everything for him I could. He rescued me from my family and gave me my first real education. He loved Byron and Byron loved him. Why would I want to hurt him?" Victoria ran her hands through her abundant black hair. She was letting it grow again, after keeping it short for the last two years. "Now our landlord is evicting us from the house I love."

"I wish I could help you." Elizabeth drew Victoria onto the sofa beside her, stroking her shoulder soothingly. "You must keep trying to reach an audience with your ideas. You're an excellent speaker. If you can get a hall, you can pull a crowd and they will listen, enthralled."

"I'm desperate," Victoria said. "The sky is falling on me."

"Victoria, they're trying to crush you. But those of us who believe in freedom, we're all free lovers at heart. We believe in the good time coming when men and women will be free of compulsion in love. When woman will no longer join with man out of fear, out of pressure from her family or his, out of economic need, but only because she wants to be with him."

"You understand me," Victoria said, seizing her hand and staring into her eyes. "I feel so very alone."

ELIZABETH WAS FRANTICALLY BUSY getting her four younger children packed and off to their various colleges and schools. She loved having the younger ones around, but their absence would free her up to write the speeches and articles she had promised and was way behind on producing. In ten days, she must begin the lecture circuit—by train to Chicago and then on loops out into the Midwestern states, back to Chicago, out again—a full six months of lecturing seven days a week and twice on Sundays. If she had a day off, she held a special meeting for women only.

Elizabeth heard that in spite of repudiating Victoria, Susan voted in the congressional election under the legal arguments Victoria had set forth in her memorial to Congress. Three weeks later, Susan was arrested, along with the men who had let her vote, led away in handcuffs. Normally Elizabeth would have rushed to Susan's side, but they were not even writing each other. She followed the trial—an obvious farce—in the papers and letters friends sent. The jury was all male. As a woman, Susan was not permitted to testify. No constitutional arguments were allowed. After a few witnesses, the judge presented a decision he had written before the trial began, directing the jury to find Susan guilty. Elizabeth wept for Susan and for herself, that they were so estranged.

But the judge made one mistake. He followed precedent in asking Susan if she had anything to say before sentence was pronounced. Susan made a ringing speech about rights and the injustice of the trial, refusing to pay her fine. She said she would gladly go to jail instead. The judge put off enforcing the sentence so that Susan could not appeal, so she neither paid the fine nor went to jail.

The remaining link between Elizabeth and Susan was Isabella, who stayed in touch with both. It seemed easier for Susan to forgive Isabella her support of Victoria than to forgive Elizabeth. Elizabeth felt sore with guilt. They had been close for so many years, it should have been she at Susan's side during the trial. The old warmth remained thrust down underneath the surface disagreement but still there, giving out an almost suffocated glow. She missed Susan daily. A dozen times a day she would think, I have to tell Susan about that, then realize she no longer could.

Grant won by a landslide and Greeley returned to New York and his sick wife, who died two days later. Elizabeth had little love for Greeley. He had opposed woman's rights in his paper, in his speeches, in his actions, in his life. When this news reached Elizabeth, she was in Topeka, Kansas, having traveled half the night. Her hotel room was endurable. She ate whenever she could in restaurants, after a bad experience when, following an exhausting day of travel and a long lecture, she was put up by sympathizers in a small town in Illinois and treated to a meal consisting of thin oatmeal, cold water and graham bread. She went to bed hungry and resolved to stay in hotels, noisy and dirty as they often were.

She knew how good a speaker she was, how she came across warm and motherly, feminine and gracious. Newspapers compared her to Queen Victoria, considered a great compliment. When a ferry crossing the Mississippi got stuck on a sandbar, she entertained the other passengers with an impromptu speech until they were tugged off and could resume the journey. One of the male passengers asked her to marry him. She told him one husband at a time was quite enough.

When roads were blocked with snow, she froze in open sleighs. She was jounced in dogcarts and coaches with broken springs, she breathed the coal smoke of locomotives and ate in dining rooms surrounded by men aiming for and missing the spittoons. Often walking into an ordinary, she felt faint from the smell of unwashed men and the reek of tobacco. On trains, the only food available was at a ten-minute stop when all the passengers rushed a cold buffet and grabbed what greasy food they could. She was making a living for herself and her family. More important, she was proselytizing for woman's rights and giving good advice on child-raising, especially the rearing of daughters. Third, just being up there on the platform, she was a living refutation of the caricature of a feminist as a skinny woman in trousers with beard and cigar. The mother of seven children, she was plump and jolly with wit and warmth. She knew that as she spoke, she left behind women who were energized, men who felt more kindly toward woman's rights, and some who were going to become active themselves in securing those rights. Everywhere—in stagecoaches, in trains, waiting in stations and in lobbies, at the long communal tables in hotels—she talked with everyone around her. As Johnny Appleseed had gone westward sowing his seeds and planting trees, she was sowing seeds too and planting what would flower and bear fruit for women—the fruit of freedom, of justice, of equality. So she soldiered on, recognizing that in spite of the hardships, in spite of the pain of her estrangement from Susan, she was enjoying herself.

THIRTY-SIX

ANTHONY GRIEVED WITH Maggie over her miscarriage, but the doctor was not pleased. "She can't take much more of this. She's a delicate woman."

It was true, she was like a fine porcelain teacup. But they needed a child. He prayed for guidance. The Lord had given Abraham Isaac when Sarah was old and not in the way of women, as the Good Book said. Surely the Lord could give him a child. It need not be a boy; he would be happy with a girl, to replace dear Lillie, who had been called to heaven.

He was now in the employ of the Committee for the Suppression of Vice of the YMCA, his work sanctioned and remunerated. The wealthy financiers and businessmen who supported the Y were backing him. "The working class is in danger of losing itself in vice, wasting their bodies in drink and loose living. Our young men could drown in pools of vice produced by immigrant vermin, polluters of our genes," a board member said. There were stirring speeches in support when he finished his report. If only Maggie were stronger, he could fully enjoy his new sense of power. From a dry goods salesman, he had transformed himself into a fist of justice.

He was stalking a purveyor of obscene rubber articles near Chinatown one Wednesday in October when he came upon a scene of chaos in a tenement. A woman was crying on the stairs, clutching a baby—a little girl as blond as the silk on an ear of corn. The woman had dirty reddish hair and a nose that looked as if it had been broken. It was hard to tell with these women how old they were—in her ragged dirty dress and unwashed face blotched with tears, she could have been twenty or thirty. If this was trouble, he was always prepared. He touched his revolver through his black frock coat. "Madam, are you all right?" He tried to be polite even with these wretched creatures.

"My sis died in the night and this is her baby. She died of consumption and now there's no one to care for the wee one. I'm living in the next building and they say I can't bring in the baby 'cause I have too many childers already. And I'm a widow, with nothing extra to spare."

"Can you look for another place to live with your children and this poor babe?"

"I don't have no money. I don't have two cents." She looked him over, her tears abating. She was thinking, he guessed, whether to try to beg from him.

"What will you do with this little babe?"

"Take her to the church and put her on the steps, I reckon. What else can I do?"

"You don't want her?"

"My sis didn't leave a penny to care for her. I have three of my own. What can I do?" Again she shrugged her bony shoulders in the dirty ragged dress.

"I'll pay you twenty dollars for her and take her away to raise as my own."

The woman sat up as if he had poked her in the behind. Her eyes met his with a suddenly appraising stare. "Twenty? She's a fine pretty babe. She's worth more than that."

So she had revealed her true character, a shameless seller of babies. "Take it or leave it. There's plenty of abandoned babies to be had."

The woman frowned at the baby. Then she held out her palm. "Twenty in cash."

Anthony counted out the money for her, but held on to it until he took the baby from her. "What's her name?"

"Bridget, but you can name her whatever. She don't know her name—she's only three months. The woman upstairs was nursing her—Sis couldn't—but she won't do it no more without you paying her."

"I'll find a wet nurse, don't worry." Not that he thought this slattern would concern herself with the baby for five minutes after he went down the steps. He took the baby and hastened toward the Bowery, where he should be able to hail a cab to take him to the ferry. The baby began to cry, feebly, and he held her close. This little child would be saved and save Maggie, all at once. He looked down at her in the cab, trying feebly to suckle on his overcoat, and he melted with pity.

They named her Adele. Maggie's mother found a wet nurse. The nursery had been set up already, so it was just a matter of putting Adele where

Lillie had once lived. Maggie took to her at once. "It's the most wonderful present in the world you've brought me, Tony."

"She'll be our own darling to raise."

"The Lord works in mysterious ways. Now he has given me a child."

"I prayed for a child for us, Maggie. I do the Lord's hard work in the ditches of filth to preserve what's right, and the Lord rewards us. The Lord's given us this babe to raise."

"Can we legally adopt her?"

"We have powerful friends. They'll make the proper arrangements. There should be no problem at all in securing Adele."

That evening, Anthony worked on his notes, updating his diary of arrests while the coal furnace heated the house and Maggie settled in the baby. He had an additional fire in the stove set into his fireplace. The wet nurse would come three times a day to feed the baby, upstairs out of his way should he be home.

Over the next weeks, his impulsive purchase proved a good one, confirming his judgment and the Lord's protection. Adele turned out to be a good baby; she did not cry nearly as much as Lillie had. She smiled readily and gurgled and cooed as Maggie amused her with a rattle. She seemed healthy and happy, and Maggie was brighter than he had seen her since Lillie took ill. He looked over at the brand-new 16-shot Winchester repeating rifle one of his backers had given him, mounted over the mantel. There were raids on which his revolver was not protection enough. Now he had this dandy powerful new weapon. The Lord did provide. He felt twice the man he had recently been.

His next seizure was one Patrick Bannon, a forty-five-year-old Irish immigrant and papist who was selling circulars for a woman's rights convention. In defiance of all decent behavior, he had his two young sons circulating the vile pamphlets. All this demanding of rights by viragos was contrary to the word of God in the Bible, contrary to nature, which clearly separated the man as head from woman created from his rib, who should cleave unto him, honor and obey and be his helpmate, as was his own dear wife. He brought Bannon before Judge Benedict. Anthony never lost a case in Benedict's court. Benedict always sided with him and always sentenced the criminal to jail. Bannon got a year and a $500 fine. That would wipe him out good.

Satan was busy night and day in the city. If Anthony had an army at his disposal, he could cleanse the city. All he could do was go out every day to fight the Lord's battles. So he went with his pistol and his notebook, feeling his strength, his vigor as never before. Sometimes he won and sometimes the police, instead of aiding him, tipped off his prey. He had an assistant now, a burly man of German descent named Bamberger, handy with his fists. He also had a few volunteers he could call on, young men from the Y. One of them had come into possession of a madam's card advertising a lewd show called the Busy Flea Dance at a brothel just below Houston. The madam charged them five dollars a head to watch a disgusting performance of four girls naked and performing obscene acts on each other, oral, anal, simulated congress with a large pink imitation organ. Anthony paid for himself, Bamberger and the young volunteer named Fred. He made mental notes so that after the arrests he could write up exactly what they did. He could not believe these creatures belonged to the same sex as his Maggie. Surely the daughters of Eve were born wicked unless saved. He could not imagine what he saw before his own eyes, mouths in the dirtiest places. He could not even look away. When the show was over, Anthony pulled his pistol and arrested everyone.

"Wrap yourself in a blanket," he said to the four prostitutes, pointing his pistol at the madam's head. "You're going to the station right now. As you are."

"I'm not going out that door without my clothes." The mulatto woman put her hands on her hips and looked him straight in the eyes. "Shoot me."

After ten minutes of these floozies screaming at him, Anthony let them get dressed and then marched them to the nearby Fourteenth Ward station. "What's up, Sally?" the policeman at the desk asked the madam.

"This gent has been pointing a pistol at my girls and me. He paid for the show, he watched the show, and then he wanted to parade my girls naked down the street."

"Are you okay, Janie?" the policeman addressed one of the prostitutes. "Have a seat, girls. You need anything?"

To Anthony's overpowering disgust, the police captain himself came out to greet the madam, with whom he seemed to have an intimate relationship. He glared at Anthony. "Who are you to go around arresting folks? You've no authority. Waving a pistol at these girls."

Anthony wrote up detailed notes on the performance, but the case was dismissed. The police often were hand in glove with the prostitutes, he reported to his backers at the Y. Something more was needed than the laws already on the books. He needed direct authority to arrest and prosecute without the agreement of a corrupt police force.

Anthony had better success against pornographers, blasphemers, free lusters and authors of books that displayed anatomy. Any discussion of the private parts, any drawings or photos of the naked body could incite dangerous longings. Once excited, such desires and fantasies were impossible to contain. He moved against two abortionists, small prey compared to Madame Restell, but he could not seem to touch her. She had powerful and rich friends who protected her as she lived openly in bloody luxury.

He did not think much of Plymouth Church—too lax. However, an attack on one minister could lead to a contempt for all, backsliding and, ultimately, atheism. He was shown a copy of *Woodhull & Claflin's Weekly,* as the smut journal was called, within a couple of days of its publication. It contained an obvious attempt to discredit the preacher of Plymouth Church, Henry Ward Beecher, known all over the United States as a Christian speaker of tremendous power, by detailing rumors of affairs. He considered Beecher full of hogwash, but the preacher was a Congregationalist and as such entitled to Anthony's full protection. Besides, Woodhull was notorious, in the papers as often as the president. It would please his backers and the Lord to put her away. Most of the issue was taken up with a scurrilous interview with Woodhull, whose name had come to his attention before as one of those free lusters, an unsexed woman who demanded that women do things not even proper for men, a slut who hung out with communists and atheists and other lowlife. But there was worse obscenity in the same issue, an account of the French Ball, a scandalous orgy attended by a mix of prominent men, whores, society ladies and lowlife—all in masks. If it were not so strongly protected by men with money, he would have moved against it. The article in question, written by Tennie C. Claflin, was about the rape of a young virgin who had been foolish enough to go to the ball and who ended up in a brothel. He did not doubt the story, but such tales could not be printed and distributed where the eyes of the innocent could fall upon them. He couldn't imagine the woman who could write such a report.

He swung into action at once with help from Beecher's parishioners, fine upstanding men in positions of authority. One bought copies of the paper and mailed it to another. The district attorney met Anthony in his office on Sunday to issue a warrant for the arrest of Woodhull and Claflin for sending obscene matter through the mails. Anthony then went with his men and officers. He waited for almost an hour. Then one of the patrolmen called out, "Here they come!" He and his men intercepted the sisters in an open carriage, with five hundred copies of the dirty rag at their feet. Oh, he could tell they were caught totally by surprise. They were taken straight to the Ludlow Street jail.

In the morning he got them moved to the jurisdiction of the U.S. commissioner Davenport—an officer of the court he could trust—who sent them back to jail. Woodhull claimed to be running for president, so it was only fitting she spend Election Day in a cell. Woodhull was the worst kind of woman, and that men called her fair only made her more dangerous. The face of an angel and the soul of a devil, one of the prosecutors said. The Reverend Beecher staunchly denied the foul story of adultery the sisters had printed, probably when a blackmail attempt failed. Anthony got them moved from Ludlow to the Tombs—a dark, filthy, overcrowded dungeon that stank of the open sewage that flowed through it—a fit place for the likes of these low women.

Their next time in court, suddenly they were represented by that notorious shyster Howe of Howe and Hummel, who specialized in getting off criminals of all stripes. Howe was a huge bear of a man—bigger than Anthony himself—who dressed like the barker of a circus on the Bowery in loud clashing colors, plaids and silks. He glittered with diamonds on stickpins and studs, on rings and pins. On his head, instead of a respectable top hat or derby, he wore in all seasons a yachting cap. Anthony had crossed swords with Howe over three belly dancers gyrating in transparent veils. Howe had got the sluts off by claiming the dance was sacred to their Islamic faith—Anthony knew all three hailed from Philadelphia but he couldn't prove they were fakes.

Besides his own suit in federal court, the sisters were being sued for libel by the gentleman Claflin claimed had deflowered a virgin at the French Ball. It was disgusting that any woman could write about such a thing, using words to describe the sexual act as if giving a recipe for roast turkey. At such moments he thought about his Maggie and his precious little daughter Adele and resolved that he would forever stand between them and such filth. Oh, he had the evil sisters, no doubt about it. No doubt at all. They were going to spend a long time in prison.

THIRTY-SEVEN

A LETTER CAME THAT SAID Freydeh's older sister Sara and family were taking a ship out of Leipzig—a recently instituted run to New York—well in time for Freydeh to meet them. She and Kezia scrubbed the three small rooms to make them as clean as they could, while Sammy hauled water up again and again. She sent Sammy out to the markets to buy pallets to put down on the floor. The day before the ship was to arrive, Sammy checked with the shipping office to make sure the ship was on schedule, for the weather had been rough and Freydeh was worried. Ships had been known to go down. It was cold already, and there had been driving rain. No snow yet, but some mornings ice crusted the mud in the street and icicles hung from the cornice past their window. This day had dawned cold but clear with a pale blue sky showing between buildings. The air smelled more of coal and less of sewage. Freydeh could scarcely choke down a bit of stale bread dipped in tea. Lately she had been drinking coffee sometimes—Sammy had taught her the habit—but this morning she was too nervous. She had not seen Sara for ten years. She inspected Sammy's cleanliness, then scrubbed Kezia until she cried that her skin was rubbing off. They put on their nicest clothes.

They arrived way too early and waited and waited. Freydeh had made sure they all wore warm clothing now that they could afford it—secondhand, but not fifth-hand, not worn out already. Kezia was bundled up so she looked like a fat dumpling, although she was still a thin child—not nearly as thin as she had been when Freydeh found her, but thinner than she ought to be. They bought hot corn and roasted chestnuts from vendors to nibble while they waited. On such a chilly morning, few strolled the paths of the park in front of Castle Garden and no one sat on the benches except a homeless man who might have been sleeping and might have been dead. Kezia ran off to watch a boat that was docking.

Freydeh chased her and dragged her back, keeping hold of her hand. Today she wasn't going to lose anybody.

At last passengers from Sara's boat began to spill out of Castle Garden. Freydeh, Sammy and Kezia pushed up close to the doors so that her sister and family could not be swept away by hawkers from boardinghouses, men seeking cheap day labor, brothel keepers—who swarmed the immigrants as they straggled through the high formidable doors of the port of entry. It seemed to Freydeh that several hundred bedraggled travelers passed her and still no one looked like her sister. Had she missed Sara? Asher she had never known well. She remembered him as religious, austere. She began to sweat, a cold sheen of fear under her dress. Finally she recognized Sara, her face more lined but sweet as ever, her dark eyes searching the crowd. Freydeh began to yell. The brother-in-law Asher was gripping a boy by the hand tightly while a little girl hung on Sara's black skirt. Sara carried a large bundle and so did Asher, a short stocky man, although thinner than she remembered him, with a great bushy beard and *payess*. The older girl, Debra, a toddler when Freydeh left, had a pack tied to her back and dragged a basket.

"Shvester, shvester!" Freydeh cried at the top of her lungs.

Sara's face changed, breaking open. "I was so afraid," she said in Yiddish, "after what happened with Shaineh, that you wouldn't meet us."

"So these are your children?"

"Chaim, Feygeleh and Debra—my oldest." She motioned Debra forward, who gave a shrug of a curtsy, eyes cast down.

"This is Samuel and this is Kezia." Sammy held out his hand to shake while Kezia stuck her thumb in her mouth, as she did when she was nervous or fearful.

Asher and Sara were staring at Sammy and Kezia, then at her, then at them again. She could tell what they were thinking: Sammy was too old to be her son by Moishe, and Kezia was too young. "They're adopted," Freydeh said. "But I love them like my own flesh and blood. Moishe gave me a baby but I lost it when he was killed. So Hashem has given me these. Come. Have you eaten?"

"Not for two days," Asher said. "We ran out of provisions. We couldn't get kosher food."

"Then we'll go home and you can eat. Can you wait that long?"

Sara was looking around. "Is it near here?"

"Not too far. We take a horsecar. Come. I have money to pay."

They all crowded onto the car, standing huddled together with the bundles in the middle for fear they would be stolen. "So many buildings,"

Asher said. "So much noise. So many people. Who are they? Where are they going?"

"I remember how it was when we came out those same doors. We didn't know where we were or what to do."

"Is it much farther?" Debra asked, speaking for the first time. Her voice reminded Freydeh of how Shaineh had sounded as a girl. It was good to hear the accents of home—although it was no longer home and never would be. Often immigrants talked of going back to their homeland once they had made their *gelt,* their money, but Jews didn't think of that.

"It's a ways. The roads are always crowded like this. Day and night," Sammy said in Yiddish. She could tell he was nervous in front of her family. She squeezed his hand.

"So many people," Sara echoed. "So much noise. And it's dirty. I thought everything would be new and clean and shining."

"We live in the dirtiest part of town, almost," Sammy said. He sounded more confident, finding a comfortable role as guide. "Over by Corlears Hook it's even worse. Five Points is worse. But where we live, there's Jews. You can find shuls and kosher butchers and bakeries and places that will hire you, if they have work."

When they got off the car and walked through the streets of their neighborhood, Asher and Sara kept staring up. "They're so tall, the buildings. You hardly see the sky. Where do people have their latrine?" Asher asked.

"You'll smell it when we go in the building," Freydeh said, taking her sister's elbow. How thin they all were. "In the courtyard. Fortunately, we face the street. But people empty their pots out the windows. Never walk too close to the buildings, especially in early morning. Don't be afraid. In a month, you'll be at home."

They labored up the steps to the top floor. "What's all this?" Asher asked of her equipment.

"I make a living with rubber goods . . . condoms."

Sara made the sign of the evil eye. "How can you do that, my sister?"

"I was left a widow with no money. I worked in a pharmacy. I saw that making condoms was something I could do. It's harder for a woman to run a business here than back in the Pale. I make good money, sister, and I keep my family. I saved enough to bring you over with your family. Be glad for what I do."

"It doesn't seem fitting for a woman," Asher said. He was no taller than Sammy and slighter.

"Back in the Pale, women run taverns and grog shops. Our mother made vodka. So? My work is better than being in a brothel, what happened to Shaineh."

Sara began to weep, beating her breast. "The shame on us!"

"Nobody needs to know, once we can get her away from the man who's keeping her. We've tracked her keeper and we know where he lives. She has a little girl by him, Sara, and you have to behave yourself when we finally find them. Here everybody can start over and over again, and nobody need know about the shame. This is a hard place. But if you're strong, you can do well, you can set up your children to do even better."

Sammy took over and briefly explained how they had been tracking Shaineh. He had followed Alfred twice but he could not keep up with the carriage. He lost him going south each time. But they would persist and they would find Shaineh and her daughter Reba. They were far too close to give up.

Freydeh heard soft giggles and turned to see Feygeleh and Kezia down on the floor playing with a doll Freydeh had made for Kezia out of odds and ends of fabric with skin of rubber and a face Kezia herself had drawn.

Freydeh fed everybody the soup she had made earlier. She would give up her bed to the family and sleep in the front room. Besides, she didn't want anybody else sleeping near her apparatus, for fear they might lurch into it in the dark and break it. She would take care of her family, but she would not let them interfere in her business.

The next day, they held a conference around the rickety kitchen table. It was warm in the little kitchen, for the stove was lit. Water was heating on it and gruel sat keeping warm. The adults, she noticed, now automatically included Sammy.

"You can help us in the rubber business, or you can look for work. It won't be easy. Times are getting harder," Sammy said. "A lot of people have been thrown out of work lately, and jobs are tight. The German Jews don't speak Yiddish, so you have to talk German with them."

"I can do that some," Asher said. "I thought all Jews spoke Yiddish."

"Not the Germans," Sammy said. He was showing off a bit, proving himself to her relatives. "There are Jews downtown who talk Ladino, nothing like Yiddish. They been here the longest. When you go around Manhattan, you hear German, you hear Yiddish, you hear Hungarian and Irish and English and Czech and Italian and even Chinese. Everybody under the sun comes here. But you got to learn English to get by and you got to speak German with the German Jews."

"How about Polish?" Sara asked. "I speak Polish."

"There are some Poles too. But they don't have the jobs you need." Sammy hit his palm on the table, looking at Asher. "Tomorrow you come with me and we'll go around and see what we can find. You're pretty skinny. Are you strong?"

"I can do whatever needs to be done, for my family," Asher said.

"I can work with you," Sara said to Freydeh. "I don't approve of it, but if I can feed my children, then I do it."

"Me too." Debra stood behind her mother. "I am thirteen. I can work as hard as anyone."

"You should be in school," Freydeh said. "There's free school here."

"The youngest children can go," Sara said. "Debra has to work. Is there enough to do for her and me, to earn our way?"

"More than enough." Freydeh put her hand over her sister's. How worn it was already. Sara was only thirty-five but looked years older. "Times are hard in the Pale?"

"Impossible," Sara said. "Neighbors were dying all around us from cholera, from hunger, from pleurisy, from consumption. People are so hungry they eat the grass of the fields and they eat the dirt of the ground."

"Here we can survive. But you have to let go of some of the old ways and the old ideas."

"I won't give up some things," Sara said. "I will not put off my *shaytl* and I will not eat *traif* and I will not give up being a Jew."

"You don't have to," Freydeh said. "You just have to stretch what you think of as natural and ordinary. There's nothing in our religion against what I do. You're just not used to such a business. But here they use these things up by the cartload. I do what I can for my children and for you."

Wednesday Freydeh went out on her rounds to the clients she serviced that day, a couple of brothels, four pharmacies and a purveyor of rubber goods. She had just entered the premises of Mr. Gillespie on Ann Street and was showing him the new item in her line, the pasha, which had little ridges on it supposed to provide extra pleasure for the woman. Another customer entered, a hulking gentleman in a rusty black frock coat with ginger whiskers and a broad high forehead. While Mr. Gillespie examined the pasha and she made out a receipt for the items he carried, the gentleman wandered around the store picking up items and putting them down, a little shy about stating his business. "I'll give the pasha a try before I order a gross of them," Gillespie said. "I'll keep this sample and let you know."

She didn't want to give up her sample, but he was a good customer. "If you need to try it out, then do it. But you'll find it a winner."

"I wouldn't mind trying it out with you, sweetheart. You're a right handsome strapping figure of a woman."

"I'm a widow with two children and I'm still mourning my husband."

He turned to the gentleman. "I'm going to be a while with this lady, so tell me what you want and I can ring it up. You don't mind waiting," he said, turning to Freydeh.

"A customer is a customer. Go ahead with him. I'll finish your receipt."

"I want a box of those." The whiskery gent pointed to the tiger condom.

"That's a real popular item. This here is the lady who makes them and she makes them right and tight."

The gentleman purchased his box, asked for a receipt—which surprised Gillespie, she could tell—and left the store. They resumed going over his order. She was just totaling it up when the gentleman entered again, this time with another man just as big and burly and a policeman. The gentleman brandished a pistol. Freydeh shrank behind a row of sporting equipment. "You're under arrest, Gillespie, for selling obscene materials. And you. The Jewess. What's your name?" He waved his pistol at Freydeh.

She did not know what to say. At first she pretended she did not understand. But her name was on the receipt she had been writing out.

"Frieda Levin, you're under arrest for selling obscene materials."

He quick-marched them down the street to the station house. She was terrified. What would happen to her? He kept waving that big pistol around. Did they shoot people here? Would she disappear forever? Would she be sent off to some place like Siberia? While she was being booked, she gave a quarter to a street urchin to run to her house with a note for Sammy, who would give the boy another quarter if he handed the note straight to him. Usually there was a kid hanging around the station hoping for just this sort of job. People wanted to contact their lawyers, their family, their business. She gave a false address to the officer—she used Big Head's address. She figured that while they wouldn't get much satisfaction about her there, they might find other things that would interest them.

She hoped the kid had delivered her note to Sammy and not just pocketed the quarter and vanished. She knew the kid wouldn't pass on the address to the police. Not that they would care. They had booked her in a perfunctory way as if annoyed. The police in her neighborhood were aware of her business and sometimes put the touch on her for free boxes, but they never bothered her. It was like hitting up the butcher for a steak or drinking free at the local saloon.

"Who was the gent who bagged me?" she asked one of the policemen.

"Anthony Comstock."

"Who's he? He didn't have a badge."

"He works for the YMCA—Young Men's Christian Association. He goes around bagging everybody who has to do with sex—booksellers, publishers, guys who sell French postcards, actresses, whores, dancers—you name it. He's one of those crazy do-gooders that want to tell you what you can do with your free time."

"Am I going to go to jail?"

"He'll try to send you to Blackwell. Depends on the judge you get. Some of them think like him. Some just dismiss his cases. They think he's a nosy piker and they don't like him any better than you or me do."

She was taken in a police wagon to the Tombs to await trial. It was a huge gloomy damp building with funny thick pillars out front and inside, like a real tomb—dark and dank and evil-smelling, as if the walls themselves sweated sewage and death. It smelled like steerage after a few days at sea in rough weather. Men howled like animals as she was led past their cells to the women's wing. She noticed an inner building separated from this one by an area with a dirt floor, where a gallows stood.

The prison guard, a stocky man with a red mustache and brown hair, said to her, "Better get some money from your family if you want to survive here. Also they can bring you blankets and food."

"They have to find me first."

"For a dollar, I'll get word to them."

"And tell the police where they are?"

He laughed. "The police don't care. You're not rolling in it, I can tell, so what's to be gained? The police would never have arrested you for what Comstock brought you in for. But he's got powerful connections, so they got to mind him."

"He took me before I could get paid by the guy he busted with me. I got only two dollars. I give you one and a note, you'll get it to my family?"

She had more than that pinned in her blouse, but she wasn't about to let on. She was sure she could be robbed in here.

After the guard had gone, a clear, cultivated American voice from the next cell said, "The guards do what they say, generally. If you buy them, they stay bought. That's the political definition of an honest man, I was told once by a man who should know."

Freydeh could not see the woman, for the walls were stone—moldy, damp with grease and grime. In one corner, toadstools were growing, poisonous she assumed. A tiny slit of window gave on the inner courtyard where she had seen the gallows. "I'm afraid," Freydeh said. "I don't know what's going to happen to me."

"Comstock got you too, is that what the guard said?"

"Yeah. I never heard of him before."

"Lucky woman. I wish I never had," another voice said. "He stuck us in here to rot. For telling the truth."

"There are two of you in there?"

"We're sisters. We were arrested together and we'll be tried together. Obscenity, they call it," the first voice said.

"My name is Freydeh. I make and sell condoms."

"Is that a good business?" the second, more sensual voice asked. "I'm called Tennie. My sister's Vickie."

"Victoria," the first voice corrected. "And tomorrow is Election Day. I was running for president when they stuck us in here. Who's going to vote for someone in jail? I can't even campaign."

"What does that man say you did?"

"Wrote two articles about prominent men—one by me, and one by Tennie. Mine told the story of a famous preacher in Brooklyn, Henry Ward Beecher, and his real life and affairs."

"I thought Christians always stuck up for their preachers."

"I'm not a Christian," Victoria said. "I believe in the spirits. They speak to me."

"Where I grew up, there was a rabbi three towns over who said angels spoke to him. I was never convinced. I'm a Jew, but a freethinker too."

"Ah, we're all freethinkers," Victoria said. "And that's why we're in here."

The next day, Sammy found her. Visitors were freely allowed, so long as they tipped the guard. Sammy came with a lawyer, a Peter Rudyard, Esq. "Billyboy says this guy can help us," Sammy said.

"You have the cash, I have the know-how. We'll get you off, Mrs. Levin. That's a promise."

"Can you get me out of here now?"

"There's bail. Can you go it?"

"Not if we have to pay you."

"Well then, you have your boy here make you comfy and we'll get to trial soon as we can."

"Someone told me that the judge makes a difference."

"He surely does, missus. I'll see what I can do. That may turn out to cost a bit too, to get the right judge."

"Sammy can pay you."

This was going to wipe out the money she had been saving to move them all to a cleaner, safer place. She'd bet Mr. Comstock ginger whiskers didn't live in a tenement. Well, she wasn't going to exhaust their money getting out sooner. Sammy could manage the condom business in the meantime and he'd teach Sara and Debra what to do. So much for Sammy's continued schooling. At least he'd had a few years. He was a good bright kid and he would pick up a lot on his own. In the meantime she would just have to sit tight. Sammy had brought her bread, cheese and apples, a blanket, a quilt, her own pillow, and a change of clothes, candles and matches. She would ask him to pick her up books in Yiddish or Russian so she had something to read. For a woman who liked to keep busy, this time was going to be hard.

The next day there was an execution, a man who had killed four women, marrying them for their money or property, then poisoning them. The gallows was set up between the inner and outer prisons and she could see the executioner, Monsieur New York, in his mask. "They say he was a butcher's apprentice before he started hanging people," the voice of Tennie said from the next cell. "The guard told me that there's people all over the roofs and upper stories waiting to see the murderer swing."

The other voice, Victoria, said, "Executions draw an enormous crowd. Some people sell places at their windows to watch over the wall."

"Not me. I seen enough death."

"You're a good woman," Victoria said. "Death shouldn't be a spectacle."

The guards were setting up chairs under a canopy for important visitors: officials, judges, wealthy men who wanted to watch. Freydeh did not. She sat down and read the German newspaper Sammy had brought her, a couple days old but better than nothing. She hoped that her sister's family would manage without her. It was a dreadful time to have been carted away to jail. She knew that Sara would not be shocked by that, the way some people might be, because they were all accustomed to the czarist police locking up Jews on trumped-up charges in order to extort money. Just when she felt as if she had her nose an inch out of poverty and could see a little way ahead, this arrest had to happen, the sky turning dark and falling on her head. All she had to look forward to were Sammy's visits every other day.

THIRTY-EIGHT

JUST BEFORE CHRISTMAS, Victoria and Tennie were transferred to the Ludlow Street jail. In the Tombs they had enjoyed the invisible company of another of Comstock's victims, but Ludlow was less unhealthy, being for federal prisoners and debtors. The walls were not as slimy as in the Tombs. They had a little more light and their lawyer saw that good chairs were brought in and a kerosene lamp to read by.

Victoria felt abandoned. No one from the woman's rights movement had come to her defense publicly except Isabella, who under a pseudonym had written that others, and among them she named Elizabeth, knew of the Beecher-Tilton affair. She also aired some of the secrets of suffragists' affairs that Victoria had considered writing about but never had. Victoria felt that she and her sister had been deserted by everyone who had previously admired and lauded them. They were outcasts again. Only Isabella remained, and she was futilely trying to get Henry to admit his guilt. Instead of confessing, Henry accused her of insanity, bringing in a doctor who said she was suffering from monomania induced by overexcitement and the influence of Mrs. Woodhull. Isabella was now threatened with being locked in an insane asylum. Victoria followed all this through letters and through the reporters who came by regularly, in hope of a story. Pearlo was also under attack and possible indictment. James was in the Tombs, in the men's section.

Finally Elizabeth jumped into the fray, defending Isabella and Victoria, stating she had known about the affair. Then one of the best lawyers in New York, Howe of Howe and Hummell, volunteered to take over their defense, although Victoria had no idea how they were ever going to pay him. He was a flamboyant man who mostly defended criminals and members of the Tweed ring, but occasionally took free speech or censorship cases. He was an old foe of Comstock. Three hearings were convened and still they were in jail. Victoria demanded the right to testify in her own and her sister's behalf, but Judge Blatchford refused, because she was a woman—thus unfit.

Victoria wept and wept. She began to refuse food. Why was she being punished? Why had the spirits deserted her, along with the women who had been her allies and her friends? She had been on the heights of money and fame, thousands had applauded her speeches, she had appeared before Congress, she had been a candidate for president. Her crime was that she had written the truth, and now she was cast down, alone except for Tennie, to rot. The newspapers said she would surely be convicted and shut up in Sing Sing for years. She was terrified. The visions she saw were not of high position but of herself grown old in a cell. She developed a deep hacking cough. Some of her hair fell out. She wondered if she was dying. Tennie kept up her spirits for a long time, always giving a cheerful funny outspoken interview to the reporters who still came by, but now she too was weak and dispirited. Instead of starving herself, Tennie ate heartily of the starchy prison food and whatever the reporters brought them, with no exercise. She was putting on weight in the enforced idleness. Sometimes when reporters came to interview them, she regained her energy. Victoria could scarcely bother. It all seemed no use. The only thing they brought that she ate were apples and oranges.

Once again they were carried off to court. Howe, wearing plaid pantaloons, a purple vest and a huge diamond on his satin scarf, asked if the Bible and Fielding and Shakespeare and Lord Byron were next to be censored. With pious vigor, he invoked freedom of the press. He poked fun at Comstock and got the audience laughing. He quoted the Bible, poetry, the Constitution and Thomas Jefferson. Comstock was livid with anger and humiliation, sitting on the edge of his seat with his back straight and his eyes fixed on Howe as if he could kill him by glaring.

Then help finally came, from Victoria's sometime lover Benjamin Butler. The senator wrote an open letter to her—copies sent to all the papers and published in several—that said the statute under which she had been arrested was misconstrued and did not apply to the *Weekly,* as it did not cover newspapers. Finally, they were released on $60,000 bail raised by selling just about everything they still owned.

They walked out into a mob of reporters. Tennie joked with them, but Victoria, leaning on her sister, said nothing. Her limbs felt flimsy. The months in jail had sapped her will. They were homeless. No hotel wanted them. They were broke. They had been turned out of their house and out of their offices. Finally they came to rest in a dingy boardinghouse where they shared a small room—containing an elderly bed, a washstand with a pitcher and basin—with each other, Zulu Maud and Byron.

At least they were free. Victoria began to eat again. The boardinghouse was so depressing, she took long walks accompanied by her children. Her physical strength began to return, but she felt as if her will had been broken. What was to become of them all? She would not return to Ohio and the life of itinerant quacks and mediums, selling whatever concoctions Buck could cook up. The food in the boardinghouse was gristle and thin broth, porridges and pasty bread—jailhouse food revisited.

She was just beginning to think seriously about what they could do when a fresh warrant was served on her and Tennie. Comstock had persuaded Luther Challis, one of the debauchers of the young virgin at the masked ball, to sue them both for libel because of Tennie's piece about him and his friend. They were once again hauled into court, with Howe defending them. At least they had a different judge.

But this time a woman came forward to defend the sisters—not one of the respectable women who had been Victoria's fair-weather friends, but the keeper of the brothel where the virgin had been brought and detained. Molly de Ford, knowing full well that she would be put out of business for her testimony, marched into court and testified that every word Tennie had written was true. This judge permitted her to testify. The jury brought a not guilty verdict. The judge scolded them, but the jury freed the sisters at last. They walked out into a group of reporters cheering them.

Victoria felt stronger. Now they were vindicated, and articles about their harassment began to appear here and there. She received her first offer in months to speak. Haggling about price made her feel better. Perhaps she could recover from this disaster. She used the money to bring out an issue of the *Weekly* attacking Comstock and all he stood for. She called the Y "the Protestant Jesuits" and published a list of books Comstock had considered obscene, works by Byron, Cervantes, Goethe, Dante, Shakespeare, Victor Hugo and Virgil.

Comstock had a great deal of influence. He had pushed Congress into enacting legislation while they were shut up in the Ludlow Street jail that greatly extended his powers. She wished she could ask Benjamin Butler to explain exactly what the new laws—openly called the Comstock Laws—

could mean to Tennie and her, but she did not have the money to take a train to Washington to see him. She was aware she still looked haggard. Her wardrobe had been sold off along with their artworks, their furniture, their linens, cutlery and fine china and books. All gone down the maw of Comstock's savage hatred of them and all they stood for.

Comstock stirred some suits from the powerful members of Plymouth Church forcing Tennie and her to return to court—until she was interviewed by another member of that church who inquired if she possessed letters written by Henry Ward Beecher that bore upon the case. She answered that she did—actually she had no letters, but if Beecher thought she did, so much the better. Obviously there were incriminating letters floating around somewhere, and if he thought she might have them, so much the better for her. The next time she was hauled into court, the judge summarily dismissed the case, saying the 1872 statute did not apply to the *Weekly* and all charges should cease. Beecher's influence over the courts was strong. Seven and a half months after the first arrest, the prosecution was vanquished and she was free—in poverty, stripped bare and in broken health. A few newspapers around the country began to defend her and connect her battle against Comstock and Beecher to freedom of the press. Late but not unwelcome.

She had an occasional lecture engagement. The National Woman Suffrage Association held a conference, but she was not invited. She was no longer respectable. The brokerage business was gone, the *Weekly* appeared only when she had a little money and something important she felt she must say. But she was too weak to push hard on anything. She attended a spiritualist convention with James where she was called upon publicly to defend her free love position. The man who had risen to confront her demanded to know if she had ever prostituted herself.

"Never," she said. "I never had sexual intercourse with any man whom I am ashamed to stand side by side with before the world. I am not ashamed of any act of my life. At the time, it was the best I knew." She said she considered herself free to have sexual intercourse with a hundred men if she chose, so long as her feelings were genuine. She demanded that everyone have the same familiarity with their sexual organs as any other part of their body, and that they not blush to discuss sex or their bodies. She stood before an audience and she could feel the dissension, alternating waves of hot and chill from the people before her. Murmurs, applause and boos. She nodded toward James, who was sitting on the platform. "This is my lover, but when I cease to love him, I will leave him."

The country had plunged into depression while the sisters had been in jail and in court. Thousands of men and women stood in lines for a little soup and some bread. At least they were not yet reduced to that. She could still keep her family in food and keep a roof over their heads, even if it was a cheap boardinghouse. Banks were failing, businesses were closing their doors. The railroads and the mines were cutting wages, indifferent to how their workers would survive when in good times they were barely paid enough to starve on. On every corner, hordes of new streetwalkers called out to passing men, women thrown out of work, women whose husbands had lost their jobs or left them to look for work or better times out west.

Annie Wood, one of those still friendly, told Victoria that respectable young women begged her to let them work in her house. Victoria came frequently for coffee and breakfast, as much to feed herself as to enjoy Annie's company. She was back with her family again—who else would have her? They had resumed their old trade in ointments and creams for the brothels. Annie said, "In times like these, ordinary working families are selling their daughters' virginity not once but again and again if they can. There's always toffs who want to buy a virgin. Some of them think it cures the clap. Poor girls. It sure does pass it on."

"How do they fake virginity?"

"Alum to tighten the opening. Some animal's blood inside."

Victoria sighed. People were so demented. "Comstock has never bothered you?"

"The chief himself protects us. He has a couple of girls here he favors. Comstock likes to cause trouble to those who can't defend themselves, but he doesn't go against those who have more power than he does. He knows his place in the chain of command."

"He's capable of very personal vendettas."

"Against you. And others. Many others." Annie sighed. "If they ever replace the chief, we'll be in trouble. I'll just retire. I've put away a good nest egg. . . . You were so canny with money, I'm surprised you didn't."

"My family eats up whatever I make. I spent for my campaign, I spent for my paper. I believed I was called to lead."

"You're not down forever. The next time you get your hands on some money, hold on." Annie nodded at her mulatto servant for more rolls and café au lait. "Have you tried my quince jam?"

Victoria looked at her friend sadly. Age was beginning to show on Annie. She kept her hair blond but there were crinkles around her eyes. "You can believe I will hold on in future. This has taken years off my life. Byron doesn't know what's happening. It's harder since his father died. Canning was the one other person who could communicate with him. But Zulu Maud knows everything that goes on, and she worries. At times, she's like a little old lady. She's far more understanding and aware than my own mother."

Annie sighed. "I'm glad I never had children. It's a load on you."

"But also comfort." Victoria slipped a roll covertly into her carryall for Zulu.

TENNIE WOULD FOLLOW her wherever she led, for Tennie was loyal and ever willing, but the rest of her family had to be supported. They were a millstone around her neck—something that dragged her down and bent her spine. But they were her family and they were loyal in their ignorant, quarrelsome way. She must make money, clear their debts, enable them to live decently again. She tried out a speech at Cooper Union on socialism and the devastation that religion wrought, thinking that in the midst of a depression such a topic would rouse the audience, but people walked out. Audiences who came to lectures did not respond to Marxian analysis. They did not want to hear Christianity attacked. She must find a subject that would satisfy audiences.

She worked through the latter part of October into November on a new speech focused on sex, "Tried as by Fire or the True and False Socially." Since people expected the worst of her, since she was notorious already, she might as well talk about what was forbidden to women and taboo in public. She would speak about the central importance of sexual expression in both men and women, and how repression distorted character and weakened the body. She connected the failure to develop and appreciate sexuality as one cause of unhealthy children. For the first time in her life, she spoke publicly about Byron and his condition, linking it to her own ignorance of her body, her marriage to a drunkard and an adulterer who at times beat her. She talked about female pleasure, insisting that women were at least as capable as men of experiencing pleasure and that orgasm was important for women. Much of women's nervous troubles were due to repression of their sexuality, a repression that began in childhood.

This speech was a success. She went from town to city to town, crisscrossing the United States, accompanied by Tennie, her children and her mother. Roxanne insisted on coming with her, saying that Vickie's health was bad and needed her support. Byron was nineteen, not bad-looking but a good-natured idiot. Zulu Maud was her darling. Victoria had taken her out of school because the other children were persecuting her for her family. Tennie and she educated Zulu Maud. Often on trains, they sat doing lessons with her. It passed the time, and Zulu was—as Victoria had been—a quick learner who enjoyed the lessons and the attention they brought her. Occasionally Victoria returned to New York City, where James was waiting, not doing much else besides sitting around with Pearlo and his other freethinker friends and writing an occasional piece for one of their journals.

Life on the road was hard. She would be one night in Kalamazoo, Michigan, the next in Jackson, the next in Lansing. They stayed in whatever hotels they could afford and ate what meals were available. Occasionally some local spiritualist or woman's rights advocate would put them up. She remembered Elizabeth's complaints about traveling hardships. Elizabeth had seen her twice in New York, but had not invited Victoria to her home; Susan had never spoken to her again. Isabella remained loyal, but she was in France, away from Beecher and his doctors and their desire to commit her to an asylum.

Occasionally she took a lover on the road, and he would travel with them for a while—some young man who struck her as intelligent, soulful. She did not expect a great deal from them, but, like Tennie, she sought a little solace and a little pleasure. She was making money, they were out of debt—Howe paid off, at last. She had clothes again instead of the same two worn dresses. She could afford a rose now and then to wear at her throat. She found to her surprise that she did not miss James. He felt very distant. Now was a time when he might have come to her aid, made money himself, volunteered to travel with her, perhaps write articles or make speeches in her defense. He complained that his war wounds, including the ball still lodged in his thigh, were bothering him. The truth was he enjoyed his life in New York, his round of discussion groups, reading freethinking journals, giving a little talk here and there, drinking a bit, playing billiards. Their sex life had never recovered from their separation in jail. He had said several times that her choosing to attack someone as prominent as Beecher was an error, but he had not said so before she wrote the piece—only after Comstock and the courts had almost crushed her.

She was weary with traveling. She was sick of the speech she had written and given well over a hundred times. Who was counting? Actually Roxanne kept count, drawing sticks in a notebook. When she had too sore a throat to speak, Tennie took over. After all, they had heard the speech so many times, even Zulu Maud could give it from memory. As it was, Zulu often opened the program by reciting poetry. She had no desire for the spotlight, but her recitation was popular and she was cute, so she obeyed and performed. At twelve, Zulu was shy with boys and did not seem to know how to flirt or even chat with them. She shrank from the presence of strangers, although she could mount the platform and recite in a clear impassioned voice that people said sounded like a smaller version of Victoria.

Victoria looked at herself as she passed a wall of mirrors in a hotel lobby in Kansas City. She was still beautiful. She had a fine slender figure and a chiseled face and black hair without a trace of white. Her eyes were as intense a blue as ever. But inside, she was not what she had been. Something had broken, beyond repair. How much longer could she continue to pull the weight of her squabbling family through the mud? For how many years could she exploit her notoriety? Did she any longer believe in anything except survival? She was frightened to the core. She had dared to do what no other woman had, and she had been punished and feared yet worse punishment. She would wake in the middle of the night soaked with a cold sweat, her heart pounding, her mouth dry, and she could not return to the comfortable numbness of sleep. She woke thinking she was back in a cell in the Tombs. She had come so close to a life in prison, she could not keep that from her nightmares.

All over the country, men were out of work and women were hungry. In every city, homeless children roamed the streets. Hoboes went from town to town riding the rails, looking for work, looking for a handout, looking, like herself, to survive. Sometimes the country felt on the verge of the revolution she had preached, and sometimes apathy was so thick, despair settling over the lives of ordinary people like a dust storm too thick to see through, too thick even to allow breathing. Only revivalists seemed to be thriving.

Word came to her via the newspapers that Theo had launched a suit against Henry Ward Beecher for adultery and alienation of Lib's affections. Theo had risen at last to strike back, but she thought him a coward. He had not come to her defense; she would not come to his. She would not offer to testify unless subpoenaed. Since he was busy denying they had ever been intimate, she doubted he would subpoena her, and she was fairly confident Beecher's lawyers wouldn't. That trial was the sensation of the country.

Pearlo wrote her as she was speaking in San Francisco that around the Brooklyn courthouse, concessions were set up where refreshments and souvenirs were sold. Men lined up every day at dawn to crowd into the limited seating in the courtroom. Thousands were turned away. Each side had teams of famous lawyers. Every word was reported in the papers. She followed the trial as she trekked up the West Coast, then back to the Midwest.

Finally, in the spring of '75, as she was leaving the stage in Brattleboro, Vermont, she was subpoenaed by Beecher's lawyers to turn over relevant letters and to appear in court to deliver them. When she returned to New York, she at once destroyed the letters from Theo she had been saving except those dealing with the writing and publication of her autobiography. She did not crave more notoriety. If Theo said they had never been lovers, fine. She didn't need that hung around her neck with all her other scandals. She would give them only the most respectable of communications. She traveled to Brooklyn with James. All eyes were on her and artists sketched her for the next day's papers, but the lawyers were deeply disappointed by the letters she produced.

While in New York, she wrote a new speech about the Beecher-Tilton scandal. She might as well make some money from it, for it had cost her enough. She imagined there would be a great deal of interest in this speech, and there was. There was.

1873 ONWARD

THIRTY-NINE

NTHONY WENT TO WASHINGTON with one thing in mind: to get a federal law passed that would outlaw obscenity in word and object once and for all, and provide him legal power to seize and prosecute writers and vendors. He was being paid $3,000 a year by the YMCA, but since the Woodhull mess, donations had dropped. Some in the leadership worried about his aggressive approach and the publicity he generated. Jesup told him not to fret, for he would back him to the hilt; in the meantime, Jesup paid for Anthony's sojourn in Washington as a lobbyist for decency.

He carried to Washington a trunk of condoms, dildos, pills and instruments for inducing abortions, obscene books and postcards. At first he had difficulty commanding the attention of anyone in Congress, because a scandal implicated a great many members, including Grant's vice president Colfax—prominent senators had been pushing stock in Union Pacific cheap to whomever in Congress would buy it. Now the scandal had broken open. However, Anthony arrived with a strategy mapped out by his powerful friends in the Y who knew whom he should approach and how. Further, he had a letter of introduction to Justice William Strong of the

Supreme Court, who had just lost the battle to write "God" into the Constitution and make Christianity the official religion. Strong drafted the new legislation and personally introduced Anthony to leading senators who would push the bill through Congress quickly—a necessity, since Congress would adjourn soon for Grant's second inauguration. Anthony was indifferent to the railroad scandal—just stocks and money. Nothing dirty there. He liked to be adequately paid and to keep his family in reasonable comfort, but otherwise he had no interest in finance. He was about the Lord's business, and he would be provided for. Justice Strong got Vice President Colfax to lend his office in the Capitol for Anthony to set up his display, inviting senators and representatives to visit his collection of horrors. They came, they saw, and he conquered.

Vice President Colfax was eager to display zeal on the side of righteousness, as were others implicated in the railroad scandal. Anthony's placard behind the items said "These are examples of what is being sent through the mail to our innocent children in boarding schools across the nation!"

Now he had the attention of the legislators. They fingered one item after another, asking him what they did. Several would not actually touch the lurid objects but poked them with a walking stick. They paid particular attention to the French postcards and the etchings, which they studied carefully. He appreciated their interest, now that he had finally aroused it. Benjamin Butler came in, looked over the table and had the audacity to wink at him, as if he were somehow involved in this smut. "Not a bad collection," the senator said in his ear, "but Colfax has a better one. You should ask to see it."

When Anthony had finished his spiel on the dangers to the youth of the nation, the senators and congressmen professed themselves ready to give him whatever law he needed. Few in Congress wanted to be seen as defending obscenity, although there were stubborn souls who insisted on blabbing about freedom of speech and the press—freedom to corrupt the innocent. He was working full-time, pressing the flesh, telling tales of his arrests and his trials, working them all. There would be inserted into the last appropriations bill before adjournment a special agent of the post office who would wield vast new powers to confiscate immoral matter in the mails and arrest those sending it: powers to search, to seize and to arrest. This special agent, everyone understood, would be him. Anthony insisted on serving without pay. If the agent were a paid office, it could be used as patronage, but if it were unpaid, then he could have it for all any politician would care. The Y would pay his salary anyhow. He had Jesup's promise.

It took him the better part of a month and a half to get everything he wanted, but on March 3, the new law made illegal the spread of vile material, banning obscenity from the mails in pretty much the way he desired. The bill passed at the last minute before inauguration almost without discussion. Two-thirds of the congressmen had no idea what they were voting for. He was beginning to develop a certain contempt for Congress. They were men, he judged, of loose morals and wavering opinions. Politics was a dubious business and he was glad he had nothing to do with it. The new law made it a crime to send through the mail erotica, contraceptive devices, medications or information, abortifacients, sex implements and ads for any of the above. Anthony returned to New York as an agent of the federal government with broad new powers. Now evildoers like Woodhull would never again escape his net. A district or circuit court judge anywhere in the United States had the right to issue a warrant to search, seize and take possession of any obscene or indecent books, papers, articles or things.

As soon as he returned, his supporters began to put pressure on the legislature to incorporate a New York Society for the Suppression of Vice. It would be independent of the Y, although several directors would be the same men who had helped him for the last year and a half. The society would receive half the fines of those arrested by him or his assistants—and he would have several. Thus, Jesup said, if contributions fell off again because of some controversial case, he would still have ample funds. The police were instructed to help the society, and the obscenity law was strengthened to include all the items listed in the federal laws and more. Now items did not have to go through the mail in New York for him to seize them and arrest their manufacturers, authors or purveyors. Woodhull had gotten off on a fluke of the previous law. That would not happen again.

He now was a powerful special agent of the post office and secretary of the Society for the Suppression of Vice. He could travel anywhere in the States and seize evildoers. The Lord had seen that he was true in his aim and had given him the power to serve. He would not flinch. He would not hesitate to examine every dirty book and picture and show that he heard of, to protect youth. It took strong willpower and an unshakable belief to carry out his work, but he was man enough to do it.

At home, things were good. Adele was a little doll baby. Maggie constantly sewed for her, dressing her up. She was cute and cheerful, although slow to learn to talk or walk. But that only showed what a good girl she was, never forward, meek and mild and gentle as a female should be, just like Maggie herself. Maggie's health had improved. He had married the ideal woman, except for her ability to bear children, and that lack was made up for by her wonderful care of Adele. He exercised his conjugal duties twice a month and Maggie bore it without complaint.

Every year he toted up for his supporters the tonnage of bad books he had burned, the arrests, the convictions. He recorded the exact number of dirty postcards, lewd pictures, improper ads and periodicals he had confiscated. He imagined a lurid mountain of trash he piled up every year—not literally, for once he had examined them, he had the books, the postcards, the pictures burned and the plates destroyed by acid. When he was through with them, he banished them from the face of the earth.

He paid off the mortgage, waiting until it was done to tell Maggie. Mostly he had the press in the palm of his hand these days, but lately some of the sporting papers, vile things, had been after him for not arresting Madame Restell, the Fifth Avenue abortionist. They claimed he went after the small fry but left the powerful alone. He hated to be criticized in the press. He paced his study. He knew that the men who supported him liked to maintain good relations with other powerful men. They had appreciated his destruction of the Woodhull gang. Madame Restell had been a particular target of the sporting press, those salacious publications that catered to young men and wrote about unfit subjects such as prostitutes and masked balls. The one good thing about them was that they hated abortionists, who they felt gave too much power to women, to cheat and cover up their adultery, to carry on and bear no consequences. On that subject alone, he agreed with them. But he had ignored their attacks on Madame Restell for years because she seemed untouchable and there were so many targets crying out for his action.

She was no back-alley quack, carrying on her bloody trade in secrecy and shame. She flaunted her sordid profession. For years she had advertised in every paper that would carry her ads, even the ones that considered themselves respectable family sheets. Her husband had been in the game with her, until he died recently. They operated under a variety of pseudonyms, but everyone knew who she was and what she did. She lived in a marble palace, a huge mansion on Fifth Avenue. He had walked by it the week before. At the side entrance, carriages drew up and heavily veiled women scurried inside. He had been told that she could, if she wished, blackmail most of the richest and most prestigious families in the city and beyond. Her connections and her clientele had shielded her from trouble with the authorities, although years ago he knew she had been arrested, tried and served a year on Blackwell's Island in the East River.

Even there, she had influence, he had been told by a police captain who cooperated with him. She had worn fine clothes, lived in a special cell, had food prepared for her and lived the life of a gracious lady behind bars. He did not doubt the story. Every high-placed man in the city and every wealthy family seemed in her debt. What disgusting scandals had been covered by her bloodletting he could only imagine. There she was living like a vulture in her castle, sinning and causing to sin countless women and the men who had impregnated them.

He would have liked to share his problem with Maggie, but the subject was too indelicate for her ears. If every woman were like his Maggie, then half the problems of the world would disappear overnight.

He arrested a free luster who had published a disgusting book of marital advice with pictures of male and female private parts that could corrupt any youth who stumbled upon it, three pornographers, the proprietor of a sexual peep show, a streetwalker who passed out broadsides displaying her bare body, a madam who specialized in masks, whips and chains, two condom makers and the proprietor of a shop that sold sex toys and dirty postcards. It was a profitable month doing the Lord's hard work, but still that abortionist weighed on his mind. The *Herald* dared insinuate he was afraid to move against her—he who had no fear of the wicked.

The year before, that one-armed pornographer Conroy had stabbed him right in the face when Anthony was arresting him. Anthony had bled mightily, needing ten stitches to stanch the wound. He had lost so much blood he had been confined to his bed for a week. But he had risen from his bed to put Conroy in jail, not only for selling pornography but for assaulting an officer of the law. Conroy would rot there for years to come. Anthony traced his scar with his fingers. He wore it as a badge of courage, proof of what he could endure and never flinch from his duty. Such a scar was a token of worth.

He fingered his scar again. How dare they imply he was a coward. He strode into the back parlor where Maggie was sitting at the pianoforte playing a hymn to amuse herself and little Adele. Adele was three now, a little doll with large pale blue eyes like bits of morning sky, strawberry blond curls and a sweet smile that showed a dimple. She had finally learned to speak, but she was never forward. The doctor said she was slow, but Maggie and Anthony considered her perfect. She was gentle, obedient, quiet, shy, everything a girl should be. If Maggie sat her down in a chair, she stayed there. He saw plenty of ill-behaved children, some who helped their parents at their evil work. He remembered one condom maker who had her whole family enrolled in her criminal activity. He saw child prostitutes, he saw eleven-year-old newsboys who had prostitutes their own age who served them, he saw children sold to young toffs to pollute their bodies and destroy their souls. He and Maggie would keep Adele safe. She was a good girl, and she would stay that way, protected, innocent.

"You don't know how vile women can be," he said to Maggie, touching her shoulder gently.

"Oh, when I was in school, there were girls with tongues as low as many of the boys, believe me, Tony. I know there are bad women. When we walk past the saloons on our way from church, I see women in those dens as well as men. I see fallen creatures selling themselves in the next neighborhood."

"You should never have to see such sights."

"Passing by corruption does not corrupt, Tony. We simply go on by."

"I'm troubled by how vile women, who should be pure, who should by their higher nature lift us up toward God, can do far more damage than men. I'm talking about so-called respectable women who interfere with God's gift of fertility. I am talking about desexed women who prattle and speechify about their rights and wrongs and want to smoke cigars and vote and hold down jobs and flaunt themselves in public. This country's on the verge of a great evil. It takes all of my effort every day, every night, to try to contain it."

Anthony was appalled at what was going on in his own fine city of Brooklyn, where respectable people moved to get away from the vice and filth of Manhattan. He had pulled Beecher's chestnuts out of the fire once by silencing that witch Woodhull, but Beecher had landed himself in muck up to his neck. Anthony thought him lax, sentimental, preaching poppycock to his congregation so they would feel good on Sundays and not think about their sins. Anthony had grown up with real religion, hellfire and brimstone, ministers who believed what they preached and made sure their flocks believed too. It wasn't easy to be a real Christian, but Beecher made it sweet and bland and smooth to swallow as blancmange.

Now that worm Theodore Tilton was suing Beecher, all their dirty laundry aired before thousands of spectators. Anthony would have gladly drowned them both like unwanted puppies. Beecher sat there in the witness chair, "I don't remember," "I can't recall," "I have no memory of that." If Anthony were in charge, he would force Beecher to remember. But he had no sympathy for Theodore Tilton, an adulterer himself who had been a cohort of Woodhull when it suited him and then run for cover when she got into trouble. This was exactly the scandal Anthony expected from those women howling about their rights. Tilton had brought such women into his house, Susan B. Anthony, Mrs. Henry Stanton, and what did he expect? His idiot wife went astray. Anthony did not doubt Beecher had seduced her, but Tilton deserved no better.

When the jury was hung after six months, he regretted the wasted trial. He could have nailed Beecher on the stand. Anthony felt as if respect for organized religion and men of the cloth had dropped several degrees. Beecher may have escaped with his income intact, but the very air of Brooklyn felt tainted by all those stories of adultery and faith betrayed. He heard that Woodhull was barging around the country giving lectures on the whole sordid affair. She wasn't breaking any laws he could dig up in recounting the story of Mrs. Tilton, doubly unfortunate in her husband and her paramour, who both abandoned her. He knew she was living in near poverty with her children, whoever the fathers actually were.

He zigzagged across the country, persecuting pornographers, abortionists, purveyors of obscene books, postcards and theater pieces. He could have filled an entire freight train with books he had burned. There were certain judges in whose courts he could always count on a conviction, judges upright and firm in their religion. Occasionally, he encountered a sleazy judge who went on about rights and free speech and he lost a case.

He came home exhausted. Sometimes the scar on his face ached where Conroy's knife had severed four arteries. He fingered it to remind himself to keep on, no matter how tired he was. Still, when he came home to Maggie, when he looked at Adele sitting demurely with her hands in her lap as Maggie had taught her, he knew she was as much his daughter as if Maggie had borne her. She was a fine little woman, silent, well behaved, eager to please. She was perfect.

FORTY

ELIZABETH WAS NOT as spry as she had been. She was carrying a lot of weight, and her joints were achy. She had as much mental energy as ever, but at sixty-one her physical strength was limited. The younger of her children were in college now, but all of them came home frequently and sometimes moved back in, like her eldest and in some ways her favorite, Neil, a scamp who was always getting into some kind of money troubles.

Susan ran the National, serving as president and keeping up with organizational and bureaucratic details that bored the stuffing out of Elizabeth. The younger women all adored Susan. They were not as comfortable with her. They called Susan "Aunt" as her own children had, but her they addressed formally. Whenever there was a state that appeared to have a chance of passing woman suffrage, she got on a train and went racketing around the state giving sometimes two speeches in a day, once, three. She could still make her voice carry to the back of the hall or to the back of the crowd without sounding shrill, but speaking outdoors was especially draining. She and Susan would canvass the state end to end. They were still losing, but the margins of defeat were lessening. They were not as close as they had been—the rift over Victoria had never completely healed. Moreover, Susan was singing only one note these days, like many of the younger women, suffrage, suffrage, suffrage, all the livelong day and all the weary night.

A woman who could not feed her family or whose children were dying of cholera would never care about the ballot box. The depression that had begun in '73 had only deepened by '76; the situation of working people was desperate. When Elizabeth went into New York, she saw soup lines stretching for blocks for a bowl of watery turnip gruel. Men and women piled into the basements of police stations to sleep on boards for the night because they had been thrown from their lodgings. Landlords grew rich on tenements where people were living twenty to a room. Bitter strikes broke out in coal mining, cigar making, textiles, the railroads, iron making. Most strikes were violently suppressed, throwing still more workers into the ranks of the hungry. Three-fifths of their wages went for food. She and Susan were looking at different worlds. In her world, the voices of the hungry, the beaten, the homeless were louder than the voices of women from comfortable homes. As she crisscrossed the country, she saw men, women and children begging in the streets, people shuffling along dressed in rags with their hands out.

Lately she had also become aware how many of the poor ended up in jail or prison. She took an interest in reform and began giving talks to prisoners. She was not afraid, and the men greeted her warmly because she did not scold them or preach to them, but discussed how prisons could be reformed and what the women's vote might mean to them when it finally arrived. She went to Sing Sing twice to speak.

Susan came to see her in Tenafly, arriving while she was celebrating the engagement of her son Gat to his fiancée. Susan had no time to join in the festivities but got right to business, plunking herself down at the dining room table that had witnessed so many of their plots and strategies. She had, if anything, grown leaner. Her nose was more prominent and her hair was sparser and iron gray now, worn in the same tight bun. Elizabeth's own hair was still abundant and curly around her face but white as parchment. As Elizabeth grew plumper, Susan grew leaner. They were more than ever Jack Sprat and his wife.

Susan ate the soup and bread Amelia put before her but could not refrain from launching at once on her mission. "The centennial celebrations in Philadelphia are going to be immense. Especially around the Fourth of July. We must demand a part."

Elizabeth groaned. "Philadelphia in July is closer to hell than I care to come, no matter what our detractors say."

"This is no time for self-indulgence, Mrs. Stanton. You are needed! Even Lucretia Mott's going to take part, at her age. She sends a special message that you should join us."

She hadn't visited her dear friend Lucretia in six months. When a woman got to Lucretia's age, no matter how hale and hearty, upon each parting a friend never could know if they would meet again. "What do you want of me this time?"

"The Beecher-Tilton scandal—not to mention Woodhull's taint—has painted the suffrage movement with an air of loose living. We need to seize the opportunity of this great patriotic festival. It's a chance to place ourselves in a more favorable light and get our message out to thousands, to millions of people."

"They'll never grant us a place in the spotlight."

"We'll demand it. In addition, it's time for a new Declaration of Rights. It should be read from the grand platform right after the Declaration of Independence."

Elizabeth frowned. "What's wrong with the old Declaration?" She was still proud of her work at Seneca Falls.

"We need something up to date."

"Susan, dear Susan, isn't it time for some of the younger women to do their part? We're old warhorses. My brain is brighter than ever but my body's dimming."

Susan glared at her. "This is a centennial, Mrs. Stanton. They won't have another one for a hundred years. I'm going directly to Philadelphia. Matilda Gage is coming too. So are many of the younger women you want to see engaged."

Elizabeth had known Matilda Joslyn Gage since 1852, just after meeting Susan. Matilda was an attractive woman—married young to a successful dry goods merchant. Matilda's home had been a way station on the Underground Railroad. She was an outspoken abolitionist who joined the woman's rights movement early and gave her full intelligence and passion to their work. Matilda had borne three daughters and one son who lived. Elizabeth noticed that sometimes they understood each other in ways Susan couldn't share. Matilda still had a close relationship with her husband. He was more supportive than Henry ever had been. She would enjoy seeing Matilda. "I can't go next week. I have too many commitments. But I'll come in a few weeks. After all, it's only May third."

"Get there as soon as you can, Mrs. Stanton. Your presence and your assistance are sorely needed. . . . By the way, I paid off the last of the *Revolution* debt last week. Six years of paying it off, Mrs. Stanton."

Elizabeth nodded, not wanting to reopen that old source of conflict. If she suffered a twinge of guilt, she wasn't going to admit it to Susan.

She did not go to Philadelphia until well into June. By then the public work on the international exhibit in Fairmount Park had been completed. The women had set up an office on Chestnut Street, where Elizabeth finally saw Lucretia, who rode in most days from her farm bringing cold chicken, hard-boiled eggs as well as fine Oolong tea to make lunch for women in the office. Elizabeth was startled by how frail, almost gaunt, Lucretia looked. We're all getting on, she thought.

Elizabeth watched Susan with the younger women. She would listen to them with great intensity, as if every word were a revelation. She treated their smallest problems and weakest notions with passionate seriousness, conversations that, even overhearing them, Elizabeth found tedious. Susan had great patience, smiling at their jokes, giving them little tasks and praising them fulsomely. She brought them along a step at a time; indeed Elizabeth could see Susan was rewarded not only with devotion but with their full participation in the movement. They became truly her disciples.

"No, Margaret, you don't seem at all forward. It's important to speak your mind. You worry that it's not ladylike, but is it admirable for a woman to lack backbone? Do you admire doormats on which people wipe their muddy boots?"

"Amanda, if he says things like that to you, perhaps he is not the suitor you should favor. If he is so critical of you now when you're courting, imagine how he will treat you when you have been married for five years."

"Oh, Phoebe, you must remember that your mother grew up in different times. You have opportunities that were closed to her. Don't judge her too harshly, but never let her clip your wings."

Coming on the scene late in the preparations, Elizabeth sat down to write the Declaration, but it turned out to be a committee affair. Every word and phrase was haggled over. Every direct, strong and militant phrase raised some woman's hackles. Elizabeth spent the better part of ten days working on draft after draft, but she found the end product much inferior to her earlier Declaration. They decided on the Fourth of July as the day they wanted a public appearance. Elizabeth wrote to General Hawley, in charge of arrangements, asking for a place on the platform and the opportunity to speak. The general refused but sent six tickets to attend.

"That's his mistake," Susan said. "We must seize the chance to speak out." Susan came up with a plan. They would rush the stage and present their Declaration, which would then have to go into the official record of the proceedings. Elizabeth and Lucretia wanted to hold a countercelebration at the First Unitarian Church instead. After a great deal of arguing and raised voices, they agreed that Elizabeth and Lucretia would open the counterfestivities and Susan and Matilda Gage would lead four younger women into the centennial with copies of the Declaration.

The Centennial Exhibition was the first world's fair ever to be mounted in the States. The women, prevented from setting up an exhibition in the main hall, raised money for their own building with its own steam engine, operated by a woman engineer from Canada. There the Declaration was printed, along with a woman's rights newspaper.

On May 6, President Grant had opened the centennial with a speech and turned on the immense Corliss steam engine, powering everything in the exhibits except the women's building. Since that day, millions had attended the Great Exhibition and the shantytown of carnival and sideshow exhibits just outside.

Harriot had come down to help. "Mother, let's go to the fair. Why not? Half the country is going."

"Don't tell Susan. She won't approve. But why not? I'm curious too."

They took the special train out to the fairgrounds. Everybody had been saying how impressive the exhibition was. Certainly it was large and crowded, covering 450 acres of asphalt laid down in Fairmount Park, with pavilions from thirty-eight nations and every state. It cost fifty cents to enter.

"This is shameful. Four dollars for a little plate of chicken." Elizabeth was incensed. "They have a captive audience and they're gouging."

Even the ice cream cost three times what it would outside. "This is outrageous in the middle of the worst depression we've lived through." Elizabeth glared around her. Most exhibits struck them as tacky. Two immense statues of little merit depicted a Pegasus and an Amazon with a horse. There was a kneeling woman made of butter. An animated wax statue of Cleopatra boasted a wing-flapping wax parrot. Cleopatra reclined, occasionally blinking, on a barge while pink cupids looked left and then right. George Washington's false teeth were on exhibit along with a new device, called a telephone. What most impressed Elizabeth was the Sholes Printing Machine. When levers were pressed, it produced type, not as clear as printing, but useful.

"Mother, that's what you need. Then maybe I can actually read the letters you write me."

"Harriot, believe me, I try. But my mind runs ahead of my hand."

The Fourth of July dawned oppressively hot and humid as if the air could be wrung out. In fifteen pounds of skirts and underskirts, Elizabeth felt faint, but when she was called upon to speak, she held forth strongly to the crowd. She said they must resume trying to get Congress to pass a new amendment to the Constitution. The church was jammed. The meeting had been under way for two hours when Susan led in the contingent from the centennial.

As soon as the original Declaration of Independence had been read, while the band was playing a march, Susan had led the delegation forward. The men standing before the platform gave way, assuming they were part of the program. Susan marched up on the stage and presented the chairman with a parchment copy of the women's own Declaration. The chairman was so startled he simply accepted it. Then they filed out of the hall, passing out copies right and left. Once outside, Susan climbed on the deserted bandstand—the band was playing within—and read the Declaration to the crowd. Matilda held an umbrella over her to shield her from the sun.

Susan was proud of their action, but Elizabeth considered it more symbolic than useful. She began a new petition drive. Within a few weeks, they gathered ten thousand signatures. But when they presented it to Congress in the fall, they were greeted with jokes and ridicule. Senator Butler arranged for Elizabeth to testify. It was humiliating. The men talked among themselves, got up, walked about, used the spittoons, smoked and ignored her.

The presidential election was approaching. Matilda, Susan and she had sent memorials to both parties, asking for a suffrage plank. The Democrats nominated Governor Samuel Tilden of New York, someone Elizabeth could actually support, for he had been instrumental in overthrowing the Tweed ring. He was as close to an honest governor as New York had seen in her adult life. Senator Blaine from Maine expected to be nominated by the Republicans, but the Union Pacific Railroad scandal stood in his way. Instead, after a huge battle in Cincinnati, the Republicans chose the governor of Ohio, one Rutherford B. Hayes, noted mostly for being inoffensive and having served honorably enough on the Union side.

The Democrats had been more open to the women than the Republicans, who took their support for granted. Tilden had a good chance of gaining the presidency. The smelly corruption of the Grant administration had annoyed many. Just that spring, an investigation revealed the Whiskey Ring had defrauded the country of millions in unpaid taxes; the scandal had been traced to the president's personal secretary and another Grant crony, a revenue agent in St. Louis. There had been scandals involving Indian reservation supply posts, a rich source of revenue. The continuing hard times made voters consider a change. Susan and Elizabeth were supporting Tilden. Spending those weeks in Philadelphia had partly mended the tear in their long weave of friendship. They wrote twice a week. Susan resumed her visits.

The whole family including Amelia crowded into the Manhattan apartment for election night so they could stay in touch with what was happening through Henry's political connections and his position on the *Sun.* By midnight, when they finally got into bed, it was clear that Tilden had won the popular vote by a considerable margin. As the *Herald* trumpeted the next morning, Samuel Tilden was now president.

However, the *Times* said the election was too close to call. Henry and Elizabeth talked more during the next weeks than they had in a decade. The election was being stolen, through the three Southern states still under Reconstruction regimes. Boards were set up in Louisiana, South Carolina and Florida that disqualified thousands of ballots for Tilden and certified ballots for Hayes even when the number of ballots exceeded the number of voters in a district. Weeks turned into months and still the election was in doubt. The election finally came down to Florida and disputed votes there. The States had no president. The Democrats were protesting fraud. Finally the election was thrown into the Supreme Court, where Republicans outnumbered Democrats. The crooked election was certified along strictly partisan lines. Rutherford Hayes became the next president while Tilden retired from public life.

The personal result of the fraudulent election for Elizabeth was that she and Henry could share a meal and an apartment without fighting. They would never again be lovers, but they might be social. They had gone their own ways for so long that their mutual bitterness had eased into a benign indifference. It was interesting to get Henry's journalistic take on political events. That was what they mainly talked about, that and their children, who were happy that their parents were on easy terms. Elizabeth still lived in Tenafly, but she was spending more time in Manhattan.

She began to feel out Susan about writing a history of the woman's rights movement thus far. Susan thought it an excellent idea. Matilda Gage volunteered to work with them on what would be a massive project, covering several volumes. Matilda was an excellent researcher and the best writer in the movement, next to herself. As they corresponded on the subject, Elizabeth found herself growing excited. Who could write such a thing if not the three of them? She did not wish to leave history to the Boston women, with their far narrower view of issues and personalities. Susan shipped trunks of papers she had been storing in Rochester. That spring, with many interruptions for touring, they sat down in Tenafly and began. After each day's work was done, they talked. Susan and Elizabeth would sit darning socks or mending. While she was fond of Matilda, her affection for Susan once again stood at the center of her days, along with her children. Her life's ragged tears were slowly being rewoven, and she was heartily glad. She had missed Susan more than she had been willing to admit. She did not ever want to quarrel seriously with her dearest friend again.

FORTY-ONE

AFTER FOUR MONTHS in the Tombs, Freydeh served eight more on Blackwell's Island in the East River. When she was brought out by boat, she was surprised at how many buildings stood on the island. It was two miles long with a smallpox hospital, a building housing typhoid and other contagious patients, a huge granite charity hospital, almshouses—one for men and one for women aged and poverty-stricken—an immense workhouse to punish the poor, a lunatic asylum and big brick buildings for children detained there and set, like everybody else who could move, to work. She had been taken past sentries to an enormous grim building of hewn stone and rubble masonry like a fort looming over her. She was checked in roughly, her clothes taken and a striped woolen uniform two sizes too big thrust at her. The floors were of cold uneven stone and all the doors and lintels were of iron. She shared a cell with three other women.

She was put to work sewing coats in a room full of women prisoners. Only one of them knew Yiddish. Most of the others spoke English, although there were two Italian women who could only communicate with each other. The women ranged in age from thirteen to sixty: prostitutes, two from panel houses where men were robbed—a panel in the wall opened while the man was occupied with the whore, and his wallet and watch stolen—thieves, pickpockets, a woman who had poisoned her lover, two women who had passed bad checks, a con woman, two abortionists, a woman who had public sex in a Bowery peep show. Several had been arrested by Comstock. The women who had been in the longest, unless they were really sad cases, bossed the others. They saw that the new prisoners and the ones they didn't like worked the hardest. Freydeh had her food taken from her at dinner the first day. The next time that happened, she punched the woman hard in the face. She was flogged by the guard, but after that, nobody took her food.

Sammy came to see her when he could. Each time he had to go through the rigmarole of getting permission and securing a place on the boat that went out to the island. He was on the list as her son, but every time they questioned him as if they had never seen him before. He was the man of the family, because Asher was depressed. He had never lived anyplace but a little village where he knew everyone, where what was expected of him was clear and the roles each played had been set in stone for generations. Sara had adapted quickly, joining in the condom business with Debra. Kezia, Chaim and Feygeleh went to school. Sammy reported that they were all good students, although Kezia got in trouble for talking and drawing pictures.

Sammy had dropped out. Freydeh felt bad about that, but nothing could be done, with her in Blackwell's and the family to support. Sara tried to find Shaineh but spoke English too badly to make herself understood. Sammy was convinced Kumble had moved Shaineh to a new location near the old burned-down place. But Sammy had little time to pursue Shaineh. Freydeh's arrest and trial had strained family resources, using up all the money they had put aside. They were still paying off the lawyer.

More women kept crowding into the prison. Times were hard outside; women resorted to amateur prostitution or thievery. Women who came in now were even thinner than Sara had been. Here at least they ate, even if the food was watery stew of turnips and potatoes. There was a scarlet fever scare in the prison, but Freydeh didn't catch it. A few prisoners were kept apart from the general population, not as punishment. They could afford individually prepared food, a comfortable bed, enough blankets, pillows, a feather quilt. The oldest woman in the prison remembered Madame Restell being locked up there twenty years before. Now in those special cells were a madam and a politician's mistress who had stabbed a rival. She caught sight of them sometimes dolled up in silks and wearing corsets and bustles as if they were going to a party.

It was cold in the prison, then airless and hot. It always stank of urine and unwashed bodies and bad food. Freydeh lost weight, but the worst thing was lack of exercise. She saw the men being taken off to break rocks and build structures on other islands, but the women were kept cooking, sewing, cleaning. She was polite to all the women and close to none. At first she could not sleep for the noise—cursing, weeping, iron doors clanging—but over time she slept when she crawled into her bunk. Sammy brought her a comb and a better blanket. He always brought newspapers and food.

Finally the day came when she could be released. Sammy came to meet her. He was taller than ever. He had become a handsome man, she realized with a shock. He would soon be thinking about women. A young woman was waiting. It took her a moment to realize that it was Debra, now just a hair shorter than Freydeh and with a woman's body. She was not exactly pretty, but she had a sweet face and a warm open smile. "Auntie Freydeh," she said, "I hope you be pleased how we done with you inside." She spoke English with an accent but she had obviously been practicing. She wore her hair up now, had a bright green skirt that looked new and a green bow on the back of her head. She would never have done that in the Pale. She even had a hat she was carrying in her hand, as if putting it on would be too much—but she had not left it behind. She was proud of it. Freydeh watched them together with a wary eye. Was something going on there? Let's see, Debra was fourteen? And Sammy was going on sixteen now.

After they took the little boat to Manhattan, she felt like a greenhorn again as if her eyes and ears would fail, overwhelmed. She had forgotten how to move through a crowd. She was buffeted until Debra and Sammy placed her between them. She smelled hot corn, roasting oysters and chestnuts, she smelled sewage and manure and human waste, she smelled slaughterhouses and glue factories, tanneries and freshly cut sawdust. It had not been quiet in the prison, but the clang of doors slamming and women's voices was silence compared to clopping hooves ringing on pavement, wheels grating and bouncing, hucksters and newsboys bellowing, harnesses jingling, street musicians scraping away on violins or playing concertinas or hurdy-gurdys, hammering, sawing, the thud of barrels being unloaded, people screaming, church bells clanging. Her head ached with it.

She had a hundred questions. "How are we doing?"

Sammy squeezed her arm. "We'll do better now you're back. We had some accidents and some product that wasn't up to standard. So we lost some customers."

"What kind of accidents?"

"A table caught fire. Sara burned herself. It was only her arm and you can't see where unless she rolls up her sleeve."

"It was such a bad time for that *momser* to arrest me." She sighed and Debra looked sideways at her with a shrug.

"No time is a good time." Sammy gave his cap a rakish tilt. "But we're surviving."

"Has he been after you?"

"We haven't seen him. He's after bigger fish these days. He travels all over the States. It was just rotten luck he ran in to you that day. If you ever see him again, run."

"Believe me, I will!" Freydeh shuddered. "He cost me a year of my life."

"And a lot of money. Money we couldn't make." Debra made that sign with her fingers people used for dollars.

"Plus the money you people spent on lawyers. Fat lot of good it did us," Freydeh said. "All that money to that shyster good-for-nothing."

"He got your sentence reduced."

"So? It was still too much for too little."

She felt exhausted by the time they got home. Sammy helped her up the four flights of steps to the top. "I'm . . . weak . . . from sitting."

"But your English got better," Sammy said. "You have less of an accent."

"I had to speak English all the time. Only one woman spoke the *mamme loshen*."

The apartment was soon crowded, for the children came home from school. The condom factory was still in the front room and Sara was tending it by herself. "So where's Asher?" Freydeh asked, slumped in a chair with her feet up on a bucket.

"You're so pale," Sara said in Yiddish. "White like a sheet, white like paper. I bet you had nothing good to eat in a year."

"Except what Sammy brought me," Freydeh said. "You made me soup and *flanken*."

"We did what we could. Times are hard," Sammy said. "Asher got laid off three weeks ago, and he hasn't found anything since."

"He could peddle something. That's what we always did when we were hard up."

"He has trouble with that," Sara said. "The streets confuse him. He gets attacked and his goods stolen. He was working in a lumberyard, but they cut back because construction is slow. He was working up by Central Park planting trees, but he couldn't understand the foreman and he got fired. They're almost all Italians."

"Where is he now?"

"He's looking for work."

Kezia said, "No he isn't. He's with some old men in the shul."

"It's a comfort to him," Sara said defensively.

Freydeh had been out of jail for less than two hours and she had found out Asher was falling apart, Sara had burned herself, Debra and Sammy were already at the point of making eyes at each other or worse, they were poor again and crowded—eight people to the three-room apartment and two of the rooms the size of closets. She cursed Comstock and his meddling, cursed him body and soul, offspring and ancestors. *A finster lebn af im.* A dark life to him. *Er zol nor anloyfen und oysgetriknt!* He should dry up like a piece of clay.

She roused herself to stand. "Well, to work. Let me at my apparatus. It knows me." She must rally her family. Fix things. That was what she was good at.

"Gladly." Sara sank into the chair Freydeh had just vacated. "I have never worked so hard in my life."

"That's not true, Mamaleh," Debra said. "You always work from dawn to well into the night."

"We all work hard," Freydeh said. "That's how we get by. Time for me to pull my weight again."

"We all know you went to prison for us, instead of us," Sammy said.

"Well, you went into this line of work—" Sara began.

"You can always do piecework making coats or dresses. We'll see how much you make in the same time," Freydeh said. "If you want to do that, don't let me stop you."

Sara fell silent in the chair. Freydeh thought her argument had silenced her older sister, but when she turned her head to look, Sara had fallen asleep from exhaustion, her head tilted back and her mouth dropped open. They had tried to keep up in her absence. But except for Sammy, they were inexperienced and Debra was just a young *maideleh* still. One of the reasons orders had slacked off, she realized, was that they had been making only the simple cheaper condoms and not the tigers or the pashas or the elephants. She put the tigers right into production first thing and corrected the formula they had been using, which reduced the tensile strength of the rubber.

It was the next day before she got outside for a short walk to the kosher butcher to get a little piece meat to make a good strong cabbage borscht. The butcher greeted her. "You do my eyes good, Mrs. Levin. So what happened by you? You got stuck on Blackwell's? It happens to the best of us. We know you just try to do for your family."

Times were hard in the neighborhood. The street kids looked starved. Guys and a woman with her children were sleeping in the filth of the alley. Even the vegetables in the pushcarts looked the worse for wear. More men were gathered on the corners and outside the saloons, a sure sign of unemployment. The coffeehouses were jammed in midday, but most of the men were reading newspapers or playing chess or just sitting, staring into empty cups. Asher seemed to have given up looking for work. Instead he went to the shul every day to pray and study. That was all fine and good in theory, but the family needed him bringing in money. She was going to have to light a fire under him, without getting Sara riled. That and she had to find out what was going on between Debra and Sammy. She was waiting for an opportunity to corner Sammy and quiz him. Kids grew up fast on these streets.

She made soup with the beef, beets, cabbage, onions and a bit of celery root. It would feed everybody along with day-old bread. That evening she worked late into the night turning out pashas. She would get her old customers back; she would find new ones. Her exhaustion had worn off and she burned with energy, free at last, back with her family and ready to go full throttle ahead.

The *untershteh*—the woman in the flat underneath—was gone, killed in a labor meeting in Tompkins Square Park, when the police charged. The papers called them dangerous communists. Her skull cracked by a club, she died at home a few days later. The husband had taken the children and vanished. Now there were newly arrived Jews from the Pale living there, twelve of them, mostly men. They slept in rows on the floor and all day looked for work. Two of them had found jobs at the docks. It was wonderful to hear Yiddish in the halls and in the yard when they went to use the latrines. Sara said there were more families in the shul Asher and she attended, recent arrivals. "Things are getting so much worse there, people are going to keep coming. I just wish they knew how hard it is here. Nobody tells you."

"Still better than there." They were in the front room vulcanizing rubber and making tigers on the mold. Kezia was painting them as they cooled.

"At least there we knew everybody. We shared what we had. You knew if you got sick, your neighbors would come in and bring soup and take your children. You knew if you died, the burial society would wash you properly and bury you the right way."

Asher said, "We're starting a burial society at the shul. It will be done right."

"Two men in the flat beneath us, they got jobs at the docks," Freydeh said helpfully.

"They're *starkers*. Big men." Asher turned his back on her, scowling.

As long as they were all living together, Asher was her problem as well as Sara's. "You got to keep trying, Asher."

Asher said nothing. Sara shook her head sadly. There was a long itchy silence in the room broken only by the neighing of a horse clopping past in the street and wagon wheels grating on the uneven stones. Someone was playing a balalaika downstairs where the men lived. Freydeh listened to the music, a song she remembered, and her fingers flew faster.

That night, she woke to voices arguing. Although the door to the tiny bedroom where Asher and Sara slept was shut, she could hear them through it. Sara was trying to get Asher to look for work. Didn't he want a place of their own? The voices rose and then stopped abruptly as something fell over. In the morning, Sara had a fresh bruise on her cheek.

That Saturday, she took Sammy and they went in search of the man who was keeping Shaineh. For seven years she had been searching for her sister and missing her time after time. Now they were close. Alfred Benedict Kumble was still living with his mother and brothers and one of their wives in the brownstone, but Sammy, in his occasional surveillance and his chats with the stableboys, had learned that Shaineh's keeper was engaged to be married. The wedding was to be in five weeks. The Kumbles were among the hundreds who took the ferries to Brooklyn every Sunday to hear Henry Ward Beecher orate. The stableboys had heard that Beecher was to marry Alfred Kumble to his bride, Beatrice Muriel Pike, in Plymouth Church.

Maybe if he was getting married, he would let Shaineh go. They followed his phaeton moving slowly through the crush of Saturday vehicles, horse-drawn trolleys, carriages, wagons, some streets almost closed with peddlers' carts, people on foot jostling each other. They could, by hurrying and at times trotting, keep up with him. The dark phaeton moved sluggishly in the torrent. Finally, it turned off on Broome Street and came to a halt. Alfred got out, nodded at his footman and went up the front stairs, unlocking the door. He was greeted effusively by a portly matron in a bright blue taffeta dress who did everything but bow to him. He disappeared inside. Down the street of once-fine houses and warehouses now crowding them, they found an oyster bar serving beer, corn cakes, oysters raw or fried and an assortment of other *traif*. They took a table where they could watch the street and ordered corn cakes and beer. Freydeh's heart was pounding from the pursuit through the streets and from excitement. She was still weak from prison. The corn cake was greasy but warm. It was late October; a chill sharpened the air. Sammy sat in a chair beside her, rather than across the table, where he too could watch the house. It had lace curtains on the parlor windows, so they could not see in. Two other men entered; a third man came out. Two heavily veiled women arrived separately and were ushered in.

"It's a house of assignation," Sammy said. "He has her stowed there."

"What's that?" She was always surprised by how much Sammy knew of the life of the streets and the city, its underside and topside too.

"Where men and women who aren't married meet each other. I mean, not to each other. Usually it's married women and bachelors or a man married to somebody else. They pay for the room for an hour or so."

"Out of the way, so no one sees them entering or leaving." Freydeh shrugged. Why would a woman who had a perfectly decent husband go off for an hour's bedding with some other man? If she hated her husband, why didn't she just walk out?

"There goes another one." A woman slipped in, having walked from the end of the block. A man and a woman left together. He put her in a cab and shortly took another.

"So what should we do?" After spending a year in jail, sometimes she found herself deferring to Sammy, as if he were a grown man—which he almost was. His voice had changed, he was five feet eight with a darkish beard he kept shaven. He did not go in for the full-bearded Jewish look of Asher. He did not even sport a mustache.

"We sit and wait till he leaves, and then we try to get inside."

She nodded, too overwrought to speak again. Was she finally going to see her sister? So many years. So much pain. And the little girl, she must be five by now? If Shaineh still had her, and her keeper had not forced her to farm the daughter out. She had not seen Shaineh in so many years, would she recognize her? They said she had yellow hair. There were no blondes in their family. Shaineh's hair had been light brown. Maybe they were pursuing the wrong woman. After all these years, how could she know? Would Shaineh even want to be found? Maybe she had adjusted to life as a kept woman and pretending not to be a Jew. Maybe she wanted to stay with this man, maybe she had fallen in love or simply settled for him and wanted no part of her past or her family.

The proprietor asked them if they didn't want something more, so they ate more corn cakes and drank another beer. And they waited, staring at the house. They waited.

Finally they saw Alfred Kumble leave. He whistled for his phaeton and the footman, who had been sitting on the curb smoking, jumped up and brought the little carriage to him. Off they went, in this case with the footman sitting beside Alfred on the seat while his master gave him some kind of instructions.

Freydeh leapt to her feet, but Sammy was halfway out the door already. They ran across to the house and rang the door. The woman opened it. "We need a room," Sammy said.

The woman looked them over with a jaundiced eye. She shrugged. "Two dollars an hour. You pay in advance. No rowdiness. This is a nice house."

Freydeh shut the door and advanced on the woman. "Never mind. You have my sister here. Shaineh. I think that man who just left, Alfred Kumble, calls her Samantha. She has a little girl."

"Not here she doesn't. And who the hell are you to come barging in here? I'm under protection of the local precinct, so don't you go bothering me or my clients. I got respectable people, people with money, coming here. Get your dirty asses out of here right now."

Freydeh seized her by the arm and twisted. Sammy went running up the steps and began banging on doors. "Police!" he yelled. "The police are coming to raid this place."

There was a great scuffling and movement upstairs. "They're lying," the woman yelled, but Freydeh pushed her down on the sofa and sat on her, stuffing one of the loose pillows in her mouth. Soon a great trampling echoed from the stairwell and men and women in various states of disarray came rushing out of the door without hesitation or conversation. Sammy called down, "There's one door locked here."

Freydeh took the slobbered pillow from the landlady's mouth. "Where's the key? Tell me, or I'll break your arms and then your legs." She gave a twist to the woman's arm as a warning.

The woman shrieked as if she had broken it already. "In my desk. Top drawer. But he'll get you for this. He's a hard one."

"I'm harder," Freydeh said. She pulled at the bell cord until it snapped. A maid appeared, saw the scene of disarray and ran off. Then she trussed the woman up hands and feet and left her on the couch bound and helpless. She found the desk, opened the drawer. A ring of keys lay there. She grabbed the ring and ran up the stairs. Sammy was standing on the third-floor landing in front of a door. He grabbed the keys from Freydeh and began trying them. The fourth key opened the door.

Freydeh pushed past him. A young woman lay on the unmade bed in a flowered dressing gown with her face in the pillow. She sat up. There was a bruise on her cheek and on her left forearm. "What?" she said.

"Shaineh! Is it you? Don't you know me? It's your big sister Freydeh," she said in Yiddish and then again in English.

The young woman stared at her. "Freydeh? What are you doing here? I looked and looked for you."

"I never got your letter till months after you came. We've been searching for you ever since." She grabbed her and hugged her. "Shaineh, get dressed, we're here to take you away. And where's your daughter?"

"He took her from me. The lady downstairs farmed her out. If he's pleased with me, sometimes the woman who has her brings her to me for an hour. So I know she's alive. She lives on Henry Street, in a house in the yard." Shaineh stood up.

"We'll get her. We'll find her and take her."

"He's dangerous. He has a terrible temper."

"So we've heard. Come on, Shaineh, get dressed. We don't have all day."

"He keeps me here. I ran away once."

"We know. We tracked you down," Sammy said. "I got the baker you worked for to tell us what he knew."

Shaineh was digging through a bureau putting on a chemise and then a taffeta dress and a woolen shawl. The only shoes she seemed to have were flimsy slippers, but those would have to do. "Hurry," Freydeh said.

"But I can't go with you." Shaineh stopped cold, turning. "Don't you see? I'm a whore."

"So, and I've been in prison. You're still my sister and Sara and Asher are here too and their kids. We'll find your daughter. It's my fault what happened to you because I didn't get your letter, from fighting with my old landlord. Now we'll make it better. At last we'll make it better, Shaineleh. Hurry!"

Shaineh was grabbing things right and left and stuffing them into a pillowcase. Freydeh wished she would just leave the silken flimsy things, for she'd have no use for them once she was out of this house of assignation and working at a regular job. Freydeh noticed that Shaineh's hair was really blond. She would ask her about that later. She was a beautiful woman, with delicate features, a fine figure, skin like a doll.

Finally Shaineh had her pillowcase stuffed and let herself be led to the hall on her tiny satin slippers. How was she going to walk in those things? It was chilly outside. Well, they would find a cab. They got her down the steps from the third floor to the second when the outside door slammed open. The landlady was running about—the maid must have untied her—and Alfred Kumble came storming in with his footman, running up the steps toward them. The footman stayed downstairs holding a bottle of champagne and a bag of foodstuffs.

"You get out of here and leave my wench alone. I'll have you put in the Tombs for this."

"We're her family," Sammy said. "This here is her older sister. We been looking for her for years and we mean to take her home." He had to crane around Shaineh to speak, standing behind her on the landing carrying the overstuffed pillowcase.

"She's mine, bought and paid for, and you get your hands off my property. She's mine! And she has nothing to do with you."

"She's my sister," Freydeh said. "She came over here to be with me, and we lost each other. Now she's found. She's no slave you can buy and sell. You people had a war about that. She's a free woman and she's our blood."

"You're a Jew. I can tell by your accent. You're a dirty Jew. You just want to take her and pimp her yourself."

"We're Jews, she's a Jew, and she's blood kin." Freydeh tried to block him, but he was a big man and shoved her aside.

"She's no Jew! She's German."

"I am too," Shaineh said. "My real name is Shaineh. The madam named me Samantha. She's my sister, he's my nephew, and I'm going with them." Shaineh struggled with him. "I'm going, I'm going to be free!"

"You're a whore and you're mine!" he bellowed, clutching her by the waist and shaking her hard. "You're trying to rob me," he yelled at Sammy behind him.

Sammy pulled his knife from his belt and lunged at Alfred, who ducked out of the way. Shaineh struggled hard but could not break free. Then she scratched at his face, tearing his cheek and trying to claw at his eyes. He cursed, shoving her away as Sammy slashed at him. She went tumbling down the steps past Freydeh. Freydeh grabbed at her to break her fall, but the silk tore in her hands and Shaineh went bumping down the steps all the way to the bottom, where she lay on the tile floor of the vestibule in a widening pool of blood from her head. She lay on her back with her limbs all twisted before the stolid footman who stood and stared.

Freydeh rushed down to her, followed by Sammy and Kumble.

"Now look what you crazy people have done!" the landlady yelled, wringing her hands. "Word of all this scandal is going to cost me my business!"

Freydeh bent over the crumpled body, touching the face, the neck, the hands. Shaineh's eyelids fluttered and her lips moved but no sound came out. Sammy and Freydeh carried her into the parlor and laid her on the sofa where Freydeh had tied up the landlady. Her head lolled to one side. A bubble of blood came from her lips and then blood trickled down to her chin.

"I think she's dying," the landlady said to the man.

"No!" Freydeh said. "She can't die. I just found her." Tears ran down her face and sobs shook her shoulders. She kept stroking Shaineh's delicate skin, her face, her soft hands so unlike hers and Sara's, her fine curls. "Shaineh, listen to me! Open your eyes, my sister, my little one, open your eyes!"

"I'm getting out of here. It's your fault for letting them in," Kumble said to the landlady. "This has to be hushed up or I'll close you down."

"I sent to you as soon as I could."

"You let this happen. I'll spread the word." Then he was out the door and gone.

Shaineh never regained consciousness. Freydeh considered calling the police, but she was too wary of them, and the landlady said, "It was an accident. I saw it all. I won't let you cause more trouble for Kumble or he'll run me out of town. He can do it."

Finally a wagon was summoned and took them back to their neighborhood with Shaineh's body. The new burial society would have immediate work. Freydeh would weep later. Once again she cursed Comstock. She had found Shaineh too late, too late to save her. Finally it was her fault. Finally it was Kumble's fault for keeping Shaineh locked in a room so she couldn't get away from him. Enough fault to spread around. Once the arrangements were made for Shaineh, Sammy and she headed for

Henry Street to find the little girl and take her, in case Alfred Kumble should have it in mind to do something with his daughter. At least maybe they could save *her*. Reba, Freydeh remembered. A little girl named Reba. She dabbed at her eyes, snuffled back her tears and walked more quickly after Sammy.

FORTY-TWO

VICTORIA WAS WEARY through and through. The only way she could make money was on the lecture circuit and the country was growing more conservative, she could feel the change. No one wanted to hear about woman's rights or messages of sexual freedom and spiritual joining. Finally she began lecturing on her interpretation of the Bible. She was frightened for herself, for Zulu Maud and helpless sweet Byron. James sat in New York with his cronies and waited for her to return with enough for them all to live on.

The next time she was there, seizing what rest she could before traveling again, he was extremely critical. "It's embarrassing, you catering to the most conservative elements. Lecturing about Revelations! What are you thinking of?"

"Money. Survival. What else?"

"You can't sell yourself that way. That's true prostitution." He was pacing with his slight limp. He was a fine-looking man, but she was no longer moved when she looked at him. "You're betraying everything we believe in."

She lay on the bed in her room in the boardinghouse where they were stabled—that was how she thought of it. Each to a stall. Ready to be taken out and galloped again, no matter how weary and saddle-sore. "I'm not sure what I believe in." James had been in jail too, but on smaller bail and for a short time. She no longer felt at one with him. "James, I think we're coming to a parting of the ways. I know we both believe that when love and desire are gone, the marriage, the partnership is over."

He stopped short. "You don't mean that. You need me."

"For what?" she asked coldly.

"To remind you of what we truly believe in." He put his hand on her shoulder, caressing her. His hand strayed down her back.

"What *you* truly believe in." She sat up, shaking off his hand. "I became notorious bleating out those ideas. I went to jail for them. I endured calumny for them. But I cannot find in myself that old belief. The spirits are no longer talking with me. I have led them into the mud and they have abandoned me. Now what I truly believe is that I must feed and clothe my children." Mine, not yours, she added mentally. You've never taken that much interest in either of them. No, when she looked at him, she simply saw bills piling up and debts coming at her. "We had a good long ride together, but it's over, James."

"You're tired. You're saying things you don't mean."

"I'm tired and I'm saying things I mean with all my heart and intellect and will."

"We'll discuss this when you return."

"There's nothing to discuss between us. I'm seeing a lawyer tomorrow."

"Don't do anything till you return from your next circuit. In the meantime, let me write a new speech for you that is far more appropriate."

"Don't bother."

She saw the lawyer and began divorce proceedings. Whether they were legally married or not, she wanted to be sure they were legally divorced. Then she went back out on the road with Tennie and Roxanne, heading toward Pennsylvania, Ohio again and Michigan this tour. Audiences would pay to hear her talk about Revelations when they would no longer pay for her message of liberation. The towns were smaller, the audiences smaller—and most of them came out because of her notoriety. She was making less for lectures and traveling farther and harder. All of her old friends had fallen away except for Annie Wood, who was preparing to retire to New Orleans to live out her life in comfort. She would take an assumed name as a widow. She would bring her mulatto maids with her. If she ran out of money, she could always take up her old profession and run a house there.

Yes, Pearlo and the freethinkers, the woman's rights advocates had disappeared from her life. Isabella had fled to France, where Theo had gone after the end of the trial. Josie had moved to Paris too. Victoria's friends had faded or moved away, and she was left as she had started, with her family. Tennie and she spoke of how they could survive, determined not to go back to Ohio with Roxanne and Buck to take up the old life.

Vanderbilt was dying, the papers said. They were in Chicago, in a cheap hotel. The *Tribune* said reporters were staked out at the new mansion on Fifth Avenue his young wife had wanted. Every week rumors of his death spread through the financial district, but every week he bestirred himself to prove he was alive. He no longer left his mansion, addressing reporters from the door or inviting a couple of them in. He had never forgiven the sisters. Still, Tennie kept all his letters and the presents he had given her, speaking of him kindly as the old boy. "I hope he's not in too much pain. He gets cross when he's hurting."

"Let his wife worry about that."

"Vickie, if it hadn't been for Ma, we'd still be his kittens, you know it."

"Sometimes I think you should have married him."

"A bit late to worry about that. Are you going to divorce James, really?"

"I am. He's cozy in Manhattan while we're knocking ourselves out in Peoria and Louisville and Sheboygan. He complains about everything I do. It isn't up to his standards. I'm betraying his ideas. He doesn't face the audiences I have to please or get booed off the stage."

Tennie began to massage Victoria's shoulders. "You're worn out. After this loop, we're going back to New York and rest for a while."

"In a boardinghouse. Will we ever again have our own quarters? A little comfort? Some pleasant furniture and carpets and beds that are our own? Ever? Or will we always be poor now and hunted. I know that monster Comstock is still after me. He sends spies to listen to my lectures to make sure I'm not talking about sex, ever."

They were in Davenport, Iowa, when the newspapers headlined the Commodore's death. They were in a sleazy hotel in Des Moines when Victoria read about the family suit. The Commodore had left 90 percent of his wealth to his son William, and a pittance to each of the other family members. He had never shown any interest in his daughters. He viewed Corny Junior as a parasite. The rest of the family was suing for what they considered their fair share of the hundred-million-plus estate. They claimed that the Commodore had been senile, even crazy in his later years, and that his will should be broken because his mind was unsound.

"Why do we even go back to New York?" Tennie asked, standing at the hotel window looking out on the dusty street and the carriages passing. "We have no home there. You're dumping the Colonel. Everything's gone and busted."

"We go to New York so we won't go back to Ohio."

"What's going to become of us? Will we have to be prostitutes or mistresses?"

Victoria pushed her face into her hands and closed her eyes tight. "I have no idea."

"I sure wish we had some of the money we spent. And what those freeloaders in our family spent like water going down the gutter and into the drain."

Dingy hotel after hotel. As the audiences grew smaller and the fees less, so were their accommodations bleaker. Roxanne acted as maid, washing, brushing, repairing. She wasn't skilled at keeping up their clothes, but at least she tried. Everything had to last. Fortunately, gaslight was kinder than sunlight to Victoria's increasingly shabby black silk dresses. The rose she wore at her neck or on her bosom now was a silk rose, not a fresh one—one more little luxury that had vanished with their money.

Back in New York, she found the notice that her divorce had not been contested and was final. Surprisingly, she also found a note from William Vanderbilt, of all people—the Commodore's son and heir—addressed to her and Tennie. She knew the Commodore had despised William for years, teasing him, sticking him out on Staten Island on a farm inherited from the Commodore's mother. He had made a profit on the farm, mostly by driving his employees until they dropped. Gradually the Commodore had begun using him as a surrogate on boards. Finally he had come to rely on William. Now he had left almost everything to him. Why did William ask them to let him know when they had arrived in New York? Victoria sent a message back saying that she and Tennie were there for two weeks.

The messenger came back: William would call on them incognito the next evening at eight. He would appreciate privacy for their conversation. Victoria bribed the boardinghouse keeper to let them have the parlor to themselves.

At eight promptly, a carriage pulled up outside and a gentleman in a long cape, his face muffled, got out and climbed the steps. The maid showed him into the parlor and Tennie shut the double doors.

"Here we are," Victoria said. "How may we help you? You know that we frequently assisted your father."

"That's why I'm here." William was not a prepossessing figure. He was a heavyset man, but without the Commodore's robust and commanding presence. His head looked too big for his body; his skin was coarse and red, his eyes small and narrowed, perennially squinting. She wondered if he was nearsighted. His voice was low and rather soft. He laid his cape carefully on a chair. "We are in court. The rest of the family is trying to break my father's will. He left the bulk of his estate to me because he believed I could increase it, and that the rest of the family would fritter it away. I believe his estimation was correct and I am fighting to maintain the will."

"The old boy had all his marbles as long as I knew him," Tennie said. "He could tell lamb from mutton any day."

"The family plans to subpoena the two of you to demonstrate that he was . . . eccentric. To be blunt, that he was crazy. They plan to question both of you about your relationships with him. The séances. The advice from his mother and his dead son—the son I was always compared to and found wanting. They plan to trot out the massages. The laying on of hands. The magnetic healing. Now that stuff is in bad repute these days. All those newspaper stories about fraudulent mediums using devices to simulate spirits. I know you never did any of that, rapping, voices, whatever. But it will look bad in court."

"I ain't afraid of courts, Willie." Tennie crossed her arms. "We've seen the inside of more courts than I can count."

"And we don't want to see any more," Victoria said firmly. "What's your plan? I gather you want to prevent the family from subpoenaing us? You would prefer that they not bring into court the letters that your father wrote me and most particularly Tennie. Even if they don't show he was incompetent, they might cause a scandal. You know he proposed to Tennie. In fact, we have that in writing."

"I'd be very interested in seeing those letters."

"I'm sure you would, but they're in a safe place." In fact they were upstairs in the lining of Tennie's trunk.

"I'd be interested in acquiring them, for the sake of the family archives. I collect memorabilia about my father."

Tennie leaned forward. "Okay, Willie, I'm interested. They mean a lot to me. But as you can see, we're not exactly rolling in it these days."

"Could you produce those letters this evening if I wrote you a check for, say, twenty thousand?"

"Forty," Victoria said.

"Twenty-five, and you produce them right now, or you may keep them. I'm only willing to go so far to pull my father's chestnuts out of the fire." He took out his checkbook and a silver pen. "Do we have a deal?"

"What about our appearances in court? That's a different matter." Victoria's heart was beating so fast she thought she might pass out. She clutched the arms of her chair, but she kept her voice level and her face expressionless. With twenty-five thousand, they could crawl out of poverty again and set themselves up. But as what? Should they restart their paper? But the country had turned conservative.

William produced his narrow foxy smile. "I have on my person two tickets first-class to Liverpool leaving two days hence, the steamship *Oceanic* on the White Star line. It makes the crossing in seven days. Do you think you would enjoy an ocean voyage and some time in England? I can wire ahead and engage very comfortable lodgings for you in a fashionable section of London. I can also set up an account into which I will deposit ten thousand pounds once I know you are in England. Then we call it quits. I only ask you do not return to this country for a decade. After that, I don't care what you do."

"Ten thousand pounds. Is that more or less than ten thousand dollars?" Tennie asked.

"It's more than twice as much." He looked at Victoria. "You can make a fresh start in England, ladies. You seem to need one."

"Two tickets won't do it. There are my two children. They must accompany us."

"Of course. Two more tickets will be in your hands tomorrow."

"Your deal is accepted," Victoria said, quelling Tennie with a gesture. "We will be on that ship. Provided the lodgings are acceptable in London and the money is deposited, we will carry out our end of the bargain. We were always reliable in our dealings with your father."

"Until you tried to blackmail him." William smirked.

"That wasn't us," Tennie said. "That was our crazy parents and sister. We knew nothing about that scheme until it was too late."

"We also have family problems." Victoria smiled slightly. "You might find it advantageous to send our parents to England. We would set them up at some distance from us, but they'd be out of your way. You don't want them called into court either. They cause scandal every time they open their mouths. But if you decide to send them on, wait until we're settled in London, please."

Victoria sat primly in her chair, taking care not to act too excited while Tennie ran upstairs to get the letters. William had guessed they were on the premises. Their lives had been too irregular of late to allow them anyplace they could stow them safely.

"I have never been abroad," Victoria said. "I look forward to the experience."

"I imagine you do," William said. "Try to stay out of the papers in London."

"It will not impact on you or your family, whatever career I decide upon. I'll probably lecture, because that's what I do best. I will, needless to say, not mention my connection to your father or to you. You can count on my silence."

"But can I count on your sister's?"

"Tennie will be silent. She wasn't the one who let out that the Commodore asked her to marry him, remember that. He told you himself, didn't he?"

William nodded. "And your parents?"

"Work through intermediaries. Make sure they don't know where the tickets are coming from. Don't send them first-class, by the way. They would cause too much of a stir. Have them told that the money is from us and that we're doing well in England."

"I appreciate your discretion."

Victoria smiled. "See that you do. And it will continue—to the grave."

Victoria told Roxanne that they had a lecture tour in England and had been sent only four tickets. She assured her mother she would send for them as soon as they could afford to, providing the lectures went well. If they didn't, Tennie and she would soon return. In two days, not only were the sisters ready to travel, but they had bought a few gowns. Annie Wood, still in Manhattan, although she had an agent scouting real estate in New Orleans, put them in touch with a source of secondhand society gowns and a seamstress who refitted them overnight. Thus they were more or less ready for the crossing, although they lacked jewels. Tennie got some decent paste from Annie.

As the *Oceanic* left New York Harbor, the sisters toasted each other with champagne. They were both free. They were unmarried, out of jail and in the money again. Zulu Maud was up on deck with Byron, leading him around as she inspected the huge white steamship. She would watch over him and keep him out of trouble.

"The Commodore came through for us one last time. He might be looking down—or more likely up, from the hot place—if it exists," Tennie said. "Lord Almighty, I am glad to be heading out. We can do it again, Vickie. Good times ahead."

"We're going to be respectable this time," Victoria said, putting down her glass with a smart rap. "No massages, no séances. I'm the widow of

Dr. Canning Woodhull. You can be the widow of whomever you want. I recommend a Civil War hero. That has a nice ring to it."

"Oh, feel the swell. I hope we don't get seasick. I think I'm too happy to get sick. Isn't champagne supposed to settle the stomach?"

"Tennie, listen to me. We must behave." This time she would not let her chance to flourish be destroyed by her family or anyone else.

"Oh, to a point. I want to have fun. We have money again. Let's enjoy it."

"We must invent a family tree. He'll send Buck and Roxanne over. We'll stow them in a suburb or a country house, some place where they can't interfere and get in our way." Victoria sipped her champagne with a frown. Then she reached for a pen and her little black notebook in which she scribbled ideas. "Let's go back at least five or six generations. We'll start before the Revolution. They were merchants. That always sounds respectable, doesn't it?"

"Sure." Tennie yawned. "Whatever you say."

FORTY-THREE

ANTHONY WENT OFF to Cleveland and Chicago to pursue pornographers, but in spite of his seizure of close to three boxcars full of filth and his putting seven men and two women in jail, he was ill at ease. He pursued a photographer of naked females all the way to Nevada. He thought of himself as God's bulldog, for once he had hold of a felon, he never let go. Still, these days he was troubled in his conscience. He was used to the calm conviction that he was the Lord's strong right arm. Yet there was a mission he had not attempted, going after a great source of evil, that female vulture Madame Restell. He must act. He would proceed against her in the way he proceeded against every criminal, by entrapping her in the commission of a crime. He must prove to the newspapers that he was brave enough to pursue evil, no matter how protected by the high and mighty. David going forth against Goliath, he was armored in virtue and right. Then why did he feel so ill? He had a cough he had not been able to shake. His limbs and torso ached. He could barely raise his arm above his head. He was so accustomed to being strong and hale that he scarcely knew what to do, away from Maggie on the road and feeling weak in all his joints, feverish some mornings. His throat was constantly dry and his voice rasped.

What mattered the tons of obscene books, dirty pictures, plates, postcards burned in pyres in Brooklyn, what mattered peep shows and dirty plays shut down, what was the use of the mounds of ungodly rubber articles he collected and destroyed, when all the time that notorious murderer of the precious unborn, defiler of the marriage bed, operated in *his* city with impunity, growing rich on the blood of infants. Last year, 72,500 pounds of bound books, 87,000 pounds of nasty pictures and photographs, 36,000 pounds of rubber articles intended for immoral purposes, 2,150 pounds of indecent playing cards, 2,875 pills and powders of abortifacients or preventives of contraception—he made no distinction. All interfered with woman's sacred duty. He had lists of men and women he had put in prison, lists of those awaiting trial—at which he would be the principal and sometimes the only witness, and a list of those who had died while he pursued them.

A month passed while he had sent letter after letter to Madame Restell in his usual persona of a young woman in trouble. No answer came, not even an acknowledgment of his pleas. She must be hard-hearted indeed to refuse her help to a frail young woman in such dire straits. He would have to go after her in person. He would be using the state statutes then, not the federal. It made little difference. He was master of both.

Although Maggie fed him corned beef that night with cabbage and potatoes, a boiled New England dinner he relished, he had little appetite. The doctor had bled and purged him, but he felt weaker. Adele sat at the table with them, eating daintily. She had fine manners, imitating Maggie. She would follow Maggie about during the daytime and sometimes one of the maids, trying to do what they did. She had not learned to read. She was still working on her alphabet blocks, tracing the letters with her sweet fingers. She was five now, as well behaved as ever. She did not talk much, an admirable thing in a female. She laughed easily, seldom cried, was as good-tempered as they could wish.

"She will be with us all her life," Maggie said to him. "She's a little slow, you know, and I don't think she could make her way."

"There's nothing wrong with a girl being slow. Too fast is the problem."

"I never worry about her getting into mischief. Not on purpose." Maggie fluffed Adele's sausage curls. "Aren't you my little darling girl?"

Adele nodded vehemently, her curls bobbing. "Mama!" she said. "Good girl."

"Finish your cabbage," Anthony said.

"Don't like."

"But you will finish it. Be a good girl, for Mommy and Papa."

Slowly, reluctantly but obediently, Adele picked up her fork and shoveled in the cabbage, endlessly chewing with watery eyes. But she ate it all.

ANTHONY DRESSED THAT DAY as he always did, in a slightly rusty rumpled black suit, one of four, a clean white shirt with stiff collar, a white bow tie. His warrants, handcuffs and his badges—federal and state—were tucked away in the pockets, and under his belt in back, his loaded revolver. He would have thought that perhaps the old hag would have retired from the bloody work, with her husband recently dead and herself close to seventy, but her ads continued in the *Herald,* vaguely worded, nothing he could proceed on—but everyone in New York knew what she did and where she did it. His fever was up again this morning and his joints ached.

Anthony had taken the train to Albany several times to secure passage of a statute with teeth against abortionists. He had gone after those legislators who opposed the new law until in fear they withdrew their objections. Most men had something to hide. He had nothing to hide, so he was fearless. Under the new statute, possession of any drug, medicine or article intended to prevent conception or cause abortion was punishable by imprisonment—up to twenty years; possession of pills, powders or instruments was a crime. No more need Anthony drag women into court and force them to testify. No witnesses other than himself and his men were needed to convict. He had her.

On a crisp January day, the sky gray with an occasional powdering of snow, he appeared at One East Fifty-second Street and rang the bell of the basement office. An older woman answered and he asked to see Madame Restell. He was shown into an office with a large well-polished desk, anatomical figures, lace curtains and green velvet chairs. A full-figured woman with dark hair marked by a single streak of white strode in and seated herself. She seemed strangely vigorous for her reputed age, moving swiftly and with authority. She was dressed respectably, but he had met women who dealt in vice and dressed like ladies before. He was unimpressed. "I have come on behalf of a lady who has a problem."

"And is the lady married or unmarried?"

"I would prefer not to say. But she is very much in need of something to help her resume her female functions."

"How old is she?"

"She is twenty-eight."

"How is her health in general?"

"She is quite healthy."

"Has she borne children?"

"Two."

She disappeared and returned with some fluid and a bottle of pills, giving him detailed instructions about exactly how the medicines were to be taken, when and how often. She made him repeat back to her the instructions. "If this does not produce the desired result, the lady will have to come to me herself. A brief operation will be required."

"How much will that cost her?"

"Two hundred payable in cash beforehand."

"Is this procedure safe?"

"With me, it is. I've lost only one patient in forty years of practice. There's not a doctor in Manhattan who can match that record. With my one failure, it was because she lied to me about how far along she was. Now I make a thorough examination before I begin."

How cold-blooded she was, boasting about her skill. He had more questions, but the woman who had answered the door came in to say her next appointment was waiting. She turned to him. "I'll be back shortly."

Apparently she had another room next to this one. He crossed to the wall and applied his ear. A married woman was purchasing something to prevent conception. When they finished, he rushed to his chair and waited for the abortionist to return. She swished in, her skirts rustling.

"How long would the lady be kept here?"

"We have a place she can sleep, where she will be watched over to make sure there are no complications. If she is fine, she can return home the next day."

"If anything goes wrong, will you help her?"

"Of course. It's the first twelve to eighteen hours when trouble occurs."

The following week, Anthony returned and purchased materials to prevent conception, claiming that the woman had turned out not to be expecting after all. She held him up for ten minutes, explaining in detail exactly how the syringe was to be used after intercourse and exactly how the powder was to be applied. She again made him repeat her instructions, adding that she very much preferred to see the woman in question and to make sure she understood her own anatomy.

The following week, he made his preparations. He brought a policeman, his deputies and reporters from the *World* and the *Tribune*. They were to wait outside for a few minutes, then the policeman would force his way in with them.

When they were all inside and had rushed into Madame's office, where she was interviewing a heavily veiled woman, she stood and glanced at them. Anthony could tell she had a pretty good notion what was happening. "You're back again. And I see you brought quite a party with you."

"I am Anthony Comstock, agent of the federal government and secretary of the Society for the Suppression of Vice." He flashed his badge. "I have a warrant to search these premises and seize materials for the prevention of or interference with conception."

She extended her hand. "May I see the warrant?"

He was startled, but complied. Then, telling the policeman to watch Restell, he grabbed the arm of the woman in the heavy black veil, who began to weep uncontrollably.

"I'm a respectable woman with four children. I came here on behalf of a friend's daughter, to inquire what could be done. I didn't mean to break any laws. If my husband learns of this, he will abandon me! I will kill myself if this comes out!"

"May I see your purse?"

There was nothing in it from Madame, no pills or powders, so she could have been telling the truth. He took her name and address. He might need her as a witness, but as he had not caught her in a felonious act, he decided to be generous. She fled at once.

Then he turned back to the gentlemen of his party. "We'll conduct a search now." They found her granddaughter playing piano upstairs, and in the kitchen two maids and a houseboy eating a lunch of sausages and sauerkraut. In their first search, they found nothing incriminating. Anthony knew there had to be a cache of pills and powders nearby, since she had absented herself briefly to fetch them on his previous visits. In a wine closet behind the bottles, they found her inventory.

She shrugged at their loot. "Take them and get them tested. There is nothing among these pills and powders that any druggist does not sell."

"Be that as it may, we found indecent rubber articles." Womb veils, condoms, syringes.

The granddaughter left off playing and came downstairs. She was in her twenties and attractive, if one didn't know her connections. She kissed her grandmother on the cheek, addressing her as Mother and asking if she should call their lawyer. Anthony ignored her and led his party on a thorough search of the house.

"See how she lives in luxury off her bloody trade," he said. She lived much better than he did, like one of the big men—like his mentor Jesup. The woodwork was intricately carved walnut. The floors were laid with Oriental carpets and one had a mosaic of marble. Some rooms had the new flocked wallpaper. Of the paintings and bronzes, only one obscene—a naked woman coming out of a seashell. Restell's grandson Charlie began following them about, alarmed. The granddaughter told him to go for Madame's lawyer. Anthony did not try to prevent him. No lawyer was going to get Restell off.

They found nothing else, although the reporters made many notes on the high style of living. Downstairs, Madame had persuaded the policeman to let her have lunch. She was sitting in her kitchen eating oysters. "So I am to go before a judge now? I would prefer to use my own carriage. I cannot gallop off, obviously, so why do you object? At least I'm entitled to that courtesy."

Anthony objected, but the policeman gave her permission. Anthony made a note not to use this officer again. He was giving the prisoner too much leeway including using her own carriage—infuriating to Anthony, as it was a better carriage than any of his mentors owned, with a pair of handsome, exquisitely curried horses drawing it, one black and one white. Madame went off to court like royalty, but she would soon have her comeuppance. "Let's see how she'll enjoy the Tombs," he said to his assistant. They traveled in their two conveyances to police court where a crowd of reporters waited. Anthony had notified the papers about the imminent arrest. Madame was speedily charged with two counts of selling articles for abortion and for contraception. She waived the examination, as her lawyer had not arrived yet. The judge set bail at $10,000 and she produced bonds from her purse. The judge, Kilbreth, who was sympathetic to Anthony, refused the bonds and insisted on security in real estate.

The scoundrel McKinley, an ex-judge who had helped get Claflin and

Woodhull out of jail, came rushing into court with the grandson, whom he sent to find someone to stand bail. They waited around until six, when Charlie came back. No one would stand bail because of the fear of the publicity, with all the reporters lurking there to write down the names of anybody who did not fear association with Madame. So Madame went off to the Tombs. Anthony went home to a delayed supper and his dear family, satisfied in the knowledge that he had begun her just punishment. He woke in the morning without fever for the first time in weeks. His head felt clear.

The next morning at his office, he perused the newspapers. "A vile business stopped," the *Tribune* trumpeted. The *Times* lauded him. He was a hero again. Over the next days, McKinley found bondsmen but the judge refused them.

In the meantime, the papers were wavering. Reporters interviewed Restell in the Tombs. She had impressed them with her bearing. They went on about how attractive she still was at sixty-seven and her air of indignation. She claimed she had given Anthony nothing he could not have bought at any druggist. "The little doctors who are behind him are envious of my fortune, because I have such a fine house in such a splendid location."

In the meantime, her fleet of lawyers tried to secure bond. They found plenty willing, but no one who would sign his legal name and be reported in the papers.

"Can't I just be put down as John Smith? I got the money right here and deeds to property."

"Your legal name or nothing," the judge said.

She kept insisting she had plenty of money to pay the bail, but the judge held firm. He was a good man, Anthony had always found. He refused to accept anything but bondsmen whose names would be legally recorded and reported. However, the game did not go on as long as Anthony would have liked. Her infernal grandson kept running around town and finally came up with two tradesmen who pledged her bond. She returned to her elegant house of vice.

When the examination of Madame Restell began, the courtroom was crammed with journalists and onlookers. Anthony had Maggie put extra starch in his shirt so it would stay crisp on the stand. He was hard on his clothes for he sweated heavily. He always wore red flannel underwear, summer or winter. It was more decent that way. Madame was dressed up in velvets and silks, wearing diamonds at her ears and leaning on her grandson, Charlie, to whom she whispered frequently. Her lawyers asked to have the proceedings closed and the public and press denied access, but the judge refused. He knew Anthony wanted as much coverage as he could get. The judge found ample evidence, all supplied by Anthony, that she should be tried. Once again, there was a scurrying for anyone who would stand surety for her bond to bail her out. Her shysters attempted to dismiss all charges, claiming lack of evidence, bringing her to one of the New York supreme courts. Restell, dressed to the nines with her grandson propping her up, was carted about from court to court in her own carriage. Her damned lawyer pleaded that he, Anthony, had to prove that the items he had seized could either prevent conception or cause an abortion. The judge refused. Anthony watched the whole proceedings from a few feet away. He kept hoping that the obstacles the judge and clerk were throwing in her path could remand her to the Tombs, but she went home, finally, once again on bail.

He heard she was shopping around for a more powerful lawyer, trying an ex-judge with more connections, a bigger reputation. The new lawyer, Stewart, was said to have agreed to represent her if she would take down her sign and travel in a less elegant and ostentatious coach. She agreed.

Anthony made a strong presentation to the grand jury—eloquent and forceful, emphasizing the danger this murderess posed to society. He was back in full voice now, strong and commanding. He could feel his own power radiating to the gentlemen listening. The grand jury indicted Restell just as he wished. He heard that she was drawing up a new will and giving away property to her grandson and granddaughter. He hoped that all the bonuses paid to bondsmen and all the fees to the myriad lawyers were draining her ill-gotten wealth. Because of the judge's rulings, she had to bribe bail bondsmen, since her own money and property could not be used as surety. He had her house watched and learned that she was sending for her new lawyer on a daily basis. She was falling apart. He could not have hoped for a better outcome. He would destroy her. She had been cool in court but now she was unraveling. She kept summoning her new lawyer or running to his office. He had put fear into her, at last. When next she came to court, she was wrapped like a mummy in layers of shawls over her gown, wan and haggard. Her age suddenly began to show.

He had to leave town the next week. A petition of free lusters and freethinkers fifty thousand strong was being presented to Congress to urge repeal of the law he had secured, which bore his name popularly, as well it should. Restell's lawyer Stewart had asked for time to have a chemist analyze the pills and powders to prove that they were not as Anthony claimed, illegal substances. Anthony pushed to have the case brought to the oyer and terminer court, where it would move more quickly and where he suspected he could get a heavier verdict against her. The trial now would begin the following Monday, so Stewart could not get a chemist in time. Anthony was taking no chances on the old witch getting off. Anthony buttered up his supporters in Congress, put on another quick display of shocking items and then rushed back on Saturday to take Sunday with his family and congregation. He was feeling fine enough to attend a birthday celebration for Budington, who was presented with a fine Moroccan leather illustrated Bible by the congregation. Monday morning Anthony would be ready to meet Restell before the bar of justice.

Anthony arrived at court in plenty of time, his wife having prepared his clothes the night before and put his papers in order. He found a scene of confusion. Two women were weeping—her granddaughter and a veiled woman. A man was with the granddaughter, apparently her husband. Were they trying to pull something? Had Restell fled? He began to sweat copiously. He would pursue her at once. Could she have left the country over the weekend? He had his man watching her house, but she might have somehow slipped out. He elbowed his way through the throng of lawyers and witnesses and court officials. "Why is Restell not here?" he thundered. Her family turned and glared at him. The granddaughter ostentatiously pulled her skirts so he would not brush them.

Her lawyer Stewart drew him aside. "The granddaughter found her body in the bathtub this morning. During the night, she slit her own throat."

"She's dead?"

Stewart turned to the family. "He wants to know if Madame is really dead."

"Tell that man that she died rather than endure the scandal of a trial. She did it for us." The granddaughter was weeping. "And she was terrified of dying in prison. She kept saying she wanted to die at home."

"You killed her!" the veiled woman screeched.

"A bloody end to a bloody life." He turned on his heel and left the court. At first, he admitted, he had felt a pang of disappointment at being denied the pleasure of bringing her to justice, but death was surely punishment enough with hell fires awaiting. He had won again. He had plenty to do, three other trials coming up, a lecture tonight to a group of businessmen who might contribute to the Society for the Suppression of Vice, a group of educators to address the next evening about the dangers facing youth. He felt his own power as he took a cab to the offices of the society. He even asked himself if he wasn't puffing up with unseemly pride at his success. But the Lord had guided his hand. He was cleaning up this city. He was cleaning up this country. Sometimes he could almost see the orderly, well-run moral society of the future, when all this talk and writing and picturing of sex would be vanquished. A great purity would reign. He felt wonderful.

Newsboys were already hawking stories of Restell's suicide. He had his driver stop so he could pick up some papers. It would be satisfying to read the accounts. No one could accuse him again of hesitating to attack the rich. Her fine mansion on Fifth Avenue, her diamond earrings and fine velvet gowns had not protected her, nor had her real estate holdings nor her carriage and matched horses nor her powerful friends including the chief of police. They had all deserted her. Vice was always alone in the end.

She lay in a coffin on ice in the parlor of her mansion, where a stream of reporters and others came through to view the body. Anthony decided to take a look for himself, to make sure it really was Restell and she was as dead as they claimed. She looked as she had when he had first met her rather than her last haggard appearances before the bar. She looked more youthful than she had any right to, her face calm and dead white, devoid of blood. Her throat was marked with a red line across it. She had severed the carotid artery and both jugular veins. A thorough job. The family—her daughter and family, her granddaughter and husband, her grandson—all glared at him and turned away, but he was not sorry for coming. He had wanted to be sure. Now he was. He had closed her down for good. Her death would serve as a bloody reminder to other abortionists what could become of them. It should be most effective. Soon he would make it impossible for a woman to effect such a crime against society and the family. His duty for the moment was done.

FORTY-FOUR

ELIZABETH THOUGHT THEY DIVIDED the work of the history up in an intelligent manner. Susan organized the materials; she had a memory for organizational details that Elizabeth not only did not recall but doubted she had paid attention to at the time. All of them researched; Matilda and she wrote. They haggled over the interpretation and then Susan would see the material through the press. They worked in Tenafly because Elizabeth was, as she said, the "least portable." In her sizable house, their work could take over what had been Theo's bedroom, now that he was marrying.

"The church is one of the primary enemies of women's liberty," Matilda said. "Why do we hold off saying so?"

Elizabeth nodded and was about to speak when Susan frowned at them over her spectacles. "We are not trying to offend the largest number of women possible. We're trying to build a suffrage movement, not whittle it down to three true believers."

"I get sick of singing the same old suffrage tune," Elizabeth said. "There's so much else wrong."

"First the vote. Then whatever we choose to attack next." Susan was adamant. But neither could Susan persuade her to confine herself to that one-note serenade. She found working on the history fascinating, but she still spent months lecturing. The next Monday, she set off again, this time to the West, where she most enjoyed traveling. The people were open to new ideas, and the vast scale of the scenery, the huge mountains of the Rockies and Sierra Nevada, the deserts stretching for days, the canyons and wild rivers excited her.

She endured many adventures on her travels, caught in snowstorms and once in Arizona, in a sandstorm. She endured floods. Forest fires trapped her briefly in a town in Northern California. Now it was early fall in Wyoming. She was riding in an omnibus with miners, cowboys, a rancher, a newspaperman, a banker and his wife, the tanned and wrinkled widow of a settler. They were telling anecdotes of children's misadventures. She was halfway through the story of how Gat and Neil had taken baby Theo up on the roof and tied him to the chimney when the omnibus gave a terrible lurch, bounded forward and toppled over, spilling the passengers onto a dry river bed. She was pinned under a wheel for hours watching helplessly while the driver slowly bled to death, his chest punctured by a rod. She wondered if she was going to die there. Two of the least injured men cut the horses loose and tried to move the coach. Their first attempt crushed the shoulder of one of the pinned cowboys. They were still trying to move the coach when they saw dust.

"I hope it ain't the Sioux," the rancher said.

They watched the dust cloud approach until at last they could see it was three men riding out to discover why the coach hadn't arrived at the next station. The five able men hoisted the carriage upright with the aid of the horses. The driver was dead. They had to amputate the leg of a middle-aged miner in order to free him from the wreckage, sawing away while he drank whiskey from a canteen, screaming, until mercifully he passed out. Finally she was freed and helped to her feet, but she could not put weight on her left leg. It buckled under her, and she had to wait for the men to come back with a wagon.

The consequences of the accident stayed with her. Whenever she went up or down stairs, that knee would give way. She had endured backaches during the last month of pregnancy, but once she had delivered, her back had always been fine. Now she had to sleep on her side with her knees drawn up. Her son Gat was living in Iowa, so she headed for him. His wife nursed and babied her. Six weeks later, she resumed her tour. It was winter now, and by the time she had talked to the last audience in the last town, she was running a fever. When she got home to New Jersey, her doctor said she had walking pneumonia and must get into bed and stay there. Five of her seven children gathered, hovering over her.

"Mother," Harriot said, assuming the role of family spokesman, "you must stop this incessant traveling. Not only do we scarcely see you, but you're driving yourself into an early grave. You must spare your health and stay home."

Amelia said the same thing more bluntly. "Let younger women hit the trail. There be forty other women can lecture. Nobody writes like thee."

Susan was after her to go out on the circuit. Elizabeth resisted, writing, "I owe it to my children to spend more of what time remains to me with them. I want to get on with our history. I want to tackle another large project." She was going to take on religion with a frontal assault. She was thinking of calling the new work *The Women's Bible.* "Neil has moved back in after his divorce. To continue the marriage would have been absurd. They no longer cared for each other and their home had become a battleground. Why live like that? She has her own money. The Civil War and then his domestic war have sapped his strength, as all this traveling has sapped mine." She was not above trying to provoke a little guilt in Susan for riding her all the time to run conventions, to go out on the lecture circuit, to write speeches for Susan to give.

In truth, she did not mind staying home in the company of family and friends. She received as many visitors as she could endure. There were pleasant evenings playing chess with Neil, playing cards with whichever of her children were there. She performed their favorite songs on her pianoforte and everyone sang. She held conversationals as she had years ago in Seneca Falls; now they argued about Marx, economics, religion and politics and national character, the frontier. Matilda had brought the treatment of Indians to the attention of Elizabeth and Harriot, who was proving to be a suffrage activist. Matilda was writing about the history of treaties with sovereign tribes the government made and then broke at will. The conversations sometimes concerned Indians now as well as expansionist ideas that were current and, Elizabeth thought, masculine and pernicious. Take, conquer, grab. Call those who resisted uncivilized. Call them savage if they fought back.

She wasn't by any means confined to the house. She went to see electric lights installed in Manhattan. She picnicked with her daughters Harriot and Margaret in Central Park to see Cleopatra's Needle just erected there. She tried out the new telephone and organized a meeting on the implications of the Edmunds Act, prohibiting polygamy in the territories. She even managed while in Chicago to see the building they called a skyscraper, ten stories tall, the Monadnock Building with walls thick as a fortress. She viewed the immense arm and hand of the Statue of Liberty in Madison Square, where it was on display. She visited Frederick Douglass to wish him well on being appointed ambassador to Haiti. She was aware that she was one of the few to fervently congratulate him on his second marriage. She didn't see that it mattered that his new wife was white, since they were obviously suited.

"I can please myself now as well as others. That's the advantage of being an old lady—that is, one with means to support herself—that makes all the difference," she told her daughters. "You have in the end only yourself. You must never lose yourself for another. Love, but hold on to your own sweet values and your own ideas. Always remember what you need and what you want."

She and Susan had tried to vote in the 1880 election, again in 1888 and this year, but were turned away. Disgusted, she threw the ballot at the recorder and stormed out. Would she ever, ever get to vote before they buried her? She had begun to doubt it, but perhaps her daughters would have that constitutional right.

Susan went to every convention. The younger women gave her scarves and jewelry, which she seldom wore. They bought her gloves and sachets. They fawned on her, kissed her, fussed over her. Sometimes Elizabeth felt a pang of jealousy but it was gone in an instant. Susan, when they traveled together, had been known to exhibit jealousy of the greater attention Elizabeth's manner and delivery brought her. Susan complained that when she was on a stage or in a room of strangers with Elizabeth, nobody listened to her. She was overshadowed and ignored. Elizabeth also knew that she had not Susan's patience with the young things. Susan adored them back. Aside from her sisters, Susan had no family ties and was all theirs. She was cool to Elizabeth's heat, thin and precise. She was the perfect aunt, and the younger women were comfortable with her.

Never before had Elizabeth had enough time to write. Some writers complained of the agony of production. Not her. Up in her room, remembering the days she had written at a table in the nursery, she gloried in the hours she had to read, to study, to write and write. This was the sunset of living. A few aches and pains were nothing compared to the freedom of her mind.

In early November news came that Lucretia was ill. Elizabeth was packed and ready to be taken to the train when a telegram came. Lucretia was dead. She wept and repacked for the funeral. They had been friends for forty years—longer even than Susan and in some ways more harmonious, probably because, she admitted to herself, Lucretia and she did not usually work together. She had loved Lucretia unstintingly for her sweet disposition, her clarity of mind, her steadfastness of purpose. She remembered standing on the bridge watching ducks in St. James's Park in London, Lucinda holding her hand while she absorbed Henry's betrayal. She remembered the afternoon in Seneca Falls when they had plotted the first woman's rights convention. She remembered Philadelphia, torrid heat and petty squabbles, then Lucretia riding in with cold chicken from her farm. She would never taste Oolong tea without thinking of Lucretia.

Among her many regular correspondents was Victoria, living in London, as was her sister—but they were not together. Victoria had brought over her parents and set them up, but she lived only with her children. She emphasized that although she had renounced some of her earlier radical causes such as free love, she lectured on and was still committed to woman's rights. She had fallen in love with an Englishman from an old and respectable banking family. A certain amount of scandal had followed her, but mostly she had been able to quash it with a lawsuit.

Elizabeth asked her what had happened to Colonel Blood. Victoria wrote that he had moved to Maine, married an heiress and gone off to South Africa to prospect. She knew nothing else nor did she wish contact with him. Her ex-husbands had gotten her into considerable trouble, and she was not looking for additional scandal.

Elizabeth heard from Isabella that the sisters were not as close. Tennie did not give a fig about the respectability Victoria was wooing so industriously. She had taken up with a multimillionaire, Francis Cook—Viscount of Montserrat—who owned palaces in Portugal and overlooking the Thames on Richmond Hill. He collected art by Rembrandt, Rubens and Van Dyck, so Tennie had taken up a passionate interest in art. Isabella also wrote, with her usual lack of discretion, that Victoria was moving heaven and earth to get her lover, John Martin, to marry her. Recently she had twisted his arm long and hard enough so that he finally introduced her to his family, who lived on an ancient estate.

Elizabeth followed Victoria's career with interest, especially since she was starting a periodical. When an English suffragist had written to query Susan about Victoria, Susan had told them to avoid contact with her. Elizabeth was sorry about that, but they had not asked her. Victoria was thus denied entrance to the woman's movement in England. They were afraid of her reputation, however she tried to conceal it. Elizabeth did not think Victoria had done anything to be regretted, however badly it turned out for her and for the movement. Victoria had been forced to retreat from her more radical positions, because she actually lived them. Elizabeth agreed with the free love position, but it got her in less trouble because she was such a respectable wife and mother. It was her anti-religious views that were beginning to heat the atmosphere. Well, she was old enough to weather any controversy. She had little to lose, besides the good opinion of people she did not respect.

Victoria had been knocked down and almost out by attacks on her. Elizabeth did not blame her for seeking shelter. So long as she advocated woman's rights, Elizabeth would support her positions and even her attempt to rewrite her own past. Colonel Blood had been a handsome man, an able and brave soldier, but he had been of no use to Victoria that Elizabeth could see. She hoped Victoria's new lover would prove more of an asset. As for Tennie, that ship would float on any tide. She was a woman whose sensuality was obvious, yet not vulgar. Something about her was natural and powerful. She could also write, when she chose to. Her articles for the *Weekly* had been pungent, with a clarity of thought and writing that surprised Elizabeth at the time. Yet she doubted that Tennie took much pride in that fluency. Probably she would live out her life happily without ever writing more than a note to a friend or relative. Susan had never trusted Tennie, but while Elizabeth did not admire her as she had Victoria nor find Tennie someone she could make into an intimate friend, she enjoyed her energy and her honesty. She was what she was, no apologies, no pretense. That was so unusual in a woman that Susan had never understood it.

The years seemed to move faster and faster. Elizabeth enjoyed a constant round of visitors, including her children and their friends and fiancés and then their spouses and, by and by, their children. She reached a friendly understanding with Henry: they could spend time with their children, have Thanksgiving and Christmas and birthdays together. She refused, however, to celebrate their anniversary, no matter what Henry or the children might suggest. It had been two decades since they were husband and wife. The legal fiction of marriage was comfortable, and so were the old folks' gossips they had. He was her best source on party politics and electoral contests. He had met Grover Cleveland and liked him. She enjoyed quizzing him about names in the news, and he relished his superior knowledge of local politicos. He loved to hold forth. When she grew weary of his stories, she would simply excuse herself, go off to her room in the Manhattan flat, shut the door and read. Her writing had a harder edge, she was well aware of that. In her old age, she was growing ever more iconoclastic. She could not take more than a few of the younger women with her, but those few were great company.

FORTY-FIVE

CORLEARS HOOK WAS an old part of the city, more dangerous than their neighborhood—dirtier, just as crowded, streets muddy with sewage and offal, dead cats, rats, pigs, dogs and horses stinking and rotting as people simply walked around them. The gangs here were notorious. Just last week, the American papers that Sammy read told of a double murder, victims' throats slit. Freydeh was nervous and Sammy kept fingering the knife in his belt. After querying neighbors and handing out more little bribes than they could afford, they found the house. The slattern who was keeping Reba, along with three other children farmed out by prostitutes, lived in a crooked old wooden house in a yard behind a tenement. The smell in the yard was intense, for not only was the privy overflowing right next to the well, but someone was keeping pigs there as well as chickens and a goat. Freydeh gagged as they waited for the woman to answer the door.

"So you say you're her aunt and her mom is dead. Why should I believe you? Little girls like her go for a pretty price."

"You will not sell her to any pimp or madam, or I'll kill you." Freydeh seized the woman's shoulder and squeezed. She was all bones. "What do you want for her?"

"Twenty dollars."

"Fifteen," Freydeh said. "We'll take her off your hands. You'll never hear from that bastard Kumble again, believe me. He's gone."

"Eighteen."

Freydeh didn't have the stomach for more haggling. "We'll come back with it."

"If she isn't here, your life will be forfeit," Sammy said. Where did he get language like that? Probably from those yellow adventure books he loved.

"Where are we going to get eighteen dollars?" he said to her once they were in the street again. "I know you saved up five, maybe six."

"You brought that pillowcase full of Shaineh's things?"

"Yeah, I didn't know what else to do with it. I thought maybe we'd bury her in something from it."

"They're washing the body right now. They won't bury her in any of that whorish stuff. She'll be buried in a plain white shroud." Freydeh walked on, thinking of Shaineh's poor body with the burial society women preparing her. "We'll go to a couple of madams and see if they want Shaineh's clothing, her lingerie, her wrappers. You take the jewelry he gave her and try to pawn it. We might get a few dollars. I thought I saw gold in there."

By late afternoon, they had disposed of what they could sell, and it was time to rush to the little cemetery, across the river in Brooklyn. The whole family went on the ferry with Shaineh's body, along with horses, a cow, a wagon heaped with bricks, two empty produce wagons and a wedding party. Asher said, "I never told them she was a *cuervah*. I told them a man was trying to rape her and she got pushed down the steps of a boardinghouse. Don't tell them different. It's a true shame on the family."

"She did what she had to, to survive." Freydeh sighed, wiping her eyes. "It was as much my fault as hers."

"We can't let him get away with this . . . this defilement and murder."

"It was an accident," Sammy said. "They were struggling at the head of the steps. She was trying to get away from him and they fought."

"He defiled her. He soiled our family," Asher said.

Freydeh decided to ignore him. To find Shaineh and immediately to lose her, it was more than she could endure. The only thing keeping her going was that they must save the little girl. She had thought that Sara and Asher would adopt her, but listening to Asher, she didn't want to give the girl into his care. He would take out on the daughter what he viewed as the shame cast upon him. What was one more child? A gift. Kezia could help care for Reba. If she could never have her baby sister back, she could have her sister's baby. Her child to raise, like Kezia and Sammy.

When they each threw a handful of dirt on the cheap pine coffin, the tears came. Had she tried hard enough? Was she too often distracted? She leaned on Sammy, taller now by several more inches, and wept. A waste. That was what she felt. Her baby sister was spent and wasted for nothing. The casual pleasure of a well-to-do man who cared for her only as one might for a fast horse or a beautiful spaniel. Who took her child from her and lodged that child in a squalid, falling-down house in a courtyard with pigs. She hated him but at least none of them need ever see his face again.

The simple ceremony was over, the grave marked by a wooden number. In a year, she hoped they would have money for a stone. Now she and Sammy must go and get the child. Sara and she hugged, returning on the ferry. The wind on the East River cut into her bones. I'm getting older, she thought, and because of that *momser* Comstock, I'm starting all over again trying to get to a warm secure place for my family. Asher was withdrawn into himself. He stood at the rail muttering, davening. The other passengers pulled away from him as if he carried plague. Shaineh was not even his sister, and he was sullen and working himself into a state. It was not so much that he grieved as that he felt sullied.

So much was different here in the New World, *goldeneh medina* that wasn't at all golden, the hard strange life that made him feel lost. She could understand that. But you had to struggle. You had to be willing to change and change more and change until you felt as if you were on a rack with your arms and legs pulled from their sockets and your head was yanked until you thought your neck would just snap like rubber pulled too far. You had to fiddle with your sense of right and wrong. But you survived. If you pushed yourself hard enough and made the right choices, you might prosper. If luck was with you and *momsers* like Comstock didn't break you. Freydeh sighed, hugging her sister and then Sammy, with Kezia clinging to her skirt as if she were afraid she might blow away into the river. Ever since she had come out of Blackwell's, Kezia had clung to her, even in sleep. She sighed, ruffling Kezia's thick black curls. "We're going to bring you a sister, Kezia."

"Will you still love me?"

"Always and forever. And she'll love you too."

When they were all back in the flat, Sammy said, "We can't go there tonight. It's after dark. We'd never get out alive."

"But if we leave her there, that bitch might sell her."

"You can't go," Asher said. "We must sit shivah for her."

Sara had already covered the mirrors. Asher had made friends in his shul and the wives of his minyan brought food to them, what they could afford.

Freydeh said nothing. She would simply walk out in the morning with Sammy and fetch the little girl. Asher was not her husband, and she had been on her own for so long she did not know if she could bring herself to obey any man. She had become something other than a wife. Sara obeyed Asher, but Freydeh wouldn't. He was not the head of her household, whether he realized that or not. She gave Sammy a look that said, It's okay.

In the kitchen setting out dishes for everyone, mismatched, a few cracked, but dishes enough, she murmured to him, "We have the eighteen, right?"

He nodded.

"We don't fight with Asher. In the morning, I go downstairs to the privy. Five minutes later, you follow. Just quiet and casual like."

Sammy nodded. "We get her tomorrow. We don't put it off."

"You're the true son of my heart. You know that, don't you?"

"If I was your real son, I couldn't marry Debra."

"No talk about marrying."

He made a sign of zipping his lip, but she knew that was not the end of this. They were old enough to marry. He was sixteen; Debra was fourteen. The age of consent in New York was ten. She must discuss this with him and with Sara before something bad happened. Children, death, marriage, it all came tumbling down at once. She could imagine a quiet life, but she had never known one. Imagine a day without a crisis. Shalom, shalom, shalom, Jews prayed all the time and where was it? In the clouds. In dreams the color of lavender and the pink cotton candy the goyim ate on the Bowery. Peace like the scent of pine needles on a June morning early. In their heads, peace, shalom, there and only there.

In the morning they left as planned. Asher was davening, lost in blissful mumbling, facing the east windows in the front room. It did not occur to him that they would disobey. They hurried through the early streets, crowded already with carts, one picking up dead animals in the street and the occasional corpse, one delivering empty barrels to a brewery, one carrying in potatoes from Long Island to the greengrocers along his route. A peddler was selling turnips, leeks, onions and carrots. There was a skim of ice on the mud of the street, but it melted quickly. The day was going to be warmer than yesterday, she could feel it. They dodged a cascade of slops from a chamber pot and headed downtown past Delancey, then east to the river. The only reasonable way to get there was to walk, and they did, at a fast pace through the mud and over the cobblestones and wooden planks. It wasn't that far, just a different world: no Jews, tougher gangs, more filth. The Patsy Conroys, the Daybreak Boys who preyed on the docks, the River Pirates all found their homes in this old, old slum along the East River where Irish and Yankees below poverty shared the rotting buildings and narrow streets deep in mud.

The old woman in her torn gray gown that had once been red, with a dirty kerchief tied around her head and her arm in a sling, answered the door again. She stared as if seeing them for the first time. "You got the money?"

"Show us the girl."

"Reba! Get your ass down here."

A dirty little barefoot girl, her long brown hair hanging in greasy hanks, came slowly, reluctantly toward the door, blinking at the light. She edged past the woman, gingerly.

"I'm your Aunt Freydeh. Did your mama ever mention me? Did she tell you my name?"

The girl shrugged, filthy thumb in mouth.

"You were lost. I've come to get you."

"Where's my mama?"

Freydeh did not want to start off by lying, but she could hardly tell the girl her mother was dead and she must go with them. The little girl squinted at Sammy suspiciously. She had already learned to mistrust men. Freydeh began, "Later on—"

"Your mother's dead," the slattern interrupted. "They take you or I'll throw you out in the street or worse. Now give me the twenty dollars for her."

"We agreed on eighteen." Freydeh held out the money but kept a grip on it.

Sammy let his coat fall open so that his knife was visible. "We'll take her now."

The woman looked indecisive. "I said twenty."

"Then you agreed to eighteen. You take it or leave it. Either way we're going home with our niece." Sammy stepped forward as if to threaten her.

The woman took the money and tucked it into a woven purse she wore under her skirts with a flash of her gray flabby legs. Freydeh picked up the child, who began to cry and tried to duck behind the woman. For a girl of five, she was severely underweight. She stank of urine and worse. The child beat feebly on her, crying and shrieking. Freydeh half expected the windows to open and people to run down as they would on her block, but nobody even looked. With Sammy in the lead, they headed for home. Freydeh gave the girl a dried apple ring to suck on, and she quieted.

Halfway there, Sammy took her. Reba began to cry again. Freydeh soothed her with more of the dried apple rings from her pocket and they marched on. At one point, the little girl said, "My mama has yellow hair. Is she coming to get me?"

Sammy looked at her and she looked back at him. Nothing to do but tell the truth. "No. But we promised her we'd take care of you for her."

"Miz Canary, she say my mama dead?"

"I'm your auntie and this is your cousin. We're going to take you home with us."

"You won't throw me in the river?"

"Why would we do that? You're our little girl now."

"Miz Canary say she throw me in the river."

"We're going to take you home and feed you and put you in clean clothes. You're going to your real family, to another little girl Kezia and your Aunt Sara and your Uncle Asher and your cousins Debra and Feygeleh, who's just your age, and Chaim. You'll have children to play with and a home to live in."

SHE NOTICED THOSE next days as Reba was cleaned up and dressed and fed, her hair cut off to get rid of the lice, the scabs on her arms and legs treated with ointment, that Asher did not look at the little girl. Sara took Reba on her lap along with her own Feygeleh. Chaim considered himself too big to sit on his mother's lap now. Sometimes on Saturdays, Asher took him to shul, and sometimes on weekday mornings for prayers before school. Chaim was still obedient and took his father's wishes as law, but she knew, from her years in the neighborhood, that would change. Kezia played with Reba like a doll. Sammy was tender with her. Debra hung back at first, but then the maternal feelings that were uncommonly developed in her took over and she began to mother Reba.

Reba would cringe if Asher or Sammy or Sara moved suddenly or lifted an arm. She did not have that reaction with Freydeh. After she had been with them for a month, she began to call Freydeh "Mama." She knew who she belonged to now.

Asher went out to look for work but seldom found it. Freydeh suspected he wanted it to find him. He was one of those men, unlike her own father, who paid little attention to his daughters and a great deal to his son. Her father had loved them all out of his overflowing generosity of spirit. She had been lucky in her parents, even though she fought with her mother. Her mother thought she had too much spirit for a girl and that would prove dangerous. She still thought her mother was wrong. A girl needed all the strength and spirit she could muster. Her mother had obviously preferred Sara and Shaineh, and she had doted on her sons. Her father had encouraged Freydeh to learn, to walk with him in the woods and listen as he told her about the different trees and birds and animals who lived there, the foxes, the wolves, the weasels, the hares, the rabbits and the deer. He showed her cocoons of moths and hornets' nests and the hives of wild bees in hollows of trees. She could never have a chance to pass on that kind of lore to her sweet adopted children, because there were no trees, no rabbits unless someone kept them in a hutch behind a building. Someday she would get them out of this slum. Comstock had cost her four years of work, but she would save, get them to a better spot. She would.

Asher was brooding about Shaineh and the shame she had brought on the family—as if anyone here knew her. If he didn't tell the story, no one would know, so what was the problem, Sara said repeatedly. He did not listen. Occasionally he would lose his temper and pound on the table in fury if she did not shut up. Nobody cared where Reba came from. So many families ended up taking in children of relatives who died, no one thought twice about it. Reba wasn't about to go shouting in the hallway that her mother had been a whore. So forget about it, maybe go and see if they're hiring at the tin factory where one of the men downstairs got a job.

Asher did not forget. He twisted thin and bitter stories about the facts of Shaineh's life and death. He ignored Reba. In three tiny rooms, that was difficult, but he was so often at the shul he could withdraw. Several times Freydeh tried to speak to him about his situation. His gaze glassed over. He did not bother to reply, simply waiting for her voice to cease as if it were an annoying noise from the street. A dog in agony. A horse or a woman being beaten. The third time she spoke to him he glared and raised his fist as if to hit her. She caught his arm and held it as they each tested their strength against the other. She was the stronger. He turned away. He was cold to all of them except his little son. She felt as if he did not know who to blame for what had happened to Shaineh. His shame gnawed away inside him like an ulcer. She tried to talk with Sara about Asher, but Sara was fiercely loyal to her husband and perhaps afraid.

Time seemed to do little to ease his bitterness. Once or twice he found work briefly but it never lasted. In the meantime, Freydeh finally confronted Sara about the attachment between Sammy and Debra. Freydeh had sent them on an errand to buy some supplies she needed. She took advantage of the privacy with the two of them gone, the younger four children in school—she had enrolled Reba, whose short hair caused her to be teased, as everyone could guess the reason for it—and Asher off at shul. "Do you think anything has happened between them?" Sara asked, wringing her hands.

"I don't think so. Sammy is a good boy. Debra's a good girl. I think holding hands and a stolen kiss is as far as it's gone."

"We should move out."

"If you can find a place cheap." She was taking only four dollars for all of them.

"I don't know what to do!"

"Will you speak to Asher?"

"He'll just start screaming. He's so destroyed by what happened to Shaineh, *zikronah l'brakhah,* may her name be blessed."

"So we'll keep this to ourselves. Even if you move out, I suspect they'll see each other. Should we think about marriage?"

"She's so young. . . . They both are." Sara was wringing her hands again. "Who needs more trouble?"

"Maybe if we betroth them, then they can marry when we think they're ready."

"Freydeh, has Sammy been bar mitzvahed?"

Freydeh sat down hard in a chair. "I took him off the streets. I never thought of it. We've been so busy trying to survive."

"We got to bar mitzvah him right away. We won't say why, just that it never happened. . . . He's circumcised, right?"

"Of course."

"So we get him bar mitzvahed. Without that, Asher will never agree."

She broke the news to Sammy, pulling him into the hall. "You got to get bar mitzvahed, Sara says."

"What for? I'm a Jew. That costs money we don't got."

"Because you and Debra are making cow eyes at each other. Because there's no chance for you with her if you don't do this. Better late than not. Asher will forbid it otherwise."

"We want to get married. Not right away. But soon."

"So then you got to do this. It means learning a bunch of Hebrew, but you're quick with languages."

"If I got to do it for her, I'll do it."

It was explained to Asher that without a man in the family, it had never happened. That seemed sufficient explanation for him and he arranged for Sammy to start studying with one of the men in his minyan. Sammy would not take the regular Hebrew classes; since he was so much older and bigger than the boys in them, he would be ashamed. The rabbi agreed that his preparation would be accelerated. Everyone accepted that he had missed his time because his father was dead and because there had been so few Jews from the Pale living in the neighborhood then. Now a couple more came every week. The shul had moved upstairs and taken over the apartment above the store.

Sammy liked learning the language, but he resented going through all what he called the rigmarole. She didn't push him about it. He understood the situation and he would do what he must, but he wasn't going to be religious like Asher. He would be something of a freethinker, like Moishe had been, like herself. Debra was a closed book to her. A good girl, hardworking, willing to do whatever she had to for her family, but showing little of what she truly thought. She was picking up English quickly, even though she couldn't go to school. When Freydeh saw her with Sammy in the street or the hallway or with one of the girls she had made friends with in the neighborhood, she was far more animated. She laughed openly, she waved her hands around and spun on her heel and leaned close to her friend to argue. She was a different girl away from her parents. Was that the girl Sammy had fallen for? Freydeh was intrigued, but would not interfere. Then she caught them in the hall together kissing against the wall with Sammy's hand under Debra's blouse. She warned them to be careful. "Enough trouble in the family already!"

Asher went out often in the evenings. They assumed he was at the shul, but one evening when Sammy was working with his Hebrew tutor, he came back and said that Asher was not there. "So where is he?" Freydeh asked Sara.

"I don't know! He doesn't smell of liquor or beer when he comes home. Could he have another woman?" Sara looked as if she might weep.

"I can't imagine that. Maybe he's so distraught he's walking and thinking. . . ."

When Asher came home that night, they were waiting for him. "Where have you been?" Sara asked, her hands on her hips. "We know you weren't at shul. Do you have a woman on the side?"

"Wife, I am going to wash away the shame on our family."

"There is no shame, but what you think is shame," Freydeh said. "Shaineh had no choice. She had a little girl to feed. He locked her up. He kept her locked up."

"Then he is a criminal and the shame should be on him." Asher turned his back on them and strode to the window to stare out at the street.

"You can't prosecute him in a court of law. Lawyers cost a lot of money. He has money. We don't."

"Keep out of my family business. You didn't protect her when she came. It's your fault, what happened to her." Every night now he went out. Sometimes he came back in an hour. Sometimes he was gone until after midnight.

"Do you think I should follow him?" Sammy asked.

Freydeh shook her head. "He's a grown man. Let him find his way."

Then one night Asher came back at ten. He was dirty and disheveled as he sat down at the table and announced, "I have dealt with it."

"Dealt with what?" Sara asked him. "You got a job?"

"I was waiting for him when he left the house of his *cuervah*. Such a man always has such a woman. I caught him and I struck him across both knees with a lead pipe. Then I left him there in the alley. . . . He will survive, but he will be lame."

"Asher, mine husband!" Sara shook him by the shoulders. "How could you do such a thing? The police will come and take you away. We'll never see you again."

"He doesn't know who I am. He never saw my face in the dark alley. No one will come after me. I thought of killing him, but I did not want to commit such an act. What I did is sufficient. I am done with him."

Freydeh was astonished. The New World had changed him too. He would never have dared seek revenge in the Pale. She was worried that somehow he could be found, but she couldn't imagine how.

He rose and walked to where Reba was sleeping on a pallet. "I spoke with the rabbi. There's a Children of Israel orphanage—"

Freydeh lunged to her feet. "She's no orphan. She has us. She has me."

"She's a child of shame."

"She's a sweet little girl who's had a hard time of it. Now she's mine." She stood glaring back at him, in his face.

"I won't live under the same roof with her."

"Then find another roof." She doubted he would. For that, he would have to get a job. At least perhaps he would begin to act like a mensch. She stood before him without wavering, and after a few minutes he turned from her, muttering. She did not regret what Asher had done, so long as no consequences landed on her and her children. She had three of them now, and soon Debra would join her family. She smiled when she thought of that. A barren woman she had been, and now she was the mother of three. The street had killed Moishe, but it had given her beautiful children. All the lines of condoms were in manufacture now; she had won back some of her lost customers and found new ones. All her effort could go into taking care of her family. Asher could carry on as he pleased, but she was the one everyone turned to when there was trouble, when something was needed, she was the one.

FINALLY

EPILOGUE

| *1902* |

ELIZABETH HAD GROWN WEAK and short of breath and quite blind. She had extracted a promise from her doctor Livonia that when she became too feeble to continue, when the pain became too much for her to work, Livonia would help her to slip out of life easily in a way that would not alarm her children or give cause for scandal. It should appear to be natural. In her recent will, she had recorded her objection to an autopsy. She requested that there should be a simple, commonsense ceremony conducted by women and then she should be buried in Woodlawn Cemetery rapidly without fuss or ostentation. She hated the ceremony of mourning that had weighed so heavily on women all through the previous century, the heavy black gowns, the weeping and wailing, the enforced withdrawal from work and society.

This was to be her last day, she decided. She had her hair dressed carefully in the morning. Snow white, it was still abundant and curly. Should she leave a note for Susan? No, that might tip her hand. They had last seen each other in the spring, when Susan visited her in the New York apartment where she had moved when Tenafly grew too much for her. She lived with her son Robert, a lawyer, and her daughter Margaret, a widow and professor of physical education at Columbia Teachers College. Susan was still passionately involved with suffrage agitation and the younger women she had brought into the movement, besides cooperating with the Woman's Christian Temperance Union on their suffrage work. Elizabeth was mistrustful of them and of their leader Frances Willard, although she did not doubt the woman's energy or organizational skills. But her dislike of organized religion had not diminished in the seven years since she published *The Woman's Bible* and shocked half her allies into distancing themselves. She was not a Christian. Several conventions of suffragists passed resolutions against her because of *The Woman's Bible,* but she would rather women did not vote than see the government at the mercy of bigots and religious zealots. The founding fathers had seen the danger of the joining of church and state and tried to secure equal rights for all citizens, Quaker, Baptist, Jew, Catholic, Protestant, infidel, agnostic: every one equal. Now organized religion was encroaching on the movement for woman's rights, eroding its edge, sapping its wild energy. Respectable women wanted to be "good." Until women ceased worrying about respectability, they would never seize their freedom—Tennie Claflin had written that in their *Weekly* decades ago, before it was suppressed.

Even now, toward what she chose should be the end, she had not been idle. Two weeks before, she had written a new essay on divorce. Until women could leave a bad relationship without forfeiting their children, they would be imprisoned. The only other woman she thought right on the mark on divorce was Victoria, who continued to write about it. They corresponded regularly. She had visited Victoria and her husband John Martin at their sumptuous Hyde Park Gate residence in London the last time she sailed to Europe. There was a woman who had retreated from scandal but never abandoned her belief in woman's rights. They enjoyed a good visit, lots of intelligent talk of politics and social issues.

Recently she had written an open letter to President Theodore Roosevelt and privately to his wife urging support for woman suffrage. She did not expect him to act, but putting a little pressure on never hurt. He was too much of a believer in woman as breeder and little else to give assistance to their cause. He was always going on about "race suicide" as if more rich white children was what the nation most needed. Still, if his wife took notice, something might be accomplished.

Her mind worked as well as ever, but her hand was cramped and her writing crabbed. She was forced to dictate. She would have liked one of those new writing machines, but her vision got in the way. Victoria had one, as well as a motorcar. Victoria was passionate about driving. Elizabeth found motorcars noisy and dusty.

Death did not frighten her. She had lived a good long time and accomplished some of what she had hoped to do. She had written essays she was proud of. She had reveled in some sweet friendships over the years. She had six living children whom she loved and who loved her back. She had darling grandchildren. Every single one of her seven children had received a college education—not easily accomplished, but she brought that off with the help of her older sister. Her daughter Harriot would carry on her work. Harriot was her truest heir.

So many of her dear friends were dead—Matilda, Lucretia, Pearlo. Henry was gone. Her eldest son Neil had died eleven years before. If she had been more superstitious, no doubt she would have been cheered by the notion of rejoining them in some eternal Sunday afternoon, an infinite vista of singing hymns and sitting around a heavenly parlor bored silly and stifling yawns. She did not believe in an afterlife. She would become one with the universe, yes, as trees gave back to the forest, as flowers wilted and dried up. A matter of chemicals. Many spiritualists who believed firmly in other levels of existence after death had lent their energy to woman's rights, and she appreciated their efforts. She also thought them fools. For a long time, she had been polite about their beliefs, but she was too old for twaddle. At least they gave women a decent role in the here and now. Victoria had been one of those believers. Elizabeth had the impression Victoria had gradually dropped those wishful theories. Once she said the spirits abandoned her after her failed run for president; another time, she said perhaps she had abandoned them.

Elizabeth was rather pleased with herself that she had shocked so many by her later writings. She might look like a kindly grandmother with white curls and a sweet round Mrs. Santa Claus face, but inside she was as fiery and radical as ever. She attacked religion, to Susan's annoyance, because revering a bunch of writing from men who had lived two thousand years ago as holy was ludicrous. Divines were always quoting certain passages in the Bible and ignoring others. The Bible maligned women, as did just about every so-called holy book she was aware of. Men put on dresses, called themselves priests and began telling women how wicked they were and that they must give up their will and desires.

When she was supposed to be resting, alone in her room, she took the powder Livonia had given her with a glass of port. It had a bitter taste, but the port sweetened her mouth. She called Harriot and Livonia and asked to stand. Livonia stood on one side and Harriot on the other as they lifted her gently out of her chair. She signaled to them to let go. She stood on her own, staring straight ahead, although she could see nothing but dim shapes. She had been too weak to dress, but she was tidy enough in her best blue dressing gown. She asked the maid Maria to lay out a handsome navy silk dress she hoped they would bury her in. She wondered if there were an audience, what she might say to them in this, the hour of her departure. Her death. Use the blunt word. The last century had used quite enough euphemisms. She hoped people would speak more honestly in this new century.

Things had changed a bit for women. They had some rights to property. Divorce had grown easier for women to obtain. More often than not, the woman was given custody of her children. She had been born into a world in which the father owned the wife and the children with the force of an absolute ruler. Women were at least on the road to owning themselves. They were still paid far less than men, but some professions were open. She had cried and pleaded for a college education. Now more women went to college every year. Increasing numbers of women attended medical schools. Women were admitted in some states to practice before the bar. In Wyoming, Colorado, Utah and Idaho women voted. Prostitution was still rampant, and thanks to Congress, it was illegal for a woman to control her body and her fertility, but they did it anyhow. Contraception might be illegal, but it was widely practiced. There was much work to do to free women, but she would have to leave those battles to others. She was laying down her heavy banner at last.

Her children were good people, useful, bright. What more could she ask for than to have used her time to move things forward? She had loved her friends. When she was young, she loved Henry fiercely. She had enjoyed her old age, famous, embattled but always with allies who grasped her intent and helped her fight on, surrounded by loving children and grandchildren who called her Queen Mother. She had a good time of it. A good run.

"I'm tired now."

Harriot grasped her elbow and with Livonia began to help her into the chair, but she shook her head. "I want to go to bed. It's time for me to sleep now."

And it was.

|*1915*|

Victoria had been widowed eighteen years before, when John had died of pneumonia. She inherited his estate and was once again an independently rich woman. She had begun editing a periodical, the *Humanitarian.* Until her death, her old friend Elizabeth contributed articles, as did many prominent feminists—as woman's rights advocates were now called—scientists and professors. She had become quite respectable. She was still passionate about causes but no longer interested in men, not in a sexual way. She had loved John. Their life together had been good, their intimacy satisfying. Now that he was gone, she devoted her affection to her daughter. Zulu Maud had occasional suitors, but no one Victoria considered worthy of her, so she discouraged them. She preferred to keep her daughter with her. After all, Victoria had been married three times, and two of those marriages she considered disastrous. It was better for a woman to remain unmarried, if she could afford to, as she often told Zulu, to maintain control of her own destiny. "My dearest, you will always have plenty of money. You don't need a man for anything but amusement."

After the turn of the century, she suspended her journal and moved with Zulu Maud to the old estate, Norton Park, on 1,100 acres in Worcestershire. The elegant house dated back to the sixteenth century. There were a number of cottages on the land and a Norman church. She invited Tennie to come live with her, as her lover Francis, who had actually married her, had died suddenly. Tennie declined. She had her own money, fine houses and a life she enjoyed. Tennie went on collecting art and occasional young men. She was still beautiful at fifty-six. She liked traveling, staying in the best hotels. She visited occasionally but said, "I don't fancy living in the country and growing moss on my back. A week or two is all I can take of the manor life, Vickie. How can you endure it? You're a hundred and ten miles from London, from the world. Who's to talk to?"

"Do you remember Demosthenes and his prophecy that I'd be a leader of my people?"

Tennie nodded. "So you ran for president. Then that sour son of a bitch Comstock stuck us in the Tombs."

"That prophecy's come true, at least here. I've started a women's agricultural college. I've improved local schools. I've converted the barn to a cultural center for plays, lectures, concerts, magic lantern shows. I've launched a fair to improve agricultural practices. I've started a Ladies' Automobile Club. . . . Let's go for a drive, now, before it starts raining again."

"You drive so fast, it makes me nervous."

"It's fun! Come on. I'll have my chauffeur drive, if that makes you more comfortable. You can see the village and my people."

"You speak like you're their queen."

"In a way, I am. . . . Queen Boadicea is said to have journeyed here to Bredon Hill to consult the Druids. Did you know the Prince of Wales came to visit me? It's a long way from the Tombs, Tennie. I just wish we'd come by some of this when we were younger."

"I still kick up my heels, Vickie. So could you, if you didn't shut yourself up. You've still got your beauty. Neither of us look twenty, but for a couple of old warhorses, we do okay."

"The house is gorgeous, isn't it? They wrote it up in *Country Life.* The gardens are a joy. I've become enamored of gardening—"

"Well, you have an army of gardeners to do the work. It isn't like planting potatoes in Ohio, is it? I have gardens at Richmond Hill, but I don't give a fig about them. I just tell the head gardener to do whatever he likes."

"I find country life satisfying, Tennie. When I drive out, the people wave to me. My neighbors are friendly. I'm accepted here, as we never were in the States."

"Well, you've invented a whole family tree back to Alexander Hamilton and probably to Julius Caesar."

"Come, let's go for a drive. I love cars. Let's go along the Avon, where Shakespeare lived, and then up into the Malvern Hills. It's lovely countryside."

They sat together in the back of the limousine while her chauffeur drove as fast as Tennie would allow. Victoria loved speed. It made her feel free. They shared a bottle of champagne with chicken and watercress sandwiches. Tennie put her hand on Victoria's arm. "Don't you ever feel as if you're pretending, as if you're back onstage playing the grande dame for an audience of stuffed shirts?"

Victoria was silent for a while. "I do think about writing my autobiography. Then leaving it when I die. I think about it often. I haven't had time to sit down and begin to write yet, but I will. When I'm a bit older. Then I'll tell the whole truth about my life—all of it as it really happened. Who I really am, who I was, what I did and believed."

As she grew older, she provided medical and dental care to the villagers, set up scholarships, gave Christmas and May Day parties on the estate. Her house was headquarters for the Peace Organization, but when the world war broke out, she supported the Allied cause. She flew the American flag over Norton, joined the Red Cross and put on events in support of the troops. She received a number of celebrity visitors every year—the prime minister among them and the president of Columbia University. Zulu Maud ran the medical and dental services and took care of their finances. She had learned about managing money over the years and increased their principal. Victoria grew interested in aviation and started a society for women pilots. She liked going up in planes, but it made Zulu Maud nervous when Victoria flew. She wished she could live on for the whole new century, with so many exciting inventions and changes.

Yes, she was an important figure in her village and in society. She was respectable, although when she visited the States, the old accusations and scandal were dug up and flung after her. She would not go again. Her adopted country was far kinder to her. Yet at times, as Tennie suggested, she felt far from her roots—attenuated. Again and again, she tried to write her true life story, but something stopped her. She could not seem to grasp how to do it. Writing essays and articles and speeches had come easily, but to write about her life stymied her. She could not find a way to express on the page all those adventures and transformations, those turns and twists and misadventures. Who would understand? She had never been entirely truthful with her husband, because what man could ever know her actual life and not judge her? They would never accept her large and small loves, that she had enjoyed the embrace of so many different men without guilt, without the need to hold on to them. In fact, she had fabricated rather a lot with John, but only for his own good and the good of their relationship, and hadn't he been happy? She had simply created a biography he could accept, no different really than ordering a meal he'd enjoy. She had known how to please him and he had pleased her. Like the Commodore with Tennie and like Colonel Blood with her, he had some sexual problems when she met him that she had easily overcome. Few men realized how common these little difficulties were. So many women were still quite inhibited. It helped to have the experiences she had enjoyed but she put them behind her and out of her history, at least for his consumption. Men could only endure so much truth. It had all worked out for the best. But someday, someday she would sit down and tell the whole truth for herself as well as for the world.

|1916|

Freydeh was living in a brownstone on the edge of Williamsburg, now part of Brooklyn. She had the whole house, with herself on the second floor, Kezia and her husband upstairs, and the common rooms on the parlor floor and the ground floor. Reba had been widowed in the Spanish-American War but she had remarried and was living farther out in Crown Heights, an area just being developed. She was a grandmother but she had just given birth to another baby with this new husband, something Freydeh had worried about because of Reba's age. The birth had been long and difficult, but baby boy and mother seemed healthy so far. Sammy and Debra lived down the block. Debra was a nurse. Sammy was in real estate with Freydeh. He ran the office and managed the buildings. He no longer did the actual carpentry, as he had for so many years.

She had taken the profits from her business and begun buying land in Brooklyn she developed herself. She had contractors she worked with regularly. Over the years she learned which ones did shoddy work, which ones tried to cheat her and failed, of course, and which ones she could trust. It had taken her ten years from the time she got out of jail to move from the ghetto with her large family, to move them across the river. By that time, their old neighborhood was crammed with Yiddish-speaking landsmen, with Jews who acted like Jews, with coffee shops and Yiddish theaters and delis that sold the kind of food she loved, with Yiddish newspapers and books. Williamsburg had plenty of Jews too. It was good to hear the *mamme loshen.* They still went back to the old neighborhood where the pickles were the best and the bialys. It had taken her another eight years to pay off their new house, and then she began buying cheap land. By that time, Sammy was an accomplished carpenter and could work on the houses as they went up. The job went better when he was on the site.

Kezia's oldest daughter Rose was with her today, helping her prepare for the seder tomorrow when the whole extended family would come together. Rose and she would need to place every table in the house end to end and then lay doors across hobbyhorses from a construction site to seat everyone, going from the front parlor all the way through to the far wall. She would have twenty-one at table, twenty-two if Danny got back from Cornell in time. Twenty-three if Feygeleh's widower came.

Rose was taking down dishes, standing on a chair. "*Bubbeleh,* how come you never got married again? Even Aunt Reba found a second husband. So did Great-auntie Sara. Didn't you want a man?"

"I was too busy. I had plenty children to love. Why should I bother?" She was ironing tablecloths to lay over the tables. "Besides, I got so used to bossing everybody around. What man would let me have my own way? I didn't need somebody interfering with my way of doing things."

"You were never lonely?"

"When am I ever alone?"

Rose shrugged. She was a pretty girl with Kezia's black hair and green eyes but tall like her father. She was getting down dishes for the seder and washing them. Standing near her, Freydeh could tell that she smoked, although her parents had forbidden it. Freydeh wouldn't say a word. Every kid needed some rebellion. All the *maidelehs* were obsessed with being skinny, so Rose probably smoked to stay thin. Grandchildren were a treat, because she wasn't responsible for them but she could love them as much as she wanted. Their mothers could do the worrying and scolding. She would never tell Rose that she had caught Kezia smooching with an Italian boy standing in the doorway of a tenement. She had scolded Kezia—curses and tears. Shame on the family. She must have sounded just like poor Asher *selig,* dead of a heart attack these twenty-five years. Sara had married again, to a big strapping man who worked on the docks and, after he was too old for that, fixed barrels and kegs. He was still working at eighty, fixing furniture now. They lived in Manhattan farther uptown off Lexington, a nice apartment. Chaim had become a rabbi out in Cleveland. Asher had been pleased but never forgave him for taking a pulpit far away. The next year he had his heart attack and died trudging through snowdrifts to shul for morning prayers.

Moishe and she had been right to escape from the Pale and come to America. Golden it wasn't, but they had a chance here, as opposed to no chance at all except to be slaughtered in a pogrom, die of cholera like her parents, *zikronim l'brakhah,* or starve to death eating grass of the field. She had seized that opportunity and now she could see her grandchildren flourishing. Rose was going to City College in the fall to be a teacher. Her brother Harry was a floor walker in Gimbel's, except he was talking of joining the army, which scared Freydeh. The army had taken Kezia's first husband. She wished Harry had gone to school and got a profession, but he liked the girls and having a good time. Now he wanted a uniform, to go off to France. He was handsome but silly.

People would ask, as Rose had, why did you stay alone? She could only laugh. She had founded a family. None of them would be poor again unless they were complete schlemiels. She had dragged them all into the middle class—never a lot of money but enough if they were careful. At seventy-four she still had her wits and much of her strength. She had even taken a little to religion in her old age, keeping the holidays—for the sake of the children, she said, but it was for herself, to celebrate the turning of the years, to celebrate her family, to celebrate being a Jew, to celebrate survival, above all survival. She was a matriarch, one without a husband but rich in love and connection. Let it continue to be so, she prayed to no one in particular. Let it continue for a while, so I can enjoy.

| *1915* |

Anthony had an enemy whose evil ways preyed on him, as had been the case with the Woodhull woman, with Restell—now it was a young harlot named Sanger. She was married but that didn't keep her from taking up with radicals and artists and writers and who knew what freethinking trash. She had been preaching her devil's gospel of preventing conception, trying to make sex free and light for women, trying to keep women from facing the consequences of their sins. Instead of carrying out the mission for which the Lord had created them, they wanted to take control of their bodies away from their husbands and their God and do exactly whatever they wished.

He had believed he thoroughly crushed that particular evil, but then the anarchist Jewess Emma Goldman started speaking about family limitation in public and even giving obscene demonstrations of the use of rubber articles to prevent conception. She was promptly jailed, but when she got out she went on with the devil's work. Lately she had passed on the mantle to young Sanger. Goldman had been a midwife; Sanger was a nurse. Women who stayed at home with their children never caused this kind of trouble.

Society needed him more than ever. He might be old, he might sometimes be weary, but his calling was more important than before, for morals were slipping. He did not always win in court these days. His favorite judges had retired. The newspapers ridiculed him when he went after those who showed paintings of naked women, as if there were any difference between dirty French postcards and dirty oils hung in a gallery or a museum. Both corrupted through the eyes. When he arrested a female bookkeeper at the Art Students League in New York because the so-called artists were advertising a show of pictures of naked ladies, the newspapers vied with each other in cartoons. They made a fuss when he had a vile play by an Irishman named Shaw—*Mrs. Warren's Profession*—closed down. They also went after him when he arrested a spiritualist, Ida Craddock, who had written a clearly obscene sex primer called *The Wedding Night* full of diagrams and so-called scientific explanations. He had her convicted in federal court. Before she could go to prison, she slashed her wrists and turned on the gas. Good riddance, but the papers made a fuss. As if any right-thinking man needed a manual to do what he should with his wife. He remembered his own beautiful wedding night with Maggie.

He suppressed a suffragette paper for printing articles about prostitution. Respectable women did not write about such things or care to read them. But the worst of the criminals he had been pursuing was the public nurse who worked on the Lower East Side out of the Henry Street Settlement House, Mrs. Sanger. She came from a pious Catholic home—her mother had been pregnant eighteen times—but she had married a free-thinking Jew, William Sanger, and been corrupted. She wrote articles about the artificial prevention of birth for *The Call,* a scurrilous socialist rag. He got the P.O. to notify *The Call* it would be seized if it continued to run her series "What Every Girl Should Know." The next issue came out with a large blank space where Sanger's column had been, headlined "What Every Girl Should Know by Order of the Post Office—NOTHING."

Then the hussy went off to France with her husband. When she returned, she wrote more obscene articles for an even more noxious rag, this one published by the Industrial Workers of the World—the Wobblies—called *The Woman Rebel.* Right on its masthead it proclaimed heresy: No Gods, No Masters. The Jewess Goldman wrote for it. He had Sanger indicted on a whole string of counts in federal court. This time he would put her away. She was part of that swarm of commies and free lovers and so-called artists who infested Greenwich Village. Misfits from every small town in the country collected there and egged each other on.

Her lawyer got her postponement after postponement. Finally the day came for trial, but Sanger did not show up. He learned she had written a pamphlet, *Family Limitation,* printed by a Wobbly press. Then she disappeared, a fugitive. However, her husband was still in his studio. Anthony suspected William Sanger must have a cache of obscene pamphlets. In the meantime, it was Thanksgiving and he took a week off in Asbury Park, where he had moved Maggie and Adele. Adele was a woman now, just as pleasant and compliant as she had been as a little girl. She was a real help to Maggie, doing a good part of the cooking. As long as she didn't get distracted, she was a fine helper. Maggie was thinner than ever and suffered from rheumatism; still she kept everything in order. He came home to a world of comfort and warmth where he could relax and be catered to. The following Monday he was ready to resume his chores and plan his attack on William Sanger.

He received a report that Margaret Sanger was in England. Somehow she had acquired a false passport and escaped him, for a while. A war was on in Europe and that might keep her there for a year or two. Now, he could not go in person to William Sanger, as the man had seen him in court when his wife was indicted. He sent his assistant. "Charlie, you pose as a dealer in condoms. You say how you admire her filthy articles and you want to help distribute her pamphlet. Get him to sell you one. Tell him we'll translate it into Jewish and Italian."

It worked. Sanger rooted around and came up with a copy, giving it to Anthony's assistant Charlie. Now he could raid Sanger's studio for more copies. They found a mother lode. He would have the pamphlet declared obscene. Then everything had to be put on the back burner when President Wilson required his presence as a delegate to the International Purity Conference in San Francisco. Preparation took most of his time through May. San Francisco was wet and chilly. He returned from the conference to the hot muggy late spring at home with a cold that turned into pneumonia. The lawyers had been wrangling over William Sanger all this time, but his trial was scheduled before the State Supreme Court of the Fourth District in September. Anthony would be ready. He was going to get this freethinker and stow him away in anticipation of the day he could lock up the wife.

The trial was tumultuous, with Sanger conducting his own defense. Anthony got angry and said bluntly that Mrs. Sanger was a heinous criminal who sought to turn every home into a brothel. He got into shouting matches with members of the public allowed into the court, including the Jewess Goldman's lover Alexander Berkman and that notorious Red, Elizabeth Gurley Flynn. When he saw who came to defend Sanger, he was surer than ever that these were dangerous elements who must be locked away. William Sanger kept making speeches, calling Anthony "a victim of an incurable sex phobia who lacked the intelligence to distinguish between pornography and scientific information."

Anthony wasn't fond of Judge McInerney, who censured him for speaking out of turn, but at least he refused to let Sanger plead free speech. The best judges, who always ruled in his favor, were gone from the bench. In the end the judge ruled that *Family Limitation* was indecent, immoral and a menace to society. "This crime is not only a violation of the laws of man but the law of God as well in your scheme to prevent motherhood. If persons would go around and urge Christian women to bear children instead of wasting their time on women's suffrage, this city and society would be better off." But all McInerney slapped on Sanger was a fine of $150 or thirty days in jail. Sanger went off to jail. Anthony went home, sick again. What was the use of winning when the penalty was a mere inconvenience?

He felt weak and feverish. He could barely make his way to New Jersey. Maggie forced him to bed. The doctor said pneumonia had returned. He was running a high fever and cooking as in an oven. The trial had worn him out, all those Reds screaming. The judge had not done his job, for he should have held them all in contempt of court. It had been a circus, and in the end Sanger was given such a light sentence it turned the trial into a farce. Anthony was bitter. He had worn himself out on the side of good, and the judge had the nerve to tell him to shut up. That thirty-day sentence made a mockery of his crusade.

The doctor said his pneumonia had taken an acute form. Maggie kept vigil at his bedside. His minister came—not a man he was as close to as he had been to Budington, but a good old-fashioned blood-and-thunder type. Anthony drifted in and out of the room. Sometimes he was in court shouting his wrath. Sometimes he was stalking a pornographer, pistol in hand. Sometimes he was lecturing on traps for the young. Sometimes he was in his bedroom, a warm September day with a hornet buzzing against the bedroom window and Maggie in a chair wiping his forehead with a damp cloth and praying. Sometimes the minister was back and prayed with her. He saw William Sanger, his face red with anger, shouting about free speech. He saw Madame Restell wrapped in silks and furs running away from him in her carriage pulled by black and white horses. He saw the shyster Howe with his diamonds twinkling in a purple and green vest and the Woodhull strumpets at the bar. He saw Victoria being led up to a scaffolding while he waited to pull on the rope.

Twice he rallied enough to pray with Maggie and the minister, sending for his secretary to dictate a report to the society. He could feel himself slipping away. The fever was burning him up. He worried a little, not about his soul but about his successor, who lacked drive. Anthony had arrested enough people during his career to fill a sixty-car passenger train. Who else could boast as good service to morality? He might be going to his reward, but the laws he had pushed through Congress were on the books to be used, and they would be, for they had teeth and claws. His successor would do his job, but he would not rejoice in being the mighty right hand of the Lord as Anthony had. Then once again he slid into the hot dark, the pool of burning mud where the sinners he had pursued were cooking like dumplings in soup. I've got you, he shouted, watching them burning naked and boiling like lobsters. I've got you once and for all!

MARGARET SANGER RETURNED to the States late in 1915, hoping that in her absence the legal situation might have changed. Comstock was dead, although his brutal laws remained on the books. Newspapers, periodicals, lecturers were openly arguing the legitimacy of contraception. The term she had first used in *The Woman Rebel,* "birth control," was everywhere now. It was suddenly respectable, even necessary, to discuss what Comstock had forbidden to be mentioned.

When she finally came to trial, she had wide public and elite support, now a sought-after lecturer and a celebrity. All charges were dropped.

A year later, with her sister Ethel—nurses, both of them—she opened the first birth control clinic in America in Brownsville, in Brooklyn. From a storefront she distributed handbills through the neighborhood in English, Yiddish and Italian. "Mothers—can you afford to have a large family? Do you want more children?" When they opened the clinic, the line of women, most with baby carriages, stretched around the block. They managed to see almost five hundred women before the police closed them down. Margaret served thirty days in the Tombs, treating it as a rest and relaxation cure. Her case was won on appeal. A few years later they opened a legal clinic unmolested.

ACKNOWLEDGMENTS

I HAVE RELIED ON many books and several interviews in doing the research for this novel. An even reasonably complete bibliography would cover at least seven or eight pages, but I wish to give particular thanks to the following: Anne M. Derousie at the Woman's Rights National Historical Park for her help on Elizabeth Cady Stanton and her time in Seneca Falls, and Michael Callahan, historian, raconteur and ranger at Castle Clinton National Monument in Manhattan.

For Victoria Woodhull, some of the most useful books were: *Other Powers: The Age of Suffrage, Spiritualism, and the Scandalous Victoria Woodhull,* by Barbara Goldsmith (Alfred A. Knopf, 1998), which I found great on all the characters; *The Woman Who Ran for President: The Many Lives of Victoria Woodhull,* by Lois Beachy Underhill (Bridge Works, 1995); *The Victoria Woodhull Reader,* edited by Madeleine Stern (M & S Press, 1974), which contains her speeches and articles; and *Notorious Victoria,* by Mary Gabriel (Algonquin Books, 1998). Not surprisingly, given her penchant for rewriting her own past, many of the stories and facts are in contradiction, and I have chosen those I thought likeliest.

For Elizabeth Cady Stanton and her friend Susan B. Anthony, I found most useful of the many biographies and histories: *The Ladies of Seneca Falls: The Birth of the Woman's Rights Movement,* by Miriam Gurko (Schocken Books, 1974); *Feminism & Suffrage: The Emergence of an Independent Women's Movement in America, 1848–1869,* by Ellen Carol DuBois (Cornell University Press, 1978); *The Elizabeth Cady Stanton–Susan B. Anthony Reader: Correspondence, Writings, Speeches,* edited by Ellen Carol DuBois (Northeastern University Press, 1981); *Extraordinary Woman: The Life of Elizabeth Cady Stanton,* by Elisabeth Griffith (Oxford University Press, 1984); *Eighty Years and More: Reminiscences, 1815–1897,* by Elizabeth Cady Stanton (Northeastern University Press, 1993; first published in 1898).

For Anthony Comstock, I relied on his own writings and on what I found to be the best biography, *Weeder in the Garden of the Lord,* by Anna Louise Bates (University Press of America, 1995), and on information from the many histories of censorship and birth control in the States.

For Freydeh, I used general histories of Jewish immigrant experience in New York, histories of Jewish life in the Pale and more specific works such as *The World of Our Mothers: The Lives of Jewish Immigrant Women,* by Sydney Stahl Weinberg (University of North Carolina Press, 1988).

Several more general books were helpful: *Rereading Sex: Battles over Sexual Knowledge and Suppression in Nineteenth-Century America,* by Helen Lefkowitz Horowitz (Alfred A. Knopf, 2002), which is outstanding; *Everyday Life in the 1800s,* by Marc McCutcheon (Writer's Digest Books, 1993), which—supplemented by *The Oxford English Dictionary* and my editor Caroline Marino's sharp eye—kept me from anachronisms; *America's Gilded Age: Intimate Portraits from an Era of Extravagance and Change,* by Milton Rugoff (Henry Holt, 1989); Luc Sante's *Low Life: Lures and Snares of Old New York* (Farrar, Straus and Giroux, 1991); *Lights and Shadows of New York Life; or, The Sights and Sensations of the Great City,* by James D. McCabe Jr. (National Publishing, 1872; facsimile edition, Farrar, Straus and Giroux, 1970); *City of Eros: New York City, Prostitution, and the Commercialization of Sex, 1790–1920,* by Timothy Gilfoyle (W. W. Norton, 1992); *Contraception and Abortion in Nineteenth-Century America,* by Janet Farrell Brodie (Cornell University Press, 1994); *Free Love and Heavenly Sinners: The Story of the Great Henry Ward Beecher*

Scandal, by Robert Shaplen (Alfred A. Knopf, 1954); and *Reverend Beecher and Mrs. Tilton: Sex and Class in Victorian America,* by Altina L. Waller (Basic Books, 1980).

Jacob Riis's photographs, although of a slightly later period, evoked the life of the streets and tenements. The Museum of Sex in New York offered concrete glimpses of some of the events and places I was writing about. The Tenement Museum of New York was also fascinating, and the guides there knowledgeable.

It has been a most interesting journey, researching and writing this novel. I hope reading it will prove as interesting to you.